THE LADIES OF SHALLOT

Glinda McKinney

This book is fiction. With the exception of a noted author and an internationally known businessman who were placed at the type of party they could reasonably have been invited to in Memphis, no characters, names, or events are based on real people or happenings. They are the sole creations of the author.

glindamckinney@att.net

To Gerald, my help and sustainer in all things.
You made this possible.

To Patty Duncan, my first reader, many-time editor, counselor, literary
adviser, steadfast supporter, friend, and author of
Ellen's Eye and *Detour to Dallas*.

To Judge McKinney, for handling the technical aspects of this book.
To Lizzy and Hailey for designing the cover.
To Hailey for formatting this book for paperback.
To Jacquie and Tucker for author photograph..

Thank you to all who showed blind faith in my writing and encouraged me
by asking when my book would be available, never giving me leave to not
finish and publish it. Could I name everyone? No. But here are a few who
know I must acknowledge them: Pauline, Fredda, Alice, Jerrie, Mot, Janet,
Bettye, Theresa, Patsy, and Altruria Teachers! Jane, you'll recognize a
certain pin that Crystal wears. Carol and Carolyn for not just volunteering
but insisting on reading the manuscript.
Dear God, let all named here have reason to be proud of their association
with this book that aspires to literary fiction.

Lines From

THE LADY OF SHALOTT
by Alfred, Lord Tennyson

Part I

. . . .

Four gray walls, and four gray towers,
Overlook a space of flowers,
And the silent isle imbowers
         The Lady of Shalott.

Part II

. . . .

She has heard a whisper say,
A curse is on her if she stay
She knows not what the curse may be,
And little other care hath she,
         The Lady of Shalott.

. . . .

And sometimes thro' the mirror blue
The knights come riding two and two:
She hath no loyal knight and true,
         The Lady of Shalott.

Part III

. . . .

His broad clear brow in sunlight glow'd;
On burnish'd hooves his war-horse trode;
         As he rode down to Camelot.

Part IV

. . . .

And at the closing of the day
She loosed the chain, and down she lay,
The Broad Stream bore her far away,
         The Lady of Shalott.

ONE- Cracked Bells and Cockleshells

C rystal saw as clear as anything the white one-piece bathing suit, modest in the style of the 1950's. It revealed shapely legs down to the almost large feet in white patent leather high-heel pumps, standing in the "pageant pretty-pose." Crystal grabbed the woman's shoulders and gave them a shake, then another. "Don't you know pretty is as pretty does?!" she said, regretting that her mother was not in fact present to receive her due shaking, instead of the hefty bag of manure she was wielding over the rose bed. Not Willette. Just cowshit. If you wanted to think of it that way.

Had she actually uttered her philippic discourse against Willette? These thirty-six rose bushes – in addition to everything else her mother had done – had gotten the place into this sorry shape. But damn if she would talk to herself over it!

And the call out of the blue this morning from Royce Menuche, Dad's old agent, wasn't helping as it should. He had an offer she couldn't refuse, for the one painting she wouldn't choose to sell. She tried to stop gritting her teeth and reflect instead on the beauty that would come from her work when the roses started blooming.

She listened to the quiet, hearing the snip each time she squeezed the blades against an unwanted stem. But she only imagined she could hear it hit the soft ground below, and the rose bush's cries for each tiny budlet that was already pouching out on its aborted branch, never to open up with the profound color and shape and scent that would have been its own.

She stood and stretched her back and out of habit, perhaps knowing it would improve her state of mind, glanced toward the break in the tall holly hedges to see Sarah's house next door. Good Grief! A man was standing in the opening where the gate used to be! Belatedly she realized she'd heard the soft thud of a fine car's door closing, and that's what had made her stand up and look. The man was big, like an ex-football player. He was in a dark suit and handsome, but handsome wasn't adequate; there was something about the way he stood, confident, looking her in the eye for the distant instant that she allowed contact. Oh. Yeah. It must be the Reverend Dr. John Half, Sarah's new minister she'd been praising to high heaven.

As if she hadn't seen him, Crystal quickly dipped a measure of insect dust and sprinkled it on a bush with the concentration of a priest and holy water, and thought about Sarah's invitation early this morning to have

Crystal over there, instead of her coming for supper at Crystal's as usual on Friday night. Crystal had been on the side porch having coffee, listening to the rain thunder down onto the covered porch. Even though she was wearing Dad's old robe and thick socks with a pair of his leather slide-ins – purchased by Willette but the scuffs done by Crystal's wearings – she was chilled and for once had been glad to go in to answer the phone. Two calls in one morning. Hmmm.

John Half, for that's who it most surely was standing there, obviously having been shooed over here by Sarah, apparently was an astute man, giving due thought whether or not to speak as she felt him watching her.

But no, she wasn't going over there, even knowing that Sarah believed she had Crystal's best interest at heart. Unlike somebody else she could name. The rain, which would nourish the wild shallots and replenish the Broad Stream River bottoms more than anything else this time of year, had stopped mid-morning. The day had turned sunny and warm and dry enough to prune the roses by the time she got home from work. The best time, between Washington's Birthday and the first week of March, was past by almost two weeks. If she wasn't at the office, it had been too cold or raining. Sarah knew roses were supposed to be trimmed before the monkey grass was cut back, and she'd already had her gardener, old Mr. Thrasher, cut hers.

Anyway, Sarah shouldn't complain – she wouldn't in any event – because Crystal kept her supplied until late fall with her favorites. In cut crystal vases the yellow and crimson roses went well with the ornate antiques and velvet curtains of Sarah's thirteen-room turreted and crenellated and curlicued mansion, the happy-ever-after house that Crystal had pictured in every fairy tale she'd ever had read to her, most by Sarah herself. Sometimes she would even make an arrangement for Sarah to take to church. She wondered if the new reverend would appreciate their home-grown quality, or if he favored hot-house precision.

Crystal had already finished trimming the roses to about two feet, then to keep out borers had bloodied the cut tips with big dollops of old red nail polish Sarah saved for her. She'd also pushed back last year's cedar mulch to work the fertilizer in, but not too close, around the roots. She would add more mulch and last, to prevent blackspot, would spray the bushes, grandiflora and hybrid teas ranging from white to deepest red.

And if history repeated itself, she'd make gallons of potpourri for Sarah and her women's church circle by spreading the petals to dry on an old sheet in an upstairs bedroom. Hell. Could she dislike Willette for doing something which provided such lasting beauty? Oh, that woman!

Behind John Half, without looking, she saw Sarah's house gleaming pale yellow with white trim in the middle of a three acre lot, which was divided by brick walkways into small gardens of tradition. They'd all been subjects of Dad's paintings. Waist high day lilies, with pint-size white blooms that opened and fell in a June sun's cycle, were depicted as umbrellas protecting toddler Crystal from raindrops, some as black as tar, threatening to mar her white fairy dress. Iris, planted at two week intervals to bloom in newly sunny areas starting in late March until mid-May, covered small Crystal sitting among them, like Joseph in his many-colored coat. All summer, foot wide elephant ears, Crystal painted crouching among them as if they were huge jungle trees, had sheltered her in games of hide and seek with Sarah feigning inability to find her. Vivid red and yellow chest-high cannas, which Crystal always called cannons because Sarah did, and that Dad painted suggesting sentries protecting a napping pre-teen Crystal, would push up when the weather got hot enough. Daisies that Sarah let Crystal pick to her heart's content, but the bouquets of which Willette disdained, would soon open their innocent white and yellow faces to the sun, as they had done painted as if a marching band behind Crystal, driving a princess carriage, in a parade. But Sarah had no roses. Well, she had no wild shallots either.

Now, spring bulbs were popping up in crayon colors in red clay pots on Sarah's wide front brick steps, and Crystal hoped the Reverend John Half was as astute as she thought, and would compliment Sarah on them.

Reverend Half, if she could trust the once-over she had given him, was taller than the six-foot high bushy row of pink camellias, a few still in bloom, on Sarah's side of the hulking holly hedge. They, along with boughs of dogwood and forsythia and early quince no doubt adorned Sarah's table tonight. A shame the azaleas weren't blooming yet. Crystal loved hers. All they required was an annual dose of iron. They were planted by her grandfather, not Willette!

Perhaps to see how her place would look to a stranger, such as the one poised in the abyss like a toy floating in a clear balloon, she glanced around. She always refused Sarah's offer to send Mr. Thrasher over to help. This visitor today was a rarity, so who was to notice if her yard looked like birds had dropped it among everything else Willette had added and Dad had collected. Hell, it was tempting to let the wild shallots take over the place. Like Sarah's, the house was Victorian, about as large and old as Sarah's, and on a three-acre lot. That's where the similarities ended. Here was peeling white paint and green shutters with slats missing, and oak doors and porch floors that needed waxing, and latticework underpinning that needed replacing and screens that needed patching. Ivory tower, my foot, she thought, remembering what it had been called by the kids at school.

If the Reverend Doctor was the insightful man Sarah had bragged on, he could see that she wasn't going anywhere the way she was dressed, muddy old oxfords, jeans bagging in the knees from kneeling at her work, a sweatshirt under Dad's authentically faded denim shirt, way too big for her. Yes, being a minister, he might know when someone wanted to be let alone. But what Sarah had in mind, that innocent standing in the vacuum between the two houses couldn't know. Sarah'd said, "Another time," when Crystal had called to say she had to do the roses. And that time would come. Sarah could chew on an idea like Vernon gnawing on a rawhide bone. But no, Crystal wasn't interested in meeting anybody any time, and Sarah knew that even if she wouldn't accept it.

When Crystal couldn't keep from it any longer and glanced back toward the passage in the hedges, the space was open to the specimen trees and still-brown Bermuda grass in Sarah's yard. Good riddance! She could return her full attention to the sorry excuse her flower garden was.

TWO - Many Towered

Acouple of weeks later, Crystal sprawled in bed and listened to the satisfying sounds of yet another spring storm that had woken her. It was only seven. Rain was pinging like zither notes on the red roof. She rolled over and snuggled under the blanket. It was Saturday and she was going back to sleep.

She woke later to raindrops splattering the long windows like eggs cracking against them, and she wondered if there was a tornado warning. Wind had set the tree limbs sweeping against the bedroom wall, in spite of the fact that a hundred years ago her great-grandfather, his journal declared, had planned for the growth of the trees and shrubs, allowing them room to grow as his family would in the house through the generations. But it had been impossible for that Victorian gentleman to envision how things would actually be in the future. The trees grew but the family didn't. And he couldn't predict, either, how things could be deliberately altered in the future. That his son, her grandfather, not thirty years later would have the house swiveled east ninety degrees, its back turned insultingly to his neighbor, thus putting the bedroom wing fifteen feet closer to the oaks and magnolias.

Mr. Thrasher was scheduled this morning to plow her garden as he did every early April. He wouldn't leave until the dirt was like cut-in pie crust. But she thought of his old mule and plow from her childhood. This nice storm, settling in to just a steady downpour, was so much better than his noisy tractor that she was actually glad he couldn't get the work done today.

At any rate, a rainy Saturday wouldn't be wasted. Though the house screamed for a full-time repairman it would have to settle for her. A cracked pane in a kitchen window stared at her like a bloodshot eye every morning and was on her to-do list, but she couldn't replace it in the rain. The basement steps were beginning to scare even her, but she couldn't repair them herself. The pocket door to the library wouldn't slide all the way in when she'd wanted some cross ventilation a few days earlier. She would tackle that with some elbow grease and WD 40, then see to the loose tiles in the downstairs bathroom.

In spite of the weather and the shape everything was in, something rejoiced, telling her it was going to be a great day. "A bitchin' day," she thought, thinking of the, to her, contradictory phrase she'd overheard from the curvy, happy teenage waitress the last time she and Sarah had stopped for a cone of soft ice cream at the Velvet Queen.

But breakfast before work she promised her rumbling stomach, looking at the clock again, seeing that the rain had lulled her until a little after eight. She went down the back stairs to the kitchen and lit a burner on the smaller of the two stoves. The kitchen had a hollow feel early mornings, as if waiting for a couple of cooks to hurry in and prepare nice meals for company. But that hadn't happened in a long time. Not since Crystal was a little girl and Willette had directed the maids, Ida and Nellie, to perform such magic.

Thinking of Willette and how she usually called on Saturday mornings tempted her to take the phone off the hook, but her mother would no doubt call Sue Elwood as she had before to drive over and tell Crystal to hang up the phone. What would it take to keep Willette at bay? Thirty miles away over swamps and the Broad Stream River and up to Memphis – not so far if you had wings – wasn't enough. And Willette didn't have wings.

She heard a vehicle on the long gravel drive. Mr. Thrasher should know he couldn't turn the dirt on a day like this. Or trim the tree, which she had also requested. And she hadn't asked him to repair the basement steps.

Then it hit her. The painting she'd dealt for the same day she'd been passed over by the Reverend was to be picked up today. Mr. Menuche had shown some collector, a Lydia Hawkins, his old catalogue from Dad's last show about twenty years ago, and she'd been taken with the very one Dad hadn't wanted to sell, according to the price he'd put on it.

But the dealing was done – the woman even wanted another painting later – and it was about time Dad's work was being sought again. But apparently she hadn't come to grips with parting with this one. She was curious then and now about Lydia Hawkins, too busy to even come and see it in person before finalizing the sale. What had attracted her to Torrence Oliver Bell's style, which even years ago had been sometimes described as old-fashioned in technique and unusual to say the least. One critic had said a few exhibited a macabre sense of humor, another had said bizarre if you looked close enough, and Dad hadn't challenged them. But their beauty was indisputable.

They made Crystal want to help the little girl catch the flowers being flailed by the wind from her hand; or wipe off the fuzz and taste the one peach that the little girl was striving to reach, dangling on the tree's bare limb that reached to high heaven; or wash the just-picked vegetables the little girl had dropped from her upturned skirt into the mud and dry her tears. Or listen for the rustle of the satin gown of the lovely Willette veiled in shadows – could it really be a lipstick smear across her face? Perhaps Lydia Hawkins knew there'd be no more and the value would naturally go up if others became interested after she started collecting them. Maybe outside was Lydia Hawkins, art aficionado.

Crystal caught sight of herself in the hall-tree mirror. Faded jeans, Dad's huge long-sleeved thermal undershirt; no shoes but a pair of Dad's old wool hunting socks, and looking down she saw a hole in one toe. Her medium-brown hair was still pulled up with purple plastic combs from her face-washing and teetering to the side in a bad imitation of Kathryn Hepburn on a bad hair day. But who cared what she looked like this morning? This painting sale was a deal already done. And anyway, Lydia Hawkins had already probably heard what Crystal accepted, not even reluctantly, that she was thought to be an oddball, although she felt as straight and narrow as the invading shallots that gave her town its name.

The phone rang just as the doorbell rang. Lydia Hawkins wouldn't get wet on the wide front porch and Willette would call back later. She lifted the handset and put it in a potted plant then walked up the curved front stairs to where "The Baby Basket" was hanging and looked at it. The painting had been there all her life. Sometimes she still saw herself reflected in it as the loved and protected baby she was then. It would be like saying good-bye to herself.

The doorbell didn't ring again. She wouldn't have guessed Lydia Hawkins to be that patient, rather that she was used to getting what she wanted when she wanted it, not even quibbling over the outlandish price of the painting, raised by Mr. Menuche for appreciation over the years. Well, aren't I the uncharitable one this morning, she thought. She went on down and opened the door.

THREE - Heard a Whisper

But it wasn't Lydia Hawkins. A man stood near the rail watching the rain. His shoulders were as wide as Crystal remembered Dad's being. He was not quite as tall as Dad or even the Reverend John Half. He had neat dark brown hair – unlike Dad's which was the very color of hers according to Sarah, until it seemingly turned gray overnight, and which he let grow, the last few years wearing it tied back with a length of twine or strip of rough cloth, befitting his artistic muse, he said.

A dark sweater clung to this man's shoulders like an old friend, like it dawned on her that she'd like to. His jeans had that been washed a million times look with the slim fit of him imbedded in them. His brown boots looked expensive and made for walking over hill and dale and through rain like today's. He wasn't the bigger-than-life image of Dad and the Reverend, but a casual emission of being in charge of his own life. She wondered.

Seeing all that in the instant before he turned to face her was maybe like seeing your life flash in front of you just before you figure to die. But she couldn't bring herself to look into his eyes to see what the man was driven by, as she felt the Reverend Half had wanted to do that evening he stood on her border and looked at her.

This man had a nice nose. She couldn't remember John Half's particularly; his whole face was what you saw. And this man had a neat beard and mustache, like so many men were wearing, except in Shallot. He had a little gray at the temples, so she knew he was at least in her generation, although she had no gray and never would. Sarah would nag her too much to ever allow it when it did come. She would know this man the next time she saw him, all right, if she ever did.

"Miss Bell? I'm Matt Hawkins."

Probably as in Mr. Lydia Hawkins. Was this anger she felt welling up? Because he had come to take her prized possession?

"Come in," she said, leaving the screen door closed as she turned back inside. That wasn't polite. But she could feel him staring at her and that wasn't polite either. Even though she had stared at him, he couldn't have known it. She hadn't even felt stared at by John Half two weeks ago. She'd just felt his considering.

It was hard to reconcile, a man in the house after so many years, since Dad died. Sure, old man Thrasher came inside to do whatever she couldn't manage with the help of her fix-it manual, but it was rare and always while she was at work. Especially unsettling because this man reminded her of Dad, why, she didn't know.

"It's stunning," he said, following her glance away from him to the painting.

She saw him cover up his surprise that the painting wasn't already packaged properly.

"Would you like me to send a professional to wrap it?" he asked.

"No. I can do it."

"If it doesn't stop raining, I'll come another time," he said.

"I wouldn't take a chance on it getting wet," she said, past her first fluttering over him, annoyed now, wondering if it showed.

"No, I'm sure," he said, "it's just that you shouldn't be expected to do it. It's not even your responsibility anymore." He gave a hint of a sarcastic smile. "Already new-owner insured."

"I'll take care of it," she said, leaving him standing there. She went upstairs and unearthed from one of Willette's closets a large box that a mink coat had been delivered in from Levy's up in Memphis, who knew how long ago, the store had been closed for years. The yellowed tissue paper still inside would make good cushioning. She went down the back stairs to the back hall, ran in the kitchen and turned off the burner, then picked her way down the basement steps to get a roll of brown wrapping paper left from Dad's stock of supplies, so old it might disintegrate the minute it saw light. A step fell through as she came back up and dislodged the paint can that was bracing it on the step below. She let out a little surprised yelp and heard the clattering. Sarah had correctly told her the steps weren't for the faint-hearted a few years ago when they went down during a tornado scare. When she came through the doorway in the back hall, Matt Hawkins was there, about to come down, and she almost bumped into him.

"You OK?" he said.

"Just a paint can I knocked over."

He followed her to the front. "Would you like me to take it down for you? The frame looks heavy."

"No, I can do it." Then she remembered long ago instruction. "But thank you." Good grief. Dust was thick on the back of the frame next to the wall. Note to self. Fire the maid. Ha ha. She braced it on the floor and used her soft shirttail to rake it off.

"Even the frame is a work of art," he said.

"It was hand carved by Dad." And it was brushed with what looked like real gold. It occurred to her the frame was probably worth several hundred dollars. She should ask extra from Lydia Hawkins for it.

After wrapping the painting on the dining room table with two layers of tissue paper and stuffing the crevices with more tissue, she secured the box with duct tape, then wrapped the entire box in the heavy paper.

"Back in a minute," she said, and went to the storage room on the enclosed back porch for a roll of heavy plastic she kept for gardening needs.

Matt Hawkins let her do it without protest or further offers, not even any small talk.

"This should protect it from the rain," she said with some satisfaction.

He smiled. "It's stopped raining. The sun's been out for a while."

Well, she deserved that. But she ignored it and darted her eyes away. She ran her hands over the plastic, testing the edges of the tape, seeing the painting in her head, knowing she would never touch it or even see it again. She was glad she wasn't the crying type.

She was relieved it had stopped raining, certain that she'd adequately protected it but believing that he wouldn't have taken a chance of getting it wet. She turned the box to him and he tested how to carry it, finally putting it under his right arm, bracing it with his left hand, and followed her to the front door.

He turned as if wanting to delay his departure or at least offer consolation, and after consideration said, "You'll miss it."

Well duh. "I'll make do," she said, opening the door, still angry as he stepped out on the porch.

She went back to the kitchen, not standing at the door as Willette would have done because it wasn't good manners to close the door on a visitor, nor waiting on the porch as Sarah would have done out of politeness as well as friendliness and curiosity until he was out of sight. The house seemed colder than it had, as if it missed the extra body heat. She circled as if in a revolving door and ran to the front to watch from a window as he put the package in the back of a medium blue Chevy Blazer. She pictured Dad driving his truck with Vernon's head hanging out the front passenger window, eyes slits against the wind. Then Matt Hawkins patted Vernon, who had come bounding down the drive like he was young. She strained to hear what he said to the little beagle, but couldn't. He'd been running a mole aground, she supposed, the day John Half had surveyed her lifestyle.

She focused on Matt Hawkins the way she used to watch through her telescope from the same window when she was a child, when the shrubs and trees were kept trimmed and the sidewalk was still visible and people came at will. He kept standing there as if he might have forgotten something, or like he might have something more to say. Which was why it wasn't polite to close the door on somebody, she figured Sarah would tsk tsk to her.

But she wanted to throw open the door and yell something like don't go yet, I wish we'd talked. But she'd inherited nothing of Dad's insight into human nature, had she, and even though she thought he'd stay, she wasn't sure. He hadn't indicated she was anything other than a participant in a business transaction. No more attention than Dad had given Sarah, on the surface.

Vernon was having a harder time letting him go than even she was. He wanted to crawl in the truck! He still missed Dad. He'd sniff Dad's boots in the back hall or curl up on the foot of Dad's bed like when he was a new puppy over thirteen years ago. And when Matt Hawkins did at last look toward the house, she jerked back from the window, like a beetle on a string pulled by a naughty boy.

The man probably thought she and Vernon were incapable of a little decorum after this clever move. Well, according to Dad, everybody had their own idea of normal for themselves. She couldn't deny Dad had been very unusual. Willette – a definite mold breaker. Sarah? Absolutely one of a kind. Where God had gotten the idea for those three, as well as her ancestors, she didn't know. And herself, she had to admit.

But she bet if Great Grandfather T. O. Bell had painted the roof Confederate gray instead of red, they'd not have razzed him. And if Grandfather T. O. Bell II had had the house turned from its original north view to face south, to oversee from its place in north Mississippi the remains of the noble Confederacy, instead of west to spite the neighbors, they'd have called it a fine Rebel sentiment. And if Dad's plans had worked out, she bet they wouldn't have faulted him either.

He hadn't left the place, that the town knew of, for close to the last six months of his life, having shown that he made no idle threats. However, if carrying out his convictions ever caused the U. S. Army any remorse they had no indication. But whenever Toliver (as they called him) Bell did whatever he did, it somehow played havoc in Shallot.

But wasn't she different? She even had a job. But she was happy to confound them by not making it clear if it was because she didn't have any money left, or had money in piles and chose to be stingy. At any rate, she knew the old-time shop owners, who waved to her through their plate-glass windows as she walked down Main Street to the brickyard, appreciated her loyalty even though she drove Sarah to the new Wal-Mart to shop. Sarah had told her that further compounding their curiosity was the fact that she was generous though she appeared so frugal, and Crystal had said can't I do anything without you blabbing?

Furthermore, they'd have to admit she stayed up-to-date on the news, even took her papers to the school recycle bin. She always paid her light bill on time at city hall, but it was usually so dark back in her wooded place they might wonder if she ever used one. And she paid her phone bill every month but answered it arbitrarily, as anybody in town who had any call to call her would attest.

She dressed neatly, they'd have to give her that, although her clothes were frequently out of style, even for Shallot. Sue said some of the ladies said they bet there were closets full of expensive clothes that hadn't been worn a time by Willette, and sometimes when Sue dropped by the office she'd say she recognized a dress Crystal had on that her mama had worn. But Sarah said they'd have a hard time faulting her for getting some use out of them.

So in spite of not trying to, she sometimes wondered just why she was even a focus of their attention. Maybe it was the contradictions. Maybe her life was so open a book they suspected something hidden. She didn't rock the boat the way her family had always done. To boil it down, maybe it was that she was a Bell. The last one. And they were maybe hoping for her to ring out whatever it was that would put her in the pantheon of the Bells preceding her. If so, she was prepared to wait them out.

She watched Matt Hawkins drive down the long gravel lane, imprisoned by the thick prickly holly hedge, as if putting the back of the house to them wasn't insult enough for the neighbors. He stopped and got out and opened the gate and she imagined she heard the squeaking hinges, although it was too far away. She seldom drove her car, but when she did she went behind the house and out the alley in back. The gate was one of her least worries. No one ever used it. Except this . . . this . . . Hawkins Delivery Man!

As he drove himself and the painting out of her life, she let the heavy panels of lace fall together at the window, the hems puddling in creamy piles on the hardwood floor. She grabbed one and instead of draping her head to pretend she was a bride, as she did when a child, she covered her face except for her eyes, like the spy that she was being. She sneezed hugely from the dust. She returned to the kitchen, deciding it was parting with the painting that had her so rattled, and made a mental note to shake the curtains out in the back yard.

She filled the tea kettle with water, stuffed the perforated stainless steel ball with tea leaves and screwed the top back on, hooked the chain to dangle the tea in the water. She made tea like Ida used to. She brought it to a rolling boil and let it steep for a good strong flavor that wouldn't dissipate when poured still warm enough to dissolve a little sugar in a crystal pitcher. With a little cold water added, and poured over a tall glass of ice with a slice of lemon, it was soothing or reviving, whichever she needed it to be, summer or winter.

She could almost hear Willette call down to the kitchen, "Ida, please bring some tea up for me. With plenty of ice." Willette always said please. Ida would roll her eyes and yell vaguely toward the back stairs, "Yessum, in a minute," even if she wasn't doing a thing. Crystal would wonder how Ida could keep from darting up those stairs. Crystal would say, "I'll do it," and Dad would say, "She can wait a minute." Ida would mutter, "Nothing to keep her from coming down to get it." But in a few minutes she'd go, carrying a glass wrapped in a linen napkin instead of sitting on a tray the way Willette wanted it.

Crystal removed the combs and dropped them in the garbage can, fluffed her hair over her cold ears, then lit the small stove's other burner to help warm the kitchen and put coffee on. If she'd asked Matt Hawkins, "Would you like coffee?" as Willette or Sarah certainly would have, would he be sitting here now, sharing it and small talk? Well, what had kept her from asking him?

She put the check on the scrubbed walnut table and as she prepared her breakfast thought of the role the money would play, not what she had given in exchange for it or who had written the check or the man who had brought it. But as she ate, she studied it curiously. It was signed by Lydia Hawkins. Not Mrs. or Miss or Ms. She wondered if Matt and Lydia Hawkins were husband and wife or mother and son. She controlled the money. She bought the painting sight unseen. And he came to fetch it.

She went to look at the stairwell landing where the picture had hung for thirty-six years. The wall could use a good painting. She took a second to appreciate the ironic pun. Yeah, she could have the three-story wall painted, which she still couldn't afford and couldn't rig scaffolding to do herself, or she could made do, just as she had without thought told Matt Hawkins she would do. Or, she could bring out the copy from the studio beside Dad's bedroom and hang it on the wall where the original had been all these years.

Lydia Hawkins couldn't know about yet another of Torrence Oliver Bell's unusual habits. Probably no one except Willette and Sarah and herself, not even Mr. Menuche, knew that Dad, as he said, "slapped up a copy" of a favorite for himself. Oh, he changed something – dress color to one Willette hated, her graceful hands to wringing hands, wilted flowers replaced fresh bloomed. Usually, it was something like that. More whimsical or inscrutable or aggravating to Willette than even the original was. Crystal wondered from time to time but certainly never asked an authority whether that meant they were actually two separate paintings. Dad didn't think so. He said nobody could buy his soul and inspiration and talent for mere money. She thought it was his joke on certain buyers who bought paintings for what he thought were the wrong reasons. Well, you had to know Dad. She was uncertain why he'd duplicated this painting, since he obviously had not planned on selling it.

She'd never paid much attention to the difference between the painting Matt Hawkins left with and the one she replaced it with, and didn't even think about it now, as she was in a hurry to get started on her work, and who else was going to know? She smiled, feeling she had regained something of herself.

A few hours later she was working in the yard, raking wet leaves away from the peonies shooting up their little pink and brown horns, pulling up carrots by their lacy green tops, and jerking marauding wild onions up by the handful, glad she'd already replaced the broken pane. The loose bathroom tiles would have to wait. Sarah must have slept late even for her and hadn't heard the truck, or she'd already have been over to find out who had come to Crystal's house so early on a low-cloud Saturday morning in April.

FOUR - A Flower of Another Color

When the voice on the phone identified itself as Lydia Hawkins, Crystal was pretty sure she was too young to be Matt's mother. But what was she talking about?

"Are you trying to pull a scam on me?"

Crystal silently repeated the word *scam*, but couldn't give it relevance.

"I didn't know there was a copy of the Toliver I bought!"

"Copy?" How did she know?

"I assumed it would be what I paid for. And now Matt tells me there's something different about it."

"Different?" Yes, but even she hadn't paid any attention to it. And who was Matt Hawkins to know the difference? An art critic? He'd only seemed to know a beautiful painting when he saw one.

"Photos of his work are catalogued. You must know that."

I may sound like an idiot, but I'm not, she almost said.

"Miss Bell, are you there?"

"I . . ."

"In this painting, the baby holds a huge red zinnia with a dragonfly circling it."

So? "I know that."

"That's not what the photo in the catalogue shows."

Well just hold your horses a minute, Crystal wanted to scream, but said, "Would you hold on a minute?" and laid the phone down, then picked it up and said "Please," and went without waiting for an answer.

Well, Dad, isn't it just like you, she thought as she rushed up to the landing. Keep the original put away and hang a copy because you like a zinnia and dragonfly better than violets and bees. A fragile nosegay of Willette's favorite, black-veined purple violets, were seized in the fat fist of the baby girl, like Jessica Lange in King Kong's grip, and being circled by huge-winged honeybee bi-planes.

The tiny, delicate blooms that gave in to early summer sun were precisely the picture Willette liked to portray of herself. But zinnias were more her in endurance if not appearance, flowering through heat and drought, but susceptible to mildewed stems as the season went on. And that was probably why Dad chose it, to aggravate her with the flower's ability to hang in there until the last small, ugly bud opened, and with the dragonfly's unflagging ability to stay aflight in all its endeavors. She went back to the phone.

"I apologize, Ms. Hawkins. I have the original hanging up here now. The one you have has always hung here, so I thought . . ."

"Do you expect me to believe that?" "You idiot" was not said but implied in Ms. Hawkins' tone. "You must have copied it."

"I couldn't even paint the wall."

"This is good, I admit."

"My father painted it."

"I want the Toliver I paid for. The one everyone knows by this title."

Again, don't say it. Everyone but you, Ms. Hawkins. And me. "Of course. Certainly. I didn't intend to deceive you."

"I could sue you for fraud."

"I don't think it would hold up in court." Of course it would.

"If I had already held the party, and someone had pointed it out to me then instead of now . . . . I would have been a laughingstock."

"Yes, I can see that." Uh oh, wrong thing to say. She could practically hear seething. "I am sorry."

"What do you suggest we do, Miss Bell?"

"Can't we just exchange paintings?"

"This is so near a likeness. It would lower the value of mine. I think we'll have to destroy it."

"No! It's the one I've loved all these years."

Crystal could sense a coming to terms in the slight hesitation on the other end of the line.

"As I love the one I bought. Eventually I would have noticed. The violets would pick up the color in my Aubusson."

The woman bought it to complement her rug? She hoped Dad was tied down in that fancy casket Willette had insisted on.

"I paid premium. You know I didn't ask Royce Menuche to bargain you down."

Now would be a good time to say you got the frame for free. The copy and the original were in identical frames, another reason she knew Dad prized that painting. But could she? Get in the same haggling category as she now knew Lydia Hawkins to be?

"Lucky for me there are two paintings titled the same."

She wanted both! Crystal would rather destroy it. "He did it hurriedly, it can't be as good."

"I don't actually want it destroyed."

Crystal stopped pacing. The woman was going to compromise.

"But it lowers the value of what I bought, so I have only one suggestion."

Of course. She would have one other suggestion. And Crystal knew what it was.

"This revelation should halve the amount I paid, don't you think? And no one the wiser?"

"All right. I'll give you a check when we exchange paintings." And now it was put up or shut up about the frame, but she still couldn't do it. Why did she insist on holding herself to a standard even when it cost her dearly, and nobody else to even know? Well, hell, could it only be that what was a few hundred dollars when you were talking several thousand you have to send back?

"And another thing. Don't make known the existence of the copy."

That was easy to promise. If people knew, wouldn't it make Dad appear even more . . . odd? Not to mention that she obviously now had her answer about the dual paintings being two separate ones, but worth only half the original value if people knew. Not that she was going to sell any more to anyone else, probably, especially now. She could see Lydia Hawkins finding some way to convey to prospective buyers that Crystal was hard to deal with. But she didn't like the idea of Dad's work going down in value for any reason. "I agree," she said. And was this why Miss, Mrs. whatever Hawkins called in person instead of getting Mr. Menuche to call.

When they hung up, Crystal went back to look again. It was so beautiful. That was all she knew. There were tender flowers of spring as well as hardy summer bloomers – purple iris, yellow pansies, pink and red geraniums, white and yellow daisies, trailing ivy, fuchsia gladioli – some like those out back now, blooming their last on the hot May day, others just coming into their own. Not a rose in the lot. Remnants of the basket the baby was sitting in and which was seemingly just plunked down in the middle of the flowers, like a foundling left by a caring but hopeless mother, were probably down in the cellar somewhere in a dark damp corner. And the baby was still around, only she was the same age now as the canvas and oil and wondered if she'd start to fade and crack and peel when it did. No, she'd be long in her grave before the painting showed its age.

She grabbed a full-skirted blue dress with nipped-in waist and rounded white pique collar and cuffs on the short sleeves and with flying fingers buttoned it over her bosom and buckled the yellowing white leather belt. Not that she would have worn them, but the starched crinoline slips had disappeared. When she was in college she'd asked her mother about them for a 'fifties party her sorority was having, but Willette said she had told Ida to burn hers the minute they had gone out of style, and added that she *hadn't* burned her bras. Could that be why she herself got a kick out of wearing these Doris Day outfits and living braless at home? Still rebelling against Willette?

The conversation with Lydia Hawkins had run her late. She rarely answered the phone any more, although it rang as seldom as the Liberty Bell, excusing herself that salesmen had started calling. Of course, there was Willette's Saturday ritual. Sarah usually just walked over, unless she was tired and needed her for something like getting the cat down from the porch roof, or help cleaning the sticky mess that boiled over when she was making apple jelly from the tree in Crystal's yard.

Sarah had gotten to the point where she slept past Crystal's leaving for work, and Crystal wouldn't accept her reason, that as she had gotten older she found it harder to get to sleep, because she didn't like to think of Sarah as getting older. But Crystal had thought in case the call was from Sarah she wouldn't want to not answer. Saying they were on good terms would be a vast understatement, for in fact they were best friends though Sarah was old enough to be her mother. Actually, almost too old to be her mother. Not like the Biblical Sarah, but old.

No, they weren't spiteful to each other as Dad and Sarah had been. The way they had been on the surface. She recalled things her Dad said, like if Sarah had a man that would put up with her she would be a lot easier to put up with, and Crystal used to wake in the middle of the night when the gate between the two yards, installed by Dad she supposed, as he was the first generation to acknowledge the Chancellors, squalled on its hinges and she would see Dad coming through it from next door, and the light in Sarah's room would go out about then. And twenty years ago Sarah was thirty years younger, as Sarah said.

And more seriously, Sarah also told her how she wished she had been more tolerant of T. Oliver, her name for him. She said she wished she'd never called the law on him. But at the time, it was the last straw of his shenanigans, no matter how she might feel about other things. And Sarah didn't think he ever held it against her. Crystal agreed. Crystal thought he just liked to stir things up because he was bored and not because he was as odd as people thought.

Crystal remembered that day only too clearly. The day the tank was delivered. A WWII relic of a tank. Gun turrets and all. Rust and camouflage. Delivered on a flatbed trailer, to be parked behind the house with all the other stuff. A milk cart, an ice wagon, a steam-boiler fire engine, an old gas street lamp, the sign off the now demolished train depot, to think of a few, some in weathered sheds and others just lying about, weathering.

Even Dad would have known Sarah wasn't going to put up with that tank. She was bound to call the law after seeing it crawl down the ramps like a mythical dragon. Its treads crunched, munched, and grazed, eating a trail six inches deep in the yard as the giant truck-tractor, after unhitching from the truck bed, pulled the tank down and behind the house.

She remembered taking matters in her own hands and trying to hide the shotgun, which she figured Dad would take with him to meet the deputy. She was darting here and there like a sentry run amuck when Dad walked right into her trying to wedge it in the butler's pantry. "I had enough of guns pointed in the war," he said patiently, lifting the gun with his large sun-browned hand. "But Sarah . . ." she said. "You ought to be able to figure out why Sarah complains," Dad said. "It's not my cast-off toy collection that bothers her."

Crystal had thought with her child's innocence then, did Sarah just want his attention? Or did he want hers? Like when she wanted Willette's and did something, played ball instead of dolls, just to get Willette to notice her? But she'd managed to put aside his advice to this day. "You've got to trust things you know, but things you feel, too. Deputy Youngblood's the little Black kid I took deer hunting and taught to slide home. I could make my point better if he handcuffed and took me in, but he'll figure out a compromise between her and me. " Then he laughed. "And not because we're brothers like they speculate around here. And I'm not his daddy, either. Point is, people'll say anything. Especially about our family.

Through the open windows that reached almost from floor to ceiling, they'd heard a car stop out front, and Dad strode heavily to the heavy wooden door and talked to Bob Youngblood. Bob went next door to talk to Sarah and came back in a few minutes and talked to Dad again. Then they'd told the truck driver to go back around and move the tank again, and there it was now, still in its final resting place out back in the side yard where Sarah couldn't see it unless she climbed up in her side tower and craned her neck out the window. It was all still so clear to Crystal, all that from so long ago, but human nature was still just a big puzzle.

But she was afraid she understood Lydia Hawkins' nature.

FIVE - A Road Runs By

She grabbed the white ballerina flats that matched the dress belt and didn't notice how they had yellowed as she stuffed a tissue in the toe of each. Willette's feet were larger than hers. Take that, Willette!

She hurried down the long drive, leaving the dusty black 1970 Cadillac, bought new the last year Willette resided there without interruption, secure in its shelter, and out onto the broken, rising and falling pieces of the sidewalk on the nearly traffic-less street of the little town.

The half-dozen houses on her street, which dead-ended on the south end of town, were big and old and perched back from the sidewalk on treed lots like birds that had grown too fat and ancient to fly away from their nests. All except hers and Sarah's had been divided into apartments where newer cars than Crystal's sat broken-down and rusted in the yards – she couldn't help thinking of the jokes about so-called southern rednecks who kept every car they ever owned – and kids played around them until the grass turned to dirt.

She and Sarah had gotten letters from a real estate agent wanting them to sell so the lots could be sub-divided and turned into a housing development. Sarah had said, "Over my dead body," and wrote a scathing answer that if she wanted her historic mansion torn down and the street turned into box houses she was capable of doing it herself, and where would the people come from to move in them, anyway? There was no interstate here! Crystal had merely torn up her letter. What would she do with her life if she didn't have this big hundred-year-old place to work herself to death on?

But she couldn't deny that on the next street over, even Shallot, Mississippi was showing it was finally out of the 'fifties and about to enter the late 'eighties – only a few years later than the rest of the world. There was a video rental, a Fax and Photo, a laundry-mat, a pizza place, a health club, and two new florists. She could see one, but two? And even a ComputerCentral rumored about to open, all occupying the front space of square brick two story buildings that had once housed businesses like Ruleman's Department Store, which even had an elevator to the second floor; and the City Café, where Dad had drunk coffee and talked with the old men until his self-incarceration; and Frank's Five and Dime, where Crystal had worked after school for one entire week until Willette found out about it and made her quit; and Morse's Drug Store and Soda Fountain with its cool Cherry Cokes, where, as strange as it seemed now, she used to hang out with the other teenagers; and the Piggly Wiggly, where Willette would send Nellie with a list, much of which she knew wouldn't be stocked in that small town grocery store. There also used to be the offices of the *Shallot Straight News*, whose slogan was "News That Can't Be Stopped," playing off the wild green onion theme.

Now in addition to the Wal-Mart out on the edge of town there was a McDonald's and a Kroger's and the concrete block building housing the new paper, *The Shallot Ballot*, whose slogan also played off the green onions, "We Can Smell the News." They simply smell, Sarah said, as she often disputed their opinion of events.

The Shallot Brickyard was on Main Street, at the end of the sidewalk and then a little farther. There Crystal kept the books and made payroll, sent reports to the home office and wrote orders for sales she herself made on the phone. She had started there thirteen years ago as clerk and she was still listed on payroll as clerk.

Mr. Elwood, the manager, liked to fish in the spring. And he liked to hunt in the fall. He also liked to smoke his cigar out in the brickyard and watch the inventory bake in the sunshine. He'd read the Jackson paper in the morning and have a long dinner at home with Sue at noon and read the Memphis paper in the afternoon. Then he'd go home early to push-mow his lawn and sit in the glider on the front patio with Sue after an early supper of leftovers from the noon meal, and see whoever passed by.

And if he continued to follow those pursuits, Crystal felt the Shallot Brickyard would do just fine this year the way it had for the past twelve. Because they were making the profit expected of them, she didn't think there was anything to worry about even though the owner's business manager, Mr. Dotkin, had been calling from Memphis the last few days asking for sales reports and inventory figures and personnel files. They'd soon be asking how many times a day the pot was flushed, Mr. Elwood said.

She had decided to ask for pay raises for Mr. Elwood and herself in the next budget. She had gotten the crew one last year, and she wasn't asking for capital improvements this year except replacement of a worn-out forklift. Home office was sending a computer. Mr. Elwood had commented that it might be more work for her to learn it than it would save her. If she'd known ComputerCentral was coming to town, she'd have requested they get the business. She usually got back with a rubber stamp approval whatever she requested. In Mr. Elwood's name, of course.

She didn't like this feeling of being late. If she hadn't gone in the garden this morning, unusual for a weekday, she wouldn't have been so last minute when the phone call came from Lydia Hawkins. She religiously went to the garden on weekend mornings, "while the dew was still on the roses," as Sarah said, quoting the old hymn, adding lately with a "you know exactly what I mean" look, that Sunday morning communion with nature was no substitute for a good reaming out by a good-looking preacher like the Reverend Dr. John Half. But it was communion to Crystal, crumbling His rich handiwork, Mississippi dirt, through her fingers and letting it produce and multiply as intended, and she said "You ought to be ashamed," to Sarah.

She worked in the vegetable garden most evenings. Saturdays in the yard she wore a big straw hat and when the sun was blazing she wore long sleeves, but nevertheless she had a light tan. Willette thought a tan was undignified for a lady and that she'd wrinkle prematurely, but Sarah said Crystal was one of those people that a little sun wouldn't hurt, like T. Oliver. And that she looked like a mummy wrapped up like that.

Sarah told her she'd read that most people had a forehead line for each decade, raising her brows to form the wrinkles, but Crystal didn't count eight, only five across and one broken. A cruel trick of nature, Sarah said, because even a tree must be felled to count its rings, but a person's age was stuck out there for the world to see. It mattered somewhat to Sarah, and was a major concern to Willette, but it didn't worry Crystal. However, she doctored each night with the best beauty unguent Sarah could buy for herself and Crystal, because according to what her mother and Sarah said, it wasn't a proper thing for a lady to get too comfortable with herself.

In summer she wore a large hat when she walked back and forth to the brickyard so everyone would remember she was her mother's daughter and give her their respect.

And wasn't it good that she chose not to let perfectly good and expensive clothes go to waste? Sarah would show her the magazines with "that pompous Mr. Blackwell's list of the worst-dressed," and tell her "that new singer with the sacrilegious name doesn't wear clothes sometimes, just underwear." Sarah always gave her clothes for her birthday and Christmas, so she could be up-to-date if she chose. Sarah had even bought her a pair of Nike walking shoes, saying she ought to be trendy like the New Yorkers she saw in the news recently wearing them with their business suits. She gladly trod to work in them and carried the shoes to match her outfit in a little canvas bag if they were of the high heel selection Willette had left.

When she entered the office, Mr. Elwood put down the morning paper and picked up his pocket watch from the desk. He looked at it and then at her. "Reckon my watch is runnin' fast." He ran it back and put it in his pocket.

"Isn't it new?" she said, and added she was sorry to be late. He was speechless for a second, then retrieved the watch and reset it.

Huh? Well for goodness sake. People really did set their watches by her! She sat down at her desk and laughed. She had thought of driving, but was pretty sure the car battery was dead. She was going to check it this weekend and bring Sarah's car over to charge it if needed. "I stayed too long in the garden." There was no need to tell him about the phone call. Nobody need know she had sold a painting, and the wrong one at that. And now she wondered what other ill might come of that. She bet Lydia Hawkins wouldn't let much get by her without satisfactory retribution. And she really didn't think money back would do the trick.

"I let the men in when I got here a few minutes ago. The time clock'll show them all checking in late."

"I'll adjust their cards."

"Oh, I'm not worried about it. But we already had a call from Mr. Dotkin this morning. He wants to know what we project our orders to be for the next three months. Now how would we do that? Wonder what's up?"

"Probably nothing. I'll make some estimates." Then she took the opportunity to reinforce the benefits of the new computer. "It won't take as long to do such as that with the computer. There'll be programs to keep up with it."

"Oh." Then he thought a minute. "How will all that information get inside the computer?"

She laughed. "That's the kicker. Somebody's got to put it in."

"Don't look at me," he said. "You know I wouldn't mind helping."

"I'll manage."

"Well, I don't know whether to worry or not," he said, looking down at the newspaper. "I was just reading here in the business section about all these hostile takeovers. You know, some company with more money than it's got good sense, trying to get a company nobody wants to sell?"

Crystal laughed again, but wheels in her head began to turn. "I doubt that. But it sounds like they may be selling us."

Mr. Elwood looked happy that they'd figured it out, then decided he wasn't going to settle for bad news like that. "No, no. I bet we're trying to decode when there's no secret message at all," he said, glad for a chance to refer to his encryption unit days in World War II.

"I expect you're right," she said, and dug into her work.

There were eight men laboring in the yard. Like the town, until recently, the company was only a shell of its former self, merely a collecting site and clearing house – no longer manufacturing its own bricks.

They depended on flatbed trucks bringing in new bricks from factories as well as used bricks from far-flung demolition sites. The men stacked them on pallets in sections according to name, age, color, type, size, and manufacturer, where they "waited for their code number to come up," Mr. Elwood said, and shipped them to their new home. Horace Smith, the new foreman, was strawboss, no pun intended Mr. Elwood told him, but obviously intending it. The men liked Horace, even though at twenty-nine he was younger than most of them and wouldn't dig in and work beside them like he was supposed to.

He wore khaki pants and shirts instead of the navy blue uniforms the men wore. The company provided them and had them laundered. And she wondered how long the company would keep that up, if it sold, although the cost was negligible to be such a good employee incentive. The dust and dirt from the bricks ground into their clothes and she knew the wives would be very unhappy if the policy changed.

Horace knew his way around the yard, which covered fifteen acres, how to repair the equipment, and how to get the orders filled on deadline by the men without their complaining about his not helping. And there were no complaints from customers he delivered to, so she let him slide by with his slacking.

Other than that she knew little about him, as he was hired by Mr. Dotkin in Memphis, except that he was stuck on himself. She was familiar with the other men and most of their families. She certainly knew the ones prone to drink up their pay on Friday nights. She gave their checks to their wives if they showed up the last Friday of the month. She first did it a few years ago when Dorrie Wilson had come in complaining that the children would go hungry and the rent wouldn't get paid unless she was given her husband's check. It seemed the right thing to do. When Jack Wilson discovered it he said Crystal was trying to run the brickyard like her daddy had tried to run the town.

"My dad didn't try to run the town," she'd said, loud enough for the rest of the men waiting in line to hear, "He did run the town." She should say more, how she was nothing like Dad and couldn't run anybody else's business with hers in such a sorry mess. But Jack interpreted her statement to mean that he was right, that she was going to run the yard the way she saw fit, and he marched out, saying, "I bet you're a women's libber, too!" and never questioned her again. She took that as permission to continue to do what she thought was right with the checks.

She liked figuring up what was due each man and imprinting it on the old check-cutter. It gave her a sense that another orderly week had passed in spite of what must be going wrong in her little hometown, much less the world, the same way the seasons rolled around in her world. Life was ordained with the few long-coat winter days, spring giving way after only three or four weeks to sweaty summer, then fall lingering to lull you into thinking winter might never come around again.

It was satisfying to believe there was very little left that could change in the life shunted to her by her parents. Let the Bell lineage fizzle with her quiet slippage into middle age. It was a rare occasion when she felt some stirring, like that one brief Saturday moment a few weeks ago, when Matt Hawkins had riled her. But there was nothing to be done about that.

Yes, she would be happy to use the computer, but she was going to do the checks as always. And tomorrow was another payday.

SIX - Steadily Weaving

Next morning she'd been in for an hour when Mr. Elwood entered. He looked relieved to see her there as usual.

"You look nice this morning," he said.

She looked up in surprise. She couldn't remember his actually commenting on her appearance before.

"That outfit reminds me of Sue when we got married."

Crystal knew he'd been married about twenty years. He'd been an old bachelor when he came from Memphis to manage the yard and met Sue, who had taught Crystal in grade school. She smoothed the skirt of the shirtwaist dress, which struck her just above the knees. It was pale blue cotton with cool short sleeves, a stand-up collar and box pleats, and buttoned down the front. It was one job to iron so she didn't wear it often. She thought Willette had worn it a time or two around the house, and Ida probably stuffed it somewhere to keep from having to iron it. But then again, Willette never wore the new off anything.

"Cedar closets keep things well," she said. They were stocked with these tailored dresses as well as Willette's evening wear and tailored suits for church and committee meetings and designer classic suits for "occasions."

"Oh, it don't look old."

"No. I didn't think you meant that."

"What I was getting at was to compliment you."

"That's just the way I took it, Mr. Elwood."

Willette still passed clothes to Crystal, though in fairness, she had to admit that Willette's purchases weren't as prestigious or numerous as before. And she actually felt bad about it because Willette still "dressed" every day of her life. What if she'd had on one of those pretty things wasting away in her closets when Matt Hawkins came to get the painting? Would he have been in such a hurry to leave? But what if by some fluke he had been attracted to her? She couldn't even imagine it and didn't want to.

After reading the morning newspaper and commenting on how glad he was that bricks were made of local commodities like good old Miss'sippi clay (never mind that a brick hadn't been made there since Reconstruction) and therefore no A-rabs could put them out of business because of the price of oil, and that they didn't need any Japanese computer-robot to run the place, he signed the stack of checks.

Then he began to fidget with a lure dangling from his vest pocket and went to the door and opened it to look out. Finally he said, "If you can do without me, I think I'll go check the water gauge down at the reservoir. I think they're opening up the spillway today."

"I believe I can manage."

"I might catch us both a mess for supper."

"Sounds good," she answered absentmindedly. The water brimming over the floodgates of the lake and foaming into the air on the huge concrete chunks at the lower lake was his favorite fishing hole, and might as well have been created by the Army Corps of Engineers for his pleasure, instead of flood control for the Mississippi River.

Not long after that, Miniver Tandy opened the door and looked around. Seeing Crystal was alone, she entered, wearing red shorts with bleach spots on one leg, flip-flops bearing the imprints of her feet and a large T-shirt with faded lettering that said, "I Don't Need No Excuse!" She kept on the large, very dark sunglasses that would have looked more at home on a Hollywood starlet. A little foil price sticker remained, as if she had just bought them and put them on in a hurry. Crystal was surprised at Miniver's garb. She was usually neatly, though casually, dressed. Her thick black hair, ordinarily in some kind of braided fashion, looked like it hadn't seen a comb all day. She left the door open enough to watch her truck parked near the front door.

"Afternoon, Miniver," Crystal said. "I've just finished writing Thomas's check."

"He be gettin' it,'" Miniver said, her head turning to look outside.

Something made Crystal halt as she began to insert the check back into its alphabetical place in the stack. "Here, you go ahead and take it," she said.

"Not my place to be gettin' his pay."

What was going on with Miniver today? She didn't even sound like herself. "Well, whatever you think, Miniver." She looked outside as Miniver got to the door. Her two children, not old enough to be in school, were waiting in the cab of the old white pickup. Their heads, covered with coarse light brown curly hair, were popping up and down as they blew bubbles through large plastic hoops and watched them fly out the windows. The truck bed was full of flattened cardboard boxes and scrap metal which Miniver picked up behind the grocery store and other businesses, and took to sell at Lazarov Recycling in North Memphis.

Miniver called out, "Don't spill that bottle of bubble soap!" and reached up to adjust the glasses. Crystal wondered why someone who worked as hard as she did, and who appeared to be sensible, would spend that kind of money on sunglasses when her worn out shoes wouldn't cost that much to replace.

"Miniver, how are things going?"

"Couldn't be better."

The bitter irony in Miniver's voice stuck between Crystal's ears and she couldn't get it to pass on through. If Miniver hadn't come in, Crystal would have given the check to Thomas anyway. "Did you come in for something in particular?"

"I got to go. The kids gettin' hot out in the truck."

"You should have brought them inside. You know I like to see them. They're cute kids."

"For mixed?"

Crystal knew her face showed her reaction to that totally unexpected response before she could suppress it.

"Oh, I know you better'n that. But what you want me to say?"

"It's just that . . . you don't seem to be yourself today. Is something wrong?"

"You sure you up to knowin'?"

She wasn't sure, but she'd asked until she was going to get the answer and not like it, like a fly always returning to the spot it had lighted on until it got swatted. She nodded.

Miniver took off her sunglasses. Her right cheekbone was raw; the hollow under her eye puckered and darker than her skin, the normally creamy white of her eye as solid red as Sarah's hibiscus. Crystal tried to contain the shock. Things like this happened.

"Says he ain't much of a man if he lets me dole out his pay to 'im."

"I'm going to call Sheriff Youngblood."

"No. It don't be happenin' again."

But Crystal saw in her eyes that it would. And she saw something else, too, and heard it in Miniver's new talk. Thomas was guilty of more than physically hurting her. Something vaguely familiar stirred in Crystal that made her want to fight for Miniver, to keep her from a familiar descending ladder.

"Miniver . . . whatever Thomas is trying to make you think . . . about yourself . . . don't fall for it."

Miniver gave her an impatient look.

Who was she to tell Miniver that Thomas made her come in today to put her where he thought she should be. Down a peg. But what if Miniver understood that? What if she was here asking for help. What could Crystal do? Nothing. "Miniver, I know things like this happen, but –"

"You don't know nothin'. You in your ivory tower, nothin' to worry about but yourself . . ."

She knew Miniver hadn't meant to say she would prefer a beating every once in a while to being as alone as Crystal was. And people still called it that? "Miniver, I feel like this was partly my fault."

"Ain't nobody responsible but me."

"I wish I could help . . . ."

"I'm goin' on now."

After she watched Miniver get in the truck with the kids and back out and drive away, she felt the crack in the sidewalk of her life deepen and widen. She put paychecks in the men's boxes in the lunchroom, locked the front office door and went home.

SEVEN - Lures and Lies

Mr. Elwood was standing at her kitchen door. Ordinarily he would have looked as happy as a kid who'd played hooky to go fishing when he had a string as nice as he pulled out of the cooler at his feet. "Crystal, I swear I don't know what's goin' on lately," he said. "You come in late one day and go home early the next."

Of course he wasn't worried or angry about her leaving early. It was just so out of line for the creature of habit that she was. "I need to turn off the burner," she said. "Would you like to come in?"

He looked surprised, like she'd asked him if he wanted to take a trip to China. She was surprised herself.

"I'll wait here," he said. "Don't want to track in."

Of course Sue would have killed him if he'd come in the house. Him a married man, her a single woman at home alone. Never mind that he was thirty years older than her. Just the propriety of it. Sue was just about Willette's equal at that.

When she returned, he said, "Is something wrong, Crystal? You know Sue and me both think a lot of you. People don't say things like that often enough."

"I appreciate it, Mr. Elwood."

"Horace locked up the yard. It should be his job as foreman, anyway. He came by the lake to tell me, like it was the biggest piece of news since Appomattox. You know I'm not fussing about you missing a few minutes of work."

"I know."

"Why, I'd be the last person . . . . Anyway, you could do the work in less time than you do, I expect, and go home early when you want."

"That right?" she said, a smile in her voice.

"And I'm not accusing you of malingering, either. Showing concern was my motive. I figured something must be wrong."

"I should have left Horace a note. Nothing's wrong."

He glanced over her shoulder. "They say you've got some really valuable things around here. You know, the paintings."

"So they say that?" Then she realized what he was getting at. "Oh, nobody would try to steal anything here."

"Towns like ours are beginning to have big city troubles."

"They say we're off the map."

"Oh, don't pay attention to what people say, blaming your daddy for things."

"I don't." But she blamed herself for what had happened to Miniver and for not coming up with some way to help her.

"Well, glad I was jumping to conclusions." He slipped four crappie off his stringer and dropped them flopping, awaiting their beheadings, into the pail of water she had brought out for him.

"Thanks for the fish. Tell Sue hello."

Between two pecan trees was an oilcloth covered table that Crystal used for potting plants, shelling beans, sorting tomatoes, or whatever. She was cleaning the fish on it, had cleaned so many she could do them automatically. Dad had taught her to hold the tail on the table, scale the fish "against the grain," lop off the head, slice down the belly, then gut it and pull out the backbone. He never was able to teach her to catch them, because he wouldn't bait the hook for her. "You'll have to do your own unpleasantries," he told her. She could catch a cricket in the house and toss it outside – bad luck to kill it Ida had warned her as a child – and she could handle worms in the garden as she worked the soil with or without gloves. She just couldn't push their twisting bodies over that sharp hook with or without gloves. And Dad had told her it was unfair to use artificial bait. She'd argued that the fish would go after something they would eat naturally, and that seemed unfair. No, he'd insisted, something made for that one thing doesn't give its victim a chance.

Mr. Elwood used lures. Made his own, just as he wanted them. But he threw back most of the fish he caught. He wasn't one to cheat nature.

Dad had usually blackened the fish outdoors in an iron skillet over a grill in the backyard, after loading them with spicy seasonings he brought from New Orleans, so she did the same. Sarah ordered the seasonings through a catalogue these days, always saying they should drive down to "Newawlens" for the next supply.

She was cleaning the last fish, wondering what Dad would have thought of her wearing the rubber kitchen gloves for this messy task, thinking of Miniver and of herself when she was her age, when she felt somebody close watching her.

"You were a million miles away," he said.

This time she looked in his eyes; she might have been trying to climb in. Though muddy brown, like a freshly-dug Mississippi stock pond, his eyes turned golden in the sun. Spots of light darted like minnows just under the surface. Blazing sunspots flicked some silent communication to her. But what? Was he blocking it or was she refusing it?

"How long have you been standing there?" And how could she not have been aware of him? Although, he seemed not to be estimating her bust and hip size the way Horace usually was when she caught him staring at her down at the brickyard. She was probably watching Matt Hawkins like that now. He wore light tan dress pants, comfortable looking yet showing precise creases down the legs. His brown leather belt matched the polished brown loafers he stood his ground in. He had on a dark blue knit tie with some little print of tan and light blue and sienna, hanging loosely from the button-down collar of the long-sleeve, light blue Oxford-cloth shirt. A little polo-playing man hovered over his left breast. He probably had a navy blazer in the truck. He was dressed to go out tonight. Not here.

"I was afraid you'd cut yourself with that fillet knife if I spoke too soon."

That ever-vigilant watchdog Vernon stood by him, nudging his leg, wanting petting, but he didn't reach down to the dog as he had when he left that April morning. He just stood and watched her. "Not much of a guard dog you have here," he finally said, then grabbed a stick for Vernon to lock his jaws on and tugged it back and forth, practically lifting the Jack Russell of the ground, then put him into ecstasies when he let it loose so Vernon could shake the stick like an animal with a broken neck and complete the "kill."

"He usually won't come near when I'm cleaning fish." With one deliberate slash she took the head off the fish and made quick work of the gutting. She scooped the offal into a pile on the newspaper covering the table and wiped the knife on the paper. The scent of fish discards permeated the air. It wasn't unpleasant yet to her, just there, like the sun and the grass. She raked an iridescent scale off her arm and another off her thigh, and became aware that she wore a pair of old Levi's that she'd cut off years ago into shorts, when the holes finally wore through. Of course, her sandals were under the table where she'd slid her feet out. To top off her ensemble she wore one of Dad's old ribbed undershirts, like Paul Newman had enticed Joann Woodward with one long hot summer. Sarah had told her that her shoulders looked as broad as a day laborer's in them. And that her breasts looked like they belonged to the same man.

"Is he afraid of that knife?"

She slashed an "x" in the air with it and laughed, feeling around with her toes for her sandals and slid her feet into them, noticing mud spatters on her legs from when she'd watered the peppers and tomatoes earlier. "Back in a minute," she said. She went into the cluttered garage for the shovel and took the fly-swarmed paper to the back and buried it in her compost heap. He stepped back as she turned on the hose and held her gloved hands under the water and slipped them off, then hosed the table carefully so as not to splatter him, and washed the knife under the hose and sheathed it. Good grief, was there anything else on the place she should wash down! But you couldn't let fish leavings just lie around. And for two cents she'd hose herself down.

"I wasn't really afraid of it," he said, smiling.

"I don't usually slice up my guests." Now where did that witty bit come from? Would he think she thought he was here to see her? Well, why was he here?

He laughed. "The smell was getting to me, though."

"Then you're no fisherman."

"No."

She fanned her shirt away from her. "I think I'm the major culprit." Now that was really witty.

Again he laughed. "You catch these?"

Her turn to laugh. "No. Why are you here?" Again, how conversational. And that was about the same thing she'd asked Miniver this afternoon. Too much to hope that he was having problems with Lydia Hawkins and had come for solace. And too irreverent for Miniver's black eye, swollen cheek.

"The painting," he said after a few seconds, as if waiting for her to finish her thoughts.

"Oh." Lydia Hawkins hadn't even bothered to contact her again as she said she would to arrange a swap. What was he to Ms. Hawkins, anyway? Husband, son, second cousin twice removed, poor relation who would do her bidding?

"Would you like to stay for supper?" some stranger asked without consulting her. She didn't know if it was to spite Lydia Hawkins or if it was because she remembered how she felt when he left the day he came for the painting. "I have plenty of pasta." She would not sit out here grilling fish under a tree like some ancient native.

With her mind being what it was these days, she'd forgotten Mr. Elwood was to bring fish and she had the pasta boiling when he got here, although she had thought eating out of the question when she remembered Miniver. But true to her selfish nature, she'd worked up an appetite and even cooked plenty for Sarah as usual, since it was Friday, although it didn't have to be Friday for her to share a meal with Sarah.

But Sarah was no doubt aware of this presence and would relinquish without regret her place at Crystal's table to him, always talking about Crystal needing a man, still threatening to bring John Half over. Yes, in spite of her curiosity, because of her misguided hopes for Crystal's love life, Sarah wouldn't take a chance on disrupting this visit.

"What? No fish?"

"I'll blacken them." What the heck.

Matt hesitated the way he had when he first came, just before he got in his truck, as if he were thinking something over. She would feel humiliated if he turned her down. The first man, and last, no doubt, she had invited to supper, even if he said no thanks, my wife, Lydia, is expecting me. Especially aggravating if he said that. Then he said, "Thanks, I'd like to."

"They won't smell as fishy," she said, already accepting that she'd say anything just to see that little smile. She lit the charcoal to heat, her method unorthodox and not reliable. She put a small pile of matches under the coals and lit them, and kept throwing matches on until they caught. He laughed and said there were such things as electric starters.

"What would be the challenge in that?" she said, laughing, too, as it became apparent the coals were catching. In a little while it would be ready for the skillet to get "red hot" as dad used to say.

He followed her in when she took the fish to the refrigerator to wait, and continued to the front of the house. Was he going to check on the painting as if he didn't trust her to have the right one again? He stopped in the large entry hall and looked around. He glanced up the stairwell to the painting and then turned to her, and she couldn't help but look him over again. He didn't feel like Ms. Hawkins' Delivery Boy.

"Lydia tried to call you the last couple of days. She thought you were trying to avoid your end of the deal."

"Oh?"

"She's very suspicious of you."

"And you?"

"I thought you forgot your phone was off the hook, like before," he said, glancing toward the plant stand.

Hell. There it was, its cord leading down the hall like a tiny water hose to the plant. She hung it up.

She owed Lydia Hawkins an apology. She owed Matt an apology. "I just don't like . . . calls," she said, "but it's a silly thing to do."

It rang immediately and she reached for it, thinking it was probably Lydia Hawkins and she might as well get it over with. But he said, "shh," and put it back in the potted plant. She looked in his eyes again and saw that the shimmers were understanding and kind and thoughtful and something else . . . independent. Something like that. No fetch and carry boy here.

EIGHT - Leave the Web, Leave the Loom

She diced vegetables and cheese to mix with the pasta for a salad, then sliced bread. More knives. Matt probably thought this was the Bates Motel.

He was sitting in a ladder-back chair at the side of the table, relaxed, sipping iced tea; he offered to help, but she didn't expect him to or want him to. Vernon, who had been favoring his right hip lately, stretched at Matt's feet.

They hardly spoke. The things she wondered about him weren't important anymore. It was answer enough that he was in her kitchen. It was exhilarating that when she glanced his way, it was as if he had been waiting for her to notice him or say something.

She didn't feel stared at tonight, although she was a sight. She'd actually hosed off her legs, done it while he was watching, then ran upstairs and was in and out of the shower before the water even got hot, and yanked on a white shirt, not one of Dad's old ones, either, and a short denim straight skirt, so faded that Willette would have put it in the Goodwill box, or rather, had her maid put it in! As she brushed her hair, she'd decided that she liked the sun streaks.

She never had company except Sarah, but Sarah expected the niceties at meals, and Willette had set a lasting example. But if Willette could be in this kitchen now, and see her like this and see him in that chair, watching her . . . well, he wouldn't be watching her anymore. Willette would naturally be who he, or any man, would watch. She would have her hair piled up with pretty ribbons instead of on her neck in a ponytail with an elastic terry band, and she would have a dainty apron over some silk hostess outfit instead of a big dish cloth tucked around her waist. And she wouldn't be actually working in the kitchen in the first place.

"The lettuce is fresh from the garden," she said. Hell. She'd had to brag on herself. Thinking of Willette did that.

He nodded toward the garden. "Looks like you eat a lot of vegetables."

"Oh, my garden's not so big." But it was. It was her hobby and exercise and second job. Bringing his food home in grocery sacks instead of from his garden was something Dad hadn't often done, and therefore she didn't. Beginning in early April the leaf lettuce and spinach came in, and other crops didn't stop until Christmas with the last of the greens and carrots.

"You could feed half the town."

She did give most of it away. But it was as easy to grow four of something as two. She'd had Sarah tell John Half she'd bring produce for him to give away, just as she had done with the former minister. The first Saturday she took a basket of spinach and onions, Sarah must have alerted him, for he'd come into the basement kitchen of the church where she was leaving them and introduced himself, adding that he'd be glad to pick up contributions at her place or even help her in the garden, but she'd said no. "No. Thank you." Sarah told her she should have let him, that he wanted to be friends. More than friends.

What would she do if the impossible happened and Preacher did get interested in her? No thanks. Anyway, according to Sarah, every single woman in the county had had a religious awakening lately, or a change of affiliation, if you went by the increased attendance. Hell, Crystal knew a good-looking man when she saw one. Preacher man. Matt. Even Horace. But John Half and Matt went about their business, not noticing or caring or at least not making an issue about how they affected the opposite sex. Horace thought every woman would fall at his feet.

John Half had been sending her the church newsletter for weeks, although she never attended. He had even sent a note, obviously referring to when Sarah had invited them both to dinner, saying he had almost come over to her house to meet her in the early spring when he'd visited Sarah, but he'd seen her working in the garden and she appeared so absorbed in her work, he'd decided not to interrupt her. Nice way to phrase it. When he had a lily delivered to her for Easter with a note thanking her for feeding the hungry, and signed simply, John, she did feel a twinge of uncertainty. Was he really interested? Maybe never having heard him preach, she couldn't get stirred up like the others did. But let one of them have him

"Sarah says I might as well be truck farming," she admitted now to Matt. There was also the peach tree, wormy because she didn't tend it, and as it was her favorite she wondered why it was always last in her ministering. There was a fig tree Dad said was left by DeSoto's men, with more distending light green tears than the birds could eat, leaving some to brown for preserve-making in late July. And the pear tree was so loaded usually that she had to prop the branches up before picking them around Labor Day. She couldn't keep up with it all, try as she may.

And there was the strawberry patch, her personal albatross, still yielding berries this late, the second week of June, five rows planted in front of the old army tank.

"I guess I do get carried away, more like buried alive, with it all."

He followed her gaze as she inadvertently turned to what she was thinking about, its presence visible through the big kitchen window, which now faced the side yard of course, since her grandfather's house-turning.

"That's a big pest-killer," he said.

She laughed. Didn't everyone have a tank in their back yard, and plant vines that yielded beautiful, delicious fruit in front of it to distract from the sight and ease the heartache it had caused?

"I guess it's some story."

"It was a real cold war."

"Is Sarah your neighbor?" he asked in a few minutes, when she didn't add more.

She liked that he didn't question her about the tank any more. "Yes." But how inadequate. She could have added Sarah was also her friend, mentor, advisor. And the only person still in the world who had her best interests at heart.

"It must have been her I caught a glimpse of as I got here. Apparently she was on her way over, but when she saw me she ducked behind the hedges."

She wanted to be frank with him, tell him Sarah would not run the risk of interfering with what she hoped was a man who had some business, hopefully to turn into social business, with Crystal. She was such an optimist. "She sees anyone coming here a mile away." After watching his smile until the last bit of it was gone, she added, "She hasn't had a lot to see lately." She did so like making him smile, even at her own expense.

They ate at the white wicker table on the screened-in porch, the back wall of which was the kitchen extension from the 1920's. The others, her mother always called verandas. Crystal had turned on the ceiling fan when they sat down but it was cool now with darkness falling. She ate with one hand and huddled with the other.

He'd rolled up his sleeves and unbuttoned the top of his shirt and slid his tie down. When, she hadn't noticed, and she marveled at that, feeling as if she'd stared at him all night.

"You're cold," he said, and stood and pulled the chain of the fan. "Do you want to go in?"

"It should be fine now," she said. Heavy June bugs thudded against the screen like creatures from *Night of the Living Dead*, and moths flapped their wide-eye-decorated wings into the screen, desperate to fling their bodies through it and into the flickering flame of the candle on the table. The breeze occasionally brought what Sarah swore was the faint roar of semis, although that river of traffic was impossible to hear they were so far from Shallot, on their way from Memphis to parts south or from the bottom of the state where the road ended, plowing north with the south's best, trying vainly to balance the sheet.

But Shallot could never be balanced again. The town had stagnated like a cypress knee in a swamp over thirty years ago, and her dad was responsible – for its death or its salvation, depending on whose point of view was being expressed.

Maybe most of the town hadn't agreed with Toliver Bell when he'd managed to have the route moved and had even quelled the call for an exit ramp for the town, necessitating a round-about to get here, so that they were actually a fifteen mile drive from the interstate. She'd always been as content with it as with the rest of her life.

She put a second serving on her plate, and like Matt, used her fingers to extract a bone that was left when she had lifted the spine from the fish. She felt hungry, down to her toes and up to her ears, like most would better describe how full they were. Willette would die of starvation before finishing one plate of food in a man's company. But Crystal was incapable of not being herself with this man, even if he made her wish she was someone else.

Unlike Willette, Sarah wouldn't think of trying to change Crystal into someone who wasn't herself, or get her to act unlike herself. Somehow Crystal thought Matt didn't want her to pretend either, and more than that, that it was her peculiar self that sustained whatever interest she held for him. That thought made her nervous. So nervous, she had almost forgotten Sarah.

She was probably insane with curiosity by now. It could have been her on the phone earlier. This porch was blocked from her side of the house by the kitchen. Crystal couldn't believe she had to take something like that into consideration but she most certainly did. They should have eaten in the kitchen where Sarah, assuming she went up in the turret and looked out its side window, could see what was going on through the kitchen window which now bared itself to her house.

She wished she'd thought of it earlier when he suggested going in. If Sarah's camera eye saw it all, she would only have to answer her questions tomorrow instead of recount it all to her. But screw it, as Sarah herself would probably say for shock value, here they were.

"Well, did you get it figured out?" he asked.

She got up and tossed a piece of bread to Vernon, who had wanted out on the steps earlier, probably to toy with a frog. He hated his dog food these days, even that for old dogs. Maybe he was in denial. A candlefly jetted in the opened door and flapped its velvety wings, its mission in life to get to the very worst place it could ever choose. Matt fanned it away from the candle.

"I'm not being very considerate of Sarah."

"How is that?"

"She can see us if we go in the kitchen. I guess I'm her life. And believe me, it's an uneventful one."

She got her laugh from him, and he said, "If it can brighten an old lady's life that easily, let's go in."

She blew out the candle and the delirious moth darted in with them like a runner stealing home. Matt put his plate and glass on the table and without much effort cupped the moth in both hands and pushed the screen door open with his hip, tossing the moth onto the porch.

Perhaps he was a kind man all-around. And perhaps the moth would only flail itself to death against the screen door, trying to get back to the wondrous light it had experienced for that one brief moment before he took its destiny in his hands.

NINE - The Starry Clusters

He put his plate in the sink when she started picking up dishes. "You don't need to help me," she said. "I'm used to doing things alone. The way I'm used to. I'll just put the food away now." Hell. She talked like she'd been living on a deserted island and had just met the man who made the new footprints on the beach.

"Then I won't insist," he said, settling down to watch. "I'm not too handy with dishes."

"You don't help Mrs. Hawkins?"

"I'm seldom there. But I wouldn't want to put one of her maids out of work."

She wouldn't try to fish out again what their relationship was if she were to die not knowing. Why didn't he tell her, if it was such that would make it all right for him to be spending the evening with her. Suddenly, she didn't want him watching her any more.

"Are you ready to exchange paintings?" she said, wiping her hands. "It's getting late." She thought she heard disappointment when he answered all right.

What did he expect her to do? Call in the clowns for after-dinner entertainment? Weren't she and Sarah enough of a departure from his evenings with Mrs. Hawkins?

"Walk with me to the truck to get the painting," he said, holding the door open.

The frustrated moth flapped drunkenly into the kitchen. It careened down into the glass chimney covering the bulb of the ceiling light and the singe was almost audible as it dropped inside and lay on what would become its worst nightmare. They'd watched the moth half the night. It had become a presence by then. A dinner companion. He'd already saved it once. She reached to flip the switch by the door to cut off the light, maybe save it again, but Matt's hand was already there and it was already dark but the moth would see no more light at the end of dark tunnels.

She was going to pull her hand away. She meant to. But the touch of him caused her to hesitate just that tiny moment, there in the dark, her hand on his, feeling with her palm the warmth of the back of his hand. It was so strange a sensation, touching him, to feel her hand flattened against another person's.

That Saturday morning in April she'd merely nodded when he came for the painting. Now, her hand over his, her forefinger had curled between two of his and she had hesitated too long.

As she attempted to retreat her hand, his swung around and gripped hers. It wasn't threatening, just sudden and sure. Then his other hand was there and in an instant they had formed a menage a trois, her hand the new lover being explored and caressed by the couple, his hands. They found the new lover's soft spots and memorized them: the shallow belly inside her palm a perfect receptacle for his thumb, the fleshy outside edge of her hand undulating between his fingertips, the heel of her hand a plump pillow under his curved fingers. And they found the rough edges of the new lover and memorized them, and with no less attention lavished on them made the lover aware that all was welcome, that no one came perfect, that the callus below the ring finger and the rough cuticle on the first finger and the strangely bent little finger, broken and not set when she played kickball despite Willette's instructions, weren't flaws, but merely the differences that help distinguish one from another.

She should pull her hand away from this caress that foretold blisses and perhaps hurtful unknowns, stuff her hand in her pocket out of harm's way. But she longed more to leave it there. When she did slip her hand from his, there was no resistance; she found that he had not been gripping it tightly at all.

What an imagination she had.

She pushed open the screen door and he followed her across the porch into the yard. Vernon had obviously been in the strawberry patch and crushed some berries under his paws, for the smell of strawberries floated across the yard. She turned toward the rows, wishing she'd had some berries picked for dessert. Matt followed in the dim light of the moon sliver and a billion stars. It wasn't much as gifts go, but she wanted to give him that, that little sample of her delicious night. They stood at the outside row – she wouldn't tempt night creatures possibly under the straw around the plants by going further – and breathed deeply as if the tank were a space capsule and they had just returned in it to mother earth.

"Vernon isn't supposed to get in the berry patch. But when he's out here chasing a rabbit he goes where he's led, tramples the plants. But doesn't it smell nice?"

"Yes, it does. Here, boy." Vernon forgot his old age hip and ran to him as if he were a puppy again and received his reward. Crystal tried to focus in the dark on the warm hands rubbing Vernon. Had the man no idea how cold she and Vernon would be later?

"Look to your left," Matt said softly.

There was a young gray-brown rabbit, its white-lined ears pointing straight up, for a few seconds still as a rock as it pretended not to be seen, before its cottonball tail bobbing up and down was all she saw as it disappeared into the dark shadows.

"Vernon will never forgive me," she said, "and that rabbit will raid my garden."

"Truth now. Aren't you secretly glad it got away?"

"Vernon couldn't catch that rabbit. With a posse."

Oh, she liked his laugh. "I grow lettuce mostly for the rabbits. It keeps them away from the other things."

"Your little smokescreen," he said.

She could sense him smiling in the dark. When he touched her hand she twined her fingers in his. What was the use of not doing it? Their hands already knew each other so well.

The dark hulk of the tank was never more confounding to her than now. "Sarah called the sheriff when she saw it being delivered," she said. When she didn't add to the story he said, "I guess they both had their reasons."

And feeling she indeed had not learned anything of human nature, she disregarded her satisfaction in the kitchen that he didn't pursue the tank battle. Now, instead, she wondered why he didn't ask what had happened. Most anybody would, surely. Was he interested in her or not?

Yes, he seemed content to be here, but she felt overwhelmed. She said the mosquitoes were out and started walking away, but he didn't move to follow.

"Can Miss Sarah see us here?" he said, looking toward her house.

"No. Unless she climbed all the way up her turret. That's why it was put here."

"That's too bad. You'll have to describe it to her, I guess."

"What?" she said, turning back.

"A kiss."

"I haven't been kissed in years!"

"That's too long."

"Nothing I could do about it. You know that's one thing you can't do for yourself." Hell. She hadn't meant it like that, but if he wanted to think she screwed herself he could. He couldn't know. Couldn't know just what lengths she'd gone to, even in her adulthood, to please her mother, who'd hinted time and again during Crystal's childhood, without saying exactly what it was that wasn't appropriate, wasn't ladylike. Yes, you could squelch just about any craving for a while. But lately, like a seventeen-year locust, dormant feelings were burrowing up . . . and that's just about how long it had been . . . .

She should tell Matt Hawkins to "kiss off," yet another pithy saying she'd overheard from the teenage girl-waitress-weatherman-philosopher at the Velvet Queen, who no doubt had no compunction about pleasing herself whenever she pleased, regardless of the consequences.

Did Matt think it would be doing her a kindness by giving her a kiss? He would bestow a kiss on a lonely spinster, or give her a kiss for dinner? "You don't owe me a kiss."

"Owe you? . . . No . . . It's probably not a good idea, anyway."

"You're probably right."

"But I'd like to," he said, shaking his head as if he were saying the wrong thing.

"I might like it," she said, hoping he didn't hear all the negatives she was feeling. She brushed a mosquito away from her arm and then slapped at one on her leg. They must have heard her call them a minute ago.

"Come on," he said, leading her toward the drive. "They'll drink you dry. Let's get the painting."

"What about the kiss?"

"I shouldn't have said that . . ."

"You don't want to kiss me now?" Well, that was probably best anyway. He'd said that.

"I still want to. I just don't know how to be, how I can be, with you."

Well, there it was. She was as odd to him as to everybody else. "Let's get what you came for."

"What I came for . . . ."

He didn't mean only the painting. She let him press her against the door of the truck. Would the hands and a kiss be only the beginning of what he wanted? And what did she want? It was so simple. Her arms went around him and her lips were on his. His mustache was a little stiff, but the beard against her chin was soft. Only when his lips had left hers did she feel his body against her, almost as if she could concentrate on only one part of him at once. Surprisingly her leg was around his and she felt the softness of the slacks protecting his skin from hers. Her bare arms and breasts covered only with the thin blouse were against his starchy-crisp shirt. His belt buckle was making an imprint against her. His hands were on her arms and she had the sensation he was trying to push her away, but she was at war to conquer him, pulling and pressing and feeling, and finally she was like a bookmark between him and the truck, before he pulled away. Which of course he could have done at will.

Why did he stop? She felt Vernon padding around their legs and said, "Get away, Vernon!" and was instantly sorry for taking out on the dog what she wanted to say to Matt. She thought she had more control. But she didn't want control. She wanted to fly again, make her head spin again, flap around like the moth dying to live. She pulled him to her again.

"Let's don't," he said when she finally gave in to his resistance again. "It's probably not the thing to do. For both of us."

"What do you mean?"

"If we were to make love . . . God. Don't think I don't want to . . . I don't want you to think maybe you just got caught up in something you're not accustomed to. But that's only my reason."

"Are you always so considerate?"

He didn't answer, and she said, "Maybe I need someone to make up my mind for me."

"I wouldn't do that. Even if I had the right to."

Why did he have to tell her? She had been willing to forget what she knew. She tried to act surprised. "So, you're married?"

"I've been separated for four years, but I'm not divorced. So that's your reason."

So Lydia wouldn't give him a divorce? Or maybe he didn't want one. But now that he'd told her what she already knew, she had no options. "I see. Let's get the painting."

He opened the tailgate and pulled out the crate with the painting. Obviously, Lydia Hawkins believed in protecting her investments.

"I like this one better," he said when they got inside, tapping the crate as he looked up at the one on the wall.

When he was gone she went in the kitchen and finished cleaning up. Just by looking around, she couldn't tell that anyone else had been there. It was as if she were a prisoner in solitary confinement.

TEN - A Red-Cross Knight

She woke to knocking at the back door. What was Dad up to now?

"Crystal? Crystal!"

Oh. Sarah.

"Are you all right, hon?"

Sarah's voice sounded more excited than worried. Crystal slipped her arms into one of Dad's old short-sleeved white shirts, which she usually wore as a summer housecoat, and usually over a pair of Willette's baby doll pajamas.

"I'm coming," she said, not loud enough for Sarah to hear. She was so tired it seemed as if she had just gotten to sleep. Why couldn't Sarah have waited a little later to hear everything?

"Crystal, now you come on down here. I'm getting worried."

Worried? "I'm coming," she yelled, glancing at the clock. Nine-fifteen. Of all things to sleep that late. No wonder Sarah was worried, especially after last night. She hurried barefoot down the back stairs and through the kitchen and opened the door. Sarah burst through like the deprived Russian housewives at a department store sale they saw on the news not long ago. Of course Sarah had a key at home, but of course the door wasn't locked, and of course Sarah wouldn't just open the door and come in without knocking anyway. Especially after last night.

"I knew you didn't have company this morning, or naturally I wouldn't have come over. But you're usually out in the garden by now. I slept late myself. I was tired when it was all over . . . . Now, I just had to see if he left you for dead or . . . ."

Crystal cut her eyes at Sarah. She ran water in the coffeepot and set it on the stove and lit a burner, then bent and lit the oven with the same match. Like last night, she sliced two thick pieces from the loaf of sourdough bread in the breadbox. On Saturdays she fed the starter mix and took enough out to make two loaves, one for her and one for Sarah.

"You slept alone," Sarah said accusingly, watching her from the very chair where Matt had sat last night.

Sarah was in a cool button-up cotton dress with butterfly sleeves and flowing skirt in mint green, which turned her light blue eyes into hazel. Her steel grey hair, always permanent curled, was brushed behind her ears for coolness as well as being complimentary to her somewhat full face. She had on her usual dab of make-up, which she ordinarily didn't bother to apply before her early morning visits over here, although she wouldn't be caught dead anywhere else without it. She didn't wear it to try to look younger, like Willette did, but just to look her best when she was out and about. And she even wore her muumuu over early summer mornings, comfy for her after she'd started gaining a few years ago. She even had on low-heeled pumps instead of sandals.

"You must have stopped watching when we came back in. We came for the painting. He left. So you dressed up for nothing."

"Silly. I knew he was gone. I'm going to a church building committee meeting this afternoon. Giving them a so-called Life Center. Depriving you of some of your inheritance."

"It won't hurt me. Give it all to them."

"Gonna buy my way into heaven."

Crystal couldn't even spar with her about that as they sometimes did other things. Sara would spend eternity there if there was one. "I won't even acknowledge that."

Sarah's eyes misted before she returned to her subject at hand. "How could you let that man leave, especially after that kiss? And you crawling up him like kudzu in July."

"Have you sent off for some night vision goggles, like in Desert Storm?" As she got out cups and saucers and poured cream, she laughed at Sarah's miffed expression. Then she took the basket and stem from the percolator and poured their coffee.

"When are you going to get a Mr. Coffee?" Sarah said as usual. "I guess my long distance vision is the only thing that's not failing." She doctored her coffee with cream and sugar. "In fact that's one thing they say improves with old age. If I didn't have you and my TV to watch, my life wouldn't be the pretty picture it is. Now I'm not going to wait for that bread dough to rise to hear all about it. So quit your fiddling. Talk."

Crystal stirred another cup of flour in the bowl. "I even used to chew gum and walk at the same time. Of course, that was before someone started giving me orders all the time."

"Oh, I don't boss you! Better check that bread under the broiler."

"You're hopeless." Crystal laughed, pulling the pan out of the oven. Butter was bubbling on the crumbly tops. "I think some strawberries are ripe. If I had thought about it before I put the toast in . . . but it would get cold."

"We'll have some," Sarah said, casually raking an invisible crumb off the table.

"All right, if you want them that bad, I'll go get some."

"They're on the porch. You know my palpitating curiosity. I had to visit the scene of the crime, so I picked berries."

"I'll be damned! To quote my dad," Crystal said laughing. "You did climb all the way up that spiral staircase last night!"

"What I can see from my own window is fair game."

"We're a pitiful pair, Sarah."

"Being there at the tank . . . I couldn't help thinking of T. Oliver . . . Damn that tank, just one more thing to interfere with our getting along . . . But Crystal, no woman touched by your dad is pitiful."

"What about Willette? She was touched by Dad."

"She's just touched."

That surprised Crystal, as Sarah never pointed out any fault of Willette's, or anybody's for that matter. She brought the berries in. Sunshine was still on them. She went to the butler's pantry to collect a crystal bowl, then ran a splash of water over the berries in a strainer and hulled them with a demitasse spoon.

"I don't want to talk about her, though. It's your man I want to hear about. He's a cross between Cooper and Costner. Oh, God, talk about the best between the old and the new."

"You'd better watch your language, Sarah. It doesn't shock me, not since I was ten. But you might forget and use it at Church some Sunday morning."

"Well, you wouldn't be there to know. The Reverend John Half isn't giving up on you, though. Your soul's not all he's after, however."

"If you don't beat all. That man's not interested in me, so don't be sacrilegious. Anyway, I thought you wanted to talk about Mr. Hawkins." She watched Sarah cut her toast into halves then halves again.

"I had to go around the world to get you to admit you wanted to, too," Sarah said, lifting her cup, sloshing a bit into the saucer as she sat it down. She rested her shaking hand on the table and steadied it with the other one. Crystal got a linen coaster from a drawer and put it under the cup in the saucer. She touched Sarah's hand and waited until the shaking stopped.

"He brought T. Oliver to mind, more than once," Sarah said. "He's nice."

"How do you know?"

"He waved at me while you were putting the pasta away, but he didn't want me to tell you," she said smugly.

"You read lips now? Or your hearing is much improved in your old age, too?"

Sarah looked smugger. "He pointed to you and shook his head a little after he waved. You know, like someone does when they want you to be quiet about something."

Crystal took her toast to the door. "Here, Vernon," she called, and held it out to him when he appeared. "Vernon likes him."

"Hell, that's no criteria," Sarah said. "He likes the postman! But did Matt like Vernon?"

Crystal watched Vernon find a place in the morning sun between the shady spots under the tree. "Petted him. Vernon's new best friend." Her own touches had gone down the drain with the dishwater. "Matt said he didn't know how to react to me, Sarah." She heard the crunch as Sarah bit down on her toast. "You didn't think that I'd . . . that he would be here this morning?"

"No. You've got to give something like that a little thought. I'm just a big talker."

"I've had years to give something like that a little thought. How much more do I need?"

"He thought you needed more."

Crystal sat down and sipped her coffee. "Why?"

"He wants more than a man-hungry spinster letting him screw her brains out."

"Good grief. I'm cutting your cable if that's what you're learning. You must have signed up for the Playboy Channel."

"Thought you couldn't be shocked." She picked up a berry, bounteously red as the polish on her nails, and plunked it into her mouth. "No, he realizes he's dealing with someone special, I think."

"I'm just different, not special."

"You're both. Anyway, he'll be back. He needs to know you want him for himself. We've got us a man with a conscience. Maybe the last one. Except for the Reverend John Half."

Crystal pulled her hair back with her usual terry-covered elastic band from one of the countless drawers and arranged it without looking. "Matt's married." She put her dishes in the sink as Sarah pushed herself up with the help of her cane. Her arthritis must be acting up from her climb last night. "Apart, but married. He didn't say why they're not divorced."

Sarah went to the door and looked out. "That dog is useless. Just useless." In slow steps she went out across the porch and back home.

ELEVEN - She Knows Not

Mercy. She was half naked. If Horace could see her now, wouldn't his prayers would be answered. She bent over and flapped her hair to fling the rain water out, and thought of Reverend John Half, and the look of indecision he'd given her through Sarah's hedges a few weeks ago. Then she thought of Matt Hawkins and the looks she'd given him Friday night, and actually sort of hummed, "gonna' wash that man right out of my hair."

She'd had enough wits about her to not get caught walking to work in the rain, but the rain, which had overtaken the morning sun before she could get a cup of coffee down on the side porch, had gotten her anyway. The Cadillac, after complaining with every blinking light on its dash, surprised her by starting, even though she hadn't carried out her threat to charge the battery with Sarah's. Another rain – just what they needed in the river bottoms around here. Whole town would be a swamp full of little wild onions if this kept up.

As she had gotten out of the car the wind blew the pelting rain in sheets before her very eyes and turned the umbrella inside out. Water had lapped her ankles in the graveled parking area. She could see only the clouded outline of the big oak tree and the small office building. Maybe she should've turned on the TV, with tornado season ramping up.

She got further soaked running to the door and standing a second to unlock it. Dammit. She was going to request an awning and a concrete walk in the next budget. No. Just an awning. She'd have the men put down a brick walk to the parking area. Wouldn't that be better at a brickyard? Mr. Elwood would smile and say something like was she trying to get them in Southern Living magazine. But he wouldn't object. He wouldn't be in this morning. He didn't like to drive in the rain. And the rest of the town appreciated it.

When she got inside, she'd locked the door behind her for some reason, although she usually didn't, then left her dripping purse hanging on a hook by the door and went straight down the short hall to the lunchroom, about the size of an old school classroom and about as spare as one, also. There was a cork bulletin board filled with safety posters and EEOC bulletins and company fliers; a beat-up desk for Horace, not that he used it; a couple of square tables with metal folding chairs around them; and a sagging fake leather couch. She saw it well, as the light was on. Strange.

Mr. Elwood told her Friday evening that Horace had locked up, and he knew only the night lights were to be left on. He'd certainly given her enough closing-up glances to know.

She would have to write a memo to Horace about the air conditioner left running and get Mr. Elwood to sign it. For a little bit she'd go back home and change into dry clothes. For even less, she'd go back home and get in bed and not come back. She shivered, brushing her shoulders as if she could brush the water out. She had on a cotton shirt and gathered skirt and sandals with no slip or hose, knowing she'd be at the office by herself because of the rain. Maybe she would go home and change at noon if it stopped raining, allowing the men to come in.

Nobody there but her, so she unbuttoned the wet shirt and took it off. She swished her skirt around trying to sling the water out, then muttered "what the hell" and stepped out of it, too.

She had just turned back toward the office to get the soft flannel shirt of Dad's she kept there to put over her shoulders when she got chilled in the old building in the winter, or in the low temperature Mr. Elwood liked in the summer, although he could sit fishing in the blazing sun all afternoon. It reached almost to her knees and would do while her clothes hung on the coat rack to dry all morning, while she was alone and catching up on her computer work.

She just about jumped out of her Vanity Fairs when she heard someone say, "That was a mighty good show." She gasped and whirled toward the voice. Horace was leaning against the doorframe of the men's room. His belt was unbuckled and the snap of his pants was undone. He was in his socks. Where the hell were his boots? Then she noticed them at the back door. He started unbuttoning his shirt.

"What do you think you're doing?!"

"Taking off my shirt like you did. I'm all wet."

She let that innuendo pass. His shiny khaki shirt was barely splattered from the rain, with just a few streaks on his pants. He must have been here a while, before the hard rain. He wasn't the umbrella type. She gave him a mean look and started putting her skirt back on, but he was watching like she was taking it off again. She grabbed it around her arms and turned toward the office.

"Where you going so fast?"

"To get dressed." She wished she hadn't answered. That somehow sounded intimate.

"Wait a minute. You don't have to go." He spoke in a rough command, but his look was as intimate as she feared her words had sounded. And she hesitated. Those were the words she had wanted to say to Matt a few weeks ago when she met him. What might have happened if she had? Or if she had said them Friday night when she had another opportunity. If she'd said, I don't care what, whether you're still married or in love or whatever, you don't have to go.

"Jeez, Crystal. Don't you know what a sight like that does to a man?"

"You've been here long enough to know you're supposed to call me Miss Bell."

He laughed. Not a good laugh like Matt's. She'd reprimanded him for the wrong thing.

"Jeez. They said you're on the road to forty. That ass don't look– "

"A lady doesn't discuss her age with– "

Again, that laugh.

Well, thank you Mother, Crystal thought, mortified, for having drummed that into me. She'd reprimanded Horace for the wrong thing again – for discussing her age and not her ass.

"Don't take it so hard," he said, moving toward her. "Your face don't give it away, either."

His arms rippled as he smoothed his curly blonde hair, not even wet. Yes, he must have listened to the weather report and parked his truck behind pallets in the back so she couldn't see it. He knew that she was the only one who came in when the rain was this bad. The men couldn't work out in the yard, unloading and stacking and loading bricks for shipment in this kind of rain. Home Office had made the rules about coming in or leaving early because of rain, having done some kind of study on cost effectiveness on the policy of working by half days. She thought she and Mr. Elwood could have saved them more money by making such decisions as needed, but wasn't certain enough to question the policy.

"I was saying she doesn't discuss her age with a man a dozen years younger than she is. Or her personal appearance with her work subordinate." She looked at the floor but still saw his rippling arms. "What are you doing here this morning?"

"I had some work."

Oh sure. He could lift a ton of bricks with those arms if he wanted to. But he was lazy. She couldn't understand a man not wanting to earn his pay. Somehow, she'd never thought of Mr. Elwood as being like that. She just thought of him as mildly incompetent, and of herself as being willing and able to take up the slack.

"I pump," he said proudly.

"You what?" Why the hell was she encouraging him!

"Pump. Pump iron. You know, lift weights. I saw you looking at my biceps."

"No, I wasn't," she said, but her gaze returned to his arm like it was a dangerous animal she had to keep an eye on.

He flexed it in a he-man magazine pose and said, "Feel it."

"No!" But she was fascinated, unable to look away from the giant muscle with the veins standing out, so close that she could almost touch it if she had the nerve.

"Come on. Touch it."

She stepped closer and put her finger on the hard mound. Just as she did, he flexed it again and she flinched as if it were going to smack her in the face. How embarrassing! His laugh showed his satisfaction. Then before she could comprehend what was happening, his hand was behind her head pulling her face to him and his other hand was squeezing her hips.

Was she too shocked to resist or did she just not want to? His mouth was hard against hers, pressing and squirming, wanting her lips apart, but she refused.

"Haven't you ever been kissed?" he asked, as if he were the one who should be aggravated.

"I wasn't kissing!" She raised her arm to hit him, but he caught it and rubbed her hand against his hard pectoral muscles, first one and then the other. Did men like that, or was Horace weird? She knew she was letting herself assume he wouldn't let her pull away, and didn't try, and he took a deep breath and groaned a little.

She was amazed. Until this weekend, it had been years since she had even touched anybody except to hug Sarah occasionally. And here she was, after holding and kissing Matt a few days ago, getting kissed and touching Horace's breast. Furthermore, unless she was sadly mistaken, she was sexually arousing him. The thought fascinated her. She hadn't even been politely friendly with him like she was with the other men at the brickyard. They knew who she was in this town and treated her respectfully. But Horace was a newcomer. She had written memos to avoid being alone with him. Maybe she had gone too far that way to keep from facing something else she might be feeling. She wondered how it would be to kiss again. Maybe even do more.

"I didn't think you'd mind a kiss. Or touching me like this," he said, moving her hand down his body, something dragging his voice down, its huskiness filling her ears.

"Well I do!" she said, jerking her hand away and realizing that he had not been making her touch him without her cooperation. Just like with Matt Friday night. "And take your hand off my ass, as you delicately put it."

He looked surprised. He was so roughly handsome maybe he wasn't used to "no."

"I know you've been wanting this like I have, all these weeks I've been here."

What if she had? Maybe this was her chance to find out if she only needed a man physically, like Matt might have suspected, because she had been alone so long. See if she was "sexed up" like Sarah said it might be, going into some lengthy explanation of how Crystal was actually now in her best years for such. Ha. She'd said that to Sarah. Ha! Then she'd reminded Sarah that her new preacher, the Reverend John Half and his famed charisma hadn't moved her. Maybe she owed it to herself to see if this would do, or if only Matt Hawkins could satisfy her, and if he was the only one who could have brought out the need in her.

And what if she did enjoy it with Horace? Was it too much to ask to have a man kissing her and his arms around her? Maybe even making love to her? Good grief, what a thought! But she didn't tell him again to move his hand. Instead, she opened her hand and rubbed her palm against his chest. "We could try another kiss."

He nodded with an I told you so look, and pulled her tight, taking her skirt and dropping it to the floor.

He started the kiss gently but soon began burrowing and she let him part her lips and put his tongue in. She moved hers to his and sort of enjoyed the sensation. Matt had not gone so far Friday night. Horace smelled familiar. Comforting. What was it? Like her favorite soap. He pulled her against him, squeezing and pressing until his uniform pants rubbed her legs like emery boards, and her breasts were flat as griddle cakes against the heat of his chest. Again, she remembered Friday night, when Matt's soft dress slacks and starched shirt kept her from feeling his flesh when she wrapped herself around him and made him kiss her. But she wasn't going to think about him now.

She vaguely wanted Horace to do more, wondering what that would be. He rubbed his hands up and down her back, but when he stopped at her bra to unfasten it, she mumbled "no," and his hands moved on, under the elastic at her waist, cupping her behind inside the soft nylon. His fingers spread out and began probing between her legs. She was too surprised to protest before he said, "Next time, wear bikinis."

Next time? He must be crazy. And she was certifiable. She had encouraged him because of the novelty of flesh against her, and knowing she brought out this desire in a man. Matt had been right about her. Or could it have been no other reason than wanting this young, desirable man? "I led you on, and I'm sorry. But I realize now I don't want this!"

"You been begging for it all these weeks."

He pulled her to the old couch across the room and pushed her down on it. The broken spring everybody knew to avoid coiled against her back. She was going to say "stop this!" in her sternest voice, but the instant vanished and his mouth fastened on hers like a suction cup, and his hand prowled into places untouched for years.

Had her body betrayed her, knowing what it needed without consulting her head, and been giving him signals that she wanted this? Was he lying? Or could he have been seeing what he wanted to see in her, what he must have seen in many women? She knew she couldn't budge him if he didn't want to get up, but she pushed at him anyway, and he backed off a little. "I think you saw what you wanted to see," she said.

"Pretty lady, I saw exactly what you wanted me to see. I know the signs."

"I wasn't thinking straight a few minutes ago."

But he was having no recriminations. One hand clamped her breast and he said, "Next time I want to see this." He pulled her underwear down as far as he could reach, then pushed them the rest of the way off with his foot.

Why didn't she try to talk him out of this? The only thing wanting to come out was a sanctimonious "I told you so" to herself.

"You wanted this bad," he said into her ear, putting his hand between her legs. "Feel that gush down there? You wanted this, all right."

"I don't want you!"

He looked surprised.

"Maybe I thought I did. I guess I did. But I told you I've changed my mind!

He unzipped his pants and slipped one leg out, nudging hers. "Spread your legs a little."

"Listen to me, Horace! I don't want this anymore. Even if I did at first!" She tried to push him away, but his iron-pumping arms didn't budge. Her back sank further into the cracked plastic like it was a gravel bed. She gave up. It had taken her too long to know what she didn't want. She had led him on, for weeks. She had gotten him in this state. Let him think it would be O.K. to do this. Oh, God, what had she done?

He shoved her leg to hang over the side. Then he was pushing and thrusting and she was caught between the jabbing springs and his jabbing body.

"Ooh, nice," he said at her ear. "Put your leg around me." He sounded calm. In charge, just like when he bossed the men. Like he knew she wouldn't mind doing what he was instructing her to do.

She heard an unfamiliar sound and realized she was moaning in a state of disbelief and disgust and pain. She had been too party-drunk to resist physically, although she knew she had garbled "No. Don't," before she'd passed out seventeen years ago. But she knew she'd had a choice not to even get into this sick sex. No reason it had to happen.

"This is good!" he groaned at her ear.

Just get it over with, she wanted to yell. If it was her fault, so be it. She'd have to live with it, and she didn't know how but she knew she would.

"Good!" he crackled out between shudders and moans, and soon collapsed on her, his hair on her face. He tried to kiss her, but she turned away.

"Oh, Crissy, that was good stuff," he said, cupping his hands around her head. "You got pretty hair. That was the first thing I noticed."

"Get off me!"

"Relax a little. You liked it. You know you did," he said, a little peevishness in his voice.

"No, I didn't!"

"You're allowed to enjoy it," he said, but got up.

She had learned a lesson. She folded her arms over her face. She had to convince him this had not been her idea and that it was not going to happen again. "No I didn't enjoy it. And I told you I didn't want this! I told you to stop but you didn't! I hope you get what's coming to you for this." She knew she was going to get what was coming to her for her part in this.

"It hurt you?" he said, something like pride in his voice. Could he still not understand?

"The sheriff – "

"The sheriff? He can't do nothing! This was your idea."

She could tell he was getting his clothes on. "It wasn't my idea! You had it planned!"

"You yellin' that way . . . First I thought it was just you enjoying it! I didn't realize you hadn't ever done it, at your age."

She wanted to jump up and run away. But she knew she'd have to see his face every day from now on. And she'd brought it on herself. She couldn't run away from that.

"We could have done things so it wouldn't hurt, if I'd known."

"You're not the first," she said spitefully, wishing she'd kept quiet.

"Sure," he said, "Sure. Nobody waits this long to do it."

But he sounded a little disappointed. Unbelievable!

"They'd have lined up, way you look. If you'd wanted to."

What was he talking about? She wished she had a gun and the strength to pull the trigger. She didn't know who she'd shoot first, him or herself.

"Hey, listen," he said, like he was doing her a favor, "You don't have to worry about none of them dread diseases. You know. I'd kill any man that made a pass at me. And I don't pick up women off the streets. Don't have to. Hey, the body's a temple. I take care of myself."

Now that he was mentioning all that, she was glad to hear it, but she wanted to scream don't show your face here again, because I can't face you again! She couldn't even have Mr. Elwood fire him without telling this. She couldn't call Bob and say throw this son of a bitch in jail and burn it down without telling her part in this. Or lying.

He rubbed his chest and put his shirt on. "Tell me when you want to give it another try." He tucked his shirt in and zipped his pants and pulled his boots on. "Gotta go home and clean up," he said, still unconvinced. "We don't want anybody to see me like this, do we?" He was almost at the door before she could think. He was so smug.

"Horace, Sheriff Youngblood doesn't have enough to keep him busy in this county."

He looked surprised and said, "What are you trying to say?"

"I'm like a sister to Bob Youngblood."

He smirked, "That n-" but she cut him off.

"You'd better not tell a soul."

"You can't be trying to make this something it wasn't, say this was rape!"

She heard the sincere disbelief in his voice.

"I don't actually know! But I could let him decide! I told you to stop. I bet I know what he'd decide!"

He smirked and said, "You wouldn't lie, I know all about you. You'd tell him the truth, that you wanted it, that you led me on."

"Don't be too sure. Don't brag around about this! Don't speak to me again unless it's business. And I don't want to catch you giving me any of those looks you used to."

"Hey, you cooperated–"

"I might have gone along at first, but I told you no! I can't take back what happened, but it's not going to happen again!"

"Are you serious?"

"I am. None of this should have happened. Get out! Or I'll call him now."

He knew better, didn't even say go ahead, just said, "Ok, it'll be our secret, more fun that way, ain't it? You'll want it again." Then he left, whistling softly.

She lay there with wooden legs and a frozen brain. Eventually she got up and washed off in the women's room, her private one because she was the only woman. French milled soap and hand lotion, luxuries she allowed herself even here, and toothbrush and toothpaste in Dad's old shaving mug on the sink, and comb and aspirins and tampons and Kotex in the cabinet, and she knew Horace had examined it all and used her soap. That's what she had smelled on him. She would put a lock on the door. No. She couldn't. Mr. Elwood would wonder and worry over it and Horace would smirk. She got a paper grocery bag from the cabinet under the sink and raked everything into it and folded down the top carefully and evenly, like it was a giant's lunch sack, and stood wondering what to do. She flung it against the wall, the sound of the precious mug breaking like a cry. Then she put on the soft shirt of her dad's and wished he was there with his arms around her instead of just his shirt. It had happened so fast! How thoroughly she must have forgotten her past, all the while believing it was never off her mind. How could she have gotten herself into this situation?

In a while she put her still damp clothes back on. She didn't go home. Sarah would notice she was home early. It would kill Sarah if she ever knew she'd encouraged Horace until it was too late; she'd think her talk had encouraged Crystal somehow. Everybody in town would notice if she went home in the middle of the morning. They would know something happened. Oh, God. If people in this town ever found out. If she thought she had been scrutinized before, she'd be under glass if they knew about this. And would they believe her lying version or Horace's?

She sat at her desk in a daze, not even jumping when the phone rang. After a few seconds she answered it, not wanting anyone to wonder if something out of the ordinary was happening on that stormy morning. It was the home office in Memphis. She said she was busy at the moment and that she'd call back. She didn't call them back.

Mr. Elwood called before eleven to tell her that maybe he should come in since they had no idea what the home office had in mind these days. But she insisted he not. "All right, if you think not," he said amiably.

Finally she didn't want to keep thinking and bringing back the mistaken morning. But her mind wouldn't go blank. Something fills a void. She thought of how her life had started changing in the spring. She let herself think of Matt. After all, she reasoned, she'd mentally contrasted Matt and Horace, and even John Half, for some reason Friday night. Friday night when she'd said without any obvious thought, something like "Maybe I need someone to make up my mind for me," and Matt had said he wouldn't even if he could. Oh, Horace had no compunction about it! He'd made up her mind for her. He'd not given her a choice . . . That's no good, you know the truth of the matter, she reminded herself.

At some point, before she could figure out what she had been doing while the clock hands crept, and she was chilled to the bone in the clothes that had stuck to her while drying, the day was over. It was still raining, mercifully keeping all away from her presence, and she knew that no one would ever even suspect the deed done today, because the clock told her she could leave without incurring anybody's curiosity.

She got her purse and walked to the door, then came back for her lunch, still in the bag, and stood thinking another minute. Then she went to the bathroom and picked up the bag of flailed items, hearing the broken pieces of Dad's mug clunking like a belated protest. She would let the fingered items be carried away with the trash. But not here. At home. She didn't put anything past Horace. Even looking in garbage to find out her secrets.

And she was almost at home before she wondered if Horace would have forced her anyway. If she had gone on back in the office, even gotten her wet clothes on and tried to leave. Would he have let her? Or was he there to get what he wanted, one way or the other. She would never know.

TWELVE - Don't Go Lightly

Though it stopped raining before she drove the car under the cover, she didn't go in the garden. The tomato plants would be bending to the ground from the beating of the rain. Ordinarily she would have re-stuck the stakes and retied the plants to them with the old panty hose Sarah saved for her. She was glad when it started raining again because Sarah wouldn't come over.

She moved around in the house on one unsuccessful errand after another, each time forgetting what she had intended to do. Finally she realized how she was hurting, just how the proverbial "run over by a truck" must feel.

She'd taken two aspirins when she got home. Oh, that ought to take care of things. She had put the sack with the contaminated items in the garbage can when she drove into the alley behind the house, and wondered if she was capable of making a mental note to replenish her supplies at work. She showered then soaked in a tub of warm water until it got cold. She put all the clothes she wore that day in a trash basket in one of the back rooms. She felt guilty about that. Maybe John Half could have found someone who needed them, they were almost new, some she bought herself, certainly not what Willette would have worn; but she never wanted to see them again. She wanted to burn them in the old trash barrel outside but couldn't because of the rain.

She puttered around the kitchen out of habit, wondering what to cook for supper, though she wasn't hungry. She wanted to eat, thinking it would help the nausea. She hadn't had anything since breakfast and her stomach growled so loudly that Vernon perked up his ears. She got several things out of the refrigerator but put them back in. She looked in the pantry and closed the door empty-handed. The phone rang but she ignored it.

Later while she was sitting reading the same words over and over on the same page of the newspaper, and her stomach had given up on food and so had Vernon, who had finally stopped walking back and forth from her chair to the kitchen and merely lay at her feet, the phone rang again and finally she gave some thought to it but didn't answer. It might be Horace. If it was Sarah needing something, she'd call back immediately. But it probably wasn't her. This was Sarah's favorite night for TV. It didn't ring again.

Before she went to bed, she looked out her open window like she always did. The night was dark, like it was covered with an opera cape. She felt as if the world had hidden from her. Instead of steaming the night up, the rain had turned the air cold, a brisk slap on her hot face to awaken her again to what she had done.

She was sleeping like a body buried in tundra. Cold heavy air pressed the sheet down on her. She squeezed herself together in a little shiver and again was aware of the tenderness of her arms and between her legs and in the small of her back and let out a little cry. It was answered by Willette's voice, inquiring, of course, rather than consoling. "Crystal, what did you get yourself into today?"

"Mother?" she thought she heard herself say. "I'm sorry. I tried not to get hurt."

But she could tell Willette didn't believe her. Willette was dressed like a 1940's actress and was straightening the seam of her stocking down the back of her wonderfully thin calf and ankle.

"A lady knows when to say no, Crystal. Don't think just because you're a child you don't know right from wrong."

"I do, Miss Davis. It wasn't my fault." She hoped her mother would hug her, just this once. But Willette reached for a large powder puff. It looked like Crystal's white fur muff that Dad had given her as a child. Willette dabbed powder over her face and shoulders, and the sweet smelling powder went up Crystal's nose until she sneezed, scattering powder about the room.

"Don't try to distract me by catching a cold. And you may call me Mother. Let me see where you've been hurt. You had better not try to hide it from me."

Where was she hurt? All over. She didn't want Willette to see the bad place, though. She would wait and tell Dad.

"I know what you're thinking, but your father can't help you with this."

"It's my leg."

"It's not your leg! You've been bad."

Willette looked disgusted. She lifted the hem of Crystal's sundress. "This is what I thought. A lady doesn't let it happen unless she is in control. She must know what she wants. And of course you couldn't make up your mind heads or tails. Look at the blood."

Crystal touched the soreness between her legs and the movement woke her up. She turned on the light almost expecting to see her mother in the room. But Willette was in Memphis.

She looked at the sheet and there was no blood, but she tore the sheet off and threw it in the corner and went into the bathroom and showered again. She put another sheet on the bed and lay there the rest of the night trying to stay awake so she wouldn't dream of her mother again. Strange, her nightmare had been of Willette and not Horace. Strange, maybe to some.

But she needed sleep more than she realized, and she was surprised when the night was over and she woke up.

She was in the kitchen making coffee, and some things had become clear to her. For one thing, she knew she couldn't go to work this morning and risk some kind of face-off with Horace. She needed a little while, even if just a day. When the clock chimed seven she went to the phone and dialed Mr. Elwood's house. She hoped he didn't hear the relief in her voice when he instead of Sue answered, or the vagueness in her story. "I won't be in this morning."

"You won't be in?"

She wouldn't average an unexpected day off work once a decade, and she knew he didn't mind but that he was again taken by surprise. If she said she was sick, Sue Elwood would be over before noon with homemade soup.

It struck her that she should go to Memphis to her doctor. Get checked over after what happened yesterday. If she needed medical attention, the sooner she got it the sooner she could put this behind her. "I have to go to Memphis on some business."
She felt better now that her life was her own again.

About 8:30, she dialed Sarah and woke her up. "I read that the older people get, the earlier they get up," Crystal said without even saying hello.

"That's only the ones that don't watch 'The Tonight Show,'" Sarah said. "I already miss Johnny. He used to have cowboy poets on. One of them was as old as I am. And they're on California time. That made him up even later."

"You sure about that?"

"Don't ask me how it works."

"Don't bet on it."

"That reminds me, when are you taking me to the new casino over at Tunica?"

"Don't bet on that either."

"Who'd have thought, a casino here in Mississippi – but why aren't you at work?"

"I need to go into town," Crystal said, glad Sarah had interrupted her own commentary, one Crystal had heard from her before. And would no doubt hear again.

"You mean Memphis?"

Crystal heard the lilt in Sarah's voice and knew what was coming. The Cadillac could usually be counted on to get about this town if needed, if the battery was in fact charged, but she never drove it anywhere else.

"Yessum. Can I use your car?"

"Certainly." Sarah was fairly elated now.

"I won't be there long. You wouldn't want – "

"Oh, yes I would," Sarah said, practically singing now.

Ordinarily she was fine with Sarah going into Memphis when she went. It wasn't just because it was Sarah's car and therefore she should invite her to go. Even if she didn't insist on going along anyway. Sarah made the most of these treks. They usually made a day of it, regardless of Crystal's protests they must get back home for this or that. They would have a nice meal at a trendy new restaurant and shop and do whatever else Sarah thought necessary while there. She was going and that was the end of discussion. "Be ready in an hour," Crystal said. Her hungry stomach made her bend over, but she still couldn't eat, so she went back upstairs to dress.

She could feel the chill in the room from last night. She couldn't decide if it was from last night's weather change or from Willette's almost real presence in the room, as if she had stepped out of the dream and spread her coolness from wall to wall.

She didn't want to have to see Willette today of all days. Just once she would like to go to Memphis and not have to contend with that. As impossible as it seemed, even if today was already ruined because of why she had to go, Willette could make it worse. But Sarah would insist on it. To Sarah's way of thinking, a young woman with character wouldn't go to town where her mother lived and not call on her. How Sarah and Willette could be so alike yet so different was amazing.

The traffic on I-55 was moving comfortably, because those headed into Memphis to work were already there. Sarah discussed every car and truck they passed. The Mercedes could take them, even if it was ten years old; how could it be that old already? And didn't anybody just stay home anymore? Regardless of Sarah's preference for others to stay home, she loved to travel. She called the hour trip to downtown Memphis travel. It was about as far north as she cared to go, but her tire prints were just about everywhere south from there. And young Crystal had been with her to many of those places, which Sarah now began recalling.

"Was it really twenty years ago we went to Atlanta to see Stone Mountain?" she asked, remembering aloud how she had talked the cook at Pittypat's Porch out of his blueberry muffin recipe and recalling the verbal directions, the secret being plenty of baking powder and barely stirring.

And Sarah was glad they'd already gone to Mobile, recalling the shrimp they bought from the vendors who boiled them on the docks. She couldn't eat like that anymore, she declared.

And wasn't it fun driving to Memphis's old train station and catching the ungodly four A.M. City of New Orleans going down from Chicago? And that lovely streetcar there that had the good fortune to be on the avenue of Desire, that they had watched glide by from its very window, was now retired. A shame.

And Sarah swore their trip to Huntsville to see the rockets was why Crystal made all A's in science that year. And every year after that. Who knew why she'd made A's before the trip.

And the same reason, Crystal's education, Sarah reminded her, was why they had gone to Oxford, sadly only a day trip because they were so fortunate to live in Faulkner country.

And wasn't their Pensacola trip a pleasant one, Sarah asked, looking over for Crystal's nod. She'd dressed Crystal in organdy and Mary Janes – the last year Crystal submitted to that regimen – telling Crystal that she could very well marry a Navy man someday, and took her to lunch with the wife of the commander of the Air Force Base (who was niece to Sarah's old college friend). Now, Sarah said wasn't it sad that their son was killed in Vietnam? He'd looked so handsome and invincible in his uniform. Wasn't it lucky that Crystal never dated any military men? One of those modern knights in shining armor. Yes, she might be a young war widow today, with nothing but plumes and medals to show. Never mind that she had nothing to show, regardless, Crystal noticed that Sarah didn't say.

And how Tupelo must have changed since they'd seen Gladys and Vernon and Elvis's humble little house. They hadn't seen Graceland in spite of Sarah's barely tamped down curiosity, because Sarah felt it would be an intrusion going into his home that so much had been written condescendingly about, and no one knowing whether he would have wanted it to be so public. But again, because she knew just about everyone in her part of the world, or so it seemed, Sarah had visited there when the man who would be king still lived in a Memphis housing project. And that just might be what allowed Sarah to grant Elvis his dignity.

"Yes, I remember," Crystal nodded, to Sarah's "do you remember?" of Savannah and Charleston and Birmingham civil rights hot spots and Hot Springs and Florida beaches in the spring. And Texas, where Sarah taught Crystal to drive, at only eleven, but tall for her age and not needing a cushion to see over the wheel. "Do you remember almost running into the Alamo?" Sarah asked now. "No. I do remember driving into the Rio Grande." "Oh, it was dry season. Thank goodness it wasn't the Mississippi. Anyway, that Lincoln was as big as a boat. Probably would have floated." In a minute she said, "I wonder if the AstroDome is still standing? It was big as a county. Maybe we should have seen a baseball game in it instead of just touring."

Yes, Sarah was responsible for Crystal's travel; but though much of it was for Crystal's edification, just as much was Sarah's curiosity, which would eventually lead to questions about this little jaunt to Memphis on a Tuesday morning.

"We ought to go traveling again, Crystal."

She was actually serious about the notion, so Crystal ignored her. The thought of encountering anything else new or different these days made Crystal's head throb .

"What's the reason for today?" Sarah asked.

"Check-up."

"My car? We haven't put five hundred miles on it since the last one."

"Me."

"Oh."

A little pause. Long enough for Sarah's curiosity to foment to a worry.

"What symptoms are you having?

"None, actually."

"Look at that car barreling on here. I remember when there wasn't a Southaven, Mississippi, just Stateline Rd. They're not moving here just because they like Mississippi. Nothing wrong with Memphis a few good ideas couldn't cure. Nothing wrong with check-ups. Even though you're the picture of health."

Crystal, used to her abrupt changes in conversation, said, "You know what a hypochondriac I am."

Sarah harrumphed and said, "You didn't even complain when you came down with appendicitis. If you hadn't burned up with fever . . ."

THIRTEEN - Yellow Fields

Doctor Chastain's office was across the street from Baptist Hospital and just a few blocks from the interstate, in a house that had been built as a small 1920's mansion. It had the misfortune to be in the path of progress as the hospital and its appendages grew. Her office was upstairs, while her partner took up the space downstairs. He'd been Dad's doctor. But Dr. Chastain had delivered her. Crystal was puzzled why Willette would have a woman doctor. She didn't trust women. It had to be a testament to Dr. Chastain's abilities. Sarah told Crystal that she was the first woman surgeon on the staff at the hospital, so Willette could've relished that distinction.

In the crowded waiting room Crystal looked through magazines she never would have at home: *People, Cosmopolitan,* even an old *National Inquirer.* Sarah also thumbed through magazines she wouldn't have at home: *Science* and *Computer,* while glancing furtively at the account on the front page of a *News Scooper* that obviously some patient had left behind on a table. Bold headlines announced "Man with Two Penises Wed in Double Ceremony to Twins With No Navels." Crystal would have picked it up and held it to the side where Sarah could read it, but she knew Sarah would be mortified for even a stranger in the room to see them with it.

Finally, after waiting over an hour because they had worked in her appointment, she was called in. Meanwhile she'd been weighed, gone downstairs to the back lab for a blood test, and squatted over a small plastic cup to give a urine sample. She missed the old nurse, Miss Perkins, who had finally married a few years ago at age fifty-five and shreded her uniforms, she said at her bridal shower. She had happily remarked to Sarah that there was still hope for Sarah to be a married woman. "Oh, I've already turned down a proposal or two," Sarah had said, not even bothering to joke or sound sarcastic and Crystal had wondered why she didn't know if that was true. But Sarah usually didn't embellish. She was going to ask her about it one of these days.

Sitting on the table, twisting the ties of her robe, she said, "It took years to get around to it again . . . but I had sex yesterday."

The tall, thin doctor who kept her hair Lucy red pushed back her glasses to look at Crystal. "Don't leave out any details. I gather they aren't pretty."

Crystal found herself relating the episode like it was a documentary. Dr. Chastain said, "I want to set you straight. You told him you had changed your mind. A man who wants to treat a woman right never has to go all the way. Those years ago you were raped, and I believe this was, too."

After the exam, she said, "You were lucky. And blessed if what he told you is true. It'll take several days to get the lab tests back."

"I believe what he said. He's pretty stuck on himself. Probably wouldn't take any chances. I guess he felt pretty safe with me."

"Did you call the sheriff? Are you going to press charges?"

"No. But what if – could he have gotten me pregnant?"

"According to the dates you've written here," she said, looking at the chart, "it's possible. But at your age, maybe it's not still sitting on ready."

"Like before."

"You know I would do what you wanted under these circumstances. Before . . ." she started, but didn't finish, just shook her head.

"If only Dad had been around." He'd been on a deep sea fishing trip, and Willette wouldn't tell her how to reach him.

Something shifted in Crystal's chest, a skipped heartbeat, for the life she'd surrendered. "I . . . I don't know . . . I was so young, and inexperienced. I've wondered. What would I have decided if I'd made the choice. I wasn't courageous."

"Don't second guess at this point. It wasn't your choice, anyway. Willette made it."

She knew one thing now. This choice, if needed, would be hers. And who said it would be a choice, anyway?

Crystal handed Sarah the *News Scooper* as they walked down the creaky back stairs to the gravel parking lot.

"You actually stuffed this in your purse for me? Nobody saw you, I hope."

"How can you read such trash?"

"I wonder how he urinates," Sarah said, flipping through the pages as she settled in the car. "Does he alternate penises or use both? I wonder if he can get them both to perform other duties."

"Obviously, since he's marrying two women! You're finally losing touch with reality."

"Haven't you learned yet there's not much that's stranger than real life?" Sarah said, ignoring her sarcasm, lost in concentration on the pictures.

"Are you ready to head back home? I've got things to do."

That got her attention. "Now, don't be so impatient. I was nice enough to come all the way up here with you –"

Crystal said "Ha!" and concentrated on backing out around the cars crowded in the small lot.

"Let's go to the Manor for lunch since we're so close to downtown," Sarah said. "Those bricks won't go back to mud without you."

Crystal hadn't eaten in more than a day and she was hungry. Very. Life was going to go on and in about a hundred years who was going to know or care one whit about yesterday's misfortune? Unless she proved to be the one-child-bears-one-child-wonder that her forebears had proven to be, she couldn't help adding as a cautionary thought. Only Sarah would care now, and before she would tell her what had happened and break her heart she would eat her own tongue. If a baby came, she would conjure up a one-night stand with prince charming, and Sarah would buy it because her love wouldn't accept anything less for Crystal these days. So girl, get over yourself! she almost said.

They went west on Union toward downtown and the river, past the Greyhound Bus station with a few homeless men and some sailors from Millington NAS walking about. Others downtown were office workers at lunch. She remembered Sarah bringing her downtown during Christmas when she was a little girl, parking in the garage on Front Street and walking through the tunnel under the street to Goldsmith's Department Store, now closed like all the rest, to see Santa and the Enchanted Forest. She never got what she asked for – that her mother would like her, or to understand why she didn't, so she could do whatever it took to change things.

It was usually Sarah who furnished her good memories. Yes, she worshipped her father whatever flaws he might have had, but she loved Sarah with an easy, daily rapport.

They parked in the bank tower garage and took the elevator to the top floor restaurant. They could see the river from their table, so Crystal knew Sarah had called for a reservation before they left home, and Sarah couldn't help commenting on some of the changes in her view. She liked the new bridge, already over a decade old, named after Hernando DeSoto, and Crystal agreed that he would have thought the span a fitting tribute. The Pyramid was a magnificent feat, according to Sarah, if the coming-at-any-moment-New Madrid Fault earthquake didn't get it. What did mere engineers know about the shifting ground of the powerful river? And Mud Island's name was well earned, deposited by the river, but with the park and river museum they had spiffed it up with it appeared to be solid enough that the river would not wash it away.

"What the river giveth it can taketh," was one of Sarah's favorite sayings. To prove it, she had taken Crystal, after driving through

Vicksburg's battle site, to visit friends whose mansion built just downriver by slaves twenty years before the War Between the States. It was now perched on a precipice dropping straight into the river. Half their plantation was now on the bottom of the Gulf of Mexico, Sarah said.

Crystal had heard it all before and just nodded and watched a half dozen barges lashed together precede a small tugboat down the wide river, while she polished off her salad of greens with raspberry dressing.

Sarah wasn't finishing her salad and Crystal's fork was poised over her plate to do it for her, when suddenly her eyes were drawn toward the entrance where several men waited to be seated, but she saw only one. He was already looking at her when she saw him. Neither of them acknowledged the other with a nod or smile. They only stared. And then she looked away, hoping he hadn't recognized her, but when she looked again a second later, he was headed their way.

She halfway thought he couldn't know her. Not only was she what Sarah called groomed today, but she wasn't the same woman he had held and kissed a few nights ago. But not even Sarah had noticed anything. Horace's fingerprints weren't all over her, after all. Her bruised arms were concealed with the long sleeves of a Willette suit, thankfully because she had known Sarah would want to dress up; Sarah had on a sky blue short-sleeved summer suit with embroidery on satin collar and hem, from Madam Rose's. She'd told Crystal she ordered it, swearing she had not driven herself up to Memphis to shop there while Crystal was at work. This Chanel – could one ever go out of style – was bought long ago when Dad could afford it and when Willette actually had a few curves, or it would never fit Crystal now. It was armor to her. But as Matt stared at her she felt she'd been dusted down to reveal all the tell-tale signs of the crime. She might not be guilty beyond a reasonable doubt, but she wasn't innocent, no longer the woman he thought he had to be so considerate of.

"Look who's here, Crystal," said Sarah, her eyes on Matt. "Imagine seeing Mr. Hawkins here," she then said to Matt rather than to Crystal.

He said "Hello, Miss Sarah," no doubt that this was she of the spying eyes. He smiled at Crystal as if he didn't even notice a difference.

She didn't say anything, afraid of blurting out what had happened with Horace. And it wasn't like there weren't other things to be contended with, anyway. Kiss. Don't kiss. Kiss.

"You're not answering the phone again," he said.

So it was him last night? Too far to drive now that the painting wasn't involved?

"I was planning to drive down there tonight if you didn't answer."

Oh. Well.

"How are you today, Miss Sarah?"

He knew he'd get an answer from her. It was obvious to all three that Sarah was in love. It wasn't important that he belonged to some other woman. And what about Mr. Perfect Reverend Dr. John Half, Crystal wanted to ask her. Sarah was at her most prim and proper. "Very well, thank you," she said demurely, and extended her hand as if she expected to be kissed like a lover of long ago on the inside of the wrist. "I'm sorry we couldn't meet the other night. Ordinarily I meet all of Crystal's friends, but I was just a tiny bit under the weather."

"I'm glad you're better."

"Yeah. She chaperones all my parties."

He smiled, and Friday night she would have enjoyed it.

"Speaking of parties, Lydia is having a grand unveiling. Would you be willing to go?"

Sarah said, "She'll go."

"I'll pick you up at seven, on the twenty-eighth."

"At seven?" she asked, as if it was an unknown number. Now she understood how Mr. Elwood felt when she sprang something so unexpected on him.

"Is she like this very often?" he asked Sarah.

"Not very. I believe it's the present company, myself excepted, that does this."

"I wish I could invite myself to lunch with you today . . ."

"Please," Sarah said.

". . . but could we make it another time? I'm taking those gentlemen to lunch," he said to Crystal. Then he spoke to Sarah again. "I do owe Crystal dinner, and I hope you'll join us, Miss Sarah. And I want to hear more about this malady of Crystal's that I've caused."

FOURTEEN - A Troop of Damsels

Crystal headed into east Memphis, turning off a broad avenue into Choctaw Greens. The large houses were sheltered from the narrow winding streets by trees and shrubs placed exactly to do that. None of them had old family lineages as hers and Sarah's did, but were fine homes built a few decades ago, and were just beginning to look ensconced in their settings. She finally turned into a drive which circled the short lawn in front of a wide porch. The house was used brick, probably from a turn-of- the-century building, and so looked old, though it wasn't particularly, and four tapered columns rose glistening white from the wide brick entrance. Sarah said. "Whatever else she is, she's class."

"You'll come in today, won't you?"

"No, I'll just sit in the arbor like I usually do. It's nice and breezy. Take as long as you want."

"That won't be long." She watched Sarah turn to go to the afternoon shade side of the house to the swing hanging under its white awning, but both stopped to look at a white gazebo instead, its columns mimicking the house portico's, with a white wooden swing hanging inside.

"That's nice," said Sarah.

And new. And not cheap, Crystal didn't say.

A Black maid in black pants and white blouse answered the bell. "How you doin', Crystal? Come on in. She's back in that hothouse."

Crystal followed her to the back of the house to a glassed-in room her mother called the Florida room, a room typical of many fine homes in Memphis. It soaked up sun in the winter, when all the straw blinds were rolled, but it did in the summer, too, even with all the blinds let down. Two ceiling fans were going in addition to air blowing through the vents. The rattan furniture with tropical print cushions was tucked under towering potted palms as if for shade.

"Well," Willette said, her tone implying all the "deep subject" admonitory phrases Crystal could think of. "Is Sarah with you?" she added without saying hello. "Go tell her to come in, for goodness' sake. She'll have a heat stroke. She can sit in the den and watch television."

"She won't come in. She's in the swing. And the new gazebo looks pretty cool."

Willette paused. Crystal could hear her deciding. Cool, as in slang for nice, or cool, as in not hot. And letting it go.

"She'll see the ceiling fan and find the switch, no doubt. I guess you two went to luncheon somewhere. I don't know why you can't drive up by yourself and let me take you to lunch."

"You look very pretty today, Mother." Of course she did. She was in a white sleeveless sundress splashed with black and pink floral patterns and white calfskin wedge sandals. There was the bare beginning of drapey skin at the low neckline and inside her arm when she raised a hand to straighten an imaginary wisp of stray hair, platinum – in the best sense of the word – and smooth.

"In this old thing?" She stood and looked across the room into a bamboo framed mirror as if to confirm it, sucking in her non-existent stomach. "I don't get to shop as often as I used to. Don't you ever go shopping? I swear, every time I see you you're wearing one of my old departeds. You'd think you're trying to be like me."

Like Willette? That would be the last thing she would want. Wouldn't it?

She looked Crystal up and down. "I used to like that suit."

Crystal would let that implication drop. "Is everything going all right with you, Mother? If you need anything . . ."

"I insist on living on my half of what your father left us. You keep yours, though what you could be doing with it is beyond me. That was one thing he did right, investing a little so you and I would be taken care of." She posed on the couch and nodded to a chair for Crystal. "I suppose I could marry again if I wanted, but I prefer to be through with men." She straightened her shoulders. "I like that they look, though."

Crystal had wondered why Willette didn't marry again. She was still beautiful and she'd seen her hide the harridan side of her nature like an Easter egg tucked away so well that it's a surprise when it shows up. And though she was closing in on sixty, Crystal figured she would pass for her older sister any day of the week.

"I'll bet you could have married," Willette said as if she had just thought of it. "You're not what one would call bad-looking. But your personality isn't exactly welcoming."

Crystal tried not to flinch as her mother looked her over. It was as thorough as John Half and Matt and Horace had looked her over, and as different as theirs had been one from the other.

"You look different," she said finally.

"I look the same as I always do."

"Has some man come into your life?" She tilted her head and squinted a little, contorting her pupils for a better look. "That usually does it to a woman. Who is it?"

"It's your imagination."

"Oh, all right. I shouldn't tease you." Then she called to the maid, "Barbara, bring us a lemonade, please. And take one to Miss Chancellor."

So much for that. Her mother had no confidence in her daughter's ability to attract a man. At this point Crystal wished her mother was correct.

After stopping at the Mall of Memphis for what Sarah said she needed, some "old lady shoes," and where Sarah tried to outfit Crystal with everything on any mannequin that Crystal even glanced at, it was almost six when she and Sarah returned home. Sarah said she was a little tired and was going to stay home and watch TV and get to bed early.

After parking the car in the garage at the back of Sarah's house, she came through the hedges and stopped practically in mid-step. "Miniver! What's happened?"

Miniver Tandy was sitting on the back porch, the two kids playing under the oak, hopping around on huge gnarled roots which pushed up like humped sea serpents under an ocean of dirt harboring what little grass the shade allowed. Miniver was sipping Diet Coke from a huge cup, a crumpled sack from Burger King on the table beside her. She was dressed in neat denim shorts and a pumpkin color tee shirt and brown leather sandals, and her thick hair was in a band at the top of her head. She looked almost like the Miniver that Crystal was used to.

"We been here a while. I hope you don't care."

"No, not a bit. Let's go inside and talk."

"Can we stay out here? The kids'll do better playin' outside."

"Mosquitoes will be bad soon."

"I rubbed them with Skin So Soft. Your dog's been under that table lookin' like he wants to eat 'em up, though."

"Hunh. He doesn't know what they are, that's all. I don't guess he's seen kids this close before." She called Vernon and he crawled from under the old metal table and sidled up. "You can pet him," she said to the children. "He won't bite." As she went back to the porch she said, "He may lick you to death, though." Then she asked Miniver if she wanted some ice for her Coke and her face.

Miniver shook her head and touched her jaw without thinking. Crystal saw her involuntary cringe and shuddered with her.

"Thomas had all weekend to drink," Miniver said, "Then, you know, yesterday, he couldn't go to work because of the rain. Yesterday was a mean day."

That was one way to describe it. A mean day all around. "Was he at work today?"

Miniver looked at her in surprise. "Don't you know? Wasn't you there?"

"No, I didn't work today."

"He kept gettin' up to go, but then he'd have another drink and pass out a while. Then he got up, come at me with a belt, like my daddy used to do me and my mama. When he fell out again, I got the kids and left. I'm not goin' back."

"I hope you mean that." But what would she do instead? "What about your mother? Could she help?" She knew some mothers would be willing.

"She's in a nursing home in demensha."

"Is that in South Carolina where you're from?"

"It's what she's got," Miniver said, a smile cracking her face.

"Oh. Dementia. I'm so sorry. I'm so out of it."

"Well, the nursing home *is* in South Carolina," Miniver said, laughing.

Crystal shook her head. "I admire you for being able to laugh."

"I don't deserve no admiration."

"There must be somewhere for battered wives. I could call the Methodist preacher. He would know."

"No. I ain't going to no place like that. I ain't puttin' my kids through that."

"I'll help you all I can. I'd give you money if I had it."

"Is that right?"

Crystal didn't know if Miniver didn't believe she would help or that she had no money. But she heard the challenge.

"I wouldn't take no money from you. I just need a couple of days. I ain't scared of work. I can go to Memphis and find a job. But ain't nobody gonna hire me with my face like this."

"You can stay here, I guess," Crystal said, surprised at herself.

Miniver looked crookedly at her through her good eye and her eye that was swollen half-closed. "No, I guess not. I think it would be too much for you."

"I want you to. I didn't mean to sound so non-committal. It's just that . . . it's just that things have been happening lately . . . I think somebody else must be living in my body."

"Now don't tell me you believe in them aliens! Nobody with any sense believes that shi – that stuff."

"Well, I don't have much sense, but I have more than that." She was half convinced Sarah believed in them, though, the way she read and reported it to her.

Miniver smiled, although she caught herself from the pain. "Good thing I'm not used to laughing much," she said.

"Maybe things will get better for you now that you've made your decision. How did you get here?"

"In my truck. I parked it behind your shed."

"That's a good place. Let's go in and put something on for supper. What do the children like?"

Miniver had been right when she answered that they didn't like much and didn't eat much. Crystal didn't know how much they were supposed to eat, but she thought it should be more when she watched them pick at their pork chops, which luckily she had in the freezer, as it was just as easy to broil several and froze them for later; and green peas out of a can, one of the vegetables she didn't grow. What did kids like? Fried chicken? She used to love Ida's. She could get Kentucky Fried Chicken tomorrow night.

After Miniver helped her clean the kitchen, she went to the truck and brought in a sack with a few clothes in it. "I left in a slight hurry," she said. "Had to leave all the jewels and furs."

Crystal liked that Miniver had a sense of humor in spite of all the uncertainty that lay before her. And what she said reminded her of something she bet Miniver didn't know about her unusual name. "Have you ever been told what your name means?"

"Huh? No. Didn't know it meant nothing. What?"

"Fur. White fur, better than mink."

"White? *White*? Ha. That's a good one. Maybe my mama had dementia twenty-three years ago."

Crystal could see her making connections and let her put whatever it was together.

In a minute Miniver said, "Thomas used to say I thought I was White. He'd be drunk, though."

Crystal felt embarrassed. In spite of what she'd thought that day Miniver came to the office with her mangled eye, would it be conceivable that he would marry a black girl, and then actually try to make her think she wasn't as good as he was? "Ancient kings and queens used to wear it. The fur."

"You mean like in old England? And Camelot? I read about that recently. Imagine that. Mama did tell me once that she gave me a good name, but I guess she'd forgot what it meant."

Her mother must not have known. Wouldn't she have realized if kids found out they'd make fun of her? Maybe she'd gotten it mixed up with Minerva. Which wasn't too usual a name itself. "I believe you're going to make it, Miniver," Crystal said as they went upstairs.

"It's amazing what a person can do if they have kids dependin' on 'em."

Yeah, some people, Crystal thought, remembering her mother's selfishness. Then she could have slapped herself for feeling sorry for herself with Miniver going through what she was. "Are you sure you want to sleep in the room with the children? They can have a room each. Got five bedrooms up here. Even a nursery on the third floor." But that was in the old days. Dad was the last to have used it. He wouldn't let Crystal be put up there, with or without a nursemaid. He said it was too hot and too far away, Sara had told her.

"They'll sleep better together like they do at home. And I'll sleep better being with them."

Next morning the aroma of coffee roused Crystal. Dad was such an early riser. Just once she would like to beat him to the kitchen. Then she fully awoke and remembered. She fished a robe out of a closet and went downstairs.

"Miniver, I've had to make my own coffee since Dad died."

"I make it strong enough to walk on."

"Maybe it'll give me some backbone," Crystal said, feeling like a rabbit being slung around by a happy hunting dog, as Mr. Elwood would say. She watched the children eat toast and jelly and scrambled eggs.

"They always eat breakfast," Miniver said, "and they believe in gettin' up early."

Just then the phone rang and Miniver finally asked her if she was going to answer it. When it stopped and rang again, she did, and heard Sarah whisper, "There's a truck parked behind your shed. Are you all right? Is someone holding you hostage?"

"I've heard it all now," Crystal said. "Come over and meet these master criminals."

She was at the back door, still wearing her early morning housedress almost before Crystal got back to the kitchen.

"Holy Mother," Sarah said as she stepped in the door.

Miniver smiled. "I ain't never been called that!"

"Sarah, this is Miniver Tandy. She's going to stay here for a few days. And this is Tommy and Tabitha."

Crystal poured Sarah some coffee and said, "They're hiding out here."

"Are you really on the lam?" Sarah asked Miniver, while moving to lay a palm on each child's head. She looked like she was bestowing a blessing on each. "Tabitha," she said, looking at the little girl who stared up as if she knew something momentous was to be revealed, "you have a lovely Biblical name."

Crystal doubted Miniver knew. She had probably named her after the little girl in the old TV show, but a Salem witch she sure wasn't. And after her own mother had tried to give her a good name.

"I know," she said proudly, "Mama told me."

"Miniver, I guess . . . you know what I thought," Crystal said. "I'm sorry."

"You'd be right. I just recently took to reading the Good Book, so don't feel bad."

FIFTEEN - Little Other Care

Sarah and Miniver were huddled like conspirators when Crystal left for work. And Vernon was eating out of the kids' hands. His dog food, no less.

Mr. Elwood stayed at Crystal's heels all day as if he were afraid she would disappear. Thomas didn't clock in and Horace made a point by looking Crystal over, letting her know he wasn't too worried she'd tell. Probably hoped she would so he could tell his version and make himself look to be a big man. But he spoke only to Mr. Elwood when he came in the office. She worked again on the projections wanted for Memphis. She was so tense she jumped when the quitting whistle she set each morning went off for the men. Mr. Elwood must have been leery of finding out what was making her not herself, because he didn't comment on it.

At home, there was a plate of sliced cucumbers marinating in vinegar and sugar on the table. A pan of squash and onion was sautéing and green beans simmering, both from the freezer – and chicken frying in an iron skillet. "You got a great garden," Miniver said as she started mashing potatoes with the old flat potato masher.

"I can't believe you found cucumbers this early," Crystal said.

"You live behind times, though. Your Mixmaster's had it. Even I had an electric hand mixer."

"I don't get out much to shop," Crystal said. "Where'd you get the chicken?" Surely she hadn't gone out shopping if she didn't want to be seen.

"Sarah brought it out of her freezer. Bet it's old as Christmas. I had to cut freezer burn off the wings."

"It smells great."

"She don't cook much anymore. I bet she don't eat right, either. She's coming over to supper. Knew you wouldn't mind, y'all being best friends."

"Good." She felt sort of like a guest. She didn't mind, though. No one was trying to take over, just acting like they would at home. Comfortable. And that was more than she had felt in days gone by when it was populated by family. This showed that she could become part of someone's life. Could she let someone become part of her life?

After Sarah went home, Crystal took Miniver to one of the closets where her mother's discarded clothes were. Miniver was bigger than

Willette in bust and hips, but shorter than Crystal, so Crystal thought some of the things would fit.

"Lordy," Miniver said. "This is just one closet?"

"I'll never wear them all, and if you get a job in Memphis you'll need some clothes."

"Old McDonald will prob'ly supply my work clothes," she said, "but if these clothes ain't gonna be worn, I guess I could take a few. Start goin' to church."

"Good luck. Having them hasn't gotten me there."

Crystal was soundly sleeping when she woke to knocking from downstairs. Was the sheriff here again? It was so long since Dad had caused a stir. Then she woke and realized someone was knocking on the front door. She glanced at the clock and was surprised that it was just ten. But that was late for someone to come, and who would come, anyway? Sarah would have called her if she needed something.

She ran down, hoping the children wouldn't wake up. Maybe she had forgotten to put the phone back on the hook, like she usually did before she went to bed in case Sarah did need her in the night. Poor Sarah. She hated to be out in the night. Crystal flung the door open.

Thomas stood there. "Where are they?" he said. He was in clean clothes, was clean-shaven, and if a person didn't know he had been drinking for days they wouldn't have suspected it. He looked younger than he did in work clothes, even with his green eyes reddened, and his sandy-colored hair was neatly combed. He looked contrite and Crystal could believe even he thought he wouldn't do it again when he said so.

Miniver was downstairs by then, Willette's silk robe exposing much of her bountiful bosom, and Crystal saw desire when Thomas looked his wife up and down.

"I won't go with you, Thomas," she said before he could ask. "I've been thinking about what I would do when you found me. I knew you would. This is a little town."

There was self-assurance in her look and her speech was so different from recently. Did even Willette's *clothes* do that to a person? Herself excluded. The phone rang and Crystal answered it. "It's Miniver's husband," she told Sarah. ". . . No, she isn't. It'll be all right. Try to go back to sleep."

"I knew Miss Crystal would help you if you asked her. I see now that she's been right all along about the check. She can give it to you from now on. All I want is for you and the kids to come on home."

"No. Whatever what you say. You've made promises before that you meant to keep." She glanced at Crystal, in admission of what Crystal had known all along. "And you have good intentions to keep this one. But you won't."

"If you don't come home, I'm leaving town. You'll never hear from me again."

"I-55's just down the road fifteen miles. You shouldn't get lost."

"I'll kill myself!"

"Do what you think is right," Miniver said.

"I can't live without you and the kids! I'll be however you want me to."

Crystal saw her waver and started to speak, but it wasn't her place. What did she know about it? But she knew her own parents hadn't been able to compromise, much less undergo major transformations in themselves, though they had professed to want to. Maybe a person could change, but she thought they had to want to for themselves, and most probably thought the other person should or would do the changing. Because changing yourself could be monumental. Risky. Look what was happening in her life when she had gotten just the least bit out of her dug-in position. But what Thomas wanted changed, what she believed he wanted changed about Miniver, couldn't ever be. It was impossible.

"Mommy, Mommy," said Tabitha from half way down the stairs. Tommy ran down to his daddy. Well, that would do it, Crystal figured. Miniver might not want to step through an unknown portal. It would be easy to believe it when Thomas said he was going to be different for the children's sake.

But Miniver said, "You kids give your daddy a bye-bye hug and then run back up to bed."

From the look on his face, Thomas was as surprised as Crystal was.

"Those children are one reason I'm not going with you, Thomas. It wouldn't be a good life for them. But there's another reason. I'm not like I was two days ago because I realize I'll not ever be what you wish I was."

Thomas glared at her and then at Crystal. "You've been talking to her, haven't you? Convinced her she's too good for me now. Just 'cause I've got a little drinkin' problem."

"Thomas," Miniver said, "I believe you love me. I wish that was enough. But you have to admit to yourself what you really want. It's probably why you started drinking so much, because you won't let yourself believe what you feel." She held out her arm. "Look this over good. What you see is what it's always going to be. You want me to be White! Don't you see? My name's the only white thing about me. There's no way on earth I'll ever be what you want. And what's more, I don't want to be."

His face went from denial to facing it and then quick denial again. But he believed Miniver wasn't going with him, because he turned and left.

"Do you want some coffee?" Crystal asked.

"No. I better go on up. The kids don't rest well after something like this."

Crystal was just drifting to sleep when she heard banging again. She didn't even think it was the law come to question her dad. She had enough going on in the present to keep her from sleeping in the past anymore. But who could it be now?

Miniver ran down the stairs with her. "It's him, Crystal. I hoped and prayed he wouldn't do this, but I know it's him."

"I'll call Sheriff Youngblood."

"No. Just don't open the door. He'll leave."

"Well, I did lock the door." She didn't bother as likely as not, but she had when he left. But just then, the old lock gave out and the door flew open. Crystal hardly recognized Thomas. His features were distorted, curiously slack and hanging for a young man, his eyes drooping like they'd fall to his cheeks, his cheeks sagging, as if needing slings to hold them up. His body swayed to and fro. How had he managed to drive?

But his body sprang to action as if a starting gun had been fired. He pushed Miniver against the wall and grabbed her throat. Crystal pulled at him but his hands were welded to Miniver's neck. Crystal couldn't move his arms at all. She kicked his legs and he finally let go of Miniver to sling Crystal away. She fell across the lamp table, feeling its edge jam into her thigh and heard the lamp crash to the floor. She scrambled up and ran to the alcove to call the sheriff. She was dialing, the old rotary phone taking forever to spin back around after each number, when he jerked the phone from her and shoved her into the wall.

Miniver dove into him and he turned his force on her again. "Black Bitch!" he said, drool dangling from his mouth. While his hand was raised for the first blow, Crystal ran to the study and got the rifle off the wall.

"Thomas," she said coldly, and he turned from Miniver. Her head was drooping and she was groaning into her hands.

In spite of his drunkenness Thomas looked shocked when he saw the gun. "Put't down," he slurred . "Don'n make me mad!"

Don't make him mad? What did it take to convince a man in this condition?

A siren undulated in the distance, getting closer. Sarah must have called Bob.

She decided to pull the trigger. She pointed it right at his heart, that twenty-two that Dad used to rabbit hunt with. Just possibly it might make Thomas think before doing something like this again. She might have a little bit of Dad in her after all. "Think before doing this again, Thomas," she said and pulled the trigger just after she heard the siren stop. She heard the empty click she knew she would. Thomas's legs buckled but his eyes focused on the gun like they were bobbers on the taut line of a fishing pole.

"She tried to shoot me!" he yelled, now made righteous as a teetotaler by fright, as Sheriff Youngblood came in. "She pulled the trigger."

"You drunken idiot. She unloaded it the minute the children got in the house," Miniver said, getting up. "She told you to think next time."

"I coulda been killed! Black bitch'uz gonna let 'er!"

"Shut up Tandy, or I'll shoot you," Bob said, pointing his .357 at Thomas's head. He looked at Crystal then at Miniver and put his gun back into its holster. "You got cartridges for this rabbit gun?" he asked Crystal.

She nodded. She kept them locked in the secret desk drawer.

"Go get one," Bob said. "You can shoot him so he'll hurt a little."

"You can't do that!" Thomas said.

"Get two," Bob said. "I'm going to shoot him, too."

"Just gimme your club," Miniver said to Bob, reaching out for it. "He don't need shootin'! This'll do it!"

They looked at her in surprise, but Bob handed it to her. She stared at her husband. Thomas had had too much by then, though – too much liquor and exertion and fright, and he dropped to the floor in a heap.

Miniver handed the club back to Bob. "I won't be like he is," she said.

"How'd you get married to somebody like this?" Bob asked. Crystal wasn't surprised he knew about them, but she saw that Miniver was.

"Well, naturally I set out looking for a drunk."

"Girl, that can happen. But this white, wife-beating trash –"

The way Miniver and Bob were glaring at each other, Crystal was afraid she'd have another fight on her hands.

"Mommy, is Daddy killed?" they heard from the top of the stairs.

They looked up to the two children sitting in the dark. How long had they been there?

"Daddy's going to be all right. He's just tired."

"I think you and Ms. Tandy need some medical attention," Bob said to Crystal as he dragged Thomas to the door. "I'll call the EMT's from the car."

"I'm all right, but Miniver –"

"No. Nothing's broken. It just takes a few days to heal."

Sarah walked in then. "You'd have needed a hospital or worse if I hadn't called Bob when I did."

"You and Crystal maybe saved my life," Miniver said, then gave Bob a dirty look.

"You pressing charges?"

"No."

"You got no sense." He glared and turned to Crystal, "Your charge will put him behind bars."

Crystal looked at Miniver.

"Crystal, the law's never been in it before. I expect he's learned a lesson."

Crystal knew Bob wouldn't like it, but she said, "I don't guess I'll do it."

"Oh, he's going to jail! DUI, breaking and entering, assault and battery, resisting arrest. But I can't keep him there forever."

"I'll be gone in a few days, anyway."

"Call me before you leave town," Bob said to Miniver. "I'll contact some agencies and see if there's some assistance they can give you."

That was the Bob Crystal knew. Then he gave Crystal a disgusted look and shook his head at her. Again, the Bob she knew.

SIXTEEN - Plumed

The thirtieth was just two days away and the Memphis office wanted all the information they'd requested by then. She had meant to send it today but was late because of the day she'd missed and was finishing it tonight. Horace could deliver it tomorrow. She'd have Mr. Elwood send him.

Mr. Elwood offered to stay late, but it would go faster if she didn't have to explain most of it to him, so she said she would call him at home if she needed him. She locked the door and went back and checked the other door. The cards reported that all the men had clocked out, but she looked around everywhere anyway, even peeking in the men's restroom after tapping on the door. She wasn't afraid to be there alone. She only wanted to know that Horace wouldn't be springing any surprise.

She was running the last report when she heard a truck pull up in front and its door open and close, and imagined she heard footsteps. She went to the door and looked through the glass pane and said "Horace, just leave – " with steel in her voice and before she realized it was Matt who was standing there. She unlocked the door and opened it. "What are you doing here?"

"Glad I'm not Horace." He waited but when she didn't respond he said, "It's the twenty-eighth. The party. Remember?"

Yes, she'd remembered the invitation. She couldn't deny that. But with all the other things going on, she'd managed to tuck its disturbing presence away when it reared its head. She hadn't thought he'd really count on her going, she supposed; she'd never actually said she'd go, and she guessed she hadn't wanted to be disappointed if he didn't show up. And she didn't want to be faced with the possibility that she might actually have to decide whether to go. Still, she'd rather it be this dilemma than Horace at the door. To say the least.

"I'm sorry . . . I had to work late. I wouldn't expect you to wait for me to finish. And then get dressed." And it would take some dressing to look like she belonged with him. He wore dark suit pants and a silk black and yellow and wine tie over a spread- collar fine white shirt. The jacket was no doubt in the truck.

"I don't mind waiting."

He didn't ask how long. What did he want? He was married and he'd already turned her down. Could it be that Lydia Hawkins had instructed him to bring her, a nice conversational topic: "Oh, there's the artist's daughter; do you believe she was that beautiful baby?" Maybe she did owe her the favor of going, after the mix-up over the painting. That was the only reason. Yeah.

"Actually, I've just finished here."

"Where's your car?"

"I walked."

"Are you alone here?"

"I gave my bodyguard the night off." Now that was really clever – for whoever was the first to say it.

Under watchful eyes she closed up shop and flipped on the night lights. Again, she felt like she was the stranger in a strange place, like she had in her kitchen the night he had eaten with her. Again, he didn't ask if he could help, he only sat in Mr. Elwood's chair, so all-seeing that she decided he could start work there in the morning if he chose.

When they were in the truck, she realized Miniver must have told him where she was, and she wondered if he still thought, as she assumed he thought, that he knew all about her life as an old maid when he saw Miniver and the kids at the door.

He pulled the truck to the front of her house as he had before. The front door opened and Sarah and Miniver and the kids and Vernon all sprouted out like one of those flower bouquets that pops up when the lid is opened.

"What'll I wear? I don't want to look like the eccentric artist's eccentric daughter," she said upstairs to Sarah and Miniver.

"Not to worry," said Sarah. "Now, you don't have a minute to shower. Just put on some Secret and some Number Five and get into this dress. Don't keep that man waiting."

"If he didn't leave when that door opened . . ." she said, but nevertheless stepped out of her clothes and into the things that Sarah had laid out for her on the bed. The dress was black cotton pique, cut straight and just above the knees and sleeveless with a low-cut square neckline. She thought Willette had culled it from her hoard of party dresses about five years earlier.

"I'm not as thin as Willette."

"You work like a Mayflower moving man," said Miniver. "You've got no fat."

"It's too short."

"You've got runner's legs," Miniver said.

"Let's see it on you," said Sarah.

"Nice and tight," Miniver said. "Girl, watch yourself tonight."

She was expecting a hallowed and ancient home on one of the avenues in Central Gardens; or even a rambling home set back a hundred yards for horses grazing out east in Germantown. But Matt veered west from I-55 to I-240 going downtown. He continued past the refinery with the smokestack blaze that could singe heaven, past warehouses and factories and railroad yards.

One high-water spring, when Crystal was still too young for a license, and they'd agreed she would pay attention to her driving while Sarah gave directions to the Old Navy Hospital grounds, to Sarah the best view of the river, they'd ended up in Arkansas. She still didn't know if Sarah had just gotten sidetracked with her usual looking about, or if she'd purposefully waited too late to tell Crystal to change lanes. This old crossing now gave the feeling of embarkation to an unknown destination when compared to the new bridge, looking like a Disney ride with its suspended approach and lighted elongated M above.

Matt did, of course, stay diligent and in the middle lane that became Riverside Drive following the east bank of the river, which was the western boundary of Memphis. Riverside was wide and rolling, although at times it was level. Every few years, the river forces would have made the land undulate because of pushing and undercutting, washing away or flooding acres of hundred year-old brick or cobblestone parking lots and riverfront parks, and requiring major building up. It was unnerving Sarah said, to know that these four lanes were just about all that separated the treacherous muddy waters from the high bluff that was the city's foundation.

Matt turned right onto Beale St. and then made a quick left into what once was the alley behind The Green Grub, known as the beer joint from hell, but which now was a fern bar, and the alley that used to host frequent robbings and stabbings now was the drive into a gleaming condominium complex, built on the bluff with a view of the millions of gallons of water moving past every day, carrying tons of earth robbed from Memphis's northern neighbors. To Sarah, it was a precarious perch for which even the view couldn't atone.

Matt didn't park in the lot. Instead he waved to the attendant in the guardhouse and drove into the area under the building and parked in one of four places marked Hawkins. A limousine was in one, a little red Mercedes with its top down in another, and the other was unused. No one else meant enough to her to offer the parking space for tonight?

Lydia Hawkins was more of everything than Crystal had imagined. Richer. Blonder. Thinner. Prettier. Nicer. They had just gotten off on the wrong foot on the phone that day, and that was understandable when you remembered what was at stake.

Crystal was going to have to recount the entire evening for Sarah, and Miniver could ask about as many questions, so better to memorize it now than suffer their recriminations later. The mayor, looking like a short heavyweight boxer, a hometown poor boy-to-success story, told her about her dad's all white high school football team driving up to South Memphis to play his all black school in 1937. It was radical, he said, actually against the law. They'd met at a horse race; he cleaned the stables and Dad bet on the horses – it too was illegal – but they had hit it off. They'd kept in touch for many years.

The University Art Department Chairman said Crystal's father's work was important in the Southern art world, that it was a shame his paintings were so few, that his art had halted at such a young age. Crystal said nothing about the rooms upstairs at home lined with his unknowns, as well as copies and drawings, nor about the workshop out back crowded with his stained glass creations, or the hand-crafted furniture. But she wondered if he would have wanted wider recognition. He'd gone to other art forms when he stopped painting, as though he couldn't not create. He'd never turned down a sale, except for this one painting, by pricing it out of the market. She wondered again why he insisted on keeping this one even though he had the copy for himself.

And there was Shelby Foote, small-boned and gray-bearded and dignified. All his books were in Sarah's possession, and all inscribed to her. Sarah had told her Dad and he had been acquaintances. Mr. Foote said, "I miss your father," then asked how her mother was doing, and said to tell Miss Chancellor that he hoped she was doing well. Maybe he would have said more, but a lady with a lot of diamonds and self-assurance came up and grabbed his arm, and asked if General Lee was as brilliant as had been written. Crystal wondered if she was a dumb as she sounded.

She excused herself and wandered out on the patio to look at the river. As she came back in she noticed a woman who seemed familiar, dark-hired, tall and somewhat glamorous and about Willette's age, sweep through the room to Mr. Foote's side. They talked amiably, looking like the grandee and the courtesan; finally she heard someone say, "God's sake, why doesn't someone rescue him from that Romance writer?" That was it.

Crystal had seen her picture on the back of more than one of Sarah's books. There would be heck to pay if she didn't meet this woman, and Sarah would want her autograph on a cocktail napkin to tuck into a book. But Sarah knew better than to expect Crystal to get it.

Crystal also recognized from newspaper pictures the Memphis businessman who had bought a pro sports team, and the man who saw that your mail got there the next day if it absolutely, positively had to be there. "Breaks the law every day" Sarah had said, admiringly. Crystal didn't know if it was really against the law to mail something first class with anybody else unless the U.S. Postal Service couldn't get it there on time, but she did know she wasn't going to ask. When a group formed around the two men, no one interrupted. Sarah later speculated, "When Fed Ex talks, everybody else listens," and Miniver told her she had the wrong commercial.

Crystal smiled back at a woman she remembered from a few classes during college, who had been the beauty queen of the day. She'd made her name and fame as a local TV news anchor before marrying into an old and important family and turning to civic endeavors. "That woman does like to get her picture taken," Sarah said not long ago. "Do you want to hear the latest about her?" "No," Crystal answered, "maybe the papers like to photograph a beautiful woman who gets things done." Diane walked over and said, "Dr. Word made freshman English seem like a different language, didn't he? Remember how he always handed out the top five grades last?" "Yes, yours was always one of them," Crystal said. "Yours was always last," Diane said, seeming content with that. "Oh, I studied a lot," Crystal muttered, trying to keep from ducking her head and shuffling her feet like an embarrassed high school nerd. "Yes," Diane said, "instead of flitting around in every contest that came along." "You were called last in those," Crystal said, also smiling.

Mother Martin of Beale Street fame, tiny and crackly, sang her blues unsubdued at the baby grand. She sought Crystal out and told her that Toliver and Willette had come to eat ribs and hear her at a place on Third close to McLemore over thirty years ago. This was a night of surprises.

Many of the guests Crystal met didn't make the connection that she was Toliver Bell's daughter, as he never signed his last name. So the party wasn't as stressful as she'd anticipated. With so many notables there she had measured herself totally out of proportion, having no claim to fame herself, just the luck of a talented parent. She had not done justice to Lydia Hawkins, who invited her as a thoughtful gesture.

She said as much to Matt on the way home and he said, "She doesn't like to share the spotlight."

While Crystal was thinking that over, he said, "I'm glad you enjoyed it."

"I wasn't invited, was I?"

"I did. Don't you remember?"

So he was the one being thoughtful. Of her if not of Lydia. At least now she could stop trying to think charitable thoughts about Lydia. Once she'd come to where Crystal and Matt were standing together and asked him to fasten her bracelet. "The latch is always coming undone," she added, moving her wrist, the diamonds heavily dangling only by a tiny chain.

The bracelet should have been worn with an armed guard. But she used it to get Matt's attention. Crystal had been around Sarah long enough to think like her. Oh, don't blame this one on Sarah.

Matt was still tied up with Lydia, his choice or hers. And she wasn't even going to think of how it might have been if that wasn't the case. She had tried to stand quietly with her arms tucked against her old dress and not be noticed by anybody. But somebody was always talking to her.

She'd tried to answer questions nicely, if they weren't too personal. There was one man who tried to pry things out of her before she ran out of one word answers and finally patience. Was she the baby? Wasn't she his only female model other than his wife? Had he ever explained that? Wasn't it years since the last sale of a painting? Was this the most ever paid for one of his works? When did he die? She'd walked away before he finished his probe, "Was it suicide?" Yes, he would be a reporter. Lydia would publicize both the purchase and the party.

"Who is Horace?" Matt said out of the dark inside the Suburban as they left the bright city lights.

She lifted her eyes from his hands on the steering wheel to the row of dark pines planted as sound and sight barriers. Some had fallen on the manmade sloping bank. A few were dead and still stood in their beds, unaware they should topple.

"He's the foreman."

He took the Hernando exit and continued west, but she didn't say anything about it being the wrong exit. If she told him about Horace, maybe she could ask why he didn't divorce Lydia. But she couldn't bring herself to make that swap.

"Do you have trouble with him?"

"No." She wouldn't give trouble with him a second chance. They were almost through the little town now, passing the large, square, red brick courthouse with its dark concrete pillars. Inside on the walls up the wide curved staircase were blazing murals of Hernando DeSoto and his fellow band of Spaniards and Indian guides, discovering the wide, marauding Mississippi River. She always wondered when she saw it, as much as she admired the man's determination and the fanciful depictions, how it was that he discovered the river, when the Natives took him to it. She asked her dad about it when she was small, and he'd answered, "The truth of what happens depends on who's doing the telling to who." She knew now how true that could be.

"Why are you interested in me?" There.

"Why shouldn't I be? Everybody at the party was."

"I'm a curiosity piece, all right."

"Who was that guy who cornered you?"

"Which one?"

He laughed. "It's a pretty night. Do you want to ride a while?"

"OK." Not, yes, yes, a thousand times yes, though she wanted to ride until the time she spent with him started to seem like a memory.

SEVENTEEN - Starry Clusters Bright

They drove west toward the river, maybe twenty miles away, on a flat, unwinding, worn-out two lane road with no yellow lines painted to the right of the faded center line. They weren't needed. You could see forever. They passed areas dark with thick, tall trees and acres of ragged spindly trees looked to be suffering from malnutrition. Sporadically the flat road became flat concrete bridges over swamps formed through the ages by the flooding of the river. The bridges seemed a mile long, with stumps and dead and living trees dripping with moss and vines and kudzu, and cypress knees already in mourning for their dying tops, eerily rising from the fog and murky waters, hiding enough snakes to populate an Indiana Jones movie.

He asked if she'd mind the windows down and she said she'd like that. The cool air whipped and swirled wisps of her hair around her face and neck like unknown things in ocean waves. The noise level of frogs and crickets was unrelenting and off the decibel scale. They passed pastures with still cattle; abandoned, falling-down half-constructed shacks; a few fine homes set back in trees at the end of long winding gravel drives; low brick houses with impractical short windows that couldn't let in a decent breeze; and mobile homes dropped forlornly in the middle of fields, now unmoving targets for a tornado to move from the still, sturdy, fixed earth.

The ground gradually became uneven, if not actually hilly. They passed a couple of faded signs noting developments on lakes designed as reservoirs as they came closer to the river. The earthen levees were covered with grass or trees or shrubs or topped by a road.

He turned south for a few more miles and then west again and just before they looked over the famed Delta's edge, drove onto a levee, slowly in the hugging dark, both watching the black lake lapping the steep bank. When he stopped, there was no vehicle in sight, not a house or boat on the water.

They got out and leaned against the truck, his thigh against hers, his arms crossed over his chest, his elbow touching her arm. From somewhere they heard bits of words. They could have been never-intercepted radio signals in code, left over from Mr. Elwood's war, circling the earth forever unless she plucked them from the atmosphere and deciphered them, to confirm what they meant and what she already knew. That she had no business being here, pretending she wasn't who she always was.

She looked at the crowded stars, hanging so vividly on nothing but black that she was almost afraid they would fall on her.

All reasons not to aside, she hoped he would kiss her again the way he had that night outside her house, and let her spread against him like lotion on a baby. She told herself she could be satisfied with that and not ask any questions or for more.

She thought no more about the stars or the dark muddy waters lapping the concrete slabs piled upon the levee like gnawed bones slung away by some giant, or the bodiless voices floating in the netherland. He had removed his jacket and tie when they left the party, like he had done in her kitchen, and rolled up his sleeves when they stopped, and now he absentmindedly slapped at a mosquito on his neck, and draped his arm over her shoulders. She was reminded of a shy boy in a dark movie theater, disguising the move.

He wasn't movie star pretty, nor even ruggedly charismatic like Reverend John Half; and he wasn't the life of the party, rather more watchful than wordy. He wasn't rich and powerful. At least, not that she knew. It seemed Lydia was the one with the money. Was that why he didn't divorce her? Could he be bought? No. Please no.

Once, he'd made a private toast before they were interrupted again. He was drinking Jack Daniels. Diane's conversation had made Crystal remember her old party days. Tonight she had swilled mineral water on the rocks with a twist of lemon, on the advice of Sarah, who kept up with what was in.

"To the Babe," he'd said in his toast. "This is the first and probably only time I'll be called a babe," she'd said. "Now don't be struck down, but I was referring to the wee babe in the basket," he said, extending his toast toward the painting. But later he'd say something like, "Hey, Babe, wanna party?" or "Say Babe, let's go to my place," and she'd say, "Do I know you?" or "Have we met?"

He now had his arm crooked around her neck, a hook around a Vaudeville jokester in an old movie being yanked from her inept performance back to real life. A plane was like a silent shooting star, they were so far from Memphis International. The voices had quieted, stopped trying to reach her. "Even the frogs are quiet," she said.

"They've gone to bed." He turned her to face him, pulling her close. "My bed isn't far from here," he said over her head. Then he tilted her face up and touched her lips with his. "Do you want to go see mine, Crystal?"

EIGHTEEN – Cautionary Tales

Even knowing he was still married, she couldn't say no. She might end up regretting it but she would regret it more if she said no.

A yipping puppy, looking for the world like a small black bear, led them in a limping run after they turned into the narrow, rutted road that stopped at the house. It was fieldstone and cedar and tucked under pines and oaks. A dock down at the lakeside sheltering a medium-sized boat was fleetingly visible in the truck lights.

"Hush, Old Ben," he said as they got out of the truck, but the puppy didn't hush and Matt didn't seem to mind.

"Isn't he just a puppy? Why did you call him Old Ben?"

"I found him in a beaver trap when I was scouting some property for the company. He has a mangled paw."

"He looks like a bear."

"Exactly. And he'll be old one day."

He said it like he expected her to know the significance of that, but she didn't know and didn't comment on it again. Old Ben tried to climb up him and got a head-scratching. When he came to her, Matt said "no" and the puppy stopped his climbing and stood with tail wagging. She didn't pet him. Vernon's puppy days had been numbered long ago. When he wanted attention he sidled up to her and got his long body rubs without any commotion.

"Can't muster up sympathy for a little crippled dog, even if it doesn't know it is?"

No. She had no sympathy for a dog lucky enough to be brought home by him. "Don't want to make Vernon jealous, going home with another dog's scent on me," she said, reaching down and rubbing his head. Is that what Matt would do, go home to Lydia with her scent on him?

The iron and glass security door closed hydraulically smooth as they entered. The room was large enough for a seating area of two large overstuffed couches around the stone fireplace that was bigger than Dad's roll-top desk, and another area with leather chairs and ottomans facing a television. Bookshelves lined a wall near a spacious dining alcove furnished with padded chairs around a glass-topped metal table that looked like something Dad would have created. There were a couple of paintings, abstract, that she didn't understand, another like Dad might have painted, and a portrait of a little girl in an antique white dress sitting in a garden, much more sedate and traditional than anything Dad had ever cast her in.

Moonlight burst through a couple of skylights in the high, beamed ceiling. It couldn't have been more different from where she'd spent her life. She liked it, but said, "This is nice." He didn't need her pronouncement that she *liked* it.

He moved to glass shelves by the TV. There was more sound equipment than on display at The Broken Record Shop in Shallot, and albums, eight tracks, and cassettes were tucked neatly against each other.

"Pick an album," he said, thumbing through them.

"Stop," she said, suddenly feeling the need to leave. They'd listen to music, then what? What they had alluded to earlier? But tomorrow would be another day. She hoped with no more complications and no more people who had come to believe that she was of importance to them, and who might be out of her life without a moment's notice.

He looked at her for a moment, then as if he didn't realize what she meant, he looked at the cover. "Johnny Mathis? I would've picked you and The Stones, for sure."

"I'm the life of the party," she said, wondering if he really thought that, remembering that she had become good at partying if for no other reason than to refute Willette's assertion that she would be a wallflower.

She stood with feet cast in stone while he slipped Johnny from his cover and onto the turntable. He pulled her hand to touch his face. In a minute he circled her arms at his waist and lightly cupped her behind with his hands. "Are we having fun yet?" he asked.

"I am." She might as well admit it. She wiped at a lipstick smudge on his shirt. "Two-timer," she said, too late realizing she meant it.

"No lips but yours have touched this shirt, My Dear."

She laughed. "Was that supposed to be Gable?" On impulse she kissed his shirt below his left shoulder, leaving only a bare suggestion of lips because she hadn't replenished her lipstick .

"You like living dangerously, huh?" He let her pull loose and dart away before he caught her and tilted her face to him. "You got me in the heart," he said, touching the spot. He kissed her on the neck. "Do you want me?"

"Yes." Before she could wonder how long he wanted her to want him. Just tonight? Forever? While it lasted? And should she tell him, but by the way, I wanted you so bad I substituted another man? He said I asked for it. Then again, he may have forced me? But yes, I do! "But."

"But what?"

But I don't know if I can let another man get that close to me, even you. Even though I've been waiting all these years for you. A man like you.

To ask. To say I've gotten you in the heart. In the heart! Hell, you may not even have meant it like that. After all, you've not gotten yourself free of your wife. But I can't tell you all this. She needed a minute to think. "I've got to go to the bathroom." She heard Willette say, "You should have asked to visit 'the powder room.'"

"Come on, I'll help you."

"I'll go by myself."

"Out this door. First door on the right."

She scrutinized herself in the mirror, a habit she'd gotten out of, although it was hard to avoid looking at herself at home. Willette'd had mirrors installed all over the house. Floor length triple folding mirrors in the bedrooms. Large mirrors and small mirrors on the walls downstairs. Gilded frames. Beveled edge wall mirrors in the bathrooms. She had never seen this image reflected before, though. And she liked it.

Unless he had trick lighting, her skin was radiant. Slight laugh lines seemed to have set in tonight just to make her smile look larger. Her eyes were like a kid's sparklers. She tried to see herself as he saw her and attempted to look dignified, but she gave up. She was just plain happy tonight and it showed.

A few minutes later she tugged up the bikini panties, just like Horace told her to do! She thought a moment. Stockings and garter belt. What a get-up. She had a drawer full of panty hose, but Sarah and Miniver had laid these out with her bra for tonight, all black, all donated by Willette as if to show Crystal what she was missing out on. It was obvious what Sarah and Miniver had been hoping. And she went along, undressed and dressed while they hovered and chatted, as if she had been naked in front of others all her life. And she had not been totally unclothed before someone since Ida used to bathe her when she was little. She was just a sex-starved fool like Matt had thought that first night, and willing to go to bed with him now he'd finally decided he wanted to and since Horace hadn't suited her.

She had to get back home and fasten doors and windows and find the crevice that all this change was coming through and stuff it with routines. One night wouldn't have been worth turning her life upside down again for, would it? There wouldn't be more than one. One night stands were her style.

In her hurry to get out and say take me home, take me away from this temptation that would be the finish of my dreams of you and not the beginning of a life with you, she brushed against a bottle which fell to the floor and broke into a million pieces. It filled the room with the intense scent of Matt.

"Are you all right in there?"

She didn't answer. She stuck her finger in a puddle and put it to her nose. It overpowered her the way he did. She could dive in, lap it up and still want more of him.

"I'm coming in," he said, opening the door. "Whoa!"

"I'm sorry."

"Only thing, now you know my secret. That stuff's supposed to be irresistible."

"It is," she mumbled, picking up pieces and putting them in the wastebasket.

"I'll clean it up later."

He leaned down as she continued to pick up the glass and placed his forehead against hers and his hands on her arms. She thought she was floating in the spilled liquid, but it was clear water, and she was being baptized in the pure water of his touch. She could try to forget the two men who with her help had made such a mess of her life.

"Come on," he said, pulling her up. They turned to leave but didn't get past the door before it was as if he couldn't wait to kiss her.

She tasted the whiskey, which she'd hated these long years, now suddenly honey to her.

"Crystal," he said against her throat. She pressed as if to let him drink from her artery. She would be a walking dead through the centuries if she could have this with him. Finally they moved down the hall to the bedroom and lay down.

She tried to wrap her leg around him but her heel caught on the cover, so she kicked off her shoes, and he pushed his off. Strange. Not even her parents or a girlfriend at a childhood slumber party had lain beside her. As a child, even when she was sick, Ida slept on a cot Dad moved into her room.

But she wanted Matt here. So this was that sweet, mysterious thing that made men and women willing, and more than that, wanting, to have that person by their side forever? Was this more than Dad or Willette or Sarah had, more than Miniver or Thomas had? Or had they started out this way? Could it start this way and then be lost? She hadn't even believed in its reality before she first saw Matt and she put up her defenses.

"Don't forget me," he said.

"No. I won't."

"Something's happening back there," he said, touching her temple.

"Something's happening to you, too," she said, laughing at her audacity.

"I'm glad you finally noticed!" he said, rolling over on her.

She kissed him. She felt she had a right to his kisses now, that she owned his mouth and could do what she pleased to it, taking charge like a greedy strip miner who had no intention of stopping until she got every ounce.

The things he would do were what her body and mind had been craving but had learned to live without until she had thought she didn't miss them. But now she was missing them and needing them.

He got up and pulled her up with a hug that made her feel welcome to his body. It made her ashamed to think about the things she wanted to do to it, like a welcomed guest who would instead plunder and leave nothing worth having. Stuff him inside her dress and pet him like a crazed woman with a doll. Wrap him inside a box and ship it to a destination she alone knew.

He didn't know her unholy thoughts and slid her zipper down. Her back under his hands was hot like melted gold in a jeweler's mold. She unbuttoned his shirt and pulled it open, and turned on the bedside lamp so she could see. She looked him over, hair, face, neck, chest down to his navel.

He slid her dress down and as he kissed down to her stomach she realized he had the same opportunity to see her. She took off his shirt and kissed his shoulders. As self-declared owner of him tonight she could do what she could free herself to do.

When he unhooked her bra, she flinched a little before she could stop. Had she taken comfort that as long as she kept part of her away from marauding eyes, part of her had not been violated? He noticed her reaction and kissed her again. Her fingers found the straps and she bared herself to him.

His kisses down her neck were like the blistering winds that scorched the Texas earth she remembered, leaving the parched land radiating heat. But then his kisses covered her breasts like gentle aloe. She wanted that forever but knew that would never satisfy the glutton she had become.

They lay on the bed again. But he didn't do what she thought he would. He just watched her a few seconds and said, "I like the way you look."

A girl had to believe her mother and not someone who loved her as much as Sarah did – but if her looks suited him, if he said they did, that was enough. As for what she thought of him, he was what she had been unable to form in her mind when she dreamed of some unknown man, but she knew he was the man she would wish to have.

"Take off your pants," she said.

He laughed but didn't take them off.

"Aren't we going to . . . you know . . ." Her assurance fled like a crooked politician who'd been found out.

He smiled. "I like that disappointed look. I didn't want to take all night getting this far." He held her hand. "I've wanted to hold you since the first minute I saw you."

"I don't believe you . . . that morning . . ."

"That morning I couldn't take my eyes off you. You must have noticed."

What had she done to deserve this? His feeling the same as she had, at least saying so. "But that night .. ."

"Did I actually turn you down? I'm usually rational."

Whatever happened between them she would never tell him about Horace; she couldn't without telling him why she tried that first kiss that led to what happened.

"After my marriage fell apart, I settled down with another woman for a couple of years."

She almost felt sorry for Lydia. "Uh huh . . ." She nodded like a movie psychiatrist who couldn't be shocked. Neutral. Nothing to her. But why tell her? It wouldn't be like him to brag about his other conquests. Would it?

"Neither wanted to get pregnant."

So he wanted to discuss that she could get pregnant? She'd probably be the happiest woman in the world if it happened. With that supposition her whole future life whizzed around inside her head like the winner of a stock car race. But her heart slid to her toes with fright. Oh, now I see what you want to discuss, and thank you so much for your kind consideration, but maybe I should mention that I'm two weeks late with my period, so even though I'm sure it's just systematic shock, there's just the slightest chance I may already be pregnant. No, scratch that, can't tell you. Then she realized the implications of what he'd said. Did she not know him at all?

Before she knew the words were forming in her mind, she said, "They both got pregnant? You and Lydia have a child? And you separated . . . and she wouldn't give you a divorce when another woman was having your child?" Or you wouldn't get one?

She had seen his expression before, similar to one of Dad's when he was troubled that she hadn't been able to figure something out, maybe about him and Sarah; or accept that a situation wasn't necessarily what it seemed and been unable to trust in what she felt to be the truth. And yet he felt a responsibility that he should have explained it all before she could mislead herself so.

"Lydia and I have never been married. We don't have a child."

So who were the women with the children? "What is she to you, then?"

"I should have told you. I'm sorry. Figured you knew her background, probably some of mine, from the company publications. Guess I thought you'd have asked if you didn't know.""

"She's not your sister. She can't be your *mother*."

He laughed. "We'll leave it at this: she's my step-mother."

"Step-mother! I don't even know the company name. She paid with a personal check, you know."

He nodded.

"So what's the name?"

"The Hawk Company."

Crystal nodded. "Yeah. I know about that company."

"Lydia finds out whatever she wants to know. She probably had you investigated. She usually does before she signs money away."

Investigated? "I hope she gave them a bonus for finding out there's nothing to find out." Oh, had she been right about that woman from the first! "So, your children . . ."

"I have a six year-old daughter, Hallie," he said, and his eyes actually grew brighter, "living in Nashville with my wife."

She tried to picture a daughter of his. Six. The age she was when she started understanding things weren't the way they should be in her home, though she knew no other home to judge it by.

He went to the chest of drawers across the room and brought her a picture. Hallie had dark brown hair and eyes and a smile that reminded her of him.

"The watercolor over the table in the living room, that's her, isn't it?"

"Yeah, a couple of years ago."

He put the framed photo back on the chest, then pointedly turned it toward the wall. When he returned to the bed, he said, "The other pregnancy . . . it was terminated. I couldn't tell her what to do. There were other things, anyway. It was already past its time when it got started."

When was she going to learn to trust herself about human nature? She'd known the kind of man he was from the first just as she'd instinctively known the kind of man Horace was from the first. "So, we're not going to do it? Make love?"

"I thought we'd finally made that decision," he said, sort of hiding behind his forearm as if she would hit him. "You're not on the pill, I take it?"

"Does an aspirin count?"

He laughed, and watched. Then he laughed again when she covered her face, realizing she'd innocently reminded him of the old joke about holding it between your knees.

"I was going to feel like a fool if you were."

She gave her shoulders a carefree shrug.

"You were just going to go along," he said, shaking his head, "Well, lucky for you I'm the kind of guy I am." He smiled a giant fake smile, and reached to the night table for a little square envelope.

NINETEEN - A Ton of Bricks

"Is Ms. Hawkins the spotted toad I think she is?"

"No, Sarah. She's beautiful. And very smart, I think. And was nice to me."

"Nice? Yes, that was smart. She was fighting fire with fire. But that phone conversation was the real Lydia Hawkins."

"She had a lot at stake with the painting."

"She had him at stake, too, and she realized it. Of course, I can sympathize with her to some extent."

"Why, I'm surprised at you," said Miniver, "siding with her against Crystal."

"It's just that I had a man taken away from me once, and I know how it feels."

"I want to hear about that sometime," said Miniver.

"So do I. But here's a news item for you," said Crystal. "They're not married. Never been."

"Did I hear you right?" said Miniver. "He's got her danglin' and a wife danglin' and now you – danglin'."

"That's not right," said Sarah.

"You're damn right, it's not right," said Miniver.

"No, I mean that can't be true. That's not like him."

How could Sarah be so sure of him, in light of this curve she just threw?

"Ms. Hawkins may be dangling, but it's a rope of her own, I'll bet. Now, about the wife, there's bound to be more to it."

"Yeah," said Miniver. "I bet you're right. Let's see, what could it be? I know. She's in a mental institution! He wouldn't divorce her in that case."

"No. He wouldn't if that were true. But I imagine it's something else, like children involved."

They both looked at Crystal with expectation on their faces. "I wish you could see yourselves," she said.

"Well?" said Miniver.

"He has a daughter. Six years old."

Sarah and Miniver looked at each other as if they were Holmes and Watson. Miniver wore Watson's self-congratulatory smile and Sarah's face showed Holmes' knowledge that solving a mystery doesn't necessarily make for a happy ending.

"I have to get ready for work. You two can drink coffee and yak all morning," Crystal said. "But don't be talking about me." She got up from the kitchen table and headed up the back stairs, stopping half way and yelling, "My ears are burning!" and joined their laughter as she went on up.

She looked through two closets before settling on something. Yesterday morning anything would have done. But today she actually wished for one of the pastel dresses gracing a perfect plastic body that Sarah had wanted to buy for her at the mall. She finally put on a navy skimmer with a small cream print that Willette probably wore to nothing more needful than getting a manicure.

She plied her face with moisturizer and under her eyes put the new miracle tightener, both "guaranteed to take ten years off," that Sarah had given her recently, adding she'd appreciate it in ten years, and even used cover coat on the dark under eye circles that showed as mementos of last night, before applying her usual barest of base. She even wished for more time to spend on her hair, but wore it loose, because she was already late even driving and didn't want to upset Mr. Elwood again. She thought of all the mornings she had merely gone through a minimal ritual and it was enough. She knew somebody was going to notice the difference.

"You sure do look fine, today. Fine."

Yesterday she would have wanted to call Bob and let him do all the law allowed, although she knew that she wouldn't have. But just let it go today. She had seen the delivery truck loaded with pallets of bricks blocking the front, waiting for Horace to deliver them, so she had turned on the side street and parked there, going in the entrance the men used. Horace was drinking coffee in the lunchroom when she went to hang up her umbrella like she used to, before their . . . encounter. Maybe that would be a workable word for it now. Last night had gone a long way in dislodging the big space that incident had taken up in her mind.

"Wishing for rain?" he said. "Me too. Another day, though. I gotta deliver that ton of bricks the boys loaded yesterday. Some bigwig's in there with Elwood. Heard 'em say we're being bought."

Mr. Elwood already here, and talking to somebody about buying them? Why should she be surprised? No more than if a sink hole swallowed up Main Street. Shouldn't it take a lot more than that to surprise her these days? But she tried not to react, didn't even say you shouldn't be listening at the office door.

She went into the office. And there was the surprise it took to surprise her. Matt sat with Mr. Elwood, who said, "We've been waiting for you."

Matt and Mr. Elwood, waiting?

"Crystal, this is Mr. Hawkins. He's buying the place."

Matt buying the brickyard?

Matt stood and was as perfect a stranger as she felt him to be.

God in Heaven. And he hadn't told her last night? She sat at her desk and arranged her purse in the bottom drawer to keep them from seeing her face.

"Mr. Hawkins, this is Miss Bell. Crystal."

"It's a beautiful name," he said. "Call me Matt."

"Mr. Hawkins called me at home to fill me in a little."

Oh. Oh? And didn't call her. God in Heaven. Was last night a figment of her imagination?

"Do you want some coffee before we get started?" he asked Matt.

"Sounds good. I had a long night."

"Crystal, would you get . . . . No, wait," Mr. Elwood said, getting up. "I'll get the coffee." He looked back at Matt. "Mr. Hawkins, she's the one who runs this place and usually makes the coffee, too. If you're going to buy it, you might as well know who's responsible for its success."

She sat back down. More like her knees buckling.

"I'm not much of a manager, but smart enough to let someone manage who is," Mr. Elwood continued, obviously taking pride in that. "Anyway, now that I think about all this, I'm past retirement age. Might as well spend all day fishing instead of half days."

"I'm the minority owner," Matt said. "My stepmother, Lydia Hawkins, is the principle stockholder, CEO. I do the legwork for her. But I have to tell you, a full day's work is what she expects."

So. This would be Lydia's retaliation?

"I don't even want to do that anymore. Haven't in a long time."

"Would you consider staying?" Matt asked Crystal.

No, she didn't want to work for Lydia Hawkins. And go through him, after seeing how he could keep secrets from her. She saw the worried look on Mr. Elwood's face when she didn't answer. He didn't want her to be unhappy or out of work. And she couldn't afford to be out of work.

"Maybe you'll like working for the new company, Crystal," Mr. Elwood said. "Maybe they'll make you manager."

"Maybe we will."

And give her a big raise and lots of holidays. No, she expected Lydia bought the company for the express purpose of flexing her muscles and putting Crystal out of work and it was hard to believe Lydia thought her such a threat. Or could be that vindictive.

"If you'll get the coffee, I'll look at the reports," Matt said to Mr. Elwood.

When Mr. Elwood left the office, they were silent, as if they both understood that there was no time to talk now, but Matt came to her desk and rubbed her shoulders until they heard Mr. Elwood returning. She wanted to jerk away but couldn't make herself, even though he had *lied* to her. Not telling was as good as lying. Oh. Back at herself.

By noon Matt had seen the computer printouts and walked over the yard with Mr. Elwood. He had looked at the personnel files and she noticed that he lingered over Horace's and Thomas's. He accepted Mr. Elwood's explanation about Thomas being in jail without comment that he had met Miniver, who of course was listed in his file as his wife. "Where is Horace?" he asked. "I didn't meet him out in the yard."

She searched the file cabinet for something as Mr. Elwood answered. "He's delivering that load of bricks to a construction site in Sledgeford." He had left after accosting her and was taking his usual time. He didn't let any surprise throw him.

Matt looked at his watch.

"He won't be back until after lunch," Mr. Elwood said. She could see the hours adding up silently in Mr. Elwood's head. An hour there and back, an hour to unload. Even if he took an hour for lunch, he was due.

Matt didn't comment, and she thought again of how Matt was, even if he wanted more information. He'd wait patiently.

"Speaking of lunch, Sue's expecting the three of us. You two ready to go?"

"I should stay here," Crystal said.

"She's dying to know what's happening. I'm not going home alone and tell her this place is sold and I'm retiring."

He got the laugh he was expecting, and said, "If the new boss doesn't mind."

"I insist."

She said, "Oh, all right." Why not? Matt wouldn't go if she refused, and would probably want her to have lunch with him. And as bad as she wanted to question him, she didn't know if she wanted the answers.

"We'll all go in my car," Mr. Elwood said.

Crystal shook her head 'no' to Matt as Mr. Elwood searched his pockets for his keys.

"I'll drive," Matt said, "I should learn my way around town."

Sue's reaction was no surprise to Crystal when she found out that her husband was "letting the new company buy him out." Sue hugged both men, her head even with her husband's, and she playfully gave an additional squeeze to Matt's shoulders. How could Sue hug a man she had never met before? Could she picture herself doing that? Sue was still thin as when she was teaching. In fact, her hair was just as black and sprayed into place as it was then. She'd found her style and was sticking to it, Sarah had said. After all, it had gotten her a husband.

Then Sue hugged her when Mr. Elwood said she would be manager, not listening when Crystal said that wasn't settled yet. Sue turned the meal into a celebration, and said she'd be tempted to a champagne toast if she wasn't a Southern Baptist.

"She's been wanting us to spend winters down on the Gulf," Mr. Elwood said.

Later, Crystal helped her clear the table and bring strawberry shortcake for dessert.

"It's homemade shortcake," Sue said, adding apologetically to Matt, "but these are California. We've finished Crystal's berries. They're to die for."

Mr. Elwood looked from her to his plate. "To die for? What does that mean?"

"Famous, are they?" Matt said.

Crystal found no relief in knowing that he wouldn't acknowledge he knew of their existence, because she knew he was about to find out a lot more on the subject whether he wanted to or not.

"Gracious yes. And not for just their taste. The way she grows them right in front of that old Army tank in her yard. Not that I've seen it in an old coon's age."

"A tank?" he said innocently, and she recognized his playfulness, like last night when they were dancing. She plopped a mound of cream on his dessert, almost landing it on his hand as he reached for his spoon. But she couldn't be mad at him, because Sue would have been very curious if he hadn't expressed curiosity about a tank in somebody's yard here in Shallot. Or anywhere.

"Torrence Oliver bought it from World War II surplus and had it shipped here on the IC Railroad. We were already off its schedule, so it had to make a special stop."

"I'll take some coffee, Sue," Mr. Elwood said, looking uncomfortably at Crystal. "I'm surprised you didn't make peach cobbler." Everyone except Sue knew he was trying to change the subject.

"Peaches aren't good yet. Not sweet if they're picked too early. He wanted to drive it through town to his place, but couldn't get it to crank, so he had to arrange for a tractor trailer to haul it."

Matt nodded, as if agreeing that would be the reasonable next step, but she had said it as if that were the most unreasonable.

"Well, he had a reason for wanting to preserve it," said Mr. Elwood. "He said it was the tank he rode in when the Third Army took Berlin."

"Now, if Patton had ridden in it, it might have had historical value for buying it," Sue said, giving in somewhat.

"I believe the government retains rights if it should need it back, like it does such surplus," said Mr. Elwood, and his face said "see, it might have some value" but Sue's face said "see how impractical he was."

"Some thought he was. . . Well, thought he shouldn't have done it. His wife for one. Crystal's mother."

"Sue, Honey," Mr. Elwood said.

"Oh, Crystal knows I don't mean anything to hurt her feelings. But the truth will out, as they say."

Was that supposed to be a comfort?

"Well, tell the rest of it, then," Mr. Elwood said.

"Oh, that some said it was a wonder the whole Third Army didn't get court marshaled, with Patton *and* Torrence Oliver in it?"

"No, Honey," he said patiently. "It wasn't like he just planned to let it rust in the back yard. He was thinking of displaying it, for the children, I believe."

"Said he was going to start up a museum, sort of, with things he'd been collecting. Crystal, I don't know how you live with all that stuff around."

"You see something long enough it becomes part of the landscape, I guess."

"Anyway, shortly after that Willette filed for divorce."

She couldn't deny it.

"They'd been separated off and on for years," Sue told Matt. "Her living up in Memphis. Then when he couldn't get the tank declared a national shrine, Torrence Oliver got it into his head he'd stage a sit-in. A live-in. He wouldn't leave the place until he got authentication."

"That same tenacity kept the interstate from running down the middle of downtown, too," said Mr. Elwood, no doubt in his voice he was one of Torrence Oliver Bell's supporters. "You didn't know you'd be given a history of the Bell family, did you?" he asked Matt.

"Oh," Sue said, brushing the whole expose` away like a pesky gnat. "Crystal knows everybody in town talks about this. I'm not telling any of her family secrets." She looked kindly at Crystal and patted her hand

"That's true enough," Crystal managed to say.

"Everybody loves Crystal like she was a member of their own family," she added.

Huh?

"I guess you may as well know all about us, Matt, you're going to be part of us," Mr. Elwood conceded.

Crystal didn't see how it could, but the day went downhill from there.

It did rain. They inventoried the inside, then Matt called Sheriff Youngblood to get information on Thomas. Crystal could tell by Matt's questions and responses that Bob filled him in on what happened that night at her house. Her secrets list was getting shorter and shorter.

By mid-afternoon the men quit working because of the rain. She and Matt and Mr. Elwood went into the lunchroom where the men sat around smoking, curious, and Matt said he'd fill them all in as soon as Horace returned. He said they'd be paid for their time.

By three o'clock Matt asked if Horace was overdue like this very often. He was, but the customers he delivered to liked him, and he got his work done or saw that the men did it, and she hoped those were the only reasons she hadn't ever reprimanded him.

Mr. Elwood mentioned the truck was always giving him trouble.

"Maybe it rained and they couldn't unload," she added, hoping in fact that he didn't return before Matt left. She looked at the clock. In a little while they could all go home. Surely Matt wouldn't keep them here on overtime waiting for Horace. Then she realized that Horace was purposely waiting. He'd think all the men would be gone because of the rain . . . .

In a few minutes the back door opened and Horace walked in. "Figured everybody'd be gone," he said, pouring a cup of coffee.

"Bring your coffee in the office," said Matt. "I want to talk to you."

"You gonna believe her side?" Horace said.

Crystal didn't say anything. To do so would imply there was something to deny.

In a few minutes Horace stormed back to the lunchroom and gave her a look that Sarah would have described as malevolent. Then he got some things out of his locker, clocked out, and left.

Matt came in and said if anyone wanted to apply for the foreman's job to let Ms. Bell know, and when he said that there would soon be a new manager to replace Mr. Elwood, who had chosen to retire, but not much else was going to change, she felt all the men adjust their focus from Matt to Mr. Elwood to her. You didn't buy a profit-making business and come in and change everything, he said. Then he added that everyone could go home and come in like always.

When the men had gone, she and Matt continued to sit, not talking, her trying to summon up the mental stamina to tell him off for not letting her know what Lydia had planned for today. She tried not to remember the last time she was alone in this room with a man. She tried to forget it was raining. She tried not to ask what had been said in the office a few minutes earlier.

"What happened in there?" she finally asked, accepting that she wasn't going to lash out at Matt, and wishing she could get up the gumption to say good-by and go home.

Matt watched her a few seconds before answering. "I fired him."

She knew he was waiting for her to ask why, but she didn't. She washed their cups at the sink instead.

"I didn't like his looks."

She dropped a cup and broke it.

"It that a signal? You breaking glass? I'm easily trained." He stood behind her and put his arms around her waist. "I hope today was as hard for you as it was for me," he said.

"No, it didn't bother me at all. Your being here this morning, announcing you're my new boss."

"You're not going to get me on sexual harassment, are you?" he said into her neck.

When she didn't answer, he said, "But, what I meant was, I hope you were bothered the same way I was," and nuzzled her neck.

Horace didn't tell him what happened.

"What did Horace think you'd tell me?"

"I have no idea. Everybody here doesn't know everything like Sue Elwood does. Or tell everything. I guess you think my father was a little off."

She knew he realized she was being evasive, but of course he let her.

"Aren't most people with a gift a little different?" he said.

"I guess you're right."

He said, "My father was. He had a gift for making money. I've always thought of him as bigger-than-life. It took me a while to come to grips with it."

She moved away and put the broken cup in the trash. She wanted them to get out of this place where she felt Horace's presence. But Matt pulled her to him and before she knew it she was kissing him and being kissed as if they were going to make love in that very place. She told herself to pull away, but it was all nice and sweet, like a peppermint stick in cellophane.

She almost wished he would steer her to the couch and make love to her. Maybe then she wouldn't feel Horace's presence in this room anymore. But she remembered his caution last night. He wasn't planning to make love to her now. He only kept kissing her neck and rubbing her thighs.

She wrapped her leg around him and pulled him even closer and they stumbled against the wall. He unbuttoned her dress and kissed her covered breast. She uncovered herself and pushed against him.

He put his hands under her skirt and moved them on her legs and stomach and she fought the urge to collapse on the floor and pull him down to her. He'd had so much and she'd had so little.

She kissed him as she unzipped his slacks and put her hand inside.

"You always surprise me," he said.

She kissed him again and started pushing his pants down, then said, "You know what I want." Like she was placing a recurring order with a supplier.

"I can wait."

"I don't want to wait." For once she was going to get what she wanted just because she wanted it and when she wanted it. She needed to see how that felt. She pulled him to her and was caught between the wall and him. But he was the one who should be caught. She moved around while they kissed and soon had him pressed against the wall.

He let her do what she wanted. She stood on her tiptoes with her dress pushed up to her waist and wrapped her leg around him as she guided him and leaned into him and felt foolish. But she took what she wanted.

"Well, you had your way with me," he said, laughing into her neck a few minutes later.

"Yes, I did, didn't I?" Had she made him do it because she knew she could, even though he'd insisted he'd rather not? No, it wasn't the same as when she'd been forced. She knew he wanted her. Then she couldn't help laughing.

"Pleased with yourself?"

"Yes." Like a child with a birthday pony. And she still remembered how that felt.

"Is that all you have to say for yourself?"

"Yes."

"Ready to get dressed?" He pulled her dress back up on her shoulders and retrieved her underwear and straightened her skirt. She started for the bathroom but stopped and watched as he picked up his slacks and headed to the other one. His shirttail covered his behind as he walked. He turned around and said, "You are bad," and grinned.

"Thanks." She darted inside. She didn't even think of asking him why he'd not told her what today would bring for her work-a-day life when they said goodbye.

"Well, if that doesn't take the cake!" said Sarah that night.

"Thomas had been telling me something was up. He figured it was being sold," said Miniver.

"Why didn't Matt tell you ahead of time about them being the ones buying the place?" said Sarah.

"You sure you know him like you think you do, Sarah?" said Miniver.

Sarah shook her head. "I believe he had a good reason. Maybe he didn't know until this morning."

"That don't sound right," Miniver said.

"I guess what's going to happen between you and him is going to happen, and that's that," Sarah said to Crystal.

"But knowing that woman's got you in her pocket . . . . I guess you could look for another job," said Miniver.

She was so tired she just let them run on, talking about her and answering their own questions, not even waiting to see if she would answer. It was strange yet very comforting to be sprawled on her bed with Miniver cross-legged on the foot and Sarah in the chaise. Familiar. Trusting. Knowlng that they only wanted good for her. Knowing they wouldn't slyly convince her she didn't deserve happiness.

"Is he going to be there tomorrow?"

"Tomorrow's Saturday, Sarah," said Miniver. "But maybe he's going to call her tomorrow."

"Why, you know he will, Miniver," said Sarah.

Finally her eyes got so heavy she thought they were going to turn inside out if she didn't close them. She gave them about the same instructions she had that morning. "Y'all can stay here and talk all night if you want to, but don't talk about me. I'm afraid I'm going to sleep."

"Well, don't mind us. Goodnight, Crystal,"

"Goodnight, Sarah."

"Goodnight, Crystal," said Miniver.

"Goodnight, Miniver," Crystal mumbled.

"Goodnight, John Boy," said Miniver.

The last thing she heard was them snickering as she let herself drift away.

TWENTY - Book It

Next morning when she walked into the kitchen, Miniver poured her some coffee and then yelled out the back door for Tabitha not to pull Vernon's tail so hard, then said, "That beagle's a saint, I swear, if he ain't bit neither of them yet."

"More of a little lamb. Never even went hunting. T. Oliver wasn't through training him when . . . ."

"Are you up and over here already? Or did you spend the night?" Crystal asked Sarah, to fill the silence and to keep Miniver from asking about Dad's death. Although she didn't mind her knowing. She wanted her to know. Miniver ought to know who her friends were, where they came from, who influenced them. But just not this morning. Even the Bell dog didn't get a normal life. Poor Vernon had his reasons for being his unusual self.

"And what if I did? Save an old lady like myself a few steps. Besides, it's way up in the morning."

Crystal looked at the clock. Nothing was happening the same way it used to. She used to be up and out early, getting everything done for herself, keeping her own web around her, not thinking or wondering a whole lot about what everybody else was doing or thinking. Now she had people here, excluding Sarah of course, who wasn't people but more of a comforting presence; and she was sleeping late, and sleeping with Matt, and no longer sleeping her life away. And she couldn't keep from accepting things she didn't want to.

"Well, you ought to sleep here," she said to Sarah. It just slipped out, sincerely, not in the little sparring tone they sometimes used with each other. She hadn't assimilated before how carefully Sarah moved, how slowly she got up, how she braced herself as she sat. Her height had dwindled. Crystal remembered backing up to Sarah all her young life and measuring against her and how she felt the day the ruler lay even on their heads. And she was getting thinner, no denying it, even if she still "had her appetite" as Sarah was fond of saying. The hair she had done each week could no longer even pretend to be streaked with black. The beautiful character in her face was being disguised by sneaking time.

"Yeah," said Miniver. "You're not no spring chicken no more."

"No, but I'm a tough old bird! And you two . . . you'd drown in a drizzle. Not enough sense to tilt your beaks down!"

"All right. I'm sorry," said Crystal.

"Yeah, Sarah, get your drawers out of your crack!" said Miniver. "We didn't mean to get you upset."

It took a second for them all to realize what she had said. Although they'd both heard the expression, hearing it in conjunction with Sarah was startling to say the least. But pretty quick Sarah began to laugh and Crystal couldn't help joining in, almost strangling on juice. Miniver looked embarrassed, which she never had over any of the aspects of her life that had been revealed to them. "Shit! I can't believe I said that! I ain't changed since I left the mountains! Ain't learned a thing being with you two!"

Sarah patted her hand. "You don't worry about that. You're learning what you need to. And you're teaching us as you go." Then she looked at Crystal. "And I've still got some tracks to make before I give it up. Now, let's change the subject."

Miniver poured more coffee and took toast out of the oven and put some on three plates while Crystal got butter and jam out.

"I've got to make tracks soon, too," Miniver said.

Crystal and Sarah looked at her as though she had told them she had booked the next space shuttle.

"Don't want to wear out my welcome."

"I don't want to hear any of that 'wearing out' stuff," said Crystal.

"Miniver, these walls would cave in now without all your busyness to hold them up," said Sarah.

"More like all my hot air. But I can stand it a while longer if y'all can, I guess," she said with an exaggerated look. Then she walked to the door to check on the children and yelled "Tabitha! Don't put his foot in your mouth! Nor yours in his!"

"Matt has a dog," Crystal said, remembering the puppy of many breeds that had followed them down the drive and taken to her. She shook her head remorsefully. They had not mentioned Matt yet this morning and she obviously couldn't stand it. Couldn't go two minutes without talking about him.

Sarah and Miniver looked at each other. "Lordy, she's got it bad!" Miniver said.

"Well, let's humor her. What kind of dog?"

"Just forget it." She stuffed her mouth with toast.

"Let us guess. If Mrs. Hawkins has anything to do with it, it's a toy poodle."

"With ribbons on his ears," added Miniver.

"You two are so smart," Crystal said, sipping her coffee with her nose in the air. "It's just a little puppy with a crippled paw. It looks like a shaggy bear cub. He named it Old Ben."

"Well, I guess it'll be old one of these days," said Sarah, with a sniff. "It happens to the best of us."

"No, you two illiterates. I'm so surprised at you," said Miniver. "Don't you know?" She picked up her coffee cup and pointedly stuck her little finger up in the air and took a loud slurp.

"Yes, Mother Superior, you are right," said Sarah, nodding. "Crystal, we've been bested by a man and by a woman from North Carolina. Will you ever forgive us, William?" she said, looking toward the ceiling.

"Oh, yeah," said Crystal. "Faulkner."

"I remember when that bear story was published," said Sarah. "And I hope I don't hurt your feelings, Miniver, but I am surprised that you know it."

"You ought to be. In school, I never reported on a book unless it was a movie."

"Well, you know my curiosity. Tell me how you did know."

"It's like this. At some point, hopefully you realize some things. It may be a little after the fact, but maybe not too late. To do something about it, I mean."

"Do you mean you've been reading literature since you grew up?"

"I guess you could put it like that. Although I didn't really grow up until a few weeks ago, and probably haven't yet. But I like to read now. By the way, good library you got here, Crystal."

"I can't believe you've taken time out to read, as much as you get done."

"I'd just fidget, otherwise. I wondered what all the fuss was about them old stories. Now I understand a little of it. Like how he did the bear, Old Ben. He didn't belittle 'im. He was saying though – or maybe because – that animal grew up in the woods, he learned what it took to survive."

"Maybe like you, Miniver," said Sarah, "so don't ever be embarrassed again about your upbringing. Roots are there to provide growth."

Crystal sipped her coffee. She'd stopped bothering to learn about life years ago; it was too much trouble, and it could break your heart. And now in spite of that, she was in it up to her neck.

"I heard that sigh, Crystal," Miniver said. "You're wrong about yourself. It all just comes so natural to you that you don't pay it any attention."

"You can't mean that, Miniver." Her life had been so out of touch with others – could she admit concentrated on herself?

"Sarah, you tell her."

"Now, don't you be bothered that you're making fools of us two old maids, Miniver," said Sarah. "Crystal, if we're not careful, this girl will put us on the cutting edge of humanity."

"Oh, you know what I'm saying, Sarah," said Miniver.

"I think I do. Crystal's always had a way of denying facts."

"Well, I'm not going to embarrass her by saying what everybody in town knows about her. But it's different from what she thinks people think."

"I've always known she has her admirers. The Methodist preacher, John Half, thinks she's a candidate for sainthood, otherwise he'd have asked her out."

"Saint Crystal!" said Miniver. "St. Crystal and John the Half-Methodist."

"Wrong story," said Sarah. "That was Salome and John the Baptist."

Again they laughed.

"If you two don't just shut up," said Crystal.

Finally, Sarah said, "By the way, Crystal's daddy knew him."

"John the Baptist!?" said Miniver, and even Crystal laughed with them.

"No."

"You mean . . .no shi – really?"

"They had a few drinks together now and then."

Miniver looked suitably impressed and even Crystal didn't hide her interest in hearing about it.

"T. Oliver was as talented in his art as any writer in his writing," Sarah said.

"I can believe that. Being here and your house is like living in the Loovie," she said, smiling.

Sarah looked in her empty coffee cup and then stood, telling them that tomorrow afternoon they were going to do something special. Right now, she was going home.

TWENTY-ONE – Red Cloaks of Market Girls

Next day, Crystal worked in the garden as usual for her Sundays. Miniver came out a little later with a pan for the tomatoes.

"I've been cleaning up some in them unused rooms, Crystal. Not that nothing's dirty. It's just that some dust has found the right spot not to be disturbed. You know that attracts hermits, don't you? Recluse. Not you. Brown spiders."

"Of course not me," Crystal said as if that were the last thing she would be. "But you don't have to do things like that, Miniver. I don't go in some of those rooms for weeks, so I just don't worry about them."

"I believe it. Years even? I found some old crinoline slips under the bed in a box marked 'linens.' I haven't ever seen one before. Just in the movies. I was vacuuming, not just being nosy, and the box just came apart."

Crystal studied a perfectly shaped red tomato. It might be as good as it looked. And then again it might not. Just like people, you couldn't tell from outside. So those slips were there all along. Why hadn't Willette let her wear them to the fifties party all those years ago? Had she not wanted Crystal's outfit to be complete?

"Anyway, I found a skirt and blouse in the wastebasket in one of the rooms. A great outfit. If you're throwing it away, would you mind if I have it?"

Crystal knew which outfit it was. She didn't want to tell Miniver no, but she didn't ever want to see it again. Miniver seemed embarrassed that it was taking her so long to decide.

"Oh, that's all right, Crystal. I shouldn't have asked. You've helped me out so much and now I'm asking for clothes off your back." She turned to go.

"Not off my back. Out of my trash. But go through all those other closets, too, like we talked about, and take what you want. That one included."

"You kids come here," Miniver called, "and help Miss Crystal with these tomatoes. Just get the red ones. We've got to hurry, cause we're going somewhere in a little while."

"Where are you going?" Crystal asked. Not that it was any of her business. It was just surprising. "You don't have to answer that, Miniver. You come and go as you want to. Of course. I was just curious. Being around Sarah, I guess."

"Why, I don't know where we're going. But you're going too. Remember, Sarah told us yesterday, and she reminded me when she called as usual to ask me and the kids to go to church."

"Why don't you go to church with her?"

"Oh, I told her whatever's good enough for you's good enough for me."

"Oh, Lord, Miniver, don't use me as an example! For anything."

"Well, when you go, we'll go."

That pressure was worse than Willette's used to be. She felt bad not to set a good example for the children in her home. But it was too late now to consider going. Thank the Good Lord. She couldn't face turning up in church and at last hearing John Half and seeing if she understood what all the fuss was about. Who knew what her new persona was capable of.

It made her feel like a child again, enjoying it as Tommy and Tabitha were, meandering on roads with Sarah, going somewhere Sarah had selected, and looking out over the cotton fields and bean fields and cornfields. And looking down gravel roads and drives that tapered off through the trees and slight hills into unknown territory, with lives that might even be stranger than hers. Of course, Crystal had figured out where they were going, and by now Miniver probably had.

They'd stopped at the Velvet Cream for hamburgers and milkshakes, like she and Sarah had done all Crystal's life, and she noticed with some trepidation that the young waitress she'd emulated so often lately was definitely pregnant. She couldn't be out of high school, and there was no ring on her finger. As they left, Sarah gave her a business card and told her if she needed help that was the place to contact.

"Sarah's got lots of connections, don't she?" Miniver commented.

"You don't know the half of them," Crystal said.

The highway had a mileage sign for Oxford and University of Mississippi, and there had been a billboard picturing Rowan Oak. They drove around the campus and then to Faulkner's home. Miniver stared at the house with its two-story, white, squared columns, four of them, hunkering on a smallish lawn behind old cedars, oaks, and magnolias. "Not as large as I expected. But classy."

"Look back here," said Sarah, leading them to the back yard and the small white house he had made his own environment for creation.

"This where he thought up all the weirdness?" Miniver asked, peering in a window.

Yes, thought Crystal, looking about, almost expecting to see the aberrated characters he had imagined lurking about with more tormented lives than hers.

"Many of them," answered Sarah. "You know he worked in Hollywood, too."

"No sh – really? I wouldn't mind knowing more about people like him one of these days," Miniver said.

"I was hoping you'd say something like that," Sarah said. "I have the perfect solution for you, and I don't want any argument."

Crystal thought she knew what Sarah had come up with, and it might be the very thing for Miniver. "You know you can't argue with her."

"Well, pray tell what you have planned for my life? I obviously ain't got no sayso."

"It won't be easy. Don't think that. Not with the children. And it'll take you a while. Four years maybe," said Sarah.

"Oh, no. Not that!"

"I'm afraid so."

"But I hate school."

"I don't think you do. I think you just hated your life during school."

"Sarah, going to school takes money."

"I'm going to pay your tuition. And enough more so you'll only have to work a few hours a week. I'd prefer to give you enough so you wouldn't have to work at all. So you'd have more time with the children."

"I'm not taking money from you!"

"I have more than enough. And nobody but Crystal to leave it to. Do you think she'd mind parting with a little of it for you?"

Now it was Crystal's turn to protest. "Sarah, we've talked about this before. Set up a hundred scholarships. Thousands. Give it to the church. What would I do with it?"

"You can give it to the church when you get it. *Then* try to keep John Half out of your pants," Sarah said smugly.

"You should be on medication," Crystal said.

"Only one stipulation about the money. You can't go giving it all to Willette."

"That beats all. What if I give it to her while you're still warm in the box?"

"Who's Willette?" said Miniver.

"My mother."

"You won't," said Sarah. "Trust me."

"Your mother? Tommy, don't climb that tree! Guess I just thought your mother was passed away."

Now that Crystal thought of it, she was surprised that Willette hadn't come up in conversation between Sarah and Miniver. With Miniver's intuition, she probably understood a story there best to wait for. But of course Sarah wouldn't bring her up. She certainly hadn't mentioned Willette to Miniver. She hadn't even thought a lot about her. Surprising what a few happy little diversions like a displaced family needing and loving you and a man wanting to make love to you can do for you. And speaking of Willette, what had she been up to? She hadn't called the house in weeks. She'd called the office a couple of times. Figured she'd have a captive audience. But at work Crystal had authority and she used it to halt conversations quickly.

"Mommy, I've got to go to the bathroom," said Tabitha.

"I swear," Miniver said, taking her by the hand. "Some people argue about giving money away and not taking it and some people ain't got a pot to you know what in." As they walked past an elderly gentleman in a light blue seersucker suit and red bow-tie, who was obviously undergoing that walking-on-hallowed-ground-introspection, she said with a big smile, "Life's a frickin' beach, ain't it?"

"Mommy, don't talk like that," said Tabitha, and put her hand across her own mouth.

"We'll get her enrolled in basic English first thing," Sarah said to the man.

"I'll do it in three!" yelled Miniver from across the yard.

Then Sarah shook hands with the man. "Hello, Dr. Winstead. How are you?"

"Fine, Miss Chancellor, and how are you?"

"Very well, and thank you for meeting me here today. This is Crystal Bell, and that was Miniver Tandy. Please take my word that she's smart and teachable. I hope you'll be her mentor."

"I'd try it with Lady Macbeth if you vouched for her," he said, turning to watch Miniver. "She'll have much of life to teach about."

Crystal could hardly keep from shaking her head to clear it. So Sarah not only had decided to enroll her. She had her career chosen. Suddenly she could see it. Miniver was going to make a difference. She'd like to sit in on a class or two of hers!

It was dark when they arrived home. The children were napping in the back seat when Crystal turned in to Sarah's long drive.

"You should have pulled in your drive, Crystal, so you and Miniver wouldn't have to carry the children."

"They're light as kites. I've carried 'em both," said Miniver.

"Don't stay up watching television," said Crystal.

"Yes, Warden."

Crystal and Miniver carried the children through the break in the thick shrubs between the two houses. The dark was impressive without a moon showing. Suddenly, Miniver jumped as something brushed against her legs, and her reaction created an echoing jump in Crystal, even though she knew it was only Vernon.

"Vernon, you scared me to death," Miniver said, as they walked to the back porch.

Approaching, Crystal sensed someone on the screened porch, sitting in the swing in the dark. And she knew who it was. But when he stood and said hello, Miniver jumped again.

TWENTY-TWO – Learning Curve

"Sorry I scared you," Matt said as they entered the porch. "Guess I was dozing."

"We came in Sarah's drive," said Crystal.

"I could have gone in and turned on the lights. The door was ajar."

Miniver examined the knob. "But I locked it. We ought to get this fixed. It probably ain't working right since . . . that night."

Crystal nodded and made a mental note, for what that would be worth these days, to have it repaired.

Then Miniver peered up at Matt. "Do you believe she hardly ever used to lock the door? With all them paintings and antiques here?" She shook her finger at Crystal and said, "Not to mention her own self," then she went inside.

Matt took Tabitha from Crystal and followed them inside and up the back stairs. They laid the children on the bed, then he and Crystal went into the hallway.

"This is a big house." Then he sort of shook his head and said, "Nothing like stating the obvious. Lots of valuables here." Then he smiled and said, "Again . . ."

"It's . . . just home."

"Miniver's right about protecting yourself. Even if you don't care about the other things."

"I love everything in it."

He looked at some pencil sketches framed and hanging on the wall. "Any gallery would display these."

Was that a hint that she could sell them and make some money? Did he know her financial status? Which was no status at all. Had Lydia filled him in? No doubt she'd run a credit check as well as her other delvings. She went on the defensive. "I don't want to let go of any more of Dad's work."

"What would he want?"

Not wanting to wake the kids she went downstairs and he followed.

"Were you expecting someone this evening? Other than me?"

She wasn't even expecting him. "Like who?"

"Are you dating someone else?"

"Yeah. I'm just stringing you along."

"Be straight with me."

"Like you are with me."

"Lydia kept all that to herself. I tried to reach you here after she called and told me."

"Oh." Miniver had adopted her phone habits. She loved dropping the receiver in the little trash basket by the table. She'd put it there for that purpose. "Why would Lydia want to own the Shallot Brickyard?"

"After the painting mix-up, she was skeptical. And nobody comes through unscathed if she believes they tried to take her."

"How did she know where I worked?"

"That background check – she would have known all about you before she even bought the painting."

"Yet she paid top dollar . . ."

"Your agent raised it for appreciation over the years. He said you wouldn't take less. Because your father had turned down offers."

"So. What blood type am I? I've always wondered."

"Hot," he said, rubbing her arm. "She only told me what she wanted me to know. That's our history. At any rate, she's always alert for a good business deal."

She remembered the surprise Lydia tried to hide when Matt introduced them to each other at her party. She was getting Crystal back with her own surprise. And she wanted to own the yard so she would own Crystal. But maybe she didn't own Matt. Maybe she would only have him left in her heart when she was Sarah's age and making decisions that by then wouldn't be important to anyone else. But if she had him in her memory only, she didn't want to be disappointed in it. She wanted him to live up to what she was letting herself believe he was.

"So you weren't expecting anyone?"

"No. Why?" She put ice in glasses and poured tea and they went onto the back porch.

"I'm probably wrong . . . you don't have a lot of drop-ins, do you?"

"I'm thinking about a swinging door."

"Someone was pulling out of your back drive into the alley as I came around the house."

Could it have been Horace? "Was it too dark for you to see."

"Yes."

"What kind of truck was it?"

"A Chevy van. Light color."

So it must not have been Horace.

"That would be big enough to carry away a lot of stuff," said

Miniver, coming out of the kitchen. "I couldn't help hearing. I saw a van like that goin' slow down the street the other day when the kids and I went for a walk. Crystal, don't you read nothing about crime these days? There's people that go and scout a place and come back later for the stuff."

"Maybe it was just some teenagers curious about this place."

"What made you think it was a truck?" Matt said.

"Probably because Sarah and I are the only ones in town without a truck."

"Miniver's right. People in that kind of business have changed. You should be more careful."

"Will you be afraid here, now?" she asked Miniver.

"After all the things I've been through? This seems like *Sanctuary*," she said, emphasizing the word so Crystal would know she was referring to the novel by Faulkner. She obviously hadn't read it. "Well, I'll have Bob drive by in the patrol car, anyway, and check with you."

"This is how scared I am," Miniver said. "I'm going to bed and sleep like a load's been lifted. Got my future planned," she told Matt. She hugged Crystal, then going through the door she turned and said, "And I don't need Deputy Dog dropping by. I'll just use that twenty-two on anybody that comes around up to no good."

"She's into it with Sheriff Youngblood," Crystal said as Miniver went up. "I don't know why they can't be friends."

They sipped tea on the kitchen porch where they'd had their first dinner, sitting in the white wicker swing, bending knees slowly in unison.

"This swing is squeaky. I never noticed before." She probably wouldn't have gotten around to oiling the chain, anyway. But enough rain blew in to saturate the wicker, restore it from the dried-out state the heat would keep it in.

"Doesn't bother me," he said.

They were holding hands like school kids, and he put his arm around her and kissed her. Dare she let herself believe that she might be the something to him that he was to her? That they'd had that same instantaneous effect on each other?

Then his hand was under her skirt on her thigh and she thought of Elvis singing about burning love. If she could feel only half what she was feeling, then maybe it would be bearable. And only half as bad if, not if but when, she lost him.

But he wasn't allowing her a choice in what she felt. Like a pressure cooker set on high heat. He was kissing and nibbling and she was almost beginning to possibly think he was feeling it all too.

TWENTY-THREE - Gray Towers

"Crystal, do you think Mr. Hawkins'll be back here today?"

"I expect so. There's a lot of unfinished business." They hadn't talked about it last night, but she thought he would show up.

Mr. Elwood's voice dropped perceptibly, like he expected Matt to overhear him. "Wonder why he fired Horace? Do you think he's going to be so arbitrary about everything? Just go about firin' and changin' on a whim?"

"I guess he had reason enough," she said, wondering just what it was. "Horace was gone all day on a half-day job."

"But he's done that before, and I guess we always felt he got enough work done anyway."

"It may have been something as simple as a personality clash."

"I guess he'll be back here today for his two weeks' severance pay. No need mailing it."

She had completely forgotten he was entitled to that. "I'm going to make out his check now and let you sign it. You can keep it on your desk for him."

"Whatever you say."

Matt didn't come in. Instead, he called from the attorney's office. A private one, she hoped. When she answered the phone, there was a pause then a voice said, "I've never heard you on the phone." She almost hung up, thinking it was Horace calling to harass her, before she realized it was Matt.

He said, "You could sell telephone sex instead of bricks."

"Thank you." What else could she say?

"I'll have to call more often."

"Yes, I hope so," she answered in as businesslike voice as she could.

"Who was that?" Mr. Elwood asked after she'd hung up, wanting to know all these days.

"Mr. Hawkins."

"What did he say?"

"That he was tied up with the attorney. And that he'd call back."

Horace came in while Mr. Elwood was at lunch. That figured. She just suddenly felt a presence. A male presence. She'd been so engrossed to concentrate on her work instead of her new life, that she hadn't heard the door open while she copied a report. Fleetingly she thought Matt had been able to get away, but almost immediately sensed that it was Horace.

He wouldn't hurt her there and then. Some of the men were still in the lunchroom. But she wanted to scream anyway, scream in fury at him for ruining her peace of mind, for having such an ego that he couldn't believe she had not wanted him.

"Your check is on Mr. Elwood's desk." It was the only thing on the desk, other than a no longer used fishing-themed ashtray, a picture of Sue that she didn't want exchanged for a more recent one or that's certainly what would be occupying the frame, a neatly folded newspaper, and a plaque commemorating twenty years with the company.

"But you wrote it. You're the one who decides."

"Not any more." The sheet of paper she held slipped through her fingers to the floor. He placed his foot on it, twisting like snuffing a cigarette.

"This check ain't all you owe me. Remember you started it."

Was that really a threat? She picked up the check from Mr. Elwood's desk and went to the door with it.

"You think I don't know what's going on? I saw his truck still here. Nobody else here but you."

She opened the door and let the check drop to the ground. "There's a strong wind today." Fury was on his face as he hurried out to chase the check.

That evening Sarah said, "We were able to get Miniver an appointment with the director of admissions at Ole Miss."

The three were sitting on the front porch – ok, veranda more accurately described it, she silently acquiesced to Willette. Dad's hand-made furniture was worthy of an art show. She never let it get dried out, wiped it with lemon oil every few weeks. The marble fern stands and side tables with hand-thrown pots Willette had collected. Add the stained glass wind-chimes made by Dad and it was a candidate for a full-color display in some designer magazine. Crystal had brought out iced tea on a painted enamel tray.

"I can't believe that school don't have higher standards," said Miniver.

"I'm proud of you," said Crystal.

Miniver ran her finger over the fanciful floral carving on the posts and the curving cradle shape of the arms on the walnut and mahogany swing Dad had built, a work of art as much as a seat. "Wonder what went on in that man's mind?" she said. "Must have been a burden to be so talented."

Sarah looked down at her hands and once again Crystal marveled at how clearly Miniver could understand things without having them diagrammed.

They were watching Tommy and Tabitha play, and Crystal couldn't remember Vernon ever being so active. "When is it?" she asked.

"Thursday afternoon. The last appointment, the last day to sign up," said Sarah. "We thought you could come home a little early and help me watch the children. Yes, I expect he was burdened."

"Who . . . oh," Miniver said, nodding, having learned to follow Sarah's broken conversations.

"I should be able to get away," said Crystal. "I'm sure I can."

"Maybe you have some pull with your new boss," said Miniver, rocking the swing until it squeaked.

"Now, don't go teasing your baby-sitter," said Sarah.

Crystal and Sarah were in the walnut rockers with the seats and backs curved to offer comfort rather than resistance, and armrests that rolled at the ends for hands to curl over naturally, with so perfectly balanced rockers that a touch of the toe kept them swaying. Crystal wondered at the creativity one man could have, and tried to comprehend the frustration of wanting to get it all out. Sarah reached over and patted Crystal's hand. "I think what's happening to you these days is wonderful. I remember some of my own experiences that might compare to what you're going through now." She glanced at Miniver, and Miniver said, "I think I'll play some hide-and-seek with the kids."

"She's real intuitive," said Sarah. "What you're going through now is agony and ecstasy both, isn't it?"

Thinking of Dad, still, Crystal thought, as Sarah either purposely or without realizing it spoke the words used to describe a great artist of long ago.

"My life used to be so simple," Crystal said.

"You wanted it to be so much, you thought it was. But a person who feels doesn't have a simple life."

"Sarah, tell me about you and Dad." Crystal was surprised by her own request, and as she looked at Sarah, she understood there had always been something that needed to be said. And marveled that she had not asked.

TWENTY-FOUR - Home Schooling

She watched Sarah as Sarah studied her face. She looked sadder than Crystal had ever seen her. Her eyes even lost the sparkle that had always announced an exuberant and adventurous woman as long as Crystal could remember.

"Maybe I will," she said. "T. Oliver. God love him. You did. And I did. We may have been all that did."

Had Willette not? She'd had her doubts. But she must have at some point.

Just the mention of his name brought some of the luster back into Sarah's eyes, and she didn't look quite so old as she had a few minutes ago. "We had this thing between us. It seems like we couldn't live with it and we couldn't live without it."

"Didn't you want to marry him?"

"It wasn't a question of wanting to or not. It was just one of those things where it's not right for either of you. I was older, for one thing. I even used to watch T. Oliver for Ida – I hardly remember her that young – so she could sneak off and see her man down across the tracks some afternoons, when Old Missus Bell would be taking her nap. Oddly enough, we grew up playing like brother and sister until I was in my teens. But we had to hide behind the shed or down in my cellar to play together – you know how our families hated each other."

"I never understood that."

"Taking different sides in wars breeds its own wars. I hate to be the one to remind you if you've forgotten," she said, putting her hand over her heart and shaking her head in mock sadness. "Your ancestors didn't support the cause."

"That's not why you and Dad couldn't see eye to eye."

"Nothing so simple. By the time we were grown, we had personal differences. Anyway, by our time, only his granny, Old Missus Bell, was living. She grew too senile to remember why, but she knew she ought to keep us apart."

"Did you know my grandmother, Dad's mother?"

"I didn't really know her. She died of consumption, TB, when he was two and I was six. Ok. Nine," she said, "if you must know. She spent her last year in a sanatorium. His daddy was always gone after that. Built his ice business. Too bad it wasn't a refrigerator business. He was killed on one of his travels. I guess you know that."

Crystal nodded. She'd read the newspaper accounts in the library desk. "Innocent Bystander, Prominent Mississipian, Caught in Shootout Between Police and Bootleggers," said the St. Louis paper. The local newspaper had speculated he could have been not so innocent.

"Then Old Missus Bell indulged T. Oliver's every whim. So some of the things that he did later . . . You know, what some people called his selfishness . . ."

"He never seemed selfish to me."

"You were the best thing that ever happened to him and he knew it. He tried to make the best decisions for you."

Sarah's tone had changed, and Crystal couldn't understand why. Sarah loved her, of that there was no doubt, and so Sarah wasn't jealous of her place in her father's life, like she understood now that Willette had been. Yes, hadn't it leaked out, like oil from a cracked cruet? Crystal remembered asking her dad to take her fishing just to have him to herself. When they returned, Willette wasn't there. She had left word with Ida that she would be at the Peabody in Memphis overnight. Oliver could join her or not. "I was supposed to take her up to Memphis for dinner," Dad had said, slapping his head with the heel of his hand as he remembered. "Hell to pay," he'd muttered, hurrying upstairs to dress for the trip to make reparations.

"That woman ought to be glad he wants to spend time with his daughter," Ida said to his disappearing back. "Go on out and play. Enjoy the dirt a while. Girl don't be six but once. Go on. She won't ever know."

"I wish you had been my mother, Sarah," said Crystal now. She saw a new intensity in Sarah's eyes.

"I wish I could have been," Sarah said.

"You two should have married, regardless of differences you had."

Sarah cleared her throat a little. "We had two chances. It would probably have been a bigger mistake than theirs. One thing, I'm not beautiful."

Crystal liked the way she had always looked, each part pretty, maybe even beautiful. But as they were laid out it wouldn't ever have been considered glamorous to magazine editors or Hollywood directors or contest judges, and she respected her enough not to gush in disagreement, but couldn't help saying, "I've always thought you were."

"Not beautiful enough to get stolen for a harem, like my Biblical namesake. Or Willette."

Pretty is as pretty does.

"Of course, to you, I am." She smiled. "I've never been out and out ugly, but knowing me all his life, I wasn't exotic, or interesting. When I was too young to know better, I thought he needed a beautiful wife to paint. And he thought so, too." She glanced at her hands on the rocker arm. "Even my hands are too big. I was never fragile."

Was that why she always kept her nails perfect? To detract from too-large hands? Crystal reached and squeezed her hand.

Sarah smiled. Remembering, she said, "Women always made over him, he was so handsome. I knew his drawbacks as well as I knew my own faults. I couldn't have lived with him painting other women, beautiful ones, any more than Willette could have."

A thought came so suddenly to Crystal she wondered that she hadn't voiced it before. Didn't artists think character showed through as well as conventional beauty? "I'm surprised Dad never painted you," she said.

"He did grow to want to," Sarah said, and gave in and pulled a lace-edged hankie from her skirt pocket and dabbed at her eyes.

"And?"

"And I wouldn't let him. I've regretted it many a time."

"You wouldn't agree to it? To be immortalized, to be the subject of a painting by an artist like him?" Then she laughed and said, "To be bought by some rich biddy who thought the color of your dress matched her couch?" and Sarah did smile at that.

"I've got to know," Crystal said. "Why not?"

"It was like the rest of our relationship. It was complicated." She stared out at the children darting about but maybe was seeing herself and Dad, because she didn't respond when Tabitha waved at her. "I guess as he matured in his painting he came to believe that physical beauty was only one aspect."

Crystal knew that the successive paintings of Willette had evolved, but she hadn't realized that it was her inner self, an ugliness, Dad was beginning to capture.

"By the time he wanted to do me – " and as Crystal snickered, she added, "I thought between Willette and me we had raised a lady."

"Sorry." And she was. She didn't want to even *think* about it.

"As I was saying, and I thought you were so interested . . ."

Crystal nodded.

"I guess I resented that he had waited so long. I was old by then. I thought. That was before I actually got old. And it was after Willette left. And I had my reputation to think about. I thought."

"What would that have to do with it?"

"Willette and you were the only ones he painted! His wife and daughter. Everybody would have known . . . if he'd painted me."

"Known what? That he loved you?"

"By then he was bringing out it seemed like the very thoughts of his subjects. Even if it was a dog resting under a tree. You knew that dog had been hot and thirsty a few minutes earlier and now it realized it was hungry, too."

"What were you trying to hide? That you were sleeping together? The way you felt about him? Who would care at that stage?"

But Sarah waved the question away. "Only the good Lord knows why I was so foolish."

"And who would have had to see it?"

"I couldn't have asked him not to display it, sell it. Should there be some near-sighted person with money to burn."

She waited a second but Crystal knew she wasn't through on the subject.

"Possibly I was just vain enough to hope someone would have bought it. Might have myself. And hung it in the middle of town."

Well, that was just the opposite of what she'd just said. She couldn't help laughing. "It would have been his masterpiece, if he had been able capture your thoughts."

When Sarah didn't reply, Crystal said, "Painting aside, back to my question. Why you two didn't marry."

Sarah seemed ready to explain more than she ever had. But then, had Crystal ever pushed her about this before?

"Another thing, important. I was wealthier than he was, from the beginning. That alone might not have been so bad if he'd become a huge success with his work, which he did, but it took him a while. But it allowed me my independence, which I liked. He wanted a clinging vine. At least until he got one. She smelled like a rose, and looked like one. A climbing rose. But she drew the life out of him, instead of just needing a little propping up from him."

". . . seven, eight, nine, ten. Ready or not, here I come," yelled Tommy, who started running around the yard looking for his mother and sister. "Am I gettin' hot?" he yelled up to Crystal and Sarah as he ran toward the porch.

"No, you're getting cold, cold . . . colder," said Crystal, and, "hot, hotter . . ." as he ran toward the shrubs.

"Maybe I oughtn't tell you all this," Sarah said.

"Yes, you should. I remember him – in spite of all you two did to antagonize each other – and don't you deny it – crossing back and forth to your house at all hours."

"You know that was only after their marriage was over. I'm not completely without morals."

"Do you mean you hung around all those years, pure as driven snow, waiting for his marriage to collapse?"

"That's not what I said."

"You're getting hot, hotter," said Crystal, laughing. "Aren't you too old to blush?"

"Sassy girl. I'll take you out of my will."

"Please do."

"No way."

"I can't understand why you two didn't get married after Willette divorced him. How you felt . . . it obviously didn't go away. Couldn't you have overcome your differences?"

"There were other things. We just couldn't reconcile them. It's one thing to love a man, and another to give in on something so important to you that you know you couldn't live with yourself if you did. And he had a solemn promise to keep, that he wouldn't break. So there you have it. I couldn't give in, but I couldn't do without him. And I won't deny that I'm glad we did that for each other."

"You're IT!" yelled Tommy as he ran around the yard and touched Miniver, who was pretending to try to run away from him.

Crystal was about to ask Sarah to tell her once and for all what could have possibly been so important that it could keep two people apart, when they knew they loved each other and finally had a chance to be together. And what sort of promise could Dad have made, probably to Willette? But the phone rang and she jumped up to answer, telling herself it wouldn't be Matt, so she wouldn't be disappointed if it wasn't. It wasn't.

"Crystal, I can hardly believe you answered. And only on the second ring."

"I was expect – hello, Mother."

"So. Expecting someone. Hmmm."

"No. I really wasn't."

"All right. Don't tell me."

It wasn't like Willette to give up without a little more prying if she really wanted to know. "What do you want, Mother?"

"I want you to come up here tomorrow."

"Tomorrow? You want me to come up there?"

"I believe that's what I said."

"You know I have to work."

"Oh, you can miss a day to take Sarah to lunch. But when your own mother wants you to, you can't."

"I didn't–"

"I'd have bet my proceeds of 'Baby' that you did."

Oh. That was what this was about. She'd found out about the sale.

"You know I rightly deserve half of that. I don't care what I was coerced into agreeing when I got the divorce."

Miniver and the children came in then laughing as they headed up to get ready for bed. Miniver saw Crystal on the phone and motioned the children to be quiet. But Willette had heard them.

"Do you have company?" Willette asked in surprise.

"No." It wasn't really a lie. They were living here.

"Do you mean you're actually watching TV? What time will you be here tomorrow?"

Inquiring about others' lives, even her own daughter's, took too much away from herself to be overly interesting. Over the years, Crystal had become grateful for that. "About one. I'll have to get some work done in the morning."

"Fine. Bring your checkbook."

Crystal went back to the porch, but Sarah had gone home. She believed Sarah was going to tell her some other things, but of course her mother had managed to interrupt. Hell. That was nonsense. All the calls she hadn't answered, and now she had run to the phone like she expected a prom invitation. She had spoiled the moment with Sarah on her own.

When was she going to stop blaming Willette for everything? Huh? Where had that come from? Well, hadn't she blamed her? Willette had made her do this or that. Willette kept her from doing this or that. But she was an adult now, had been for years. Shouldn't she start acting like one? Yes. And tomorrow, she'd let Willette start acting like the adult she was, also.

TWENTY-FIVE - Her Own Mischance

Mr. Elwood looked up with a question on his face, but instantly erased it and merely nodded when she said she needed the afternoon off. He sat down with his paper, didn't open it, but started going through invoices.

She was busy all morning, but not too busy to notice that Matt didn't call. Maybe Lydia Hawkins had sent him to Timbuktu she was so worried about Crystal getting him. She sarcastically 'humphed' to herself and got another thoughtful nod from Mr. Elwood.

When she got to her mother's Barbara let her in and looked inquisitively outside. "Where's Miz Sarah? She not with you?"

"Not today."

"I was hoping you would be astute enough to leave her at home," said Willette as she came into the room, "She thinks she's your Siamese twin, I declare."

For once, instead of insisting on coming, Sarah had only offered to come when she found out Crystal had to see her mother. She was happy to stay at home with Miniver and the kids. Crystal hardly knew how to act without Sarah rattling away next to her in the car. But Sarah had told her to be careful what she agreed to with Willette, and Miniver said she had a bad feeling about her, even though she'd hardly heard about her, and maybe that was the give-away.

Sarah usually stopped short of actually saying what she'd like to about Willette, Crystal knew, but she'd let herself today. "She probably heard about the painting and thinks she'd entitled to something from it. She doesn't know she's already gotten more than she ever deserved or was meant to get. Oh, never mind. Tell her I inquired about her health. Never mind that, either. She'd probably take offense."

Now on impulse, Crystal said, "Sarah said to tell you she inquired about your health."

"Oh, I'll bet she did. She'd be glad if I was on my deathbed, no doubt. Tell her I'm very well. She's not sick, by chance?"

"She's like a spring chicken. Her own words. I'll tell her you asked."

Barbara walked out of the room shaking her head. "I'll bring lemonade to the sun porch," she said.

"The Florida room," said Willette. "She knows it's the Florida room." She raised her voice where Barbara could hear her in the kitchen. "Bring it to the living room." Then she said to Crystal, "It's too hot out in the Florida room today. It's too hot for anything. How do you make it in that old house with only window units?"

It was a rhetorical question, of course. She didn't wait for an answer, just headed into the living room talking about how it was almost too hot to live. If she had really wanted an answer, Crystal would remind her about the big trees stirring the breeze and blowing it and the smell of magnolias into the long windows, and the huge attic fan sucking air in upstairs like a wind tunnel. When the air it drew in became really hot, she turned on the window units until she decided she'd rather have hot air and sweat than be cold and clammy.

But she'd been thinking lately about the paintings. Was all that temperature change bad for them? She'd read where they needed a controlled climate. She ought to look into it. Might have to cave in and get central air.

As she sipped lemonade, Crystal realized Willette was looking her over very carefully. She controlled her urge to squirm like when she was little. She tried to pretend she didn't realize her mother was so interested in her. But Willette knew her too well.

"You're trying to act as if nothing has happened. But as usual, I'll get to the bottom of it."

Crystal crossed and uncrossed her legs and almost knocked over her tall glass as she reached for it.

"Nerves. You're guilty. It never fails."

Willette was poised on the new but old-style camelback sofa, her back straight, legs angled, one crossed over the other, together from knees to ankles, like she was being photographed by Miss America chroniclers.

"Guilty of what?" Crystal said, then clamped her teeth together. When would she learn to make a lying denial if necessary, instead of answering with questions that Willette, like a good lawyer, already know the answer to.

"I only know part of it as of now."

Willette walked to an elaborately framed painting on the wall across the room. She stood next to herself of thirty-eight years ago. In the background a white sash with half-obscured letters partially spelling a state, "Missi," lay crumpled on a trophy with "Secon," the last letter "d" hidden because the loving cup was lying sideways on a wooden folding chair. Did it indicate that the awards were almost immaterial, or did it show her disappointment? She was beautiful now as then. The painting showed only her surface beauty. No undertones of inner peace. No hints of malice or selfishness. Dad had not known her so well then as he would eventually. Was it possible it had not always been there? Maybe something had happened to break her, break her spirit that all was well between her and Dad. Could it be? But what would that have to do with her? What did she ever do to Willette to make her feel the way she did about her?

Willette reached to straighten an imaginary tilt of the painting. "I'm your mother. You shouldn't try to keep things from me."

"What things?" She'd never learn. And why couldn't she say the same to Willette? What are you keeping from me? What made you the way you are? What happened?

"What else have you made from your father's paintings that you haven't shared with me?"

"Nothing. That was the only one."

"You know, I could probably win those paintings if I challenged the will in court. I was his inspiration." She gave the painting one last glance, as if she hated it, then returned to the couch.

Crystal couldn't argue with her. She couldn't remember him with a brush in his hand after Willette divorced him. Like maybe he was punishing himself. He hadn't sat around in a stupor, for sure, even when he didn't leave the place for that last several months, but he hadn't painted. But it was like he had to do something with his hands, some breaking and cutting and twisting and sawing and carving. Most of the stained glass creations were in the shed out back where he'd done them, leaning against the walls in blazing rainbows when the sun hit the west window. And the porch furniture. And even though few in number, he'd made whimsical yard decorations with likely looking odds and ends. An artist, standing on his head, palette turned upright, created with a drive shaft, hubcap, and tractor bolts, among other reclaimed auto parts. An artist whose life had been turned upside down. Maybe Willette did deserve the paintings. She probably would be able to sell them some day. Then she could take care of herself.

"I could cut them in little pieces," Willette said quietly.

"Why would you do that?"

"That's all he cared about. Painting."

"I don't believe that." She had actually refuted Willette.

"You're right. Eventually it was painting and you. Finally only you."

Was Willette admitting she had been jealous of Dad's work and his child? Her own child? "Is that why you never . . . ." But she couldn't say it: is that why you never liked me? Or was she saying she was jealous because she seldom was the subject of the art, or because Dad spent less time with her then?

"You know he stopped painting when I left."

And Crystal had always thought her leaving was why he stopped, too. Now, she wondered if it was because he was disgusted with himself for taking so long to realize that Sarah was as worthy for her character as Willette was for her beauty.

"You think I disliked you because he never painted us together, that you became his inspiration. What kind of mother would I be if I didn't like you because of a little thing like that? Strangely, I've usually been able to read you, Crystal."

Why would that be strange, Crystal wondered, and resisted saying she was wrong this once.

"So when is the next art auction?"

"I don't plan to sell another one." For one thing, she didn't know of anyone else wanting one. Even Lydia Hawkins probably wouldn't want another, now. And she didn't want her to have any more.

"I saw the party coverage on the society page. I was humiliated, as you surely can relate to."

Well, thank you Mother.

"But you obviously don't care. I was trying to decide whether to call Mrs. Hawkins or my lawyer, when she called me."

"You have a new lawyer? A woman?" She could hardly believe it. Besides not liking other women, she enjoyed preening in front of men too much to deal with a mere woman.

"Don't be silly. Mrs. Hawkins called me."

"You know her?"

"I do now. She's a gracious woman. She apologized for not inviting me to the party. I was Oliver's wife, and I should have been included, of course. You were there."

"She didn't even invite me." Oh, hell. She knew Willette had backed her into the corner that she had planned all along, when Willette gave her a very innocent look and said, "Do you mean to say that you crashed the party?"

"No."

"I didn't think so. Tell me about him."

"He works for her."

"It's more like she has him in her Gucci handbag. I've inquired around. His father left everything under her control. He gets his part, but she's boss."

She quieted then and Crystal felt herself being looked over again by her mother like she was trying to see something there that she hadn't before. Then she wrinkled her brows together and said, "What are you going to do with the money from 'Baby'? Finally get a new wardrobe and makeover?"

Something was wrong here. Real wrong. Wasn't it against nature for a mother not to love her child? And wasn't it against some heavenly law for a mother to actually want to torment her own child? Yes, she would tell Willette what she had done with the money from the sale of the painting, and with most of the money she had earned for the last few years. She would be sorry then for all the cruelties against her daughter. She would love her then. She forgot she had planned to tell her so they would hopefully begin to live like the adults they were.

"Did you hear me? Mrs. Hawkins wants to talk to you," Willette was saying.

"I doubt if we have anything to talk about."

"I expect you do. She wants to buy another painting."

"I don't want to sell any more to her."

"For everything your father made me go through, I deserve every cent, or at least half, of all that we can get from his sanctified talent."

"You've gotten it all, Mother. Most of it, anyway. The monthly dividends, most of what I earn, most of the proceeds from the painting."

"I don't know what you're talking about. I've gotten my half, which I deserved."

"You continued to live in the style you always did. It wasn't enough, what was left. I can't even understand how we were provided for the way we were. Ash Cooper must be the best money manager in the world. The ice plant hadn't made money in decades. And Dad hadn't sold a painting in years. He hadn't wanted to, then when he needed to, nobody wanted one. I guess that's one reason he ki –"

"Don't say it! Those were mean lies. It was an accident."

She was shocked at Willette's denial, and even more shocked at her own newly acquired willingness to accept what she had always known. Suicide. Not an accident. Why? Why had he done it? Had she not accepted it because she might wonder if he loved her, why would he kill himself? If she had wondered about that, she didn't any more. He had loved her with all his heart. Sarah had told her so. "I guess he'd be glad if he could know his name and style are back in vogue now."

"So you've been giving me your share, too, all these years." Willette sat down, dropped down, really, onto the couch she had just stood up from, but Crystal looked away and didn't answer her. "Why did you do it?"

Why? Had she sacrificed everything out of love for her mother who didn't love her? Had she really sacrificed? No. She had been content to be productive. Had she done it to make her mother love her? No, that couldn't be, because she had never intended for Willette to find out. Why then?

"You know why you did it. You didn't do it because you loved me. You didn't even do it to be a martyr. You did it for your sainted father. You couldn't let him be less than perfect in a bargain he made with me. You had to uphold his word so I couldn't say that he had fallen down on yet another promise."

Willette did know her well. What she was saying was true. And she wished even now she had been able to make herself keep the truth from her mother.

"And I'll bet he let me down on another promise. He told you, didn't he? Didn't he!"

"Told me what?"

Willette closed her hands together in what looked almost like a prayer clasp, then let her fingers twine together, and finally swiveled her shoulders to rest her hands on her thigh as contestants were taught to do patiently in interviews with judges. "Nothing important," she finally said.

Crystal felt dwarfed at the depth of feelings that must have been between Dad and Willette. Love or hate or jealousy or whatever. She wanted to leave. She didn't like seeing Willette looking as if she had lost control of the situation.

"I know you want to leave. And you can. I told Lydia Hawkins you'd be there this afternoon. In light of what you've told me about our finances, I'm more convinced than ever that you have to sell while the selling's good. Art collectors are capricious. And some are simply stupid when it comes to recognizing talent. We're lucky Lydia Hawkins contacted Mr. Menuche."

The more Crystal thought about it, she agreed. Selling was what an artist worked for, wasn't it? Even Matt thought so. Dad had been pleased to do it until the later years. Sarah wouldn't even have stopped him from selling the unborn painting of herself. She could have Ash Cooper invest the money for Willette and have that worry off herself.

TWENTY-SIX - The River Lie

The guard instructed her to park in one of the Hawkins spots. A woman of about fifty in a dark blue tailored dress and sensible shoes let her in. She identified herself as Mrs. Morris, Ms. Hawkins' assistant, and asked her to be seated while she went for Ms. Hawkins. Crystal stood, looking around and saw again the large room facing the river, a million dollar view (probably not quite that much in Memphis). The hot western sun couldn't even ruin it. The windows were covered with panels now to temper it, not left open like the night of the party. She noticed things she hadn't that night. Three white couches and white carpet over light wood floors centering the largest seating area. Tables displaying art of various genres. A large glass-fronted case displaying Chinese vases. A colorful Chinese screen on a wall. On the largest wall, the Aubusson was displayed as a hanging piece. So, ok, it wasn't as bad as she'd thought. And "Baby," looking larger than its three by four feet was in its own special place, out of harm's way of the fading afternoon sun, thank goodness.

"What does the eye signify? It's almost hidden in the shrubs in the background."

Crystal was startled, of course, both from considering the painting with such concentration in its new setting as well as her undetected entrance. That had been Lydia's intent, she felt sure.

"I didn't think this painting was known to be ulterior, shall we say. It appears to have been painted as if it were for viewing in a straightforward manner, taking it in as simply a beautiful idyllic portrait."

Crystal was surprised Lydia had looked that deeply. More likely she had read the articles written about it. The eye was virtually hidden, almost could be taken as another berry on the holly hedge, except for the fact that it *was* an eye, and blue-green. Crystal had assumed it was her father's quirky way of humiliating the Chancellors, signifying their spying, but making it so small and hard to detect so as to further mock them by saying how insignificant it was to him. "I'm not sure." Now she knew it was Sarah's. But she wondered about the motive. He wouldn't have done it to taunt Sarah as being on the outside looking in.

"Certainly not the eye of God. That would have been in the cloud so subtly above the baby's basket. Now what could it indicate? It's almost unnoticeable, but definitely there."

That was in the critiques, also.

"It was not the artist's style to include anything of insignificance," Lydia read from a pamphlet Crystal recognized as being from a showing. "Could it be the proverbial 'evil eye'?"

She walked next to Crystal and perused the painting. "But Mr. Menuche said this was the artist's favorite, that it couldn't forecast bad luck for his only child."

She paused enough that Crystal wondered if she meant bad luck was coming anyway.

She sat down and motioned Crystal to.

"The baby's outside in the basket, mother not present, no nanny on a bench. Not even a pet dog looking out for it. Could that be portentous?"

Now, that wasn't in the reviews.

"At any rate, I'm surprised, really, that it remained in the family so long."

"This is a suitable spot for it." Yes, she was content it was here. Lydia Hawkins obviously had an appreciation for it and other art. She looked like a piece of work, herself. Oh. Give it to her. A piece of artwork. She wore a peach colored suit with designer-clean lines; a hammered bronze necklace that was no doubt a pre-Columbian find; her hair loose and perfectly dependent on the cut, making it probably the best haircut in the world; her legs bare, maybe a concession to the heat which Crystal had long given in to, but most probably the newest trend if Lydia was doing it; backless brown alligator pumps. Lydia knew how to display the best.

They agreed on two more purchases, Mr. Menuche selecting them, with the price to be the mid-point of two independent appraisals. One sale would take place quickly, and the other next year. They shook hands on the deal, and each knew the other would willingly be boiled in oil rather than let the other say she didn't keep her word. There was more at stake than mere color and canvas and cash.

When Lydia said, "So you two are seeing each other," Crystal realized why Lydia wanted her there in person, again not dealing with Mr. Menuche. A chance to appraise her. To question her.

Crystal didn't want to think that Lydia and Matt had discussed her, even that he told Lydia he was seeing her. And she didn't want to talk about Matt with Lydia. But she didn't leave when Lydia started telling about them.

"He's the one who introduced me to his father. It was our second date and he took me to dinner with 'the old man.' That's what Matt called him, but he was only twenty-one years older than Matt. Matt gets more like him as the years go by."

And how old was she? Older than Matt. Late forties but not looking it.

"Matt looked like a fraternity pledge beside him. Which he was. I fell for Daniel that night."

"So it really wasn't his money."

"It didn't hurt. Hawkins Investments. Hawkins Plaza in mid-town. Hawk's Nest Mall out east. Hawk Tower in the medical center. The Second Street Building. You can hardly look around this town without seeing something he financed or built."

No wonder Matt had been surprised she didn't know the company was in the family.

"He had the one thing Matt lacks. Or won't acknowledge. Ambition. It wouldn't be from fear of failure . . . maybe fear of comparison."

Maybe fear of not being there for his daughter.

"Before I went after him I talked to Matt about how I felt. He said he understood."

She wondered. He'd said something about his father being bigger than life, and having to learn to live with it. Did he feel he didn't want to compete with him even in love? No. He wouldn't want Lydia if she didn't want him, not enough to compete with her ambition.

"Daniel wouldn't get involved with me until he knew Matt and I were through, that it was all right with Matt."

So, was Matt's father selfish or considerate? This was Lydia's version. But if he was like Matt was now, as Lydia said, he wouldn't have hurt his son deliberately.

"There wasn't anything between Matt and me while his father was alive."

Why was that not hard to believe?

"When Matt married – you know about that, don't you? I wouldn't say either of them is over that yet. She wanted a career. He wanted kids and a place in the country."

Matt wouldn't keep anybody he cared about from going after what they loved.

"He got the country place and she got the kid. And some country."

"Why are you telling me this?"

"For your own good. I'd been working for the company for years. Daniel left me in control after he learned that Matt had spent a small fortune on her and then couldn't live with her. Not financially sound. I have approval on any major project he would undertake. Not that I've had to approve anything, to this point."

Crystal ignored her sarcasm, kept herself from saying that he was putting his daughter first, rather than trying to put together business deals that would make more money they didn't need and cost too much time.

"Nevertheless. Even his wife wants him back."

Crystal tried not to give away whether she knew that or not.

"But I'm the one who'll have him. He'd be married to me now, if I hadn't made a mistake."

Crystal watched her walk to the glass terrace doors and look as if she were seeing the view. "Don't say you weren't warned."

Crystal left then. She had heard too much of what she already knew, and learned too much of what she had suspected. Lydia was the one who had chosen not to bear his child.

But Lydia wasn't the only one who had made a "mistake." Just how much of a person's background could someone dig up? Was her talk today some kind of warning that she'd tell Matt about Crystal? Did she know the whole story? A frightened college sophomore drinking and partying and rebelling against her mother, and not knowing she wasn't responsible for her own date rape, a term she'd never even heard of then?

And what of Lydia's understanding that she would end up with Matt? Although his wife wanted him back.

Well, he had made no promises to her. The few things he had said and the things they had done together might be the stuff of ordinary events for ordinary people, and not the outrageous, cosmic flights she took them for. What did she know? She only knew what she felt in her own heart.

It was almost ten and she was worn to a frazzle when she drove into the lane and looked for Miniver and the children's bedroom lights. Miniver had finally begun to sleep in a room by herself, and her light was still on. It felt good to know somebody was waiting up for her. Her body wasn't behaving like it always had before so much started happening in her life, when she could go non-stop from wake-up to lying-down. Yesterday she had spotted, and was expecting to get back her cycle any day. She felt she had hardly had a decent night's sleep all summer. And it wasn't because someone else was in the house. She'd grown accustomed to their noise and ramblings cut off at night like a curtain drop at a play. It was comforting to know that she was sheltering and befriending. And in fact she did sleep soundly. So what was the deal?

Matt had gone by the office and then come by the house during the afternoon, Miniver said, but didn't stay when she told him Crystal had gone to Memphis to see her mother. Then later Miniver thought he had come back because a vehicle pulled in the driveway, but it backed out and left, so it was someone just turning around in the drive. Must be someone living around close, because it was a light Chevy van, maybe the same one Matt saw.

Crystal was glad to know it wasn't Horace. She thought she saw his truck behind her as she came into town tonight, although she was in Sarah's Mercedes. But she used it exclusively now; it was as if the old Coupe de Ville had decided the only safe place for it was at home under its own cover since that Monday with Horace. But hopefully she was just paranoid thinking it was Horace. Crazy sounding that she hoped for that.

TWENTY-SEVEN - A Bow Shot

When she entered the office next morning, Matt and Mr. Elwood were sitting at the computer. She wasn't late, so what was Mr. Elwood doing here already? And he never touched the computer. He'd even refused his free course offered with its purchase.

"Matt was just showing me a few things. You know, Crystal, it is real simple when it's shown to you."

"I'd just as soon learn to fly a jet plane," he'd said when she offered to teach him. And now, this.

"I should have listened to Crystal," he said to Matt. "Crystal, it ain't any harder than learning all those codes." Then he turned back to Matt. "When I told him I was in secrets in the war, he said this would be a piece of cake." He smiled, remembering earlier days. "I enlisted when I was seventeen. Not too smart. But learning makes you feel young."

Matt nodded interestedly and smiled at Mr. Elwood's self-deprecation, then showed him how to save the file and got up. "We should have waited for you. I just thought we could get started putting some stats in."

"It's your business. You can put the stats wherever you want."

"Uh oh. I don't like the sound of that," he said.

"It's not that we thought you couldn't get things done. Matt and I decided yesterday to get here early this morning. We're going fishing this afternoon, and we didn't want to leave you covered up."

"Maybe we'll bring you some fish," Matt said.

"I don't need any," she said, and didn't add you said you didn't like fishing.

Mr. Elwood gave her a look but only said, "This young man says he doesn't like fishing. Too busy. I say he just doesn't know how relaxing it is."

She thumbed through a stack of papers, for what she knew not, as it hit her: she had cultivated Mr. Elwood's insecurity until she had taken away his initiative, had him dependent on her for his every official thought. How embarrassing. And Matt was helping him gain back some pride in his work to remember in his retirement, as he did from his first career.

"I'll get you some coffee," Mr. Elwood said.

"No, I'll get it," Matt said.

"I'll get it," she said.

"It won't hurt to let someone do something for you sometimes," Mr. Elwood said to her, like Miniver did. "Now, I'm going to get it. Matt, do you want some more?"

"Thanks."

"What's wrong?" Matt asked as Mr. Elwood went into the lunchroom.

"I hadn't realized I've been such a tyrant."

"I can't see you as that."

"I drained him of responsibility and initiative . . ."

"It's just that you're so efficient."

"I've always done things myself, the way I want – "

"Hold up, Crystal," said Mr. Elwood, coming back in the office with the coffee. "Let him find out any little foible on his own. Supposing you had one." He smiled and so did Matt.

"Don't say I didn't warn you," she told Matt, more seriously than she meant to. "And I'm set in my ways."

After work as she walked down the lane to the house, the depleted azalea blossoms, still imbedded, not yet disintegrating and returning to the earth, caught her eye instead of anything else that was coming into bloom. Some things didn't know when their day was over.

She heard Tommy and Tabitha in the backyard and went to see. They were studying something in a large tub of water. "Crystal, c'mere, c'mere," they shouted, jumping and waving her over. Inside the twenty gallon galvanized washtub that used to be in the basement – she hoped Miniver hadn't broken her neck on those stairs fetching it – were two turtles on a large rock, their long necks extended and eyes bugged to take in their new home. Vernon would bark and back away and Tommy was darting like a fencer, trying to poke them with a stick. He managed to touch one, and its head and feet tucked under in defensive subjugation.

"Who's gonna feed'em?" asked Miniver. "Look like they'd snap off the hand that came near 'em. Tommy, stop pokin'."

"Who's gonna shell 'em so we can eat 'em?" said Sarah.

Crystal had noticed Sarah was talking a lot like Miniver these days.

"Sarah, wouldn't it be better you settin' an example for me, instead of you pickin' up my bad habits?" said Miniver.

When Sarah gave Miniver a smug smile and said, "To which habits are you referring, Miniver?" Miniver said, "Oh. I get the point."

"We won't eat Bert and Ernie," said Tabitha, pulling on Sarah.

"Don't kill our turtles!" yelled Tommy.

"They're our pets," said Tabitha. "Don't worry, we won't eat you!" she yelled into the water.

"Where did they come from?" Crystal asked.

"From where did they come?" said Miniver.

"Matt brought them," said Sarah.

Crystal was surprised. The kids obviously loved them, but they were wild things now out of their habitat. What could have prompted him?

"Oh, he didn't catch them," Miniver said. "He bought them."

That was a surprise, too. No, she bet she knew where he got them and why.

"The store where they bought ice and bait," said Miniver.

So Matt wouldn't use artificial bait.

"The man had them in a little fish tank. Matt thought they'd be better off here for a while."

"Dad bought me a snake there when I was little," Crystal said.

"He better not be bringing one of those things here!" said Miniver.

"Oh, it was a baby grass snake. It was going to die there," said Crystal.

"Its descendants are probably listening to us now," said Sarah.

Miniver jumped in a metal lawn chair the kids had dragged back there.

"Snakes can't hear!" said Tommy.

"Feel better now?" said Sarah to Miniver, and Crystal laughed as Miniver put it all together, and said, "Not one bit!"

"Sissy!" said Tommy.

"And where is the man who caused this tempest in a tub?" asked Sarah.

"Do you mean you actually darkened your own doorway this afternoon?" said Crystal.

Sarah ignored her but Miniver said, "I told her to take a nap here when the kids did but she went home instead. She overslept."

Sarah gave her a dirty look.

"He brought fish, too. They're in the freezer."

"Did you invite him to supper?" said Sarah.

"I did. He said not if I was going to make turtle soup. Or fish. I guess he don't – doesn't like fish."

"He only likes to fish," said Sarah. "Well, he has the right bait."

"Bet he could hook about anything he wanted!" said Miniver, taking Sarah's bait.

They gave each other looks as Crystal gave them both dirty looks.

"No, I happen to know he likes to eat fish," said Sarah. "Just not after catching them, I guess. We'd better go inside and see what else we have to cook for supper." But nevertheless she sat down in the chair

Miniver had vacated. "We won't cook up your new pets," she told the children. Tommy gave her a big smile and Tabitha gave her a big kiss.

"Matt said he'd be back and bring supper," Miniver said.

Again, Crystal listened to them like she was going to owe them a bread-and-butter note for being such considerate hostesses to her. It seemed like this house that used to be her home and only hers was getting to be a stranger and stranger place. But she didn't feel like a stranger in it now. It wasn't that. She felt welcome. Real welcome.

She went in to change clothes and saw the ironing board set up in the kitchen and clothes on hangers hooked over the doorframe. The clothes she had worn the day she toyed with her life with Horace were clean again and neatly pressed and hanging innocently between the children's clothes. The old rack Nellie used to hang freshly ironed laundry on, which Crystal didn't need for her few items, was down in the basement, hidden pretty good if Miniver didn't spot it when she went down to get the tub. But she wasn't going to tell Miniver. She might think Crystal didn't want her to hang clothes over the doorframe. But the way Miniver did it was fine with her.

She hurried up and ran back down barefooted in shorts and tee-shirt. She felt free and light like she never had before. She couldn't understand it. She had more complications now than ever, but she was so happy she felt like a child running naked with not a care in the world.

She looked outside at a sudden commotion. Matt was getting out of his truck and carrying two large pizza boxes. Everybody ran up to him and talked at once – even Vernon barked – but she stopped behind the screen door, greedily watching as he looked around for her.

If it wouldn't deprive her of even more, she could lock the door now and never go out again, preserving the happiness that was seeping out of every pore. She looked down almost expecting a puddle of it to have drizzled down and collected at her feet.

Then she saw that from across the yard he had found her inside the screen door, and she went out to them all, trying not to smile out loud.

TWENTY-EIGHT - A Carol, Mournful

She was rushing home during her lunch break to meet the art dealer, Mr. Menuche. After the mix-up over "Baby," he obviously wasn't taking any chances on another wrong painting turning up in Lydia Hawkins' living room.

Not wanting to be long away from the office, Crystal had driven Sarah's car. Lately, she found herself more willing to accede to Sarah's insistences that she drive. She was sitting at a red light thinking about Matt when he'd brought the turtles and pizza a few nights ago. The kids wanted him to look at the turtles' new home. Miniver wanted to talk to him about going back to school. Sarah wanted his opinion on a new back pain. Vernon pawed at his leg for a rubbing. He managed to give all their fair share.

She hoped the walls of the kitchen had soaked the sounds and sights and smells of that good night, and would bounce them back to her on command at some future hour when the reality of it wasn't to be had.

She didn't notice the traffic light had turned green when she realized a truck was speeding up behind her. She could only gasp and try to keep her head from bouncing against the steering wheel.

The impact would have thrown her into the windshield she thought, if her seat belt hadn't been fastened. She put the car in park and turned off the ignition and got out, neck already stiff. Massaging it, she walked back to the truck.

"You ought to go when a light turns green," said Horace. "Were you asleep? Or maybe daydreaming?" He leaned against his dented hood. "You know, about rainy days and Mondays?"

He had been following her. He'd rammed her car deliberately! "I'm calling the sheriff," she said. "You did this on purpose."

"There's witnesses," he said, nodding toward the stores across the street. "It's your own fault if you get hit from behind when you just sit there after the light changes."

She rubbed her neck and followed his gaze. A couple of clerks were standing in the door of the Fred's Dollar Store and no doubt would back him up that she was just sitting there, even though it couldn't have been more than a few seconds.

"Wonder how damaged my truck is?" He barely glanced at it. "Lucky you. It looks like just the bumper and hood'll have to be replaced.

A car stopped and John Half got out. "Miss Bell, are you hurt? Should I call for an ambulance?"

"No. No, my neck's just a little stiff."

"Hell, your neck's always been stiff," said Horace.

"That's no way to talk to a lady," said John Half.

"Just who are you, mister?"

"I'm John Half. And you?"

"I'm somebody that knows her better than you do, it's obvious," Horace said, but backing away a little as he said it. He was several inches shorter than John Half and even for all his working out he looked like the kid brother against Mr. All-American.

"I doubt that," John Half said.

She wanted to face Horace down, especially in light of his intimidation at the heft of John Half, but she couldn't bring herself to accept what she'd have to, telling it all and having it retold until the day she died. And after, even though she'd not know about it! Like they still talked about Dad and her grandfathers. It would be the bell toll they had been waiting on from her. "Horace, get your truck repaired and send me the bill at the office," she said.

"Don't you want to call the sheriff?"

He knew whatever he did, short of trying to repeat what he'd done that day at the office, he was home free. He knew she wasn't going to tell what happened. Not to Bob or anybody. And that's why she couldn't ask the clerks what they saw. They must be curious as to why he deliberately did it. She had to get away before they came over and got to talking. "No. I guess I shouldn't have been just sitting here."

"Miss Bell, excuse me for insisting, but you should call Bob Youngblood," said John Half as he looked at the vehicles. "And if you're at fault, which appears unlikely, your insurance will probably require two estimates and pay the average of the two."

"Are you a lawyer?" Horace said, reaching for his door handle.

"No," he answered, then turned to Crystal, "but I was hit a few months ago up in Memphis. That's what was required then."

That was what she and Lydia Hawkins were doing about the painting. And the dealer was at home waiting for her. "That sounds fair. Send me the estimates, Horace."

"How do I know you'll – "

"Miss Bell wouldn't go back on her word," said John Half.

Horace cast wary eyes, as if he would have to try to dodge a blow any minute. So he wasn't too sure about his strength with a man opposing him. Only helpless women! Oh, just forget it.

A siren sounded in the distance and Horace appeared to deliberate as he glanced at his watch. "All right. I'm in a hurry now. Late for a job interview." As he got in his truck, he said, "Some people get put out of work for no reason. By the way, I don't think I'm hurt bad."

Deep down she knew she was going to have to face him again.

"He shouldn't have left," said John Half, looking as if he wanted to offer his arm for her to lean on.

"It was probably my fault."

He stood by her waiting for the patrol car as the wailing got louder. "Will it be all right if I call tonight to see how you're feeling?"

"I'm not hurt, just a sore neck."

"I've been wanting to call . . . ."

Dear God. Was what Sarah said about John Half being romantically interested in her actually true? She didn't have to answer him, because Bob screeched his patrol car to a halt and jumped out.

"Crystal, you hurt?"

"No. Just Sarah's car."

"You the guilty party, John?"

"Oh, no. Not him," she said quickly. "Somebody else. But he had to leave. It was my fault."

"Something's screwy here," Bob said. "Looks to me like you're the one got rear-ended. Unless you backed into him at the light. So what happened? He shouldn't have left the scene."

"There was hardly any damage. I'll pay his bill."

"That's a good way to get sued, Crystal, just outright saying you're at fault. And I don't see how you were."

"I'd be a witness that they agreed on things," John Half said, "and that Horace wasn't hurt."

"It's not what the law says, but if you want it that way, Crystal . . . and it's a little late now. Horace, huh?'

"Thanks, Bob. I have to hurry home. I'm expecting someone." She got in her car and finally remembered to say thank you to John Half.

On her way back to work after meeting Mr. Menuche, she thought about what he had told her about her father's work. Word was out about his paintings being on the market again and how it had been under-appreciated and retained in the private family collection for the last two decades. Lydia

Hawkins had already leaked the report of this purchase to the news, he said, although he'd been working on a news release he wanted to show Crystal. Sell now if she ever was, he said. And she had to agree.

She rubbed her stiff neck and felt a little sick to her stomach.

When she'd told Sarah and Miniver what had happened at the light, they were surprised that she had let Horace drive away before Bob got there. And Sarah was angry that Crystal hadn't let them call the EMT's. And when Crystal said she was paying for the repairs, Sarah got downright indignant. "Not a chance. I've paid that insurance for years. Now I'm going to collect on it for once. Couldn't file when you drove into the Rio Grande."

"What!" said Miniver.

No use arguing. She didn't have money to throw around, anyway, even if she sold more paintings. But she'd pay Sarah's next premium or wring her neck.

"And we're buying a new car just as soon as we can get around to it," Sarah said.

Miniver was real indignant that Crystal could be thought at fault. "Didn't anybody here but me have to pass a test to get their license? If you're hit from the rear, it ain't your fault. Isn't. Hardly ever."

"I did what I thought was best," Crystal said, slumping wearily.

"It's all right," said Sarah, patting Crystal's arm. "Let's forget about it."

By the time she reached the office, her breasts were tender and her stomach was cramping so she went in the restroom to look. A large red whelp crossed her chest where the seat belt had burned her as it stopped her lurch. Blood stained her underwear. Her period must be starting at last. She was thankful she'd replaced her stock, and had bought a lock for the cabinet while she was at it. But she'd never had cramping like this. Finally she told Mr. Elwood that her neck was hurting and she going home to lie down.

He already knew about the accident, of course. Sue had heard about it and told him when he went home for lunch. A clerk at Fred's Dollar Store was a friend of hers and had called to tell her about it. He said, "You did what you thought you should, but I think Horace was at fault. Sue's friend said it was like he rammed you on purpose. It seems farfetched, but he may hold you responsible for him getting fired."

"Oh, no. It was accidental."

By the time she got back home, she was pretty sure of what was happening. She remembered her first night with Matt when a little recessive part of her brain had told her she might be pregnant, but she hadn't listened to it since. She'd convinced herself it was shock and stress keeping her body upset and from returning to normal.

Sarah and Miniver helped her upstairs to bed and Sarah called Dr. Chastain, who confirmed Sarah and Miniver's new suspicions that it might be a miscarriage. But they couldn't talk her into going to see Dr. Chastain. She couldn't bear the thought of having it confirmed that Horace had killed life in her body today. How he could have smirked and gotten what he would have thought was the last laugh if he'd only left her alone.

It wouldn't have been Horace's. It would have been hers. Her life would never have gone back to the way it used to be, but what was so great about it, anyway?

Only now, now that it was all over, did she wonder what would have happened between her and Matt if this hadn't happened today. Would she have told him what went on? No, she'd already realized she couldn't do that. Could she have let him think it was his? No, she couldn't have done that either. She would have simply gone away and had her baby and tried to make a new life for them. What would Sarah have done without her? Reluctantly, she faced the ease with which she let herself accept that she didn't have to think about any of the alternatives now.

As she lay in bed, Sarah looked at her with curiosity but didn't say anything. But Miniver got to figuring out how long it had been since Crystal was out with Matt that first night, and innocently said something about how she wouldn't have thought it could be long enough. But she didn't ask questions. Later, when Miniver left for the drugstore to get a prescription for sleep which Dr. Chastain called in for Crystal, and which all concerned knew she wouldn't take, and after exchanging glances with Sarah and saying she'd take the kids and buy them an ice cream soda while there, Sarah said, "Do you want to talk about it? It might make you feel better."

"You wouldn't understand," Crystal said. "Losing a baby . . . ." She would have taken a vow of silence if she could take back what she said, when she saw the look on Sarah's face.

"Don't tell me I couldn't understand," Sarah said. She got up as Crystal held out her arms for the woman who was so dear to her.

"I'm sorry," Crystal said, unable to imagine what similarity to this Sarah might have undergone, as Sarah sat on the bed and leaned against her. "Do you want to talk to me about it, Sarah? It might make you feel better."

Sarah patted Crystal's arm, letting Crystal know she understood that she was being gently prodded with her own words. "I could tell you," Sarah said. "It would make me feel better. But it's a story with many complications, and I don't know if it would make you feel any better."

"I want to hear all about it."

"Then I'm going to tell you. It's a story that started almost forty years ago. But I didn't know then there would be a situation where I'd need to tell more than I needed to keep my word."

"That long ago?"

"Like your mother, you can't keep quiet. Are you going to let me talk or not?"

Crystal nodded.

"I had an affair with a man I knew wasn't for me in the long-run."

Then like Miniver had earlier with her, Crystal got to figuring when that could have been. Must have been just before Dad and Willette married. Maybe Sarah went with someone on the rebound.

"I got pregnant when I was almost forty-five years old."

TWENTY-NINE - Enlightenment

Crystal opened her mouth and closed it.

"The man was married, I might add, when I found out about my condition."

Crystal couldn't open her mouth now although she had a hundred questions.

"I went away. Even I didn't have the nerve to face all I would have had to here in the 1950's. It wouldn't be much better today, would it?"

Crystal shook her head, in agreement with that point while negating that what Sarah was revealing could be true.

"I put out for community consumption that I was going to care for an aunt who was ill. But the man, he knew it wasn't like me to stay away without contacting him, in spite of my independence, and in spite of the fact that he had married, because we were friends, too, in addition to our being . . . ." She looked away. "I hate to say the word, but it can't be denied. Lovers."

"Who?" Crystal said, but Sarah said, "Just wait now." She cleared her throat and continued. "He knew every place I might go. You see, we had previously discussed that possibility, not a possible pregnancy – no, lovers seldom discussed such realities those years ago, I think – but the possibility of my going away, to make things easier on the bride, who might eventually realize that we had been close and come to resent it. However, we had come to the conclusion that I shouldn't go."

"Why should that have bothered her? That you were 'close?' She's the one who got him."

"You'll understand," Sarah said. "Naturally, he wondered what happened to change my mind, and concluded it might just be what it was. He found me, actually at my aunt's in Memphis. You see, we knew all about each other's families, having known each other for so long."

This was hard to believe. She actually loved someone else at some point besides Dad?

"We talked about all the possibilities. Abortion – which wasn't available on demand, then. My keeping the baby, which was unthinkable then. Divorce. But I didn't think his wife should have to pay for my mistake."

"Sarah," Crystal got out, "I don't understand."

"Hush, now, before I forget something. Now, this is important. We hadn't married before because we knew each other well enough to believe all the reasons it wouldn't work. But we couldn't stay away from each other. Anyway, he decided he should divorce so we could marry now that we had a reason above ourselves, our selfish selves, to make it work. And their marriage could almost be an annulment, he said." She blinked at Crystal. "Lord, don't the complications just go on and on?"

Crystal could hardly nod in agreement. What was the final outcome?

"They had just gotten back from a month's honeymoon, where he said they'd found out each other's ideas of the marriage bed weren't anywhere near meeting. He left me there and went home to tell her, and the you-know-what hit the fan, if I might paraphrase Miniver."

This story was supposed to make her feel better? Obviously the plan had fallen through. Sarah had never married. What had happened to the baby? Did she miscarry? Her heart was breaking for Sarah.

"His wife wanted that marriage more than anyone knew, probably even more after all the enlightenment. She said she would kill herself, and then we could try to live a happy life with that on our consciences, but that when the child found out what it had caused, and she guaranteed that to happen, it would realize it was to blame. And that the child would never live down the scandal."

"She couldn't have done something so evil."

"To her it would have been justice. I never doubted she could manage it even from the grave, if she did kill herself. And I didn't doubt she would. I didn't know her so well then."

Something uncomfortable had begun moving around in Crystal's head, like heartburn of the brain. She had to have the rest of the story to counter the sense of apprehension that she understood more of this than she possibly could.

"And deep down, I thought he still loved his wife. She was polished to a shine, knew all the right answers. She was a Miss America runner-up, after all."

About anyone else, or at any other time, Sarah would have paused and Crystal would have given an apropos, to them, snicker. But not now. Not now. Miss America runner-up? She knew someone of that ilk. She knew her very well. Mississippi had more than its share of Miss Americas and runner-ups, but another one here in Shallot?

"It didn't work out, as you know, because I've been single all my life." She patted Crystal on the leg. "Are you feeling better now?"

"No! I'm about to have a stroke. Don't you stop now!"

"Oh. Didn't I finish the story? Neither he nor I would consider ending the pregnancy. It was a girl. "

Sarah looked peaceful now, like it was the perfect outcome for all concerned.

"A girl?"

"Beautiful and healthy. We did the only thing the three of us could, for once in our lives, unselfishly agree on. What we thought would be best for the baby."

But the wife had wanted them to abort before that. It was unsaid, but might as well have been spoken. Yes, she knew someone whose idea of a solution for that kind of problem was to simply end it. The life. Not the problem.

"I couldn't bear to let my baby be adopted by strangers and not ever getting to see her."

"Sarah . . . ."

"Do you want to hear the rest?"

"Yes."

"I finally agreed with the only option his wife left open. To let them have my baby."

How could she have done that? She was wealthy, she could have gone away with the baby . . . But this was her home. And wouldn't his wife have seen that the story got out? People would have talked . . . and Sarah couldn't have abided that talk about her baby. And she obviously didn't want to leave . . . the father . . .

"I stayed in Memphis to have the baby, while they went away to New Orleans for a year so that nobody knew Willette wasn't the mother. I was settled back here when they brought you back home. I watched my baby girl grow up–"

"I don't believe you! I don't believe you could do that!"

Sarah patted Crystal's hand. "I had no choice under the circumstances."

"You were wealthy! You could have gone away . . ."

"And left my home . . . I would have, if I thought it would have been best for you. But someone always finds out if there's no father . . . I couldn't take that chance that you'd be made unhappy . . ."

"You let me grow up believing she was my mother . . ."

"You had your father, and he was so good to you and loved you better than he ever did Willette or me."

"And she hated me."

"I thought she would love you. She wanted you so badly. But here's a fact. I can't say I could have loved you more if I had actually been able to keep you."

Crystal rolled over and faced the wall. She wanted to tell Sarah that what they had done was so stupid, she could never understand how they came up with that solution. She wanted to tell her how plain old mad she was for having this cruelty done to her. She wanted to say she didn't love and admire Sarah any more. But she had more reason to love her now, although she couldn't love her more than she already did. And more reason to admire her, for making what she thought would be the best decision for her baby, although it meant Sarah's sacrifice as a mother. She tried to envision how her life would have been if she could have grown up not only with her dad but also with Sarah as her mother. She saw the three of them on picnics and having cookies and milk in the kitchen. Instead, both she and Sarah had been lonely old maids. And in spite of getting her way, Willette had been unhappy and lonely.

And Dad had been unhappy and lonely so much of his life. No wonder he'd been such a great artist, if great anguish helped fuel that talent.

"I caused a hell of a lot of trouble, didn't I?" Crystal said. "I ruined a lot of lives."

"Biggest display of hubris I've seen since Scarlet O'Hara," Sarah said, just as Miniver knocked and walked in with the medicine.

"Huh?" Miniver said. "Is she breaking out with something now? I swear – I don't know what next!"

"Yes. A case of self-importance. The best cure is the comeuppance that usually follows."

"Oh. I gotcha," said Miniver. "What's she's worryin' over now is bullshit, right? Not to change the subject, Crystal, but I just want to say from the bottom of my heart how sorry I am that this happened to you. I just know you would have made the best mother there could be. And Sarah could have been like its grandmother. That would've been the happiest baby in the world."

"Miniver, you have a way of saying the right thing at the right time," Crystal said. She rolled over and took Sarah's hand. "I'm sorry, Sarah."

"Miniver, you didn't change the subject, it would appear," said Sarah.

"You mean I just cured her?" She gave her a pill and a glass of water.

"Just the water," Crystal said, and Miniver and Sarah didn't argue.

"Are you gonna tell Matt about this?" said Miniver.

"No."

"I think you ought to," Miniver said, "but it's not for me to say." Then she realized what she'd just said and put her finger to her head. Then she said to Sarah, "Can't you just tell he loves kids and is good to his daughter, the way he is with Tommy and Tabitha?"

"Yes. But I guess it wasn't meant to be."

Crystal was now so used to them talking about her over her head that it was almost like she was taking part in their conversation. But she needed to let this all soak in. She rolled over and went to sleep.

THIRTY - Singing Her Song

She lay there when she awoke and let the bed absorb her. She felt as un-alive as the faded flowers on the sheets. When she heard Tommy and Tabitha whispering in the hall outside her door, wondering if she was awake and should they ask to come in, she didn't even call to them but went back to sleep. Later as the door closed she woke and saw a tray with coffee and toast and sliced ripe tomatoes. She rolled over, so tired that if she didn't sleep until she couldn't sleep any more, she would never be able to get out of the bed again.

It seemed only a few minutes later when Miniver, holding the tray of untouched food, asked, "Crystal, do you want something for lunch?"

She mumbled "uh uh" then woke briefly later to Miniver saying something about the way drunks sleep off a binge, and she felt Sarah's cool soft touch on her forehead. A good idea, a bottle of whiskey. When they left she'd get up and get one. But she dropped off again until she felt someone shaking her, jostling her, trying to wake her from the sleep she so needed. Willette always had to have her way! No. She didn't anymore. She wasn't her mother now. She mumbled, "Leave me alone, Willette."

"It's me. You ought to eat something."

It didn't sound like Willette. She tried to open her eyes.

"Crystal, you can't just sleep from now on. You got to get over this."

"Oh. Miniver."

"Aren't you hungry?"

"You know, I think I am."

"Feel better?"

"I really do. Where's Sarah?"

"She went home for a nap. I'll open a can of soup and bring it up for you."

"I'll get dressed and come down."

"Sure you feel like it?"

"Uh huh. I feel better than I have in a while." That was true. What had happened was a tragedy. She had lost a child, but because of it she could give Sarah her child back.

"Matt called yesterday and today. He was worried, wondering if you were hurt in the accident."

"You mean I've been in here that long?"

"Better part of two days."

Well, she had to believe Miniver. "What did you tell him?"

"I knew you didn't want him to think you were injured. He'd probably have come over. So I said you had the flu."

Crystal laughed. "In July?"

"Hey, I didn't have time to think. He said there's a lot of it going around."

After eating, she went next door. "Sarah?" she called as she opened the door and looked in the large dark rooms to the right and left of the entry hall of Sarah's house. Each room was furnished in originals from when it was built, fit for a tour that could be starting any minute, and a guide entertaining them with intimate anecdotes. "Where are you hiding in this museum?"

"I'm up here," Sarah called, "in the tester bedroom." Crystal could hear the history talking: "And in the next bedroom, the first Sarah Chancellor, wife of Josephus Chancellor, who built the house in 1870 as a gift for his bride – who came up from New Orleans with four wagons of furnishings – died after giving birth to the couple's only child, just one year to the day after their marriage. It continued the family trend, one child per generation, a boy, until the present Sarah Chancellor broke the mold." In more ways than one.

"Were you still napping?" she asked as she went up the wide stairs.

"No. I don't sleep *all* afternoon. Like someone I could name." Sarah was sitting on the edge of the high bed, and had already smoothed the heavily embroidered damask comforter which matched the drapes and the half canopy.

"Well, I'm up now. And I'm feeling a lot better. Mom."

"Mom, huh? I always pictured myself as a 'mommy' type," Sarah said, trying, not hard, to extinguish the glow on her face.

"Not in this life," said Crystal, herself unsuccessful in keeping happiness out of her voice.

"Rebellion already. Kneel on the priedieu and say a dozen Hail Marys."

"I bet this prayer bench is two hundred years old. It probably wouldn't hold me even if I could say a Hail Mary," said Crystal. "And what would the Reverend John Half say if he heard you instructing me in Catholicism?"

"By the way, the Reverend John Half called to inquire about you last night. He was real concerned. He said he would call again tonight. Sounds to me like he's priming to make his move."

"Sounds like wishful thinking on your part. Don't mothers always think men are after their daughters?" No, Willette never thought it. She knelt on the low narrow bench and looked at the Bible on its shelf at the top of the straight back. It was open. The Psalms. And the velvet cushion under her bare knees was warm with body heat. "The Reverend Half would be real proud to know that you've been praying."

"I pray."

Crystal studied her own hands folded over the Bible on the high shelf. "What do you pray for?"

"I used to pray that somehow you'd find out I was your mother. But now I know the truth of that old saying, that you'd better be careful what you pray for."

"Are you saying you wish I didn't know?" She'd rather have Sarah the way she'd always been than have her unhappy that she'd broken her word.

"I'm saying I'd rather you not know than have you lose your own child in order to find out."

"I'm glad I know, Sarah." She got up from the prayer bench and climbed to sit next to Sarah. Her feet dangled a foot above the floor and Sarah's were resting on the stepping bench. Crystal swung her feet like a little girl. "I always wished my mother would just hug me. Just because she loved me."

"Your mother loves you, child."

She put her arm around Crystal's waist and then Crystal slouched over and put her head on Sarah's shoulder. Sarah wrapped both arms around her then and squeezed her hard.

"I love you, Mommy," Crystal whispered.

THIRTY-ONE - The Eddy Whirls

"Woman, you have a lot of secrets."

"Don't men like mysterious women?"

"Maybe."

"If you want to know anything, just ask anybody in town, like Sue said. My life's an open book."

He looked as if he wanted to scoff at that. "So you recovered speedily from the flu."

"The forty-eight hour flu. You said yourself there was a lot of it going around."

"Hell. I wasn't going to interrogate Miniver."

He had called while she was at Sarah's and Miniver told him she was feeling better. So he'd dropped by later and asked if she felt like going for a drive. Now they were on the road to his place and she was wishing she had said no.

He reached for her hand and held it. "Why didn't you tell me what Horace did?"

Her heart almost stopped. "How did you find out?"

"Half the town saw it, the way I heard."

"Oh, the accident," she said before she caught herself.

"Are we talking about two different things?"

She looked out the window, realizing she was a little disappointed that he hadn't learned what happened that day at the office. She was so tired of guarding.

"Never mind," he said, glancing at her. "Lean back and relax. I guess you're still convalescing."

They were driving into the sun, almost due west toward the river, and though the air conditioning was on high she felt the late sun beating in through the windshield. It felt good, like summer heat does for a while outside after being in Arctic cold air conditioning. She closed her eyes against the glare and almost dropped off to sleep.

When they got to his place her shirt was stuck to the back of the seat. He un-pried her and led her to the bedroom. He told her to lie down and stretched out beside her. The room was cold, Arctic cold again, and she wanted to snuggle for warmth as well as to feel him close to her, but didn't, because she didn't think she was up to what he might want, what she hoped he would want.

"You look like a sleepy little girl. And you've been sick. Let's just take a nap."

"Are you sure?"

"Don't look so relieved. I might get the idea you prefer sleep."

No. She wouldn't trade making love with him for three magic wishes granted her. Much less sleep. He closed his eyes. She tried to stay awake to watch him sleep. But before she knew it she was out, too. When she woke it was dark and she was sprawled all over him. In the faint glow from the clock radio she saw that he was watching her wake, enjoying the surprised look that must be on her face. She wanted to forget what she had been through the last couple of days and beg him to do whatever his heart desired with her for the rest of the night. But she unraveled from him and said, "I'm hungry."

"Taking me for granted?" He rolled off the bed and pulled her up, then flipped on the lamp and stared at her. "You always look this good after a car wreck? And the flu?"

She rubbed sleep out of her eyes and fought the impulse to turn her back to him in spite of his trying to make her feel better. She'd seen herself enough mornings to know how she looked now. Automatically, she reached up to push back her hair, but he did it for her. "It's soft," he said, pulling his fingers through it. "I'd have done this that first Saturday morning"

She actually giggled. "I threw those damn combs away."

He smiled. "I can make scrambled eggs or fried eggs."

"But I want an omelet."

"Can we sing with you, Crystal?" said Tabitha, dancing around Crystal as she picked tomatoes. It was a bountiful crop. Not even any blossom end rot.

"Was I singing?"

"I ain't singin'!" said Tommy, jumping back, yelling, "Only sissies sing sissy ole songs!"

"I'm not a sissy!" yelled Crystal as Tabitha did.

"Sissy, sissy, you're both sissies!" sang Tommy, jumping around them.

"We'll show you sissies!" said Crystal, grabbing Tabitha's hand and leading her to gallop after Tommy. They caught him, with his cooperation, and she said to Tabitha as she grabbed him up, "What should we do with him, Sheena?"

"Who's Sheena?" both children said.

"Queen of the Amazon." She looked toward the large rusting wash tub now home to the turtles, out behind the tank. "Should we throw him to the crocodiles?"

"Yeah, yeah!" yelled Tabitha.

Tommy kicked the air in pretend terror. "No! Don't throw me to the crocodiles."

"Are you sorry you called us sissies?" Tabitha yelled as Crystal swung him out over the tub and they watched the ominous mounds of the creatures in the dark water.

"Sissy, sissy!" he called, trying to jump from Crystal's clutches into the tub. "Help me, Miss Sarah!" he yelled as she came through the hedges. "They're feeding me to the crocodiles!" He made an effort to dangle his feet even closer to the water.

"You're enjoying this too much!" Crystal said, and stood him on the ground.

"You know turtles are meat eaters," Sarah said, mysteriously. "She felt Tommy's arm like the witch did Hansel, then said, "Nah, you're too bony."

"I wasn't worried. Bert and Ernie wouldn't eat me."

"Crystal wouldn't drop you in!" said Tabitha.

"Yeah, she's too sissy!" Tommy said, taunting, daring her by running close and then jumping back.

"I'm gonna tell Mama you called us sissies," Tabitha said, and poked out her tongue.

"Can we get in the pool?" Tabitha asked as Tommy jerked his shirt off and hopped into the child's wading pool that Miniver and Sarah had put in the back yard and that Crystal wished she'd thought of.

"Yes," Sarah said. "I've a good mind to get in, too."

They went to the round table under the shade and sorted the tomatoes and planned supper. Supper was different now. The children's appetites had grown, and Sarah always ate with them, and Miniver was one of those people with such high metabolism that she had to eat to keep any weight on. And these days Crystal ate more than she ever had. She wondered how she used to be satisfied with a small baked potato and a salad, or a cup of butterbeans and an ear of corn, or a small pork chop or steak and sliced tomatoes and cucumbers.

Miniver did most of the cooking, pulling out large pans that hadn't been hot in years. She would make chicken and dumplings or pan fried steak and gravy, or cook hamburgers on the grill to go with two or three vegetables. Then after a couple of days she'd serve all the leftovers and then start all over again.

"The kids are out of the pool," Sarah said, coming into the kitchen.

Crystal had a cookbook propped open, picturing a mouthwatering meatloaf decked out with pimento and green pepper rings, and nice little sprigs of parsley around the platter. "I've just put a meatloaf in the oven. Let's get the kids bathed while it cooks."

"It smells good," Sarah said a while later as they pulled it out of the oven.

"Looks pretty dry though."

"We'll get out the ketchup. The children seem to like anything as long as ketchup's on top."

"I guess we should go ahead and feed them," Crystal said. She went to the door and called them to leave their checker game on the back porch until later. "Sarah, I'm sort of worried about Miniver."

"I am, too. But I was determined to hold out as long as you could."

"If she's not here when the kids finish eating, I think I'll call Bob."

"She could have had a wreck."

"We'd probably have heard about it. The car's in your name. Bob would have heard and called us. Maybe something like a flat tire . . . ."

"Where's Mama?" Tommy asked as they sat down. "She said she'd be back for supper."

"When is she getting home?" asked Tabitha.

"She'll probably get here any minute," said Crystal. "And she'll check your plates, so eat your supper."

"What is it?" asked Tommy, poking the meatloaf with his fork and reaching for the ketchup bottle.

"We've got to say blessing," said Tabitha, giving Tommy a superior look. "All hold hands." She bowed her head but kept her eye on Tommy to see that he was, too. "God is great, God is good, and we thank Him for our food. Amen," she said, while Tommy said "Give us bread and give us meat, give us gravy, let's eat!" and Tabitha said, "I'm telling Mama!"

"Amen," said Sarah, and whispered, "It's meatloaf. Eat it so you won't hurt Crystal's feelings."

"I heard that," Crystal said.

THIRTY-TWO – The Highway

As soon as the kids had brushed their teeth, she called Bob while Sarah read them a story. "I'm getting worried about Miniver."

"What's happened to her?" he asked, and Crystal was surprised to hear the anxiety in his voice.

"I don't know. Nothing, I hope, but she's late getting home."

"So that's it. She was supposed to call me when she got back."

"Oh?" Then she said with sudden understanding, "Oh."

"She said she was going to tell you about it – nothing much to tell, not as much as I'd like. When was she to be back?"

"We expected her before supper –"

"It's almost eight! Why didn't you call me sooner?"

"You obviously know Miniver. If we'd called to report her missing and she walked in the door a minute later . . ."

"I don't want you and Miss Sarah to worry. It's probably nothing but a flat. I'm going to put out a bulletin and head over toward Oxford now. I'll let you know as soon as I find her."

"What did he say?" Sarah asked, coming down the stairs.

"He's going to look for her. Said it's probably a flat. But he was real worried about her."

"Is that so?"

"Yeah. Wasn't that nice of him," Crystal said, following Sarah as she walked to the front door and opened it to look out.

"We have a real thoughtful sheriff."

"If I wasn't so worried I'd be real put out with you two."

"Who two?" Sarah said, heading to the back door, opening it to look out.

"You and Miniver, keeping secrets from me."

"He comes by every day to check on us is all. It was your idea."

"Well why didn't one of you tell me?"

"Miniver was afraid you'd be disappointed . . . her still married," Sarah said, heading to the front again.

"Well, I couldn't be more pleased."

"So far, they're just friends. But I think he cares for her. Don't you?"

"You should have heard him."

"Well, he'll find her and everything's going to be all right."

"Let's sit at the kitchen table," Crystal said.

They drank iced tea and listened for the kids and the phone. Sarah would get up every little while and say "tea just goes right through me." About ten the phone rang and Crystal raced to it. Sarah sat at the table like she knew it was bad news she didn't want confirmed.

"He's found her," Crystal said when she returned to the kitchen, seeing Sarah staring out the window over the sink. "They're taking her to the hospital. The Med up in Memphis. She'll be all right."

Sarah dropped into a kitchen chair and sat as still as if she'd been flash-frozen. "Oh my Lord! She was in a wreck?"

"It wasn't exactly a wreck. Rather, not just a wreck."

"What happened?"

"A man ran her off the highway then beat her up. One of those lonesome stretches on her way home."

"God in Heaven! Did he want the car? Why didn't she just let him have it? I'm going to give her an earful."

Crystal wet a tea towel for Sarah to hold to her face. "Try to stay calm. I wouldn't want my new mom to have a heart attack."

"Don't worry about me. What all's wrong with Miniver?"

"They think her wrist might be broken. And maybe a concussion. And a turned ankle."

"Was Thomas responsible, do you think?"

"He's still behind bars."

"Oh, God. Was she, . . I hate to even think of it . . . was she . . ."

"She says not." But that possibility hit her that Miniver could have been raped and it weakened her knees and she dropped to a chair, also.

Sarah reached for Crystal's hand. "My heart still breaks for you, my precious girl. What took so long for Miniver to be found?"

"He hopped in the back seat and held a knife to her. He made her drive the car into the woods and hide it before he beat her. She was unconscious. When she came to, she was disoriented and the car was bogged down in the swamp. She got lost before she found the road. She had just wandered back when Bob found her."

"Who would do a thing like that to Miniver? Why?"

The only description Miniver had given of the truck was that it was a dark color. "Bob said Miniver didn't have a clue who or why. He said it must have been random."

"Should we go up to the hospital?"

"No. Miniver said she didn't want the kids to see her tonight the way she looks. And it would upset them if they didn't get to see her."

Sarah opened her mouth but Crystal cut her off. "And before you say it, I'm not going and leave you and the kids here. She'll be all right. Bob is with her."

"Who could have done it?" Sarah said again.

"Bob said he would let us know if they're going to keep her overnight."

"Well. Let's make some coffee. It might be a while."

An hour later Crystal was drinking her second cup of coffee. They were at the kitchen table and Sarah's first cup was still sitting there cold. Sarah's head was resting on her crossed arms on the table and she snored like a little tea pot that didn't want to whistle. Crystal thought about waking her and putting her to bed, but she knew she wouldn't want to go up until they heard more about Miniver.

Just then the phone rang and Crystal almost fell off her chair it startled her so even though she was expecting it. Sarah shifted a bit and turned her head in the opposite direction and continued her soft snoring as Crystal hurried to the front to answer it.

It was Bob, saying he and Miniver would be there within an hour. The doctor wanted to watch her overnight but she said no. Bob said the county would pick up the tab, but she wanted to be home when the kids got up in the morning. "You know how she is when she makes up her mind," he said. She would be sore for a few days, and had required three stitches on her forehead. Both wrists were sprained, neither broken, and her turned ankle was hurting and very swollen. She needed to be on crutches for a few days but wouldn't be able to lift anything heavier than a loaded fork for now. Which was going to complicate being on crutches.

When Crystal woke Sarah and told her, she said, "Oh, no. We have to keep her in bed. I don't think it's possible."

Crystal found a gown for Sarah and put her to bed. She didn't even have to make it, or change sheets that had been on it for years. Miniver had seen to washings and changings and having things deathbed clean and ready since she'd been there. Then Crystal went down to wait and stared into a cup of coffee without thinking to drink it.

THIRTY-THREE – Chanted Lowly

Next morning, after Sarah had gone home to bathe and change clothes, and the kids were fed and playing in the yard, she checked again on Miniver.

"Well, haven't the tides turned?" Miniver said.

"Yeah. Seems like yesterday you were waiting on me."

"I want a bell to ring and you'd better get your butt up here," Miniver said. "Pronto."

Crystal hugged her. Miniver wouldn't let anybody scare her. "Ready for breakfast?"

"Are you cooking it?"

"I cook just fine for one. It's quantities that throw me."

"Just bring me some oatmeal," Miniver said, touching her tender jaw.

When Crystal returned with the oatmeal she watched Miniver wince in pain as she took a bite.

"Is the oatmeal that hard?"

"Don't make me laugh. It hurts."

"Does it hurt to talk?" It was only a few weeks ago when Miniver couldn't laugh because of her husband beating her.

"Nope."

"Did you recognize the man, Miniver?"

"Yeah."

"I hope Bob finds him."

"I didn't tell them who it was. I said he had a stocking on his face."

"Why didn't you tell?"

"Better not to."

"How could that be? Who was it? Can't you tell me?"

Miniver stirred more brown sugar into her oatmeal. "Everything can get to be a big mess." She looked up into Crystal's face. "It wasn't me meant to get stopped."

"What?" How could she know that? And who . . . . "Oh, God! It was Horace!"

Miniver put a spoon of oatmeal in her mouth.

"I'm going to call Bob. We can't let Horace get away with this. He's more dangerous than I thought."

"Yeah, he's dangerous, all right. But we ain't tellin' Bob. Horace told me I ought to be real quiet and stay home and look after my kids, that you never know what might happen."

"We have to turn him in!"

"Nuh uh. I ain't taking no chances with my kids," she said, shaking her head.

"But Miniver, we can't watch them every second." How and when did Horace turn into a man who would beat women and threaten children? He'd never been in trouble, according to his background check, which would have been pretty thorough because as foreman he handled company money. "And what if he hurts somebody else? Maybe Sarah?"

"He said he wasn't going to hurt me. Hard to tell who's behind the wheel with them tinted windows. And I was wearing your clothes. That outfit I got out of the trash. And I had my hair pulled back straight like you do a lot. It happened so fast at first, I believe him when he said I wasn't who he thought I was."

"I'm so sorry. He . . . it's obvious . . . he thought you were me until it was too late." If only the new car had come, he might not have known it was Sarah's. This might not have . . . . Damnation. Still wishing for sunshine in a tornado.

"When I wasn't you, he slapped me real hard to let me know I'd better not turn him in."

"From the looks of you he did more than that."

"No, I actually did most of it to myself. Split my head trying to get out of the car in a panic before I realized he didn't mean me no real harm. Busted it on the door facing and knocked myself out."

"What about your stomach? Didn't he hit you?"

"I gather you hit yourself there with your fist," said Sarah, walking into the room.

"Shit, no," she said with disgust. "I didn't think of unfastening the damn seat belt when I tried to jump out. And I had my to-go cup wedged in between the belt and my tummy. You know, that hard plastic one with the top. Big enough to end a county drought?"

"What about your wrists?"

"I was so scared at first, thinking I was gonna get raped or murdered. Then I got mad. To think that Horace had slapped me. And to think what he might have planned to do to Crystal, although he said he only wanted to talk. I started clawing at his face for all I was worth."

"Good for you!" said Sarah. "So it was Horace? That bastard."

Miniver did a fake reel backward at that coming from Sarah, then nodded and said, "He squeezed my wrists so hard I thought they were crushed. He's strong as a horse. No way I could have gotten loose if he hadn't let me."

Yes. Crystal believed that. "What about your ankle?"

"Hell. I turned it running around like a lost nanny goat. After I almost stepped on a snake. Broad Stream River swamp's no place to get lost in."

Sarah said to Crystal, "So Horace blames you for his troubles. But why didn't you tell Bob who it was, Miniver?"

"Bob can't hold him from now on. I'm not even *thinking* of putting my kids in danger."

Horace hadn't wanted to hurt anyone but her, and he claimed not to want to even hurt her. If she went to Bob and told him everything now, and something did happen to Tommy or Tabitha, she couldn't live with herself. Would Horace actually hurt children?

She rushed across the room to look out the window and saw them making mud pies and throwing them into the tub with the turtles, which were sunning on a rock pile in the middle. She went downstairs and took some bread for the children to feed their pets. She wondered how long turtles would live in a tub filled with rainwater and mud pies. Maybe forever. It was reasonably close to what they were used to.

She went back in and stood at the phone, picked it up, hung it up, picked it up again and dialed half the numbers to Bob's office, then hung it up. She didn't dare call until Miniver agreed. She went back to the kitchen, cursing herself for a coward and an accomplice to Miniver's injuries.

Sarah called out the bedroom window, "If you children see a man on the place I want you to run inside real fast. Your mama said to yell bloody murder."

"I'm scared now!" yelled Tabitha.

"You sissy!" yelled Tommy.

"It's a game," said Crystal through the window, "but don't forget to play it. Okay?"

"All right," yelled Tommy. "It'll be fun!"

Crystal wondered if she should take the gun down where it would be handy and not behind lock and key where it had been since Miniver and the children arrived. No. That might put them in yet another type of danger.

She was standing there thinking of a hundred ways a child could get hurt when she heard the kids scream. One of them actually yelled "bloody murder." She ran outside without even thinking about the gun.

THIRTY-FOUR - In the Boat

On each side of Matt, the children had stopped yelling and were laughing.

"We're playing a game," Tabitha told Matt.

"Did we play the game good?" Tommy asked Crystal.

"I'd give you a whippin' if I could get down there!" Miniver yelled out the upstairs window, where she was apparently balancing on one foot. "You know better'n to holler like that if it was just Matt. You scared the sh – you scared me to death!"

"What's going on?" Matt asked.

"It's a game I'll tell you about," said Crystal. "Do you want to come in and have some coffee?"

"Sure, if that's what it takes."

Sarah walked down the porch steps as they went up. "Do you want to stay and have some coffee with us?" Crystal asked her. "No," Sarah said, continuing to walk. "I'm going home for a while. This place is too wild for me. I need some peace and quiet."

"Don't you watch MTV!" yelled Miniver out the window again.

"You come over Matt, if it gets too much for you," Sarah said.

"Take a nap," Crystal told her.

"Or if it gets too boring for you," Sarah added.

"Sure will," he said. He pecked Crystal a kiss and then said, "Not boring here."

"So what brings you here?"

"You."

"That's good. But anything else specifically?"

"Mr. Elwood sent me, to be specific. Not that I wouldn't have come on my own."

"Good Grief. I forgot to go to work today!"

"Well, the day wasn't exactly over yet. But we didn't want you to think we could handle it without you." He dodged as if she were going to jab him.

"I can't believe I forgot about work."

"You forgot. Tell me what's going on?"

"Am I fired?"

"Not unless you fire yourself. You're the new manager."

The new manager. Maybe Lydia thought Crystal wouldn't like taking orders from Matt. Or that she would feel indebted for the promotion.

"If you want the job."

"When does she want to know?"

"Mr. Elwood wants to leave in a month."

"Oh."

"Or rather, Sue wants him to. She said top executives give a month's notice."

They both smiled and made no comment.

She poured coffee and asked if he wanted toast. She made herself some, too, although she'd had breakfast. She couldn't eat enough lately. Getting like Miniver.

"So what's going on around here?"

"Well, I can't go in today, for starters. I have to stay around here and look after Miniver and the kids."

Just then the bell tinkled from upstairs. "Service!" yelled Miniver. "I want tea!"

"Why don't you go up and visit Miniver while I make her tea. She can tell you what happened. She'd tell you anyway, even if I did."

"All right." He walked to the stairs and yelled up, "I'm coming up. Are you decent?"

"Hell no!" she yelled down. "Hurry up!"

When Crystal called Mr. Elwood and told him she was going to take a few days of vacation starting today, without missing a beat he said that was a good idea to get some of it out of the way while he was still there, and that he'd probably forgotten that's what she'd decided. Need to retire when you forget such, he said. Of course, he knew better. But of course, he couldn't let her bear the responsibility. Or chide her. It wasn't in his realm of possibilities. "I'm going to miss you," she said. And with that, they both understood that she was going to accept.

Sarah and Miniver told Crystal she wasn't going to make a liar of herself. They told her to go out of town for a few days but she had given them a look to let them know they had finally gone off the deep end. Miniver was still mostly hopping on one foot when she had to get around, two days after the "accident." So a day at the Memphis Zoo was a compromise.

Dad had brought her when she was about five. He'd taken a sketchbook from the picnic basket Ida had packed – Willette'd told them not to eat any concession stand food so naturally they'd had a hotdog – and had sketched Crystal looking at a lion pacing behind bars. Somehow he'd caught her feelings of sorrow mingled with fascination, and the lion's frustration as well as resignation when he'd painted it later on a larger scale.

"The Cage" had been bought, she assumed before he'd had a chance to make his own copy, if he'd wanted one, because there wasn't one around, and Willette had said it was only fitting that a fur coat for her should come of it. He'd painted Crystal in a Victorian dress and long curled hair, although her hair had been short, and as it was fall she was in the brown loafers, knee socks, sweater set and plaid skirt that Willette kept her in, mimicking the private school in Memphis that Willette envisioned her attending. The cage was more bird cage than zoo cage, with palms and orchids springing from pots in a sitting room rather than a zoo. But in the finished sketch and painting the girl was in the cage and the lion rested outside. Sarah had the small drawing on a gold-leafed easel on a table in her parlor. Crystal understood it now.

But the day occupying her mind now was eventful, too. Sarah had made it a point to be there to demonstrate her support, and brought Crystal along, of course. Before that day, she couldn't even have brought Tabitha and Tommy with her, she thought with new insight.

Tommy, climbing on one of the huge animal statues outside the new entrance, yelled, "There's your name!" and pointed to the engraved donor plate adorning the base of the statue. "Hawkins. Just like yours."

Crystal looked at it, recognizing the hawk insignia and said, "You're a good reader, Tommy," then looked at Matt.

"We're into animals," he said, laughing. "The name thing, I guess."

Inside, Tommy and Tabitha hopped around on bricks making a walkway. "Hey, there it is again!" Tommy said.

"We're into bricks, too, I guess," Matt said, picking Tabitha up and putting her on his shoulder.

Now there were more natural settings and open spaces for the animals than she remembered. She was especially glad for the gorillas. She remembered their sensitive-appearing eyes, one even watching TV as if it understood the soap opera that the zoo worker had tuned in for it. Sarah had let her put money into a machine that melted black wax into a mold and forced out your very own toy gorilla. She bet she still had it in a drawer somewhere with every other little memento Sarah had ever given her. The black velvet painting of Elvis that both had known but not said would aggravate Willette no end, and the Rebel flag featuring Lee's face Sarah had bought for her anyway although she said Crystal's grandfathers would turn in their graves. Had she kept all those things because Willette had usually given her collectable dolls she couldn't play with? Or had there been some awareness in her young self that Sarah was more to her than met the eye?

Maybe it was only because Sarah loved her and showed it.

"Wonder what happened to monkey island?" Matt said, after she'd been quiet for a while.

"Remember when one would escape?" she said, picturing the news cameras trying to capture it on film in one of the treed back yards of the homes on North Parkway.

The children seemed to be feeling the adventure she had under the trees so big and limby and leafy they actually could be heard "singing" in the breeze over the wide paths. They were playing hunters, of course, and Tabitha said, "No, pretend you're using a camera! It would be bad to shoot the animals." "Ok, but my camera goes 'bang,'" yelled Tommy.

Inside the subterranean aquarium it was cool and quiet until Tommy and Tabitha spied the huge Mississippi River catfish napping contentedly in the bottom of the largest tank. "It's bigger than Granmama's pig up in North Carolina," said Tommy. "And there's turtles," said Tabitha. "They look like Bert and Ernie, our very own turtles."

"Can we go on the rides?" Tommy asked, hearing the steam whistle.

"Ohhh! I'm telling! We're not to ask for anything!" said Tabitha.

After the children rode all the kiddie rides, they chased chipmunks under the trees as they headed to the snack bar for hotdogs. While they were eating, Tabitha started crying and said, "I wish Mama could have come on our vacation."

"Don't be a sissy!" said Tommy.

"Do you want to take her a gift?" Matt asked.

"Uh huh. That'll make her feel better," said Tabitha.

In the gift shop the children picked out a dainty, scalloped, gold-edged china cup and saucer with "Memphis Zoo" printed in gold to take to Miniver. "You should take something to Sarah," said Matt. "We wouldn't want her feelings to be hurt."

"Yeah, she's like a mama for Crystal," said Tabitha.

THIRTY-FIVE – The Loosed Chain

Fall wasn't in the air yet, not even a hint, though there'd been one really cool, rainy day and night that a hurricane down on the Gulf was responsible for. But it was mid-August and school would be starting soon, so people began to talk about how it wouldn't be long before fall was here.

Crystal and Sarah were helping Miniver pack her belongings into her old white truck. Their new apartment just off the campus in Oxford was furnished with the basics, and Crystal and Sarah had given her some odds and ends. She had some kitchen items from her house with Thomas which they had divided before he left for Louisiana. He had told Miniver when he got out of jail that he had changed, and was taken aback when she reminded him that she had, too. A few days later when he called to tell her he was going to work on an oil rig in the Gulf, he said he wondered how she'd feel if the platform exploded and he burned to death or if he fell overboard and drowned. She had told him he'd always be the kids' father, so he'd better stop smoking and drinking.

The kids ran to the tank and took a package of saltines to throw in for Bert and Ernie. They had begged to take the turtles with them, but must have known they couldn't, because when Crystal suggested they be put back in the lake, that they might be missing the rest of the turtles, they thought it was a good idea. They could go back to their school, Tabitha said, just like the three of them were about to do, and Tommy said, "You sissy, turtles don't swim in a school. It's fish that do that."

When the kids hugged Vernon he started shrilly barking his heart out. Crystal hadn't heard him do that in ages. The kids and Sarah said he knew they were leaving. She didn't doubt it.

Sarah told all three of them she wanted some school papers with smiley faces for her refrigerator door.

Tommy would be in kindergarten, and Tabitha would be in pre-school. Tabitha had been singing the ABC song for days, and it sounded something like Abby-seed-e-f-g, h-I-jackle-amino-pee. When she sang it, she would stop there and laugh.

"We'll be down to see you in a couple of weeks," Sarah called as they went down the long drive, now used regularly. The kids yelled 'bye' and waved until they were out of sight.

"I feel like I've sent my own kids off to boarding school," Crystal said. "I'll never understand how a parent could do that." Her throat filled with a lump before she knew it. And she blinked furiously. She hated that. Not doing it, but that Sarah saw; how little this hurt must be compared to what she felt when Crystal went off to college, with her unable to claim parental goodbyes. "I'm sorry," she said.

"It's all right. I watched from my front porch when you left for college," Sarah said. "And you ran over and hugged me. Don't you remember?"

"Mostly I remember being glad to get away on my own. Away from Willette."

"I can believe you there. But the way she wanted you before you were born, I couldn't believe she wouldn't love you. If I'd known . . . but once it was done, it was too late."

She wanted to console Sarah by saying it was all right, she understood. And that Sarah had countered Willette's pin pricks with her own affection and attention. But she'd always been able to be truthful to her, and she wasn't going to start lying to her now, not now when she knew what they really were to each other, and say, "Oh, I'd have probably been this way if Willette hadn't influenced me. You know. Reclusive. Self-absorbed. Insecure. Work-aholic so I wouldn't have to face it all." But no need in beating herself up. Nor in holding Willette or Sarah or even Dad to blame. She was old enough to know better and to do better and certainly now could understand a lot of it. Maybe she had already started doing better.

So she hugged Sarah and said, "It's all right," and Sarah looked at her with gratitude. "I should go on to work," Crystal said. "Will you be all right by yourself today?"

They continued to stand, looking down the drive, waiting to see if it would fill up again with the old white truck full of life.

"Lord. I can't believe it was my own idea to send those sweet things away."

"Miniver could have whiled away her life here . . ." Crystal answered.

"I was just wishing."

Crystal turned to look at the fading house. For a while now, it had fairly glowed. "Things have to change and so do we, I know now."

"Maybe there's another change just around the corner."

"Like I said, I'm going to work."

THIRTY-SIX - The Silent Nights

The office already looked changed. Somewhat changed, that is. Mr. Elwood's stuffed fish had already been taken home. Wonder what Sue had done with it? But its outline on the faded paint was still there, just as the outline of Crystal had been left on her wall when she sold herself, her painting, and seemed to have started all this. Mr. Elwood was still there reading the paper, but he was at her old desk and she sat at his. And he had a computer on it now, of course. The men in the yard were still stacking bricks, but now a stamp on the machinery and a new painting on the front door showed the same insignia she remembered from the zoo, an outline of a hawk gripping a bird in its talons. Crystal would bet Lydia Hawkins came up with that insignia when she became CEO. Lydia had signed the memo about initiating the stamping, saying it was company policy that the Hawkins brand went on everything they owned, on the same day that Crystal was made manager. Crystal expected a tattoo appointment any day now for herself.

Matt had brought craftsmen to assess the old kilns and had recommended they be put to use making special-order bricks. Crystal agreed. She'd inquired about the possibility a few years earlier of utilizing the old ovens to make new "used" bricks for home-builders, but it was one of her few suggestions to be turned down by the former owner. Mr. Elwood was staying on until they hired two office workers.

At any rate, Crystal was actually looking forward to the extra help. She reflected that she was becoming downright laid-back about accepting help in her middle age. And she never would have guessed how nervous the new job would make her. She supposed that discovering her true relation to Sarah, and Horace's acts, topped off by Miniver and the kids moving, was too much for an old stick-in-the-mud. Not to mention Matt. It was the only explanation she had for the way she felt.

Right now, she wished she hadn't had that cup of coffee a few minutes ago. She knew now what Sarah meant when she said she felt swimmy-headed. Maybe she needed glasses. She was the right age for the eyes to go, wasn't she?

"Are you all right?" Mr. Elwood asked.

"Not used to my own cooking again," she said. In a few minutes the feeling passed and she got back to work.

These days, she wore her coolest clothes to work and still felt like butter in a hot skillet. And when she stepped outside, heat sealed around her like the lid on a pan.

At home she turned on the air conditioners until the drone drove her crazy. She believed if she didn't soon feel the cool night wind of fall on her skin it would dry and crack and float to the ground.

She gathered the few tomatoes and squash and beans the garden still produced, after resting from the office, and had Sarah call John Half to pick them up the next day. He tucked a note into her screen door handle saying Sarah had kept him informed about her recovery from the accident and that he hoped to see her soon. And p.s., please allow him to help her with the gardening, with his phone number. Another day a gift basket of garden hand tools was left on her porch with a note that he couldn't resist giving the new florist some business. Must not know there are two, she thought, aggravated at his gesture for some reason she couldn't quite name. A couple of days later, there was a pot of green houseplants, guaranteed almost carefree, he said in the note, and added that, news to "un-informed" him, there were actually two new florists in town, and he didn't want to make a difference in them.

Surprisingly, she took joy in the new tools as she used them and found a suitable place in the kitchen for the plant where she saw it each day.

She hadn't mowed the yard since Miniver left. Now that she thought about it, she hadn't done it since Miniver had been there. Miniver stayed busy. Crystal called old Mr. Thrasher to do it. He always tried to make a deal with her and now he was booked, but said he would work her yard in. Straggly Dallas and Johnson grasses and dandelions thrived in the sun. Bermuda browned from lack of watering. The wild onions were more than Sarah could take. And she said snakes were probably in the weeds by now. Crystal didn't tell her she'd spotted a grass snake, sure enough, its red tongue flicking, at the trench alongside the garden a few days after seeing a shed skin, almost translucent, lying in wads like crumpled tissue paper straightened out somewhat, as if it had had to work peeling out of it. Or perhaps Vernon had played with it, on the ground next to the now uninhabited tub, almost as if in disdain that the turtles were no longer there. The only good snake was a dead one, to Sarah. She had berated Dad to Crystal for bringing that one home so long ago from the bait shop and then turning it loose. In fact, Sarah carried her walking cane these days, though her arthritis wasn't bothering her in this heat, and made Crystal smile, saying it was her weapon, like the broad's club in the B.C. comic strip. Not that Crystal loved them; she just tried to keep her philosophy like Dad's, which was to respect the Earth's creatures.

The house was last painted ten or twelve years ago, and heat was curling the peeling paint. Winds spawned by the hurricane a couple of weeks earlier had split a huge limb off the Southern magnolia in the front yard. The big flowers were turning brown and Sarah said they reminded her of the magnolia ropes the day after, faded and signifying all the festivities were over, that she and the other girls twined together like clover chains when she was in school. She didn't like to think about being young so long ago. Next, they reminded her of dead funeral flowers, and she didn't like to think about being as old as she was. Crystal called Mr. Thrasher to cut the limb off and haul it away, and the chainsaw rattled their nerves.

If she had the willpower to tackle getting the house painted, she would do it, now that she had a little money to spare. But she didn't.

And she and Sarah missed Miniver and the kids more every day instead of becoming accustomed to their absence. Vernon lay around with an even more hangdog expression.

She and Sarah had driven to the lake and tipped the turtles off the rock in the cooler of water back into the muddy water they had come from. Sarah swore she even missed them.

Crystal didn't see Matt much, between Lydia keeping him busy buying new companies and taming them and the days he spent in Nashville. With his daughter. Not his wife, she told herself. His daughter. Hallie.

Crystal asked no questions about his wife. Or even his daughter. What she didn't know couldn't hurt her, she had decided. But he'd volunteered some information, and she wondered if this "telling" bore significance. His wife had left him to pursue a career, just as Lydia had informed her, and was very successful. It required her to be away from home a lot, and she didn't like leaving their daughter with a housekeeper. He didn't like her doing that either. "Hallie wants us to get back together," he said. "Though she never puts it in so many words. She doesn't remember that we were together."

And your wife? Crystal didn't ask. And she didn't say she must want it, or you want it, or maybe both of you want it, because you've never divorced. She tried not to think how much happier his daughter would be if they did get back together.

"Fight for him," Sarah said, reminding her that T. Oliver had stayed with Willette for Crystal's sake, and that not a whole lot of good had resulted from that sorry state of affairs. "And he might have more reason to be with you than you realize," she added. But Crystal couldn't see herself winning. She'd be like Sarah, in the end.

When he told her Hallie was in a special school, she assumed it was one for gifted students, and couldn't stop her hand from clasping her heart when she heard the rest: a school for deaf children. Hearing-impaired, these days, he added. "She was a month early. Her lungs weren't fully developed. She was in intensive care for a week. They think the antibiotics affected her hearing."

She was just getting over the shock and distress of learning that when he shocked her further by adding, "I'm going to Nashville for Labor Day weekend. I'd like you to come. I want you to meet Hallie." She managed to say she wouldn't want to take time away from his daughter, while thinking how much she'd like to meet Hallie, but how afraid she'd be of it. What if Hallie didn't like her? And she didn't want to face what it might mean, his wanting her to meet his daughter.

And there was Sarah. She didn't want to leave her alone that long. Sarah had lost a lot of her vitality lately without the daily company of Miniver and the kids.

But it was Crystal who constantly worried Sarah, she discovered. Sarah told her Miniver had diagnosed Crystal's lethargy and physical discomforts as Chronic Fatigue Syndrome, when she described Crystal's symptoms to Miniver over the phone. "You know, the Yuppie Flu, the latest 'in' disease. But I'm not so sure," Sarah added in agreement when Crystal just shook her head in amazed denial and said, "There's nothing wrong with me but hot weather."

Actually it was a comfort knowing that Sarah and she were entitled to worry about each other now, like they had always done anyway.

She still felt responsible for Willette. She put half the money for the second painting in Willette's account, and called her every few days, which she had never done before. It was almost as if she felt sorry for her. She didn't tell Willette she knew. Besides knowing Sarah took for granted that she wouldn't tell, she did know the pain of humiliation, and she didn't want to inflict that even on Willette.

It was Saturday afternoon and Sarah, cooling herself with an elaborate folding Chinese fan, sat under the oak in the rattan chair Crystal had put there. Crystal was sorting the tomatoes and peppers. Much more than they needed, as usual.

"You're not going to spend the afternoon in the kitchen with those tomatoes, are you?" Sarah said.

"No. Let's take them to John Half for his soup kitchen, as Miniver called it." She'd written him notes for his gifts, but had not heard from him in a few days, and she guessed she had become accustomed to hearing from him, appreciating that here was yet another person who had her best interests at heart.

Sarah perked up. "That'll get us out of the house for a few minutes. We haven't even been to the grocery store since those younguns left."

With Sarah's love of going, she could care less where they went. But Crystal thought going anywhere she didn't have to was too much trouble because she felt queasy so often. Going through what she had, getting pregnant and then the miscarriage, had really thrown her body for a loop. Her hormones without doubt would return to normal soon and she'd feel better.

"Sarah, get on that new pantsuit you ordered from Madam Rose's," she said on impulse. "And some comfortable shoes."

"Are we going to dress up and walk to church with the tomatoes? This heat has boiled your brain, girl."

"No. We're going to the Casino!"

"I can't believe it!" said Sarah. But she got up quickly, and added, "You wear that dress I ordered you, too. A couple of things you've been wearing have gotten a little snug on you."

"I gained while Miniver was here doing so much cooking."

"It's the answer to a prayer," Sarah said later in the car, ignoring Crystal's sarcastic look. "The Casino's just a stone's throw from us. But I figured I'd have to drive myself up to Memphis and get on a bus with one of those senior citizen's groups. And you know how I hate being around old people."

"You ought to be ashamed," said Crystal as they pulled into the parking lot between the parsonage and the Methodist Church.

THIRTY-SEVEN - To Many Towered Camelot

Sarah had called ahead as Crystal suspected she would, because John Half came out to meet them. "You're like a fresh cut rose, Miss Sarah," he said, helping her out of the car.

Sarah patted his arm. "Thank you, John." Sarah was as informal as a faded bathrobe with her, and as down to earth as well water in a bucket with Miniver. And she would be the stately benefactor to the church with John Half when he was her pastor, but today he was simply her friend.

"And how does Crystal look?" Sarah said, segueing into the matchmaker that she wanted to be.

He considered his reply, only looking in her eyes, though he'd already apparently taken her in. "Like lemonade over ice," he said. Her dress was the palest yellow, and on her shoulder was an antique pin, diamond chips shaped in a square to represent a block of ice, with gold tongs grasping it.

Sarah laughed. "She should. The Bells owned the icehouse. She still owns what's left of it."

Just another tax and upkeep burden she would have thought at some earlier date, but she had come to feel differently although like the brickyard, until it was so recently infused with new blood and guts, no ice had been made in the Shallot plant to supplicate the dry bones of the town for decades.

"That's an unusual pin," he said.

Crystal nodded and touched it, not remembering ever wearing it before, but it had just seemed right today with this dress. Apparently she had acquired some residual fashion sense from Willette. Or appreciation for her family history. "We should be going," she said. Even she noticed his reaction. He'd like them to stay and visit. But he only said, "This produce will be much appreciated. Our committee has a long list of needy."

"We're going to Tunica," Sarah said, confessing instead of ignoring Crystal's warning look.

Just the slightest smile formed as he said, "You know your church doesn't condone that place."

"I know, John," she said, wearing a false shamed look. "But you know I'm a person who has to find out things for herself. I'm worried about Crystal though. She has an addictive personality. I'll have to really watch out for her."

"Sarah . . ." said Crystal.

"It may be too much of a job for me," she said.

"Maybe I could go with you to help out," John Half said as if conspiring with Sarah.

Had Sarah already invited him? She wouldn't put it past her.

"At any rate, I suppose I really should see what I've preached against," he said to Crystal. "Mind if I tag along? Fodder for a sermon."

"You'd go to a gambling casino?"

"See how unaware she is? You're more than welcome to go with us for your research. And to hang on to Crystal for me."

"I'll be gentle with her," he said to Sarah, and "I promise not to gamble," he said to Crystal. Then he turned and winked at Sarah. "Just let me get these tomatoes inside. The caretaker's here to distribute them."

Crystal took a few turns on county and state highways then drove several miles west toward the Mississippi River and Tunica County, whose voters had passed the gambling referendum, with the stipulation that any gambling must be on water. They entered the Delta where land was flat and rich with black dirt as far as the eye could see, at least as far as the levee covered with trees, built to protect that very delta from the high water that over ages had deposited the dirt. Green cotton stalks were thick in fields on each side, full of green-apple-colored ears. As they passed a large ginning complex beside a railroad track, Sarah said, "This is one of the few gins still in operation around here." Crystal mused, as if everyone didn't know that; but maybe John Half wasn't aware, being a newcomer from somewhere up north, not too far, she reflected, for Sarah didn't hold it against him.

Sarah sat in the back seat, having instructed John that they would go in her new car to try it out "on the road," rather than in his car as he offered, and that Crystal would drive as usual and that he would join her up front. "She's never had an accident that was her fault," she added. As they bumped over the track, the Mercedes and its tires muffling it well, Sarah noted, "This is the track that goes from Chicago through Memphis to New Orleans. Crystal and I rode it. They write songs about it." Maybe John didn't know. Sarah wasn't one to ramble for *no* reason. "City of New Orleans," she said. "One of the Guthrie boys." She hummed a few bars, then said,". . . 'Gone five hundred miles before the day is done' . . . Don't miss the turn at Highway 61 – that's not part of the song, John."

"Yeah, I think I've heard it before," he said, turning back to her, laughter in his voice.

In a minute, Sarah said, "Who'd ever have thought there'd be a gambling casino in Mississippi of all places? Regardless that cotton can't support the economy anymore."

"Yes, a drastic remedy," John answered.

Crystal turned south at the two-lane US Highway 61, falling in behind a new coach carrying passengers from Memphis to the Casino, according to its advertising.

"They make several runs a day, Sarah said. "I've heard they serve free drinks. At the casino. And they have slot machines by the hundreds. The casino floats, supposedly, in a canal dug from the river. It's attached to land by a long dock."

"You know an awful lot about it. Sure you haven't been sneaking over here?" John teased.

"It's open twenty-four hours a day, just like Vegas." Sarah them mused that if Columbus had been familiar with a delta this flat he'd never have set out to prove the earth was round. There was a long stretch with pecan groves on both sides of the road. "They'll cut them down to widen the road because of the casino," Sarah said as if she'd already seen the plans. "If I owned them, I'd chain myself to one to prevent it. Trees like that don't spring up as quick as a casino does."

"I seem to remember hearing that you helped stop one highway, already," John said.

They turned off the highway at Tunica, the little town long famous in North Mississippi and Memphis for its fishing camps and poverty, particularly that centered at an area called Sugar Ditch, "probably the most un-aptly named few acres in the world," Sarah said. "Yes, I've learned of it," he said. "If this casino can better their lives with jobs, or if its tax money can educate them . . . the lawmakers seemed to think it would be possible to justify."

"Just somehow inappropriate, though, isn't it," said Sarah, "out here on the richest dirt in the world."

Crystal nodded in agreement as she followed the bus. The new road, barely wide enough for two lanes of traffic to and from the Mississippi River, lay on a cotton field like an inappropriate black satin ribbon on a gift package.

"The law keeps it hidden now, having to be on water, but they'll be sprouting up before they can be stopped, like toadstools in a fairy ring," Sarah said, her sadness obvious.

The parking lot, several acres, was packed, traffic backed up, a guard directing cars. "Go to the front," Sarah said. "We'll park there."

"Your car might get towed," John said, finally amazed at something she said.

"You haven't traveled with Sarah," Crystal said, laughing, stopping at the front.

A guard checked her name and said, "Break the Bank, Miss Chancellor," and motioned them into a slot twenty feet from the door.

"I called in a marker," Sarah said slyly to John.

"She probably owns half the joint," Crystal said. "Or sold them the land to put it on."

Sarah said, "I just happen to know a few people."

"My arm's getting tired," Sarah said, much later, putting three quarters into the slot and pulling the handle. "Are you two ready to eat?"

"Thought you'd never ask," said John.

Crystal's stomach had already gnawed on itself. It was after eight, but she hadn't wanted to interrupt Sarah's good time.

They pushed their way through the narrow lanes between the machines, wound their way down the stairs and into the dining room where they were ushered to a table near a window facing the river. The sun was hovering at the brink across the River on the Arkansas side, a ripe tomato just before it sank, leaving pink and orange layers that morphed into the smudged purple of eggplant, and finally, before they finished eating and left their table, nothing but the black sky and black water and the running lights of an occasional boat.

Crystal hoped Sarah would be ready to go home after dinner, a buffet that Crystal would have liked to sample everything on, to her surprise, but Sarah was making the most of this trip. She was watching Sarah put dollar coins into a machine – so far Sarah had won a little and lost it back – when she heard a familiar voice behind them. She turned and saw only his back. She had stared at it enough occasions to know it. He was explaining to a beautiful brunet what must show in the three windows to win. Crystal didn't think that was important to the woman looking up at him. Was it his wife or ex-wife or whatever he called her? Probably not. This woman had to be in her early twenties.

Just then the machine beside Sarah paid off and Matt and the woman turned to look at the commotion, and he looked from her to John Half. And Crystal looked from Matt to the woman. She knew what he was thinking about her and John. Just what she was thinking about him and the woman.

Just then Sarah turned to Crystal with a fifty and asked her to get change, saw Matt and gave him a wonderful hello, then noticing the woman, her expression went blank. "I suppose we should go?" she asked Crystal.

"Hello," Matt said, encompassing them both, then offered his hand to John Half and introduced himself.

"John Half," John said as they shook hands, and Crystal noticed he didn't begin his name with Reverend or Brother or Doctor or whatever he used as a man of God. He hadn't that day with Horace, either. She knew it wasn't that they were in a gambling place and he thought it would call attention to himself or would be embarrassed. She sensed that he wanted to appear to be her date. And she was glad.

"Sarah and Crystal, this is Beverly Harris. Beverly, this is Sarah Chancellor and Crystal Bell. And John Half."

"How do you do?" said Sarah before turning to John. "I'm afraid I'm getting tired. If you'll scoop up my coins we'll be going. You two are probably ready to get me home, anyway."

Crystal didn't refute her. If Matt was so busy choosing between her and his wife and Lydia and now some woman named Beverly, she would remove herself from the competition. She'd lose, never mind the trip he wanted to take her on. And he'd feel better thinking another man was interested in her. He was that sort of man, she thought, never wondering at the disparity in her thinking. "Good night," she said.

As they passed the last few machines, Sarah dragging, her mood obvious, John said, "Sarah, the machines are supposed to be paying off better now than recently, because the percentages were too low."

"Well, does that show they can be rigged or they can be rigged," said Sarah. "No use putting more money in."

He added in explanation, "I've read all kinds of publications about these places. You know, so my rhetoric will be informed. Anyway, this weekend, and this weekend only," he added like a pitchman, "you have a good chance of winning again. They're practically giving it away."

"I'm out of the mood."

"Go ahead," Crystal said, knowing what put her out of the mood. "Those coins won't do you any good once we leave." Like John Half, she didn't want to see Sarah leave unhappy. Even if she didn't win, maybe she'd go home with the memory of how much fun she'd had blowing a hundred dollars tonight instead of what they'd just seen.

"All right, if you'll pull the lever for me," she said to John.

"Sarah, I'll do it for you," he said. "Sock it to 'em," he added, looking sideways at Crystal. He had no sooner let the lever go back than coins poured out, filling the trough almost to overflowing.

"You can give it to the needy," Sarah said, happy again.

He kissed her on the cheek in exuberance, then turned and gave Crystal a kiss on the cheek also. She looked away in embarrassment. Right into Matt's eyes a few yards away.

THIRTY-EIGHT - Want to Believe

When she arrived at the office Monday morning, he was sitting at her old desk, a Seven-Eleven cup of coffee in his hand.

"I didn't know you were a gambler," he said.

"Sometimes you decide to take a chance."

"Are you seeing him? John Half."

Did he mean that the way it sounded? A little hurt? But he wasn't exactly alone Saturday night.

He watched her answer an early call instead of his question, then said, "Don't you have anything to ask me?"

"Okay. Why were you at the casino with a beautiful Beverly?"

He laughed. "See, that wasn't too hard, was it? Now, here's my story. It was work."

"Fine," Crystal said. "I'd better get to work, too." No problem.

He touched her arm and said, "I'm sorry I joked. But it's true. Her father owns a company Lydia wants to bring in. They were at the blackjack tables. Such as that . . . it's part of my job." Then he nodded to her, "Now, it's your turn."

"Why didn't you call yesterday?"

"I did. You didn't answer."

She was outside most of the day. Well, why didn't you come? she would like to ask. Maybe it was, after all, because she was with another man Saturday night. She watched him let her consider yet not find anything to say

"Like I knew at the start. This isn't a simple thing we've gotten into, is it? I don't know why I'm not divorced. Except she says she doesn't want one. Why haven't I gotten one, anyway? Gone ahead with my life."

He looked at her as if she would provide the answer, but she didn't.

"Maybe I didn't want it bad enough to make her unhappy. Or it may be because my daughter doesn't want it."

"Maybe it's both. And more." She didn't like her answer but there it was.

"Then again, maybe I never thought it would matter if I was still married. That there might be anyone else, someone who'd knock me off my feet . . ."

No, no, she didn't want to hear this from him. That she would be the reason he would divorce – if he did. Yes, she did. She wanted him to do it. For her. No. His daughter – do that to her? She couldn't want to do that to Hallie.

"But that would be putting responsibility on someone who hadn't asked for it, don't you think?" he said, absolving her.

She nodded without meaning to, and she was sure he noticed the readiness with which she took herself out of the equation. Maybe to cover it up, she returned to the former subject. "I'm not dating him. He's Sarah's preacher at the Methodist church."

"All right, if that's your story."

"It's sad but true. Sarah hijacked him. You know how she is."

"I know he was there to be with you."

"What? You're as unsound as Sarah."

"There's no mistaking that look."

"What look?"

"The one a man gives another man who cares about his woman."

Mr. Elwood entered and their conversation ended. But her thoughts continued to rotate back and forth between her hopes and fears like a perpetual motion clock.

"If you don't go to Nashville with him, I'll send you out for a switch and I'll use it," Sarah said that night when she heard his explanation about the other woman.

"I want to and I don't want to. But I can't go."

"Don't be so wishy-washy. The only way you'll know for yourself what you can and can't do, you know what I mean – about his daughter – is to go."

Crystal continued washing dishes.

"When are you getting a dishwasher?"

"Maybe I will. I can afford one now."

"We both know you won't. But you can go."

She didn't say she wouldn't go because she didn't want to leave her alone.

"Miniver and the children are coming."

"Don't you ever think to tell me anything? Anything useful?"

"We were going to surprise you."

"Oh."

"So you're going."

"Yes, hell yes! I'm going!"

"Atta girl! Be a good opportunity to tell him."

"Tell what?"

But Sarah just sat there eating a whole tomato that she had peeled and sprinkled with a little salt. "Like everything else," she said, contemplating it as if it were poor Yorick's skull, "don't they just get sweeter the closer they get to playing out?"

"Tell him what, Sarah?"

"You know, it's been thirty-seven years, but I still remember how it was when I was expecting you." She sucked on the tomato and dabbed at a dribble of juice on her chin with a paper napkin left from Miniver's shopping. Miniver had tucked one inside the children's cloth napkins saying it would be a crime if they stained the fine ones.

Crystal had always wanted Willette to talk about how she'd waited impatiently for her, what she went through. But naturally Willette hadn't. How could she have? She wouldn't have, at any rate. Unless it had been a week's labor. And then Crystal would have heard about it. "Tell me about it, Sarah. Mom."

Sarah put the tomato down and rubbed with the napkin at the tomato's juice that had dripped onto the table, watching the flimsy paper disintegrate into ineffectiveness, as she sorted out what she would say. "Well, for one thing, I felt queasy in the morning for about three months. Just queasy. Not actually throwing-up-guts nauseated, as Miniver would say."

Just queasy, huh?

"In spite of that, I still ate and gained weight. Never lost it all, either. Til' here I am in my old age."

Gained weight? Crystal sat up straight and sucked her stomach in, and that made the buttons strain over her breasts. "Oh, you've still got your girlish figure," she said absentmindedly.

"True," Sarah said. They both laughed, then she added, "That's more than I can say about you these days."

"You always said I needed to gain some," Crystal said, dumping her last few bites into the garbage.

"Just about anything would hurt my feelings. Like people were trying to run my life. Conspiring against me. Of course, Willette *was*. But most of it was hormones."

Well, Crystal knew how that was. Hers were sure acting up lately.

"I got so hot I wished I could move into the ice house."

Crystal felt sweat trickle down the center of her back and between her puffed breasts. She wanted to reach for the folded newspaper and fan herself, but didn't.

"I convinced myself that it was because of upheaval. Like T. Oliver's plan to get married."

Well, Crystal knew about upheaval, too.

"For those three months I never suspected I was pregnant, because I continued to see some of the right signs. I found out later that's not too unusual."

She'd heard more than she wanted to. But Sarah wouldn't say all this just to make her worry. And anyway, she'd had a miscarriage all those weeks ago. Hadn't she?

"Any of this sound familiar?"

No. It couldn't be. She wanted to run away from Sarah's words, like she had run that day the tank was delivered, before she'd accepted that her father wasn't like other fathers and never would be, and before she realized he needed her love even more because of it. She'd even stopped disliking herself for having felt disloyal to him, after he'd spoken so bluntly to her about life and its options, or lack of them.

And she'd accepted that she'd lost her baby those weeks ago. And now, in spite of Matt's care . . . except that day at the office, when she'd made him. What would she say to him? But that was a week before the accident that she'd assumed had made her miscarry. Oh. God.

"We'd better get up to see Dr. Chastain tomorrow, don't you think?" said Sarah. "Find out if you got pregnant again so quickly, or if you didn't lose the baby when we thought you did?"

Could a person be at the bottom of a black hole while floating on a cloud? Absolutely. "I'll take tomorrow afternoon off."

"You ought to be on vitamins. Folic acid. Getting extra calcium, too. At your age, they'll want to give you a test for all those things that could happen."

She wasn't going to take any damned tests.

"I wouldn't take them. Just unnecessary worry. Your body is as healthy as a twenty-year-old's."

Crystal folded her arms across her stomach, resisting the urge to rub it.

"Besides, what good would it do? They don't know you if they think you'd not want your child. Whatever the circumstance."

"Just how long were you going to wait before letting me in on this?"

"I figured you'd notice labor pains."

THIRTY-NINE - Bridle Bells Ring

Miniver and the kids came as soon as school was out on Friday, as she and Sarah had already planned. Didn't family do that? Spend holidays together, she said.

Vernon barked like they were that elusive rabbit he'd been after all summer when he saw the children. And she and Sarah and Miniver hugged in a triangle and then Crystal and Sarah took turns hugging Tommy and Tabitha when they ran up to them after they got through hugging Vernon. "Can we go see Bert and Ernie?" Tabitha asked

"We'll drive right down to the lake," Sarah said.

"But you know we might not be able to really see them," Crystal said.

"Can we take some bread?" Tabitha asked.

"They're not sissies!" Tommy said. "They catch insects now!"

But he threw bread crumbs into the lake, too.

When they got back home, they cooked hamburgers and corn on the cob wrapped in foil on the grill. "They'll be ready for hamburgers again Monday," Miniver said as they watched the kids and Vernon playing around the roots of the big oak. "Got to cook hamburgers for Labor Day."

"We'll cook steaks for Labor Day," Sarah said.

"I can tell you two haven't used this grill since we left," said Miniver. "I bet you haven't used the oven either," she added, laughing.

Then Sarah looked smug and said, "But Crystal has something in her oven, as they say."

"What?" Crystal said.

Miniver looked shocked, and shrieked, "Do you mean it?! You mean her oven?"

"Sure do."

"I can't believe you'd talk that way, Sarah," said Miniver. "Using that trashy phrase." She turned her nose up. "But you really mean it?!"

"My oven?" Crystal said.

Miniver rubbed her stomach in little circles. "I've had something in mine twice."

"Oh. That oven." She looked down and let herself touch her stomach. She spread her hand and smiled.

"What?! You mean it's true?"

"Unless her doctor's a quack. We're having a baby!" Sarah said.

Miniver practically squealed. "You can buy her things, and rock her on the front porch!"

Sarah crossed her arms in front of her stomach, palms up, in a pose almost as if she were already holding an infant. "I deserve a grandchild," she said, more to herself than either of them. Then she brought herself back to include them. "And she's going to call me Grandma, not Grandmother."

"Or maybe even Granny," said Miniver.

"But she's not going to call me Sarah."

"Damn right," Miniver said. "You'll be more of a grandmother than Willette ever will."

Crystal couldn't help putting her arm over Sarah's shoulder as Sarah said softly, "Damn right."

"I bet Matt will be happy," said Miniver.

Sarah nodded in agreement.

But Crystal knew something they would never know. The ultrasound and exam left no chance it was Matt's. The due date coincided precisely from that day with Horace.

"When are you telling him?" Miniver asked.

"I don't know. But if either of you mentions it . . ."

To convince them she shouldn't, couldn't, go on the trip, she would have to tell them the truth. So she convinced herself that a few days with Matt – what could it hurt? In view of the fact that she'd have to quit her job and light out to somewhere in a few weeks, just like Sarah had done all those years ago, this would be the last opportunity to be with him. Was it an unnatural thought that she, pregnant with another man's child, wanted to spend a weekend with a married man, and that she deserved it? Hadn't she earned it with her previous life?

Crystal hadn't been to Nashville since she was a child. Interstate 40 had been under construction in the mid-sixties and Sarah wanted to see where the determination came from on the part of some to drive it straight through the heart of Memphis. Though Sarah had only lived in Memphis when she was waiting Crystal's birth, she said her inherited property there, and taxes she paid on it, gave her citizenship. She also said what happened there affected them in Shallot eventually. It might not exactly be Camelot, but it was their shining city.

To Crystal, the drive had been about dodging huge Caterpillar earth movers and concrete trucks and gravel trucks.

This morning, Matt had picked her up at ten. They crossed over long stretches of murky wetlands with an occasional red-tailed hawk circling. Cotton fields, bolls not opened yet, lined other miles. The 55 MPH speed limit gave her plenty of gazing time out the windows so she didn't just stare at him. She'd like to hold out her arm and say, go ahead, pinch me if I'm not dreaming.

A couple of hours later he asked if she was ready for lunch, a good place was not far ahead and it was about the halfway point. She was hungry, even though she'd eaten a piece of toast for breakfast and didn't "puke her toes right up," as Miniver said she did when she was pregnant.

Back on the interstate, full and content and relaxed, she noticed dozens of fallen trees on the bank, as if a giant hand had flailed down from the sky and knocked them over in a rage. Of course, that was what had happened. A tornado. It made her think of the most powerful tornado that had come through Shallot, uprooting and pillaging. It had demolished the school building not an hour after classes were out for the day. The very day that Dad had followed Willette to Memphis when she was angry that he had taken Crystal fishing. When the dark clouds suddenly grew darker and the huge trees started swaying like giants in grass skirts and hail had started pelting her like pebbles, Sarah had come running through the gate and grabbed her up from her pile of dirt pies and the two of them and Ida and Nellie had hovered in the basement with a kerosene lantern and listened to the storm's roar.

They had sung church songs they knew by heart. First Ida, in her expressive contralto, then Sarah, in her trained soprano – she'd had singing lessons as a child, and at that time still sang in the church choir – and finally Crystal and Nellie joined in with weak and trembling voices. Even after it was quiet they stayed there, maybe just enjoying feeling safe, maybe not wanting to see what havoc had been wrought. And hungry, they had opened a quart jar of spiced peaches that Ida had canned a few weeks earlier. They pried them out of the sticky, sweet liquid with their fingers and flicked off the prickly brown cloves tucked into them and took huge sucking bites from the whole, juicy peaches until they were down to the rough pits.

Was that why she loved peaches so much? But she didn't take care of the tree now. Didn't she think she deserved it? Maybe not. After all, she'd thought she was responsible for Willette being angry at Dad that day. The storm was probably already in Memphis by the time they left their refuge and Sarah went home.

Miraculously no lines were down in their area and the phone was ringing as they emerged, Dad calling, worried. After Ida assured him all was well, he asked to speak to Crystal. She wanted him to come home, but answered his question when he asked by saying she wasn't scared at all. She hadn't wanted to anger Willette anymore. Willette didn't ask to speak to her. "Tell Mother to have a good time," she said. She wanted to say, tell her I'm sorry, but somehow hadn't wanted Dad to know that she understood she was the cause and enabler of their trouble.

When tornadoes were expected now, she went to Sarah's basement, where they had battery operated lanterns and radio, and sat in recliners which Sarah'd had put there for that purpose, centered on a braided rug with a nice table between them, and ate pretzels and drank Cokes until the storms were over. For the most part, their tornadoes came up from Texas, ominous and noisy like a herd of runaway cattle, striking like a branding iron. Whatever they encountered was left looking like only one thing – like it had been hit by a tornado. Or run over by a herd of cattle. But with a surgeon's precision, the last one had lifted a puppy from a trailer park it demolished between Shallot and Memphis, and set it down in the branches of a tree miles away. It was found the next day, whimpering yet unhurt.

"You're quiet," Matt said, patting her leg.

"I was just thinking of Sarah."

"She's a fine lady."

They descended into the Tennessee River valley and she could see the river's course for miles north and south, one wooded ridge after another. She had seen the river with Sarah where it made a wide curve down into Alabama, when they had gone to Florence to visit Ivy Green. The kids in first grade had started, among other things, calling her dad the Cracked Bell, and Sarah had used the trip to take her mind off it as well as to point out how easy her life was compared to some. "Just about anything can be overcome," Sarah had said as they walked down the gravel paths to stand at the seminal places in the young Helen Keller's life. It had appeared so peaceful then, empty of what books and movies had depicted of her tortured early life. Crystal hoped Sarah's lesson had finally taken hold.

The green rolling hills of middle Tennessee seemingly propelled their vehicle up and down like cars on the old wooden Zippin Pippin Roller Coaster at the Memphis Fairgrounds that Elvis had loved so, each descent giving them momentum to climb the next height. They crossed river after river, some more than once because of their windings.

Traffic was getting thick. I-40 was joined by I-440 under construction. To their left now she could see the square-looking capitol with its white dome resting on a tall-columned box, sitting on a hill on the north edge of downtown.

They exited east at Broadway, which she remembered as being the main thoroughfare, and passed the old stone train station with its huge clock tower. The rundown train sheds behind it told the story that it wasn't being used as intended anymore, even if the sign on the station hadn't announced that it was now a restaurant and hotel. She mentally compared this beauty to the remaining rundown station in Memphis, but credited the Memphis one for still fulfilling its promise.

The streets were bustling, though it was Saturday and state workers as well as other office workers were not present. Tourists and their cameras were on the sidewalks and a couple of tour buses cruised in the slow lanes.

There were also a few homeless men. There was never one in Shallot. If one had found his unbeaten pathway there, a church would have housed him for the night, fed him, re-clothed him, and Bob would have ushered him out of town the next day if the homeless person had managed to put up with being stared at that long.

As they waited for a light to change, a man with a 'will work for food' sign peered into the Suburban. "Nice truck," they could tell he was saying. "Can you help a veteran?" She couldn't ignore the man and reached for her purse.

"He'll probably buy booze," Matt said.

"I can't pass him by–"

Matt took a ten from some bills in the console and rolled down the window. "This is from her," he said, putting it in the grimy outstretched fingers.

"Bless you, M'am," the man said. "I don't drink, just down on my luck."

The light changed as the bill dropped from his shaky fingers and he bent to pick it up. Crystal saw a flat whiskey bottle jutting out his back pocket.

A car honked impatiently and as soon as the man had backed away, Matt pulled through the light.

"You were right," she said.

"You're right to be generous."

"Miniver would have demanded her money back," she said, laughing.

"Miniver would've…"

He didn't finish, but she did it for him, "Miniver would've realized the kind of person he was."

"I guess she learned the hard way."

She smiled just to think of Miniver.

"What would Sarah have done?"

"She'd have had him arrested."

He laughed.

"Me, I might as well have been hibernating in a cave."

"It was an ivory tower."

"Not you, too," she said.

"More of us should give people the benefit of doubt," he said.

It could cause you plenty of trouble. She'd learned that the hard way.

FORTY - Loyal Knight and True

Matt was with his daughter. He'd invited Crystal to go with them but she wouldn't. She wondered where Green Hills Mall was; it could be named for any of the many tree-covered hills in and around the city. What kind of mother would have the father take the daughter shopping for school clothes? Even Willette had seen to that with Crystal. Much to Crystal's regret. But she knew the answer. The mother who had Matt for the father of her child could do it, would know he would enlist an experienced saleslady, as he told Crystal he was going to do if she didn't come. But she had no experience at letting little girls have what they liked, did she?

She lay across the king size bed in the cool room she had brazenly said they would share and tugged a pillow under her head and realized that she could go to sleep. Dr. Chastain had confirmed Sarah's investigations, she would need the right nutrition, supplements, extra rest and sleep. It seemed now that she had known forever there was a new life she was responsible for. How could she have been so oblivious? But that was the way she'd lived most of her life. Not seeing what was under her own nose unless she was forced to. Sarah being her mother, Willette's jealousy because of it, and yes, Dad's suicide because he couldn't live any longer with his life's failures and his refusal to fix them.

Later when she rolled over and woke up, for a second she couldn't remember where she was. Then she stretched under the light blanket, snug. A winter squirrel in a leaf-stuffed hollow. But how did the blanket get there? The room was dark, the curtains closed, and she hadn't closed them either. Then she saw Matt asleep in a chair, legs stretched out and crossed, fingers laced across his stomach, loafers sprawled where he'd toed them off.

She got up quietly and went to the bathroom – *that* was happening more frequently. She'd gone to sleep on the bedspread and didn't like the feeling that others may have lain on it. She undressed and stepped into the shower.

In a few minutes he tapped on the door. "Can I come in?"

"I'm in the shower."

"Thought I timed it about right."

"All right," she said, turning her back to him.

"Want me to scrub your back?"

She was embarrassed, her faults exposed, her hands over her breasts revealing to her their slight heaviness, compared to the way they were, say, when she wasn't pregnant. "No. Do you really want to?"

"Wouldn't have asked," he said.

"OK," she said, as if agreeing to twenty lashes instead.

He unbuttoned and pulled off his blue striped shirt and stepped out of his dark navy slacks and hooked them over the door. He pulled off his socks and stood there a minute in his white cotton boxers before getting out of them, and as usual looked her over the way she was doing him, and she was thinking this was getting to be a habit.

Suddenly she wanted him to see her in all her exposed nakedness, and inside her, too, even the baby if she could still be honest with herself, all that he had missed to this point, though he seemed to have determined things about her that even she didn't know, and that he believed even if she didn't. She wanted to tell him all the rest, the things she knew about her failings. But she'd tried before, hadn't she? Now, she'd just let him see her for what he wanted her to be, and if he did choose her over his daughter and she couldn't do the moral thing, he had only himself to blame. He'd understand she was helpless when it came to him.

Finally, smiling indulgently, he asked, "Seen enough?" as if he were the one wanting to bare himself.

"Did you?"

"I did." He stepped in and adjusted the nozzle and kissed her on the forehead. "That back scrub offer's good." He soaped the thick bath cloth and starting at her neck, made soothing circles all the way across her shoulders and down her back time and again. Was this part of making love? She could see how this could almost satisfy. If she didn't already know what the real thing was with him.

She leaned her back against his chest and he closed his arms across her breasts, their new tenderness causing her to draw breath sharply.

"Sorry," he said, loosening his arms.

"It's all right," she said happily.

"Masochist."

"How many times do I have to remind you? I'm weird."

"Sorry. I don't have whips and chains." He kissed her neck. "Is this hurting?"

"Yes. I love it."

He cupped her head and lightly kneaded with his fingertips. "Does this hurt enough?"

"No. More."

"What about this?" he said, moving his hands down, splaying them across her hips.

She felt him wanting her, and she turned to him, But true to his earlier care, having learned from two women who had their own needs, he got out and reached for a little packet in his shaving case.

FORTY-ONE - A Song That Echoes Clearly

The woman was mesmerizing. Crystal felt guiltily helpless not to watch, like a callous but innocent youth taken to see a stripper by his worldly friend. Every action must have been carefully rehearsed because her act was going as if it were the most spontaneous performance the audience could have hoped for. Every hand gesture appeared to be a move that happened of its own volition, but that would have been missed, yes, if not done. The red cowboy boots stepped her around to cover the entire small stage in equal parts, not to slight anyone watching from any corner of the room, the fringe on them swaying and lifting and then settling in place before she haughtily stomped and strutted again.

She looked the audience in the eye. It was obvious that she loved the people whose eyes were on her. She wanted their adulation, and she was letting it show. She must be what they called a natural.

She was at ease with the musicians and generously deferred to them when they had the spotlight, though it was obvious to all she was the attraction.

Every shake of her beautiful head seemed necessary to complete the words she was singing. She was without doubt enjoying her dream-come-true of being selected as the next inductee into the Grand Ole Opry, as she had informed the audience.

And Crystal assumed each one of them felt like she did, that she had called them to her and whispered the good news to them personally, like each was her best friend.

Yes, in spite of being so uncomfortable about being there, almost as if spying, Crystal was as taken with the singer and her performance as were the rest of them. She was finally to her biggest hit now, as she informed the audience, but their frantic burst of applause at the first note would have made that clear anyway, and even Crystal recognized the tune. Miniver forever hummed it around the house and had a tape she played on her boombox. Miniver had told her and Sarah about growing up back in the mountains of North Carolina listening to whatever music they could pick up on their radio. She liked country as well as anything else, maybe better. She'd met Thomas at a country music hang-out where she was a waitress when he was on a road construction crew there. And she was going to be in shock when Crystal told her who the singer of "The Lost Country Girl" was.

Only Matt appeared not to be drawn in. With screened eyes, his head tilted at a skeptical angle, he sipped a beer or drew on a cigarette. She'd never seen him smoke. He held the little matchbook and idly slid the cover up and down under the flap. He didn't applaud after the songs, instead lifting his beer or cigarette to his mouth.

Crystal toyed with the idea of thinking it was inconsiderate of him not to at least acknowledge her talent. His wife's talent.

Even if "she done him wrong" like the song was about, it was a performance that deserved recognition. The others at the tables, lined up on each side of a runway extension of the stage in the long room, apparently realized they were seeing a show that was going to be one they could tell about one day, when Helen Hawke was no doubt leaving her boot prints in cement in the Walkway of Stars on Music Valley Drive, which Miniver said was the Nashville equivalent of Hollywood's homage to the big time.

Helen Hawke had involved Crystal so in the "I'm here and he's there like I thought I wanted but now I don't think I can stand it" lyrics that she almost felt sorry for her. She figured it was a true testament to Helen's talent that she was drawn in with the rest of them in spite of her reasons not to be.

After the set, Helen, in her boots and jeans and black leather vest – not so skimpy that it required a blouse under it, showing enough but not enough to embarrass the older members of the audience – glided to their table amidst smiles and friendly shoulder touches and quick hand clasps with those at tables in her path and then sat as close to Matt as possible. "You told me you were bringing someone," she said without peevishness, "but I didn't know it was a beautiful woman."

Well, with her so beautiful, she could afford to be generous.

Then she quickly kissed Matt on the mouth and turned to Crystal and extended her hand, asking, "Have you been friends long?" Crystal couldn't think of an answer, but Matt said, "We're not friends."

"Oh, business for Lydia, then," Helen said, and Matt, who was about to speak, waited patiently as Helen smilingly turned to sign autographs for a teenage girl and a woman who must be close to Sarah's age. Helen appealed to all ages. Then Helen asked, "How did it go this afternoon?"

"Just fine," Matt said. "And Crystal isn't business."

Helen ignored his response but said, "You and Hallie always have such a good time together, just the two of you."

Crystal figured it was Helen's way of asking if she went shopping with them.

"She said she hadn't seen you since yesterday morning," was all Matt said.

"Even when I'm not touring, she's in bed when I get home from my shows. I have interviews or personal appearances some mornings. Maybe a recording session," she said more or less to Crystal. Then she said to Matt, "You understand now, don't you? Why what we've discussed, why it would be for the best?"

Crystal wondered why she didn't let him know that she wanted him for herself, in addition to wanting him back for their daughter's sake. Didn't Helen realize it would be hard for a mortal man to turn her down?

As she signed yet another autograph on a paper napkin a waiter brought, Helen smiled at the two middle-aged couples, looking to be from the heart of America, that he indicated, and in that close proximity, Crystal saw that Helen's smile was sincere. The request made her happy. Crystal empathized with the people who were too shy to come in person with their requests. But Helen apparently appreciated that much of her success depended upon people like them. Had she really wanted it, this singing life, more than a family life with Matt and Hallie? She glanced at Matt, who was still scrutinizing Helen. "You're happy, aren't you?" he said.

"Almost," Helen answered. "You didn't applaud."

"You're a great performer," he said. "One of the best."

She didn't look too pleased at that, and Crystal thought she must have wondered, as she did, if he had meant it the way it sounded. Crystal waited for her to say well don't you *know* I wrote the song about you? Don't you know this was something I had to do or regret it all my life and don't you know we couldn't have lived like that forever? But you've been patient and gave me the time to see if I could do it and now I want what I might have had to give up for a while to get this? But all she said was, "I have to get ready for the next set," and kissed him on the cheek, as if she knew not to push. And obviously she wasn't going to bare her heart here in this place in front of Crystal. But strangely, Crystal didn't hold it against Helen, her understanding of situations and self-control, like she did Lydia and Willette for their cool appraisals.

"Bye, Crystal," Helen said. "Thanks for coming to see my show." Not one question to her about her and Matt's relationship, no recrimination to Matt about Crystal.

FORTY-TWO - Last Song

They left the Nashville Palace, which Miniver had informed Matt was where many of the big stars got their start, having no indication he knew one so personally, and added that he should make sure to take Crystal there. He had listened as if it were all news to him and promised to do it.

Now Crystal couldn't help wondering why he hadn't told her who his wife was. Was he still hurting, as Lydia said, that Helen had left him for personal fulfillment? Maybe. Was he bitter that she'd achieved all this success? No, he'd supported her and her entourage with his wealth, according to Lydia, paying the band's salary, recording expenses, road expenses, who knew what all. Was he feeling guilty that he had not been willing to stay with Helen, sacrifice his work and way of life for her? She might not have even asked him to do that. Now that Helen had made it big, if they got back together people might think he wouldn't let Helen go. Crystal made herself stop contemplating.

As they crossed the meandering Cumberland River, Matt said, "This town, what it stands for, to find success among all the ones who don't . . . It means everything to her."

"Not everything."

He drove downtown and through Printer's Alley. Crystal said no when he asked if she'd like to go in one of the nightclubs. For a person with talent like Helen's, it would be hard to hide that talent under a bushel and not let it take her where it would.

"Want to park and walk?"

"Umm. Not unless you want to." She wouldn't say how tired she was feeling.

"We'll just crawl down Broadway with all the rest of the traffic," he said.

Sarah as well as Miniver would never forgive her for not going in Tootsie's Orchid Lounge, in the thick of things on Broadway where it had been through the rise of country music. "All the great ones have hung out in there," Miniver had said. "Willie practically lived there." "And Kris," added Sarah, "wrote some good ones at that bar." Miniver had looked shocked. "I'm surprised you know Nelson and Kristofferson. I figured the real opera would be more your style." "Well, it is, I suppose. But I like the Opry, too. '. . . ribbon . . . . . hair . . .'" she had hummed-sung in a croaky voice. Now

Crystal looked out the window at the garish neon sign on the purple-fronted, fabled honky-tonk filled with tourists, drinkers, country music lovers, and would-be music greats, and put her window down and heard the invisible twanging guitars from inside, like she and Sarah had heard so many years ago while walking down the sidewalk, politely ignoring the man in the door who tried to beckon them in. "Come in, little ladies. Hear some music. All ages welcome." Of course they had gone on by, like market girls on a mission, as usual not there to actually participate in the experience, just to see it.

"You liked her," Matt said in the new quietness as they turned right off Broadway, leaving the brightly lit shrines to country music behind, just a little east of the I40 entrance, and entered James Robertson Parkway to circle down to the capitol.

A place in this ascendancy was what Helen had wanted enough to leave this man. To break up her family. But this was the sacred place from which the country music world would bow to her if her talent was enough, and if luck found her in the right place at the right time. Crystal admired her for having a dream and the nerve to follow it.

"When did Helen decide to try all this? Didn't you know when you married her? Didn't you want her to?" Well, he started this discussion.

"She was her church soloist. That was the extent of it when I met her. She sang at my father and Lydia's wedding."

So he'd known her for a long while. So she was young. And still young.

"She was still in high school in Memphis. Then she went to Vanderbilt here in Nashville. When she was a junior, a guitar player forming a band heard her sing in a choral group and asked if she'd be their lead. I happened to see them at a little place on West End while I was here on business. We went out together when I was here after that."

So she was majoring in Nashville and country music while she was in college.

"When she graduated she gave it up and moved back to Memphis. Lydia hired her as her assistant. That's how we hooked up again."

And so Helen had tried to give it up. She knew she wanted Matt and she had tried.

"About a year later, after we married, the band asked her to come back. Their new singer hadn't worked out."

"Is it the same band she has now?"

He nodded.

So she was loyal.

"They were beginning to get a lot of attention when we found out we were expecting Hallie."

So that's why Helen hadn't wanted her pregnancy then. Her new career must have been put on hold by it. But she loved her daughter and wanted what was best for her.

"She told the band to find another singer, but they wouldn't. They did sessions and back-ups. Drove trucks and cooked hamburgers for a couple of years until she could rejoin them."

So the band was depending on her, too. Of course, that wouldn't be reason enough. But it showed they knew what a talent she was, and that she'd probably not be able to suppress it forever.

"Eventually, they had to make the move back to Nashville or give it up."

"But you didn't ask her not to go." Of course not. And he would have done the financing of their first album, according to Lydia's veiled revelations.

He shook his head no. "For a while we tried to make long-distance work. At first Hallie was with me. But Helen wanted her when she wasn't touring, and Hallie missed her mother; I'm sure you understand that."

It wasn't necessary at this point to tell all the ways she was glad to be missing Willette back then, even while ravaging her heart to find some way to get her to return to her and Dad.

"There aren't many weeks I haven't seen Hallie."

"Did Helen ask you . . . did she ask you to follow her here?"

"No. I could have opened an office here. But I didn't."

Helen had known, like he did. And she still understood and only reminded for Hallie's sake. You couldn't ask, it had to be given.

Helen had known that he would continue to put his all into his daughter's life. That he would be patient while she followed her dream and realized she had to have him, too. And that's what he was doing until he'd stood in the rain on her porch and left with her heart as well as the painting of her, and left his heart with her, at least that part that didn't belong to Hallie, and that part that she believed he hadn't even known was still waiting for Helen.

"Yes, I do like her," she said, though he may have forgotten he'd asked. Maybe some would think it was all manipulation on Helen's part, but she didn't. It was just what it was.

"What am I gonna do with you?" he said, patting her thigh.

He was kidding, but wasn't that the real question? This between them wasn't supposed to have happened.

"Let's go back to the room," he said.

In the room, he pinned her against the door. "Crystal . . ." he said, filtering his helplessness about the whole situation to her. "I don't know what's right anymore." His eyes poured over her, saying what they hadn't before. If he couldn't choose the right thing, he believed she could.

For one split second she wondered if her decision would have been the same if she weren't carrying Horace's baby. She hoped it would have been. They couldn't have lived happily for long, knowing he had given up his daughter for her. He couldn't be in two places at the same time.

His mouth was on hers before the sob that she didn't know had started was finished. It confirmed their unspoken words. Then she lay her head against him and said, "It's all right. It's the right thing."

"I'm sorry. I don't want you to be hurt."

She nodded, "I know." They hugged and patted each other's back like people did at funerals: It'll be all right, eventually. We'll learn to live without each other. Life will go on.

But wasn't it supposed to take all weekend for her to make up her mind? "Can't we have tonight?" she said.

"Tonight. Or forever. If you still want it. If you think it's – ."

"The right thing? I don't care. I deserve this weekend."

"You deserve it? You deserve whatever you want. I can't believe you think I'm what you deserve."

"I'm the judge of that."

Just hearing him laugh softly at something she said made her happy. Life was supposed to be that way. In the future she would try to find happiness in simple things. Perhaps only in her baby's smile.

He was still hugging her loosely, but he pulled her tighter, kissing her forehead. She could have him but couldn't. She put her teeth against his collarbone. The most vulnerable of the body's bones she'd heard, bared to her.

"You'll be all right, Crystal. If I thought different , . ."

"I will be," she said. "But not now." Then she kissed him for all the nights she wouldn't have him.

He pulled the spread and top sheet back. She liked that. They sat on the side of the bed and pushed their shoes off and lay down on their backs, with his arm under her neck, and watched the ceiling for a few minutes. Then she lifted her leg across his. It was so comfortable now, now that it was too late. She imagined that it would have been like this every night, comfy beside him and drifting off to sleep, after making love like there would be no tomorrow. Or softly and quickly, like there would be all the tomorrows in the world. She couldn't believe she had to stifle a yawn!

"Go on to sleep," he said.

"Not tonight." But she was tired. Like if she couldn't close her eyes for a few minutes she would just drop off the earth.

"Just for a while. You're tired."

"Well, I do want to be awake. . ."

Smiling, he rolled onto his side as she did, with his stomach to her back and rubbed her neck and shoulders. Soon something like a large fist closed around her consciousness, and she was asleep with the feel of his breath on her shoulder.

She awoke as she went to sleep, with her back against his stomach. His hand was on her breast. He wasn't quite awake yet. But she knew her body was becoming part of his sleeping mind as her breaths became deeper and put her body tighter against his. His hand moved on her and his next breath was deep and she thought maybe contented. "You awake?" he said, and she turned over and kissed his eyes and mouth and his leg wrapped around her.

For a short while she let herself imagine she was the one he would always do these things with, these kisses and touches. His weight only against her and the moistness and sounds only created between them. Then she wished for him and Helen to be happy, or she'd have given him up for only half of what he deserved.

FORTY-THREE - Lend Her Grace

When she awoke again, it was daylight and she heard the shower. She hoped he wouldn't be long. Every day her wait tolerance grew shorter. The water stopped and she gave him a minute to dry off, then threw back the sheet and started getting up. Then she heard the hair dryer. "Oh, no," she muttered, lying back down. But he was quick and the dryer went off. She swung her legs over the side of the bed, then heard the electric razor. Maybe this wouldn't take long.

The noise stopped. She put her legs over the edge again and then she heard water. Brushing his teeth!

She forgot all about how – probably because she was around the men at the brickyard so much who worked and sweated, and she understood that and didn't think less of them for it – how she loved drawing in his fresh scent, how one of the best things about him was how clean he always was. Sparkling clean. Scrubbed down clean. The water went off and she flew up, feeling anger at him. Anger? This too would have been part of everyday life with him.

The door opened as she was about to knock. He stood there with a towel wrapped around him. He looked her up and down. She wore nothing but the polish Miniver had put on her toenails, and was fighting the urge to hold herself like a toddler who has to go potty *now*! She grabbed the towel from around him and held it in front of her as she raced in and shut the door. "Sorry," she heard through running water she turned on.

She didn't answer.

She took a long cool shower because the bathroom was warm. Then she brushed her teeth and put lotion all over. She wished she had her make-up. She was running out of things to do.

She must have looked so silly, needing to go so bad she forgot she was naked. Practically had her legs crossed. Finally she wrapped in a towel, too hot for the robe hanging on the door, and he stood up when she came into the room. She stared. He was in a light gray suit and tie and a dark shirt. He was beautiful.

"Crystal, I want to ask you something. Are you pregnant?"

"What? . . . No! Why . . ." She thought quickly enough not to finish asking what made him ask that.

"I've experienced it, you know." He laughed as she said "Really." Then he said, "Well, as close as a man can come to it. It's just that . .

.You've, . . ." he tilted his head in an embarrassed admission, "it looks good – you've gained a little weight. You get hungry. Your breasts were tender…"

She stared at her pink toenails. The moment of truth. Or not. "If you'd been eating Miniver's cooking this summer you'd have gained, too."

He was silent, waiting for answers to the rest of his observations.

"I guess all my appetites have increased." Then she squirmed even as she knew she would say it, embarrassed to say something like this, even though it was a lie, even though they were talking about her being pregnant for heaven's sake. "It's almost time for my period. I get tender then. Hormones, I guess."

He considered it all as she spoke it. Then he nodded thoughtfully.

Then she spoke the truth if she ever had. "And wouldn't I be the happiest girl in the world if I were pregnant with your child?"

"You might deny it though, knowing you, thinking . . . I don't want to say this. About how it would affect my life with Hallie . . . if you and I didn't break it off . . ."

"There's no need for me to consider those things."

He nodded thoughtfully again.

When she could take her eyes off him, she turned back into the bathroom. But he was across the floor before she could close the door and pulled her to him. "I know what you're thinking," he said.

"No you don't."

"If you could meet yourself as a stranger like I did that Saturday…"

"They'd think I'm strange, all right."

"You're not cursed with a strange malady. Give yourself a chance. Give someone a chance to know you."

She didn't want anyone else to know her.

"The first look at you – it isn't enough and people sense it. That's the thing, Crystal."

"What's so great about me! I'm an old maid in a little Mississippi town in the Broad Stream River swamp. My family's half crazy and I probably am, too. My house is falling down around me. I work until I can't think about my life. . . Helen's a big star, beautiful. How could you have been interested in me?"

He held her back a little from him to look into her eyes. "My darling Crystal. You've saved the brickyard all these years, all those jobs.

Your love for Sarah has given her a reason to live and be happy. You've kept your father's legacy intact. You give away food by the baskets. You opened your home to a family who needed you."

"I didn't have a choice."

"Yes. You did. But you've done what you thought was the right thing. With your drive, you could have gone anywhere and been a success. But hey, you're a rock star in your hometown."

"So that's why they stare."

"No. It's probably because you're as beautiful outside as you are inside."

"Huh?"

"That's what I saw that first morning, but all I knew about you was that you were selling a painting. But you've got to accept that or it's . . . just no good. People tend to eventually see us as we see ourselves."

"I was thinking you're beautiful."

"Well, you're wrong about that."

But she used to love it when Dad called her his pretty girl. "So you were wrong in what you just said."

"Didn't you ever wonder why your dad stopped painting you? Weren't you about twelve? I suspect as you grew into a beautiful young woman with a certain allure he just didn't want to paint his own daughter in artistic poses. And he wouldn't have wanted to go on depicting you in the outlandish ways he had done as you got old enough to be embarrassed by it."

That couldn't possibly be true. But yes, Dad had not even suggested painting her portrait as she grew older. She had wondered why. She would never agree with Matt that it was because she was beautiful! But it could be that he would have found it awkward to paint a young woman rather than his child. Or maybe he did finally realize that she was tired of posing, even when he took photos to go by at times.

"I wish I knew what happened to you, Crystal, to make you see yourself as no one else does."

Whatever she was, ugly or beautiful, Willette was what happened. It was the inflection in her voice, the positive way she conveyed the negative feelings: "You're just not what people expect of you, Crystal." And it was the way Willette would assess her when she wanted to look pretty for something special, touch her own hair and say something like, "I'd have styled yours if you had asked me," or "It's a shame you couldn't have inherited some of my features." Willette, beautiful Miss America runner-up, was the one she had believed. How could she have known of Willette's insecurities?

She was supposed to tell Matt that Willette had left her so little self-esteem she'd subjected herself to date rape? And then begged for it, as Horace believed. She could get past it now. Matt was telling her these things he believed, so she would, too.

She smiled, not remembering having felt normal and pretty. "You'll be late for Hallie," she said. What else was there to say? She'd gone to sleep knowing what morning would bring, and now she could face it a little better. She was glad their decision had been reached before she met Hallie. "She's expecting you to take her to church."

"You'd have liked her."

"I like her," she said. "In fact, I love her. You go on." She touched his face. "I will be all right. You've seen to that."

Their cinerary embrace was a sweet and gentle place for all that remained of what she'd hoped for until this moment in spite of trying not to, a commiseration with each other over a mutual loss. The change was already feeling natural and permanent.

FORTY-FOUR - Epistolary

After she dressed, she started pacing. What to do? What to do? Their original plans were to stay through tomorrow's holiday celebration, a picnic for the three of them and then the symphony concert and fireworks on the riverfront. He'd told her that Hallie felt the booms of the fireworks so that it was almost as if she heard them. Crystal, regretting that Hallie would never hear her mother sing, had actually looked forward to it for Hallie's sake, in spite of how uneasy she'd felt at the thought of meeting her. But now they were old plans. That was before she knew what she'd known all along, and before he gave her a chance to not do the right thing for Hallie, without ever setting eyes on her. She couldn't stay here any longer.

She wanted to go home and cry on Sarah's sympathetic shoulder. Let her make everything better as she always had, like a mother should. And then get a good talking to from Miniver, and then do what she had to do. And that was to stand on her own two feet.

She wrote a note for Matt. "I'm going home. My life will never be the same. For that I thank you. Crystal."

FORTY-FIVE - Winding Down

S he called down and had the desk arrange for a rental car and was in the lobby waiting for it to be delivered when the desk clerk motioned her to a phone, saying she had a call. She answered the phone with the certain knowledge that something bad had happened to one of the people in her life that she had come to care about, or to the one she had cared about all her life and left at home.

"Crystal?"

"Bob? What is it?"

"You're not alone, are you?"

"What's happened?" She sensed the deliberation.

"Crystal . . . somebody broke into your house."

Why hadn't she listened to advice about changing the locks!? "Are Sarah and Miniver and the kids all right?" But any window in the house was an open entrance.

"Miniver and the kids weren't there."

"Why? Where were they?" Miniver wouldn't have gone away from the house. Oh. Her mother. Something must have happened to her.

"Gone to North Carolina. She got a call. Her mama was in a nursing home, you know."

He had something to tell her that she couldn't bear to hear, and he was putting it off.

"She was going to miss her mama's funeral to stay here with Miz Sarah. She said one thing her mama taught her was to keep her word. But Miz Sarah told her she wouldn't have it. And that you wouldn't want her to."

"That's right. She couldn't miss her own mother's funeral."

"Miz Sarah gave her the keys to the new Mercedes and said impress the home folk while you're there."

"Naturally." Crystal liked hearing all this.

"I said I would look in on Miz Sarah and I did."

Again, more she would have known already.

"Miz Sarah said we weren't to interrupt your trip."

And more. So all right. If someone broke in and took the paintings, maybe they could be found. If not, she'd learn to live without them. Or chase them to the ends of the earth.

"But I couldn't be there all the time."

No. No.

"She's in the hospital, Crystal, pretty bad."

"Which hospital?"

"Baptist South."

"I'll be there as soon as possible."

"I called about flights. There's not one until three-thirty this afternoon."

"I've rented a car. I'll be there before then." She looked at Dad's thin Baume and Mercier on the black leather band on her wrist. Willette had given it to him. Most of its expired time was done on Crystal's wrist. It just wasn't his style and Willette must have known it, but wanted him to have it because it was her style. He liked big, clunky, Timex watches. His last few years he'd worn a heavyweight Rolex, but she had thought it wasn't like him to spend so much on a watch for himself and she had told him she liked it. "Got it for my birthday," he'd said, looking at it for a long moment. But now that she knew things, she knew Sarah gave it to him. "It's eleven now. I'll be there before three."

"If you get stopped, have the trooper call me. Do you want to know what happened?"

She saw a white Ford park out front and the uniformed driver get out and indicate he was delivering it, showing papers and the keys to the doorman. "Yes." She didn't really. "But my car just got here." And she'd still rather speculate than know if it was the worst.

FORTY-SIX - Her Last Song, A Lady of Shallot

"Sarah. Mom. It's me, Crystal."

She kissed the sagging cheek and held Sarah's hands. There was a slight tremble in the fingers. The skin was smooth and cool and blank white. They'd removed her nail polish. There was hardly any color to her nails, hardly any distinction between the white half-moons and the pale pink middles and creamy tips. Her hair was white, as if it had never been any other color. Crystal had denied it. Just seeing what she wanted to see.

Her lips normally had some color, even without lipstick, because of protecting herself from the sun so much all her life. And she still had bright eyes. "The sun fades everything," she had told Crystal, "even lips and eyes." Maybe time would do it too, but if so, time had spared Sarah there. But now her lips were like the white roses in her garden. She wished Sarah would open her eyes and let that light shine out of the white skin and white hair and white sheets.

"Sarah . . ."

Suddenly Sarah opened her eyes and blue flashed through the blankness. "I want to hold my baby," she said.

"I'm here" Crystal said, and leaned into the opening arms.

"No. Not you. I want my little baby."

Crystal swallowed instead of sobbing. "Sarah, Mom, you're confused a little. It's me, Crystal."

"Oh, Crystal. My baby. You got back in time."

"Mom," Crystal said, and with her ear barely touching Sarah's breast, heard the last nurturing breath escape from her body. She'd read in some ancient book when she was a child that the last exhalation of breath was almost a musical note. It was not music to her ears. Only an exhaling of life.

Sarah had only been holding onto that last formality until Crystal arrived. For a long while Crystal sat beside Sarah's bed and watched the face and body of the woman who had been her friend, protector, mentor and mother. She was who had kept Crystal sane, at least whatever sanity she had, and had kept her own sanity while having to give her child to a woman she detested.

Crystal watched without hope that there would be life after this death. On this earth. That the still figure would turn to her and say, "Oh, I guess I'll stay around a little longer since you need me so, Crystal." She didn't want to give her over to a world that didn't need her. By watching, maybe she could give Sarah's spirit a last parting knowledge that her mere presence, in life or death, could give Crystal the persistence to do what she must, for the one who would come after them.

In a little while she noticed the nurse watching her outside the glass walls of the ICU. She'd probably been there the whole time. The monitoring machines must have alerted her that Sarah was beyond her help. She came into the room then and said, "I'm so sorry."

"Thank you for giving me this time with her. Will you tell Sheriff Youngblood? And John Half." They were both down the hall in the waiting room.

FORTY-SEVEN - Thro' the Purple Night

"I found her on the steps leading to her turret room."

"She must have heard something at my house and gone up to get a better view."

Bob let her continue, as he drove.

"That curiosity of hers. I told her a dozen times to stay off those stairs. But she was going to see what she could see. She wanted to know everything."

"You don't seem to be afflicted with the same trait."

"What do you mean by that?"

"Nothing derogatory. You just seem to be figuring it all out for yourself instead of asking what happened."

"Tell me," she said. "I can't even think any more."

"I rode with her on the way to the hospital. I didn't think she was up to answering too many questions."

So he didn't know what happened?

"But she talked. Mostly about some private things."

Oh. She could feel him trying to decide whether to say it outright, wondering whether she knew about Sarah's relationship to her.

"Doubt if anybody else knew," he said. "Might even have been secret from you."

She watched him exit I-55 for the twisting miles of two-lane to Shallot. "I haven't known long. Not long enough."

"I've got to tell you, I always thought you and she were more alike than any two turtle doves on a wire could be."

"Did everybody?"

"Don't know about that. And I won't be discussing it with anybody. But it wouldn't be anything for you to be ashamed of."

"I was happy to learn she was my mother."

He glanced at her, nodded, understanding what an understatement it must be. "Both of you had every right to be proud of the other. And proud of the old man, too."

"So she told it all." Sarah must have been totally lost, disoriented, to have talked about it.

"Not that. But she didn't need to. No way you're not Oliver Bell's blood."

"She must have lost her will-power because of pain or something. She took care to keep it secret."

"No. I think she wanted to say it. Like she knew it was her last chance."

Bob patted her arm and she uncurled her hands and covered his hand with hers. "I'm glad it was you with her. Not just because you won't tell it. You were Dad's friend. Almost like a son."

He laughed. "Yeah. But no truth to those rumors."

"I'd be glad if there was."

"But my daddy wouldn't!"

Bob and John had stayed by her side at the hospital while she made arrangements for Sarah to be taken to Shallot, and then followed Crystal to the rental agency to return the car. There would be no Sarah at home for Crystal to thank for insisting that she let the bank send her a credit card last year. Today was her first use of it. No Sarah to appreciate that irony. Her money hadn't been good enough for them. She had at long last entered the plastic age.

She felt like she had been in a time warp whizzing from one new age to another. The time of men, trouble with Horace and joy with Matt. The time of friendship with Miniver. A child's world of love reciprocated with Tommy and Tabitha. The age of acceptance with Willette. The glorious and too quick world of motherly love from Sarah. Accepting a new world that would accompany her own baby.

And now, the world she would have to face without Sarah. She hadn't been through doing things for her. Or giving her all the little things a mother deserved from her daughter. A card on Mother's Day. A corsage for Easter. Only a cup and saucer from the zoo. That was all. But hadn't Sarah loved it.

She was glad she had chosen to ride home with Bob. John had stood by Sarah's bedside, and had placed his hand upon Sarah's and had taken Crystal's hand in his other and said a silent prayer, then "I'm so sorry, Crystal." It didn't sound like a platitude, or words of comfort said by a preacher. It sounded like a feeling that came from Sarah through him to her. She'd felt herself wanting him to hug her; maybe more of Sarah's soul could pass through him to her before it all departed.

Later he said, "I'll drive you home if you'd like," and she had recognized it as his saying less than he would. He wanted to drive her home. He wanted to drive her home and sit with her, and comfort her if that was possible. But he understood without her having to reject his offer, only nodding and saying he would call.

She and Bob were almost home before Bob decided he should break in on her solitude and said, "Here's what I know. This morning, when she didn't answer the phone, I went on over there. I knew she should be up getting ready for church."

"Wouldn't miss."

"Don't many of the women in town miss, these days. Some of the Baptists even switching, I hear."

"I don't see it," Crystal would have said before today. But now she only said, "Sarah thought if he was Catholic he'd be Pope."

Bob laughed and she could tell he thought she'd be all right now. He could tell her the rest.

"They had tied Vernon up."

"He didn't know how friendly Vernon was, missed a man's company." She remembered how he'd practically licked Matt that first day.

"Maybe Vernon knew they weren't friendly. Anyway, Sarah was able to tell me she'd seen a light at your house and thought you were back early, so she was going over when she heard Vernon whining. She called him but he didn't come. She knew something was wrong, so she went up to the turret room to see what she could see."

"Those winding stairs . . .they were too steep for her!"

"You were right, I guess. She had fallen."

So if it was Horace, and she had little doubt it was, he had in effect killed Sarah. "Was she able to describe him at all?"

She felt Bob's scrutinizing, though he only glanced her way. "No. But I've been referring to 'them.' You keep saying 'him.'"

"I do?"

"Do you have an idea who it could have been?"

"I wish I knew who it was."

It was dark when she and Bob pulled into the alley behind her house. Bob unlocked the door and followed her in to look around. Along with all the other paintings, her copy of "Baby" was gone. Horace – most likely Horace – had taken the earliest painting of her. There had been no Madonnaesque painting of Willette holding her as an infant. She'd always imagined she remembered Dad and the spring day that painting was born.

The studio was cleansed of paintings, drawings, prints, folios of sketches. It was as if he had robbed her of another family member. Her entire life had now been violated by Horace.

"I'll do my best to catch whoever did this to you and Sarah."

She took her eyes from the blank walls. "I hope you do." Before I do.

"I don't like leaving you alone."

"I'm used to it." And now she really was alone.

As Bob left, he told her he'd gotten Mr. Thrasher to install a new lock on her back door to replace the broken one. He gave her the key and she remembered he hadn't asked for hers when they came in, but she hadn't even noticed it then. "You ought to have the front lock replaced, to match this one," he said. "Hard to keep up with two keys. Already supposed to have replaced it, anyway, according to Miniver."

"Uh huh," she said. "First thing."

"Yeah, I know, after the first hundred."

She lay on the couch and stared at a crack in the plaster ceiling twelve feet up. The phone rang twice, but she didn't answer. It was probably John. But no matter who it was it wouldn't change a thing.

Later, she sat at the kitchen table and made herself eat crackers and milk because she had more than just herself to worry about needing sustenance. And she checked to make sure all the doors were locked, although she thought there couldn't be much of value left in the withering old house. At nine she went to bed and Vernon trundled to Dad's room as usual. He'd be snoring soon.

Something woke her, and she could hardly believe she had been asleep. If she was asleep, maybe she woke up because she had to go to the bathroom. She stood and through her open bedroom door noticed a faint light from somewhere downstairs. She thought she had turned them all off. As she headed to the bathroom she heard a noise downstairs. It was a step on the oak floor, and then another. Then the next step was muffled by the carpet runner on the stairs.

FORTY-EIGHT - What the Curse May Be

Frozen to the floor like a dry tongue on an ice cube, it was surprising to know she could be so unresponsive to her own needs. She needed to scream! But Sarah had been the only one close enough to have a chance of hearing, even if she could manage to get one out. What she needed was to get her feet loose and run! But where? Down the hall to the back stairs to the kitchen and out the door! No. She couldn't make it that far without him hearing her.

She heard it again, now on the squeaky third step from the top. He was not even thinking, or didn't care if he woke her. Didn't everybody know to walk on the inside of old steps if you didn't want them to squeak?! It was Horace, must be. Probably thought she'd be glad to see him!

Her feet finally broke the floor's grip and she sprang across the room and grabbed the heavy silver candlestick on the dresser. The twelve-inch taper fell out and rolled across the floor, in the dark and stillness making the noise of a falling redwood.

"Crystal? Did I wake you?"

She couldn't believe it.

"It's your mother."

She was still standing there holding the empty candlestick when Willette came into the room and flicked on the light.

"I knocked. When you didn't answer I let myself in the front door with my key. I couldn't believe it still worked. Don't you ever change anything?"

Crystal stared at her. Turned out like she was going to dinner at a casual but nice restaurant. Flowing pants of light blue silk shantung, drawstring waist, and matching sleeveless top – no, her arms didn't sag – and dark blue flats. Hair in control. White button earrings and matching necklace. Make-up minimal yet effective. And wasn't it just like her to have gone to the front door.

"I assumed you must have taken a sleeping pill, so I came on up."

"What are you doing here?"

"Naturally I came when I heard about Sarah."

"How did you hear?"

"Sue Elwood called me as soon as she found out about it. A weekend down at the coast doesn't stop her finding out what happens here. She'd have been here by now if she was within a hundred miles. They're coming back tomorrow. She's a busybody as I've said, but she does what's expected."

"How did Sue find out?" Crystal hadn't even thought of calling her and Mr. Elwood. Maybe she'd have thought of it tomorrow. Maybe she'd even have thought of calling Willette. No. She wouldn't have.

"She calls her friend Lavinia every day. The black lady who works at Fred's Dollar Store. She looks after Sue's cat when they're out of town. I know more about her than I ever intended. She gets headaches when she's off her hormones. Imagine that she thought I'd be interested in that."

"Lavinia gets headaches?" Bizarre conversation to be having with Willette!

"Not Lavinia. Sue! You get more like Sarah . . . ."

Crystal smiled as Willette clamped her lips together. "You came to console me?"

"I came to pay my respects, knowing how close you two were. And so you wouldn't be alone."

"Oh."

"Any mother would do the same."

Was Willette fishing?

"I didn't want you to be alone," she repeated.

She hadn't cared about that when Dad died. She had driven down from Memphis and returned each night. But then Sarah had been next door.

"I couldn't face this house when . . . when Oliver . . . when he . . . I couldn't bear to sleep in it."

"He didn't do it here."

"That's not why."

"He was out at the lake . . . the first time he'd left here in months."

"Thoughtful of you to the end . . ."

Could Willette still be harboring that? That rivalry or jealousy or whatever lurked in what passed for a heart?

"I couldn't think of being in this house without him. All his clothes, his art . . . even his personal scent."

She had loved Dad, or whatever love was for her, hadn't she? It must have been wrenching for Willette with her possessive ways and self-centered constitution and lack of introspection, with his not being the way she wanted him to be and to feel that he loved his child, who wasn't hers, more than he did her, and maybe still loved another woman. But back to the present. Was it possible she didn't know about the rest of what happened here? The theft of the paintings? Crystal would have bet that's why she was back. But Willette would want to do the correct thing. And she would want to keep up the front. "All his things were a comfort to me," Crystal said.

"I'll go to my old bedroom. I suppose we'll need to change the sheets."

"Ida changed them after you left," Crystal said sarcastically.

"That would figure. Probably did it without even being asked," Willette said without missing a beat. "She would never change them every day as I wanted. Anyway," she added, almost smiling, "Hasn't that been almost twenty years? I still like them fresh."

Crystal followed her into the room. "This room has been dusted," Willette said, merely glancing around, although Crystal expected her to swipe a table top with a fingertip. They turned back the spread and Willette inhaled and said, "Why, these are freshly laundered sheets. Why didn't you admit you were expecting me?"

Crystal didn't answer that she had prepared the room last week for Miniver's visit, and it hadn't taken much; Miniver had left everything cleaned to a fare-the-well. Crystal had put her in this room, the nicest. Miniver had changed the sheets before she left, obviously thinking she wouldn't get back to stay another night, because these were white and Crystal had put floral ones on. Poor Miniver. She would blame herself for all that had happened. Crystal wondered how she was going to convince Miniver that it wasn't her fault. If it was anyone's, it was her own. And she dreaded the children finding out. Maybe they wouldn't understand. Yes, they would, since they'd be coming from their own grandmother's funeral. And they'd spent more time with Sarah than they had with their own grandmother.

She wanted to throw herself on the bed and kick and scream. Sarah was gone, gone forever, and Willette was worried about sheets! "How can you think of sheets?"

"I was only trying to get your mind off things for a little while. It's horrible to think of."

Maybe she was trying to help. In her own way.

"I'll see you in the morning, Crystal. We should both get to bed."

Crystal turned and left, didn't even say good night. If that had been Sarah, her mother Sarah, she would crawl in bed with her and they would curl up together until they both felt better. As she entered her room, she heard Willette call out, "I expect you'll be up first. I don't like my coffee strong."

FORTY-NINE - His Broad Clear Brow

Crystal sat carefully at the table trying to keep her first cup of coffee down.

"My God, you look ill," Willette said, coming into the room in a light pink cotton duster, three-quarter sleeves and just below the knees. She wasn't made up yet, but her hair was combed neatly and the robe color complimented her skin.

Crystal used sheer willpower to force the coffee down. She pulled the lightweight tan robe tight to ward off Willette's stares, and tried to ignore her when she said, "That was your father's. It's too big for you, not flattering at all. Makes you look heavy and nauseated."

"Who would I be trying to impress?"

"It's how you live by yourself that speaks loudest about you."

Crystal had to agree – wasn't she a living example of it this minute – but said, "What do you want for breakfast?"

"Three prunes and a bowl of bran flakes."

"I'll have to go to the store. Or maybe Sarah has . . . I'll go over there and look."

"I assumed you wouldn't have any such thing. So I brought my own. It's in a bag in the car. You can get it in a few minutes. Fortunately for you, you didn't inherit my constitution."

"Well, you don't have to look so disappointed. I was spared your looks as well."

Willette said appreciatively, "Now where did you get that cynicism? More of Sarah rubbed off on you."

"I can only hope so."

She was wondering if she could simply tell Willette she knew Sarah was her mother and stop all her fishing, but Willette would probably deny it, assured the last proof of it had gone with Sarah, when the doorbell rang, startling them both. After a moment Crystal stood slowly, carefully, but Willette said, "Good Lord! You're not going to the door like that? I'll go."

"It's probably Bob."

She recognized John Half's voice saying the kitchen was just fine when Willette said she'd get Crystal to come to the front parlor. Hearing his voice without seeing him made her cock her head toward the door. Like smooth custard spreads to fill the shell, his voice, though soft, filled the hall.

She could imagine it filling a sanctuary. Another line from Sarah's favorite hymn, to which she often alluded, and which Crystal remembered from when Willette used to take her to church, both dressed the way Willette thought they should – and that took "Sunday best" to a whole new height – came to mind: "He speaks, and the sound of His voice is so sweet the birds hush their singing."

"Crystal, your minister has come to offer his condolences." Willette's voice was a mixture of surprise and envy. "When did you start going back to church? How long have you been at First Methodist, Reverend Half?"

"Please call me John."

Crystal could tell Willette thought she had some things figured out.

"I didn't start back," said Crystal.

"I'm Sarah's minister," John said. "I'm Crystal's friend."

"I see."

He lightly touched Crystal's shoulder, then sat but didn't speak right away, almost as if he didn't want to share their grief with Willette.

But Willette didn't leave, and he finally placed his hand on hers. "Crystal, I'm so very sorry," and though they were almost the same words as at the hospital, these words were his alone, no Sarah migrating through him to her.

She barely nodded, staring at his hand, not really minding it there, and blinked several times, hoping the tears forming would dissipate before they rolled down her cheeks. She didn't know why she didn't want Willette to see her tears for Sarah, nor the depth of her grief. Maybe she knew not to show emotion to Willette, who used that, another person's vulnerability, to control a situation.

"Crystal . . . Sarah and I hit it off immediately when I began my ministry here. You know we were close."

John wasn't asking for her sympathy. He was trying to tell her something privately. She finally looked at his face. He knew. He had been Sarah's "father confessor." He was trying to ease her pain of losing her mother and being unable to let the world know. Crystal gave him a little smile. It was so good to have someone here in Willette's presence who knew and didn't hate her for it. "Thank you, John."

"Would you care for coffee, Reverend Half?" Willette said as she got a cup and saucer out of a cabinet.

For pity's sake! Her formality!

Willette brought the coffee to him and sat down. A very good excuse to get in on the conversation and learn all she could about Sarah and

John Half and Crystal. But the intimacies were over, and he became the minister of Sarah, a beloved church member who needed him for her final preparations.

After he left, Willette said she wished he'd called first so they could have been dressed presentably. "No man with that . . . that . . . presence, should be a preacher," she added. "It's a distraction."

"You mean his sex appeal? Sarah said it was a drawing card."

"So he's the man in your life. I thought it was . . . I am surprised. And just as impressed."

This would be very pleasant, bringing Willette down. Even at Crystal's own expense. "He's not in my life."

"You could never pull the wool over my eyes. And it was plainly on his face. Plain as day," she added, as if she had to hear it again to believe it.

Crystal didn't refute her again. It was true, she acceded. Sarah said so. Even Matt thought so. Crystal came close to telling Willette that she couldn't find it any harder to believe than she herself did.

But that would all change if he found out about her pregnancy. What would he think? That it was a character flaw, to say the least, that ran in Sarah's blood? But if Crystal was the daughter she never was able to claim, he was the son she was never able to have. When Sarah told Crystal about her birth circumstances, it was fresh on Sarah's mind, and now that Crystal thought about it Sarah had probably talked it over with him both as her surrogate son and as her religious counselor – would God forgive her for breaking her word, she would have wanted to know. Possibly she would have told Crystal, with his counsel and encouragement, even if she had not thought Crystal was suffering a miscarriage. She couldn't imagine this man advising Sarah against it, even though it meant breaking an oath. Blood and mothers and fathers were sacred, too. But he would never know she was carrying on the tradition. She would be gone from here before anything became obvious about her state of being.

FIFTY - Under Tower and Balcony

Taylor's Funeral Home on Main St. was in a house that had been converted many years ago when the town grew a little, and the few private homes on the square were purchased for businesses. It was the only funeral home in town. The preparatory and storage facility had been added on the back and the large yard was graveled parking area. A large awning covered the front entry at the concrete circle driveway. The floors squeaked under the carpet inside all the doorways because of the many footsteps that had passed through the portals. Death brought more visitors than life had to the moderate house.

Just about everyone in town was coming through today. The air conditioner couldn't keep up with the relentless September summer that entered the doors continually opening to the hot bodies. A line stretched outside. Crystal wasn't surprised. Everyone knew Sarah was the person who signified what the town was: its history, its tradition, its wealth, its charity, its backbone. They didn't have to have been old school friends or in her book club or garden club or church circle. They simply knew it by living in her atmosphere.

Crystal, hot in a black suit and feeling pale, was standing at the head of the casket where they came by for a last glimpse of Sarah, and then stopped to shake Crystal's hand and talk as if they conversed with her every day. All accepted that she was in lieu of family and gave her their condolences. They spoke to Willette also, with more formal yet familiar greetings and lack of surprise to see her.

Willette sat in a flame-stitched wine-on-wine wingback chair against the wall not far from Crystal. She had sent Mr. Taylor to Morris Furniture and Appliance. She had insisted on going with Crystal earlier to finalize arrangements, and had found little to her liking. "You should update some things, Charles," she told him. "Some of these chairs have seen too much use. I recognize them from before." She didn't care that the furniture store was closed for the holiday. "Alan Morris won't turn down business. And get them in wine or forest green. Either will be a complement to the beige chairs you may keep." Willette wore a navy suit, short sleeved, while confessing that she felt formal occasions like this called for long sleeves but this was the style now. In her pearls and seated in the wine colored chair she looked very regal and cool in spite of the heat.

Charles Taylor obviously remembered Willette's expectations as well as her charm. He hadn't challenged her suggestion at all, apparently only relieved that she gave permission to keep the beige chairs. And he had placed a new chair exactly where he must have known she'd want it.

Crystal remembered Willette at Dad's funeral services. Although Willette was not his widow, only his ex-wife then, she'd also received condolences, appearing composed standing by Crystal's side. She had refused to look at the casket, closed in deference to his injury, after the first time when just the two of them had stood there. "Why was it like this?" she had asked the spring bouquet lying on top of the oak box. Crystal had thought then she meant why did he choose to die that way, but it was possible she meant why did their life together turn out the way it had.

Sarah had not attended visitation, only Dad's funeral, sitting in the last row, and also remained in the background at the cemetery and at the gathering afterward at home for the meal. But she had been with Crystal almost continuously otherwise. Crystal hadn't even realized then how much Dad had actually meant to Sarah, and now she regretted that she hadn't been aware enough to give back to Sarah a little support. Crystal thought of something she could do to help make up for that, for her own peace of mind even if Sarah or Dad never knew.

FIFTY-ONE – Heavily the Low Sky Raining

Sarah was lying in state, but it was Labor Day nonetheless, and fireworks were going off all over town. Crystal and Willette sat on the front porch and caught glimpses above the trees of exploding rockets and flares and star bombs expansively bursting in the night air. It gave Willette a headache. "It's enough to wake the dead," she said. Then in as much of an apology as Crystal figured she could allow herself, added, "I forget how sensitive you are."

Earlier when they were eating supper, a casserole that someone from Sarah's church circle had brought, Willette said, "I wonder what arrangements Sarah made for all her money? She probably gave it to her church."

Crystal knew Willette was trying to find out what she knew, but she said nothing.

"No, that would be too reasonable. She probably heard butterflies migrate and left her gardens to them."

"What would be unreasonable about that?"

"This tastes just like my old chicken casserole recipe. I used to have Ida make it when I had to take a dish for bereavement. Toast the almonds first."

"I loved Ida's caramel pound cake," Crystal said, too tired to think ahead and keep from falling into a conversation as she knew Willette intended.

"That was my recipe, too! The sugar had to be browned in a seasoned iron skillet, and I didn't let her use the pan for anything else, or the sugar would stick and burn."

"Where did you learn that?"

"From my mother, who learned it from her cook."

So that's why Crystal's attempts to make the cake had failed. After a couple of efforts she'd given up.

"She probably gave it to the ACLU."

You just couldn't derail Willette where money was concerned, or where Sarah was concerned.

"I expect she did."

"No. I expect she left it to you. Is that a breeze finally? It's hot for this late at night. Seems like I remember the breezes being cooler on this porch."

"The last storm got another of the trees. That makes a difference."

"I'm sure she left the bulk of it to you."

"What makes you think that?" Yeah, just tell me the reason you think that.

"You know how eccentric she could be."

"So it would be crazy for her to leave me some money?"

"Well, just look at what's happened around here. You don't seem to have done so well with what your father left you."

Crystal was weary, about to fall into Willette's trap and get angry and tell her everything she wanted to know, and maybe betray Sarah. What would Sarah want her to do? Let Willette know Sarah had broken her promise that she had kept when it would have been easier to break it than to keep it? Or would Sarah want Crystal to come out with it at last. Get the last laugh. But Sarah wasn't cruel. Not even to Willette.

"But I didn't mean that," Willette said, daintily fluffing her skirt up over her knees. She had taken her panty hose off earlier, and Crystal stared at her legs. They were smooth and firm and well-shaped. They'd still look good in a swimsuit lineup. She wished she and Willette had some kind of something, some simpatico, maybe, if not love or even friendship. If they had it, she'd tell her, gladly, how great she looked. It would vindicate Willette's reason for living. If she told her, Willette would probably say something about Crystal's legs being too long and thin, like Dad's. Willette was considering something, and didn't even appear aware that Crystal's mouth almost dropped when she added, "No. In light of what you told me a few weeks ago . . . . I guess you've managed. Very well."

That was quite a concession. What was going on with Willette?

After a few minutes of their silence highlighting the clatter of insects on the screen, Crystal turned off the porch light and the charging bugs calmed down a little.

"But . . . Sarah might have left some sort of . . . I don't know . . . letter or something, to you . . . . You know how she disliked me. She never forgave me for taking away . . . But understandably, I couldn't have allowed her and your father's friendship to continue. After all, he was my husband. It just wasn't done in those days. I wouldn't even allow it these days."

Without the porch light, the illumination that drained through the lace curtains was the color of gray starch water, after Ida would strain it through cheesecloth to get out the lumps for the laundry. Crystal couldn't see Willette's face clearly.

"I'll caution you," Willette continued, her voice uncertain, almost halting, like it was being cut by the slow blades of the old Hunter ceiling fan, still moving in silence after decades, "she might have left lies. To try to come between us."

Crystal actually laughed. "She couldn't do that."

"I'm relieved to hear you say that, Crystal."

"Willette, we're already so far apart nothing could make a difference."

"Please don't say that . . . I tried . . ."

Willette's efforts to make their relationship appear to have been close were surprising and somehow made her feel sad. She wished she hadn't laughed. But it had apparently gone over Willette's head. "Maybe you did. Maybe I didn't try hard enough to be a good daughter. But I don't want to talk about it tonight." She stood and picked up the plates and casserole. "I need to go to bed."

"You're right. Today has been hard," Willette said, picking up the glasses and they went inside. "I feel sapped."

Crystal supposed it had been nerve-racking for her, if she really was worried about Crystal discovering the truth. "Go on up. I'll put the food in the refrigerator and wash these plates."

"I can't believe you don't have a dishwasher," Willette said. She turned away, then added, "I should help."

What had gotten into her? Was Willette at last maturing into someone who could care? Willette wasn't lazy – she worked hard on the things that meant something to her. But she seemingly had always assumed the things she didn't want to do would just get done. By somebody. And now she was offering to help wash dishes? Crystal tried to keep the surprise out of her face and voice. "It won't take me a minute."

As Willette started up the stairs, Crystal added, "But thanks," and realized it was not the rote nicety that Willette had drilled into her as a girl.

As she dropped onto her bed later and lay still without even a sheet covering her so as not to hold in her own heat, Crystal wondered what could be going on in Willette's mind, as she lay in bed in a house she had left so long ago, leaving in it a tormented husband and the young girl who thought she herself was to blame.

FIFTY-TWO - In the Lighted Palace

"Now, who is that?" Willette said in the morning as she looked over Crystal's shoulder. "God. I'll bet he has an interesting story." She smoothed the skirt of her short-sleeved linen suit, trimmed with satin at all the hems and pearl buttons at the bodice, matching her pearl necklace and earrings.

Crystal turned slowly, expecting to see Matt, from Willette's reaction. Who else in Shallot could put that sparkle in Willette's eye? She vaguely felt guilty for not calling him, but had decided it would sound like, not an excuse, certainly, to talk to him – because he cared about Sarah even after knowing her so short a time, and he would know Crystal could use his support through this – but a sign that she intended to keep their ties when she should just let it go after their decision had been made. But Mr. Elwood would no doubt mention it when he spoke to him, and he would come.

But as she turned, Willette was saying, "He looks like a model for healthy living. Working out, I think it's called."

Crystal's bones locked together as if braced for a hard blow when Horace, in a tan suit, shirt collar unbuttoned, neck so muscular a tie would choke him, approached and extended his hand. She turned away as Willette introduced herself, Mrs. Oliver Bell, as if a widow, instead of Mrs. Willette Bell, divorcee, and took his hand.

He said he was the former, with emphasis on the word, foreman at the brickyard. He was handy at a lot of things, he added, although "a new man has come into the business," and it seems "Crystal appreciates his work more."

Crystal turned to face him as he looked her up and down, and she wished she had worn another of the black suits, rather than the black sheath with brocade at the cap sleeves and hem that Willette bought for her. "I knew you wouldn't have anything suitable to wear," Willette had said when the doorbell rang at eight this morning, "so I had the girl at Madam Rose's select something for you." "Plenty of suits here," Crystal had said, but felt perspiration – she didn't even think sweat in Willette's presence – roll under her arms just thinking of the long sleeves on most of them, and wondered at Willette's gesture. Was it thoughtful or just another bossy put down? And good grief. She had it driven from Memphis to Shallot. "I followed my intuition and got a size bigger than you've been wearing."

Your old things, mostly, Crystal didn't say and confirm what Willette already knew, and didn't comment either on her perceived weight gain.

Willette scrutinized Horace but said nothing.

He didn't hold any grudges, he continued, and wanted to offer his condolences. "It's sad when the town loses a fine woman like Miz. Chancellor. Especially in an accident like that. And me planning to see if she could set me up in business, since we had so much in common."

Had he been planning on telling Sarah about what happened, his version, and blackmailing her into saving Crystal's reputation? But she remained silent. If she said anything, it would turn into everything she wanted to say.

Now Willette was wearing a look that said "What could the two of you have had in common?"

"See, we both admired Crystal so much, and wanted what was best for her." He reached out to touch Crystal's arm, but she turned away enough that even he realized he shouldn't go further. "I'm really sorry, Crystal." And that at least sounded true.

Just then, Mr. Elwood and Sue entered, Sue waving from down the center aisle. Crystal sensed by Willette's sigh that she thought it was inappropriate.

Horace said, "I can't stay for the service. Got some business to take care of."

"Don't tell me he's the man in your life," Willette said as he went out the side door. "Looks aren't everything, you know."

Just before being engulfed in Sue's hug and Mr. Elwood's handshake, Crystal managed to say, "I didn't say I had one."

Crystal was glad she set the funeral for the Methodist Church instead of Taylor's as most were these days. It would never have held them all. Sarah would have been pleased. In addition to her church being important in her life, Sarah's years, filled with fine antiques and manicured flower beds and the hush of life's finer things, seemed more suited to the polished oak pews with deep gold velvet cushions, carved chancel rail, wine-colored carpet runner, stained glass windows and neatly mown grass, instead of hodge-podge hedges and metal folding chairs for overflow from the plain oak pews, and the portable pulpit which made it convenient for Mr. Taylor to arrange for various crowds.

Sarah would also have been happy with this large attendance and the things John Half said about her, and with the long motorcade that followed to the cemetery a mile out of town. Crystal and Willette and

Sarah's two elderly distant cousins were the only ones to sit in the pew reserved for family.

Try as she would, Crystal hadn't been able to keep tears from rolling during the entire service. For the longest, she hadn't wiped at them because she didn't want to draw attention to herself. Then she'd decided Sarah would be glad that she couldn't help crying for her, and so she wiped at them.

FIFTY-THREE – They Read Her Name

As people began to get in their cars to form a cortege, Willette turned toward the side of the church, obviously thinking burial would be at the church cemetery.

"Why aren't we staying?" she asked.

"Didn't you read the morning paper? I changed my mind." She probably should have told her, but she hadn't been up to the recriminations she had known would be forthcoming. "Burial will be at the old Torrence Graveyard off Bell Road south of town."

"You mean . . . how can that be? She's not a family member!"

"I want her there, and since I'm the only one in the family, there's no problem with it." She got in the limo and turned away from Willette, who had of course gotten in, and watched out the window as they journeyed down the freshly black-topped narrow road that was overhung by a canopy of fully-leafed tree branches, beautiful enough for a bride to be traveling on to meet her groom.

There was a space on one side of Dad, and two on the other. Crystal had decided to be a little circumspect for Sarah, since she had been so all her life about her private life. Sarah would be in the outer one, then, when her own time came, she'd be planted between them, and she thought they would have been pleased with the arrangement.

"I'm not getting out," Willette said when they got there. "I can't believe you'd humiliate me this way."

"I don't intend that. I'm only honoring Sarah."

"She would have been happy at her church cemetery!"

"Get out or not."

Willette peered out the window to see where the grave was prepared. A path stood open between two rows of people from the car to the site. "Next to him!"

"Not exactly. Room for me between them."

"My God! What are people going to think?"

Crystal knew she wished she hadn't asked that question. Willette touched her cheek and said, "Randall, it's too hot in here!" The driver had already gotten out, but the motor was running and the air on.

"People know that they were best friends. They think I'm a little strange," Crystal said. Hadn't Willette even contributed to that reputation for her? "Maybe this proves it." But it sure did feel right to her.

As Randall opened the door of the limousine, Crystal caught sight of Matt's truck parked along the road with the rest of the motorcade. He was walking to the door where she was half in and half out, and Willette was saying that at least Crystal saved the correct space for her, his wife, on the other side, and Crystal was thinking with surprise that Willette intended to be buried next to the man she had distanced herself from.

Matt took over from Randall and helped her out. She managed to say, "How did you know?" He clasped her to him. "Mr. Elwood called. I'm glad I knew Sarah. I'm sorry this happened."

Randall helped Willette get out and Crystal watched her look from Matt to her and felt a brief pleasure at Willette's expression.

Crystal could sense Matt behind her as she sat in the shade under the tent, in a chair placed on green carpeting to cover the fresh dirt that had gotten scattered about, wishing to God that Sarah could just be back there with her as John said the final eulogy. She was shocked at how she saw him now, continuing God's ritual, having discarded the protection of sacred garments, which she'd never seen him in before today, yet had imagined him in after that first day at her hedges. Sarah would be pleased to know that Crystal had finally come to appreciate his . . . presentation . . . in spite of the bizarre fact that it was at Sarah's burial service, as he committed her to earth. And she couldn't help accusing herself of being on the down side of normal, forgetting what she had managed to convince herself of with Matt's help the other night. And here was Matt behind her, could touch her shoulder, and she half expected him to, and she was entertaining as worldly thoughts about John Half as any woman in town had probably ever dared. Dear Lord. Was it going to become necessary to have herself locked away, the final end most had probably predicted for her family?

At the church John had reminded them of Sarah's generosity and family background and faith, and her stewardship of worldly goods and maintenance of home and garden as if she were preserving it for generations who would come after her. He didn't say that she was the last of her family. He didn't lie before God for the benefit of anyone. Now, after the appropriate rites, he gave only a brief glimpse of the heart of Sarah: "She trusted God to help her make decisions. She assimilated the changing of her world. She didn't look back once she had done what she felt was the thing God wanted her to do. She was steadfast with her love. For these traits, I believe she already has begun receiving her rewards."

Then the Reverend did an unusual thing. He moved to stand in front of Crystal and reached to hold her hands, the leaned to her side and whispered, "You've done the right thing. She'd have chosen this."

She was aware of Matt stepping back a little so he couldn't hear, and Willette leaning toward her a little trying to hear, and a whispered crowd response which seemed to form the question: "What'd he say?"

FIFTY-FOUR – By Garden Wall and Gallery

Gradually the crowd left after breaking into several groups standing in the sparse noon shade of the large oaks, to talk and catch up on other business.

Many people who shook her hand in sympathy remembered her father kindly – anyone who had invective kindly refrained – the proximity obviously bringing him to mind, then greeted Willette politely as they had the day before.

Suddenly it was just her and Willette, with Matt and John, who shook hands as the limousine driver, who had the motor running, walked up. "No hurry," he said to Crystal, "I'm just letting it get cool inside. Can I speak to you a minute, John?"

As John walked to the car, Matt stood patiently.

Instinctively, considering her attitude toward Willette she was sure, he didn't say anything personal. She hated to give him up. Although she'd expected from the first that she would have to. But Sarah and him both? It might be more than she could bear. She might go crazy. No, she had a child to think about.

Willette was watching him like a judge at a contest. "Crystal, I don't believe I've met your friend."

"Hello, I'm Matt Hawkins. You must be Mrs. Bell," he said, as he took her extended hand.

"How did you know?" Willette asked. "Do you think Crystal favors me?"

True to form, turning the conversation to herself.

"You're exactly like the portraits your husband painted of you, Mrs. Bell."

"Oh. How kind you are."

A runway smile.

"Call me Willette. Please. Now let me think. Hawkins. Your wife bought the paintings?"

What an act!

"My father's widow," he said.

"And you knew Sarah?"

Crystal decided to end some of her speculation before it spawned a multitude. "Mrs. Hawkins bought the brickyard, Willette. Sue told you, I'm sure. Matt is my new boss."

"Oh. The man Horace Smith mentioned. And Crystal, you may call me Mother."

"Have you seen Horace?" Matt asked Crystal, his surprise and concern apparent.

"He was at the funeral home," Willette said. "I will say I don't doubt you had reason to let him go."

"He didn't cause any trouble, did he?" Matt asked Crystal.

Crystal was apparently out of the conversation as far as Willette was concerned. "No. But he reeked of overstating things. And no man should be so proud of himself."

John returned and after a moment said, "Crystal, I'm sorry to be so blunt, but Randall asked me to remind you that they won't cover the grave as long as you're here." She didn't mind his bluntness. It was better than hem-hawing around when something needed to be told. Sarah had seen this in the beginning. He nodded toward the back of the graveyard where two men were leaning against a backhoe, and said to Matt, as if he might not understand the custom there, "The family comes back later, after the grave is covered and flowers are placed. Sarah had to explain it to me when I was new here. It spares the family the finality of seeing . . ." but here he did give way, and Crystal didn't mind that either. No use in saying words that weren't going to do anything but hurt. "Anyway," he finished, "it's a good reason for them to come back later in private."

"We should be leaving, regardless," said Willette. "I'm sure people have already arrived for lunch."

John had offered the church hall, the usual choice to hold the usual meal after a funeral in Shallot but had agreed with Crystal on her decision.

Crystal knew Sarah would have been very content to have the gathering at her place. One last time for her to have it shown off. The house was already in perfect dying condition because that's the way she kept it. The yard was manicured as usual. Extra tables and chairs and tents that Willette had helped her order were set up already under the stately trees of Sarah's lawn.

Now Willette answered John, "It's too hot to stay here another minute." She touched under her eyes. "The humidity."

"All right," Crystal said, feeling like a popsicle melting into a sticky mess. She thought she might topple if she didn't find a cool place. She actually swayed enough for them to notice, and both men grabbed to steady her.

"I'll take you home," they both said.

"Randall will take us," said Willette. "And don't you two look so disappointed. A lady always returns with the man who brought her. Especially if he's in a limousine."

"Willette," Crystal said.

"Crystal doesn't understand how humor can be appropriate on such an occasion. I believe Sarah would appreciate it."

She was right, curse her.

"The church ladies will already have their best casseroles and pies set out. Everyone in Sarah's circle will try to outdo the other one, knowing I'll be there. They remember how famous I was for mine."

She headed for the limo but turned. "You two are invited to supper. Be there about seven. And no, you can't bring a thing."

"Ida cooked those casseroles," Crystal announced, a childish attempt, she realized too late, to get back at Willette for taking charge, inviting the two men to her home without consulting her. But since when had Willette consulted her about anything.

"I heard that," Willette said, but clearly not angry. A lady shouldn't have to stand over a hot stove. Didn't all gentlemen agree? And she still thought she was Crystal's mother and had some rights.

When they crossed into Crystal's yard after two o'clock, Willette sent Randall on sudden errands, important errands, she said. She made a list of the kind of gin, vodka and vermouth she wanted. She told Crystal she should have martini makings on hand for guests even if she didn't like them. Martinis, not guests, she added, and by then Crystal was getting used to her subtle and satirical sense of humor, and wondering if she'd had it all along and Crystal couldn't see it, or wasn't allowed to partake of it.

"And let's see, a good bourbon," she added to Randall as she wrote. "No. Make that Jack Daniels. Matt looks like a plain whiskey man to me. Like your father," she said to Crystal. "And white wine. Knight's Cross. John will probably appreciate that. He doesn't strike me as an abstainer." Then Randall was to buy Manzanilla olives and some fresh boiled shrimp at Seessel's, and have them packed in ice. She handed him the list. Did Crystal have Tabasco and tomato catsup? she remembered to ask. Yes, good. She'd make the sauce. What about fresh lemons? No? "Then bring two dozen, Randall. Have the produce manager pick them out."

Crystal watched him add to it the list with quick scribbles. 2 doz lem prod man. He didn't want to risk not doing it the way she wanted. He walked to the door.

"That's a lot of lemons for cocktail sauce," Crystal muttered.

"I want to make a pitcher of lemonade tomorrow. We'll sit on the porch and drink it, like Oliver and I used to do."

"I'll be going back to the cemetery."

"It won't take you all day." she added, going to the window and looking out.

So she did miss him. How could she miss someone she was so miserable with? Angry if he spent a few minutes chatting across the hedges with Sarah. Or fishing, or painting. Or playing with his daughter. Was that love? Maybe she didn't love Matt. She didn't mind that he was good to Helen or spent weekends with his daughter or went fishing with Mr. Elwood or put in the extra hours it took to do a good job. She admired him for it.

"Do you still have your homemade bread around? It would be good with the shrimp."

Good with the . . . what was going on? Willette had come close to approving something she did. "No." She hadn't been here to feed the roux and make the loaves Saturday, and neither had Miniver, of course. The starter was probably ruined. She hadn't even thought of it, sitting in its big earthenware bowl in the hall pantry.

"Buy some butter rolls at the store bakery," she called to Randall from the door. "The kind they make there. Ask the lady. She'll know."

Crystal went to the porch and saw Randall's worried look. "Cloverleaf," she said and he nodded and left in the black limo. "I thought we were having leftover casseroles," she mumbled.

"We're tired of that, aren't we, by now? You hardly ate a thimbleful at lunch. I suppose you still like shrimp."

Willette noticed her eating? She turned her back to her and started thumbing through the florist cards in the manila envelope that Randall had brought in. No telling what else Willette might notice if she got looking closely.

"Oh, don't worry about those now. We'll send thank-yous next week."

Crystal put them back on the table. "I'm going back to the cemetery to see the grave and the flowers."

"Don't do that either. You look as if you'll faint if you don't get some rest. You should take a nap. I'm going up to take one. And then have a cool bath."

She couldn't believe Willette wasn't pestering her for details about Matt. She must have resigned herself to wait until night to find out. She still believed she could manipulate any man.

"I'm going," she said to Willette's back as she climbed the stairs, hoping the Cadillac would start. Willette had been doing the driving in her BMW. Miniver must have been starting it from time to time because it fired right up.

She didn't stay long. Just long enough to see the once beautiful floral sprays in wilting piles on the grave, in spite of the lush shade that had worked its way over, and to say to Sarah, "I don't understand that woman."

When she returned home she left a note for Randall on the screendoor to put the shrimp and lemons in the refrigerator and the rolls and liquor on the counter and to keep the money left from the three hundred she'd given him. And, "Thank you so much."

She went to Sarah's, climbed the stairs, and lay on the tester bed until she heard Willette calling her from next door. That was highly unlikely, but she thought she did. When she went back through the hedges and into the kitchen, Willette was in a turquoise sleeveless two-piece dress, jewelry of turquoise stones, tan sandals embroidered with turquoise, and fresh make-up. Some wonderful rare scent wafted from her.

"Don't look at me that way. Aren't you going to change?"

Crystal looked down at the wrinkled black sheath. It was a badge.

Willette pulled a large linen cloth from a drawer and tucked it around her waist. "This is my way of getting through life, putting death away as soon as possible. Where's your tape player? I'd like some music."

"There's the radio. Unless you want to play my old Eagles albums."

"Heavens. No. Oliver's old LP's will do. Empty some ice in a bowl. Get the large etched one that Mayor and Mrs. Shelton gave Oliver and me for a wedding gift. In the butler pantry. It's big enough for ice, with the shrimp bowl in the middle."

Crystal caught herself before commenting in surprise that Willette would so specifically remember such a thing. And asking why she hadn't taken it with her.

"And fill the ice bucket for the drinks," Willette added, rinsing and slicing a couple of lemons. "Please."

Crystal waited for her to say something about the ice trays she had to empty, like why didn't she have a newer refrigerator with an icemaker, but she didn't. She only kept assembling her makings for the cocktail sauce.

Crystal went to the pantry and brought back a new bottle of Worcestershire Sauce and Tabasco. She'd stocked both since Miniver had done so much cooking before they moved out. Crystal got the glass juicer out and pushed the lemon halves down over the ridged top, catching the juice in the glass dish under it.

Willette was humming, something Crystal didn't know. Maybe it wasn't even a real tune. She seemed happy. Not exactly celebrating, but happy. "Scrape the seeds out, then dump the lemon flesh that's left into the bowl. I like the texture. Why don't you make us a salad of whatever fresh vegetables you have?"

The doorbell rang. "It's John I expect. I'd have bet he'd be first."

"Matt probably won't show up at all. There's no reason for him to."

"The bet's on," said Willette.

FIFTY-FIVE – In the Golden Galaxy

Willette won the bet. And Crystal had a pleasant evening, though she felt strange about it, like a meatball in sweet and sour sauce, riding that wave of laughter and sorrow. Not only because it was Sarah's being gone that brought it about, but that she was also almost enjoying an evening with Willette in the same room. She thought it was probably because they had Sarah to talk about. She seemed to be propelling the good times forward the way she always had. Crystal didn't tell any stories, nor did Matt. But Willette told, surprisingly to Crystal's way of thinking, a story about Sarah. They had run into each other at the rose show in Memphis, and Willette announced to Sarah that she had already made arrangements to purchase the winning entry, as the money would be going to charity, and the winning entry turned out to be Pink Chance, a new hybrid by none other than Sarah and her gardener, Mr. Thrasher. Good Grief! She wondered if it was still in the garden. It must be the one with the luscious petals that turned back like full pink lips and smelled like a rose ought to smell. She'd try to stop cursing those roses. John told gentle stories of his missteps in a community prone to the status quo and Sarah's practical way of setting him straight.

Finally, when she was beginning to wonder if Willette had both men in such thrall that they'd be unable to leave, although she had detected from both men that they realized she was tired, John said he should leave, that the next day, Wednesday, was his busiest of the week.

"Even more than Sunday?" Willette asked.

He would make hospital rounds in Memphis, he said, then at six would have the mid-week supper and prayer service, and after that a meeting of the building committee for a youth center, thanks to Sarah's earlier generosity. Then embarrassed, he said that he wasn't supposed to have made her contribution public, according to her wishes. He added that he didn't believe, however, that she'd mind Willette and Matt knowing, and he assumed Crystal already knew, and she nodded, but he said this would be a reminder for him to be more faithful to bear in mind what God's servant Sarah wanted.

"She'd be glad for me to know of it," said Willette, shrugging her shoulders, and Crystal agreed. Sarah would not mind if Willette knew of her generosity which was intended to be secret yet slipped out anyway.

"Actually, she told me," said Matt. Now he looked uneasy at the surprise all around. "She was complementing Crystal when she said it."

Now Crystal was embarrassed.

Willette said, "I'm not surprised, knowing you were to be her boss."

"It wasn't that. Anyone could see the job Crystal had been doing. Lydia certainly did."

"Pray tell, then," Willette said, almost too disinterestedly.

John then showed suppressed surprise at Willette's disinterest. Sarah had not laid blame where it was due. "If you don't mind, Crystal. That is, Matt, if you think it would be appropriate."

Willette looked at both the men. "Some habits are hard to break." Then she looked at Crystal. "I'm sorry. To have implied anything not consistent to your generous nature."

In front of witnesses. This must be costing Willette dearly. Or it could be she wouldn't let Sarah get ahead of her. "Let's just drop it," Crystal said, almost embarrassed for Willette, and beginning to realize the meaning of "a hollow victory."

But Willette wouldn't let it drop. "Oh, if I knew Sarah, and I did, it was about how she was leaving most if not all of her estate to Crystal, and how Crystal didn't want it and certainly wouldn't mind a little something being tithed to the church from it."

"At the risk of embarrassing Crystal," Matt said, and raised his glass to her, "I guess you did know Sarah. And we all know Crystal."

"To Crystal," John said, and "to Sarah." After sipping, he put his wineglass on a silver coaster and stood, adding that he didn't want to break up the party, but that he should be going. "Not that it was a party, of course."

"Crystal, walk the good preacher to the door before he's as embarrassed as you," said Willette. "Anyway, Matt and I want to be alone."

Against her better judgment, Crystal did. She didn't want Willette to be alone with Matt, but she didn't want to be alone with him, either. There was no chance John would be allowed by Willette to walk himself to the door.

At the front door John said, "Come out with me a minute," indicating that they sit on the step, and reached for her hand. "I don't think of you as one of my flock. Of course, you're not. Even if you were, I wouldn't think of you in that way."

She thought of saying good night and going inside, leaving him with his words that were going to mutate into intimate confessions.

"I'm not ashamed to be a man of God. Not with Horace the day of the accident, not at the casino with Matt. I'm sure you realize why I didn't tell them."

She had to accept Matt's and Sarah's view. He had only wanted to be known as a man interested in a woman. "Sarah had her suspicions," she said.

"She knew," he said, squeezing her hand. "I'd like to pray for you, if you'll let me. But not as a minister."

"Do. Sarah may be the only other person who has ever prayed for me." She didn't know if he wanted her to bow her head and close her eyes or not, but she watched him. He looked up at the glittering stars and the big piece of moon, now the pale blue color of blood coursing through veins, and started talking as if God were his best friend, in addition to being his heavenly Father, like Sarah had been her best friend, and then her mother, and as if he knew God would do anything for him, just as she knew about Sarah.

"God," he said, "I'd like to talk to you about Crystal. I don't think she'd ask for divine intervention for herself. I'm praying that you'll look after her. Give her the strength to realize that she is a person, full unto herself. Give her the awareness that her life is precious to so many for her friendship and her charity, and going beyond her duty to her town without ever asking what it costs her."

She couldn't say she was surprised by his faith. No wonder Sarah had thought he hung that moon up there. But she was astonished to hear what he believed about her, and she felt humbled to be presented so grandly to God.

Then he brought her hand to his face. "Is it all right if I open my heart to God, also, though it concerns you?" She nodded before she had time to give it rational thought, so she guessed she didn't want to think rationally, and he continued talking to his God and friend. "Father, you know I'm not so unselfish. I'm at the center of too many of my own prayers. I don't know the full extent of Crystal and Matt's relationship. I think it was strong, and it might still be. But if I can trust the insight you've given me, a crossroad has been reached between them. A decision made that will lead them in separate ways. I believe they both have their reasons. Heal their hearts. You know I'm in love with Crystal." He turned to her and said, "I love you, Crystal." He kissed her hand then put it back against his cheek, and turned back to God. "I want to make Crystal happy, and I pray that's in Your plan. If it is, give her something to determine that by, because I can't."

She didn't know if it was his words or God's work, but she felt an opening in her heart for something, even if it was only for understanding that she had someone who would be willing to shoulder some of her emptiness if she would let him. He squeezed her hand and left, and she remembered seeing him in a new light this afternoon as she felt this awakening now.

When she returned inside, Willette said, patting Matt's hand flirtatiously, "Not that we minded too much, but you were gone so long we thought you'd eloped."

Matt said he should leave and as Crystal hesitated just one split second about getting up, Willette said, "Don't wait up, Crystal," and laughing like she must have when she had gotten her way after all, all those years ago, started leading him to the door.

"Crystal . . . ," Matt said, hesitating.

"I'm glad you came," she said. That wasn't enough. What if he hadn't been the one to come for the painting and they'd never met? "I'm glad you came," she said again, holding her hand out to him, putting them back to the day when she didn't, when he had introduced himself to her. He took it with his left hand and covered it with his right, and she remembered the night in the kitchen when their hands had fallen in love. There was no need to say more.

FIFTY-SIX - Settlings

B y week's end, Crystal wondered how long Willette thought she need stay to be considered "proper." If it was much longer, Crystal was going to turn the house over to her and go to Sarah's.

She wished Matt and Mr. Elwood hadn't been so accommodating, insisting she take some time off. There was already one new "girl" at the office, as Mr. Elwood said, Miss Annie Crull, seventy-five if a day, who wanted to supplement her teacher's retirement income with a part time job, which she happily revealed paid more than the pension. Miss Crull had taught senior English, and she made much ado about her trip to Stratford-on-Avon and London one summer. Crystal had enjoyed studying the Shakespearean families even more treacherous and dysfunctional than her own.

The new foreman, a company man sent from Memphis, was also working out well, though not as personable with the customers as Horace had been, Mr. Elwood confided.

It wasn't that Crystal's time with Willette was going as she figured it would, a truce with skirmishes that made her want to turn the house over to her; on the contrary, it was merely the unpredictability of what Willette would say next. For example, she hadn't railed about the monetary loss of the paintings other than when she first found out that insurance would only pay the standard few thousand, because there wasn't a separate theft rider on them. Crystal had thought she couldn't afford such a big premium on something unnecessary in a place like Shallot. She now wondered how she could have been so foolish. She had extra coverage for fire – a big old house with outdated wiring – she wasn't that stupid.

But in fact, Willette said how lucky they'd been that the paintings were only stolen and not destroyed, as they would have been in a fire. Even though they'd have received more compensation than they would now, there was still some chance they could be recovered. Then Willette cursed the thief to eternal damnation, not solely because of the loss of the art, which she predicted would be sent to a foreign country and sold for a fraction of its worth, but also because of Oliver's being robbed of his new chance to be placed in the art world where he deserved. She also threw in her belief that the thief had killed Sarah as surely as if he'd heaved her over the stairs. She also speculated that it was possible they'd be contacted to buy back the paintings, that they were "kidnapped for ransom."

Crystal chose not to tell her that she'd probably met the thief at the funeral home. The more she thought about it, the more certain she was that Horace had done it. She didn't think he knew anything about art, but he would have heard. According to Sue, "They were in that big old house just waiting for someone to realize they were theirs for the taking, now that the news was out about how valuable they were. Everybody knew there's a black market for art. Asia mostly, and Columbian drug dealers."

Did everybody know that but Crystal? And she'd written Sue's opinions off, like she'd done Mr. Elwood's concern when he brought the fish to her on the day Matt exchanged the paintings, and then Miniver's dire forecasts. How determined she'd been that her little world was behind its own protective hedges left there for her by Dad and his father and his father.

And back to Willette, rather than beating her own self up, there was also Willette's reaction to Miniver and the kids when they returned, two days after the funeral, driving up in Sarah's new Mercedes. The kids flew out and Vernon shrieked like a hound dog treeing a possum. Miniver's head hung worse than it had when Thomas had beaten her.

"You must be Sarah's maid," Willette said from her chair on the porch, jumping to conclusions the way only she could do, as Crystal ran down the steps to meet them.

"You must be Willette," said Miniver from the yard, some of her feisty self making a resurgence.

"You can call me Mrs. Bell."

"Yes, Your Highness," Crystal heard Miniver mutter.

"I assume that, as Sarah apparently loaned you her car. I wondered why you didn't go over and get it to drive, Crystal."

Crystal decided to let Miniver and Willette have at each other for a minute, and get it out of their systems. It was bound to happen.

"You know what they say about assume. It makes an –" said Miniver.

. . . Ass out of "u" and me! Crystal finished soundlessly. "Wait!" Crystal said, losing nerve. "Miniver is not Sarah's maid."

"Oh. She cleans for *you*, then. I thought this place had had some attention lately." Then switching again to Miniver, "I'll take up some things with you about the proper way to do things."

Miniver had been subdued. Met her match. Maybe she was thrown off because of what had happened to Sarah.

"No," said, Crystal, but Willette ignored her.

"First, do you usually bring your children to work with you? My Barbara would never do that. And it's almost ten o'clock. The day's half gone. Whatever your work, you should be professional about it."

"Now there's something we agree on," Miniver said, reviving, but by then Crystal knew she had to set things clear. "Willette, this is my friend Miniver. She was looking after Sarah –" Crystal stopped, realizing she was fanning the flames for Willette and rubbing salt in Miniver's wounds.

"With friends like that," said Willette, and Miniver sat down on the bottom step and put her head in her hands. Crystal could see Willette putting together why she thought Miniver had the car. "Not even considering your imposition, borrowing her car to go away in, you should have never left Sarah alone." Then she looked toward the kids sprawling in the grass with Vernon.

"Oh, Jesus, why did I leave? Why did I think I had to?"

Crystal sat by her and put her arm around her. "She wanted you to," she said.

"Sarah was very trusting," said Willette. "Sometimes one simply cannot afford that."

Crystal debated seconding that. Sarah had trusted Willette, and had been repaid with thorns for roses. But she didn't say it. Now still wasn't the time. Miniver didn't deserve to have to hear all that would be said and share in all that would have to be endured.

"Nothing other than a death in the family would have absolved you from your duty," Willette said almost in afterthought.

"Exactly," said Crystal to Willette.

"Oh," said Willette, taken aback, "then you did what you must." Then she went inside.

Crystal and Miniver stayed outside in the porch swing and watched the kids play with Vernon. Finally Miniver said, "I guess it was something that was meant to be, with it all happening that way. But mainly, if that woman in there thought I was to blame, I know Sarah isn't blaming me, and you're not either. Y'all and her are about as far apart as anybody could be."

Eventually they went in to make lunch. Willette was pouring something from a mixing bowl into ice cube trays. "This is one of my specialties. It's lemon sherbet. I thought the children might like it. This kitchen is sweltering with the oak tree gone. No shade from the afternoon sun now. You should put up an awning, Crystal."

She turned her back to them to put the trays into the freezer and they looked at each other, Miniver with a "what's this" look, and Crystal with an astonished shrug.

In the afternoon while Willette napped and they were on the way to the cemetery, Miniver said she'd known immediately who Willette was by how she was dressed, and how she looked sitting in the high-backed rattan lounge chair before she ever spoke a word. "She's just the woman who could have picked out all them – those – clothes and barely got the new off. She turned that front porch chair into a throne. No shit, Crystal, she's real classy. But she be cold. I mean," and she imitated Willette's refined drawl as she corrected herself, "may I call her a real iceberg?"

After they laughed, Crystal feeling a bit disloyal, Miniver said, "But maybe Willette isn't so bad."

Crystal wasn't ready to hear that, because Miniver was intuitive, as Sarah had said.

"Anyway, she's your mother; well, she was your mother once, and I'm going to respect her."

Miniver knew.

"Girl, don't look so surprised. It was obvious after I got to know you both. You and Sarah. I haven't even come close figuring out how it happened, but I don't know how the whole town didn't recognize it. Maybe I just had the perspective of a newcomer. Or maybe it's something so hard to imagine."

"If I had only known, all those years."

"Things happen for a reason." She laughed. "You've heard that I expect." She turned around and said, "Tommy, put that window up. Vernon's liable to lose his tongue the way he's hanging out."

Crystal smiled, thinking of the irony. Vernon, Dad's dog, riding in Sarah's car, to where Dad and Sarah were now, next to each other for longer than they'd ever been before.

"As I said, I never figured out the whys and wherefores," Miniver said, turning back to the front, "but I think I know when you found out."

Crystal turned onto the treed lane and stared ahead into the shadows.

"This is a beautiful place," Miniver said as the cemetery appeared in view. "It was when you thought you lost your own baby, wasn't it?"

"Uh huh. I'll tell you all about it someday."

"I'll nag it out of you if you wait too long. Oh, I'm going to watch my language, too. I reverted some, being away from you two and the college scene. Oh Lordy, I hope I'm not too far behind in my classes. I feel guilty even thinking of that now."

"Sarah would want you to think of school."

"How times change," Willette said after Miniver and the children left in the evening in her old white truck, replacing its parking space with the Mercedes in Sarah's garage. "When Sarah attended school there, a person like Miniver couldn't have gone. And now, Sarah has paid her way."

"Sarah changed with the times, if they were for the better."

"I can't help preferring most things as I remember them. Though not such as what we're discussing now, I suppose. People deserve their chances."

Crystal felt a faint bit of admiration for Willette's having gotten to that point.

A couple of evenings later they sat inside reading the newspaper, because a large hole had appeared in the screen of the porch and mosquitoes came in like they were invited. Willette deduced that one of the children had gouged a hole in the screen. She said you couldn't trust children; perhaps they didn't really mean to be destructive, but their curiosity or energy would tell on them every time. A probing stick would go through the screen like a fork through meringue.

Crystal told her the screen was fifteen years old and that a good-sized wasp could fly right through it without meaning to. She said she would cut a piece from a roll in the basement and patch it tomorrow.

"I'm going home tomorrow. I have appointments for all kinds of things."

"I didn't expect you to stay this long. I mean . . . I understand that you don't like to come here. It must have been a sacrifice."

"Crystal, sometimes it doesn't hurt to simply go through the rituals. You don't have to be brutally honest at all costs. For myself, if honesty hurts me, I'd rather not hear it. And I get more that way as the years go by."

Was Willette telling her that she suspected Crystal knew Sarah was her mother, and that she would be hurt, not just angry, if Crystal told her she knew the truth?

Suddenly Crystal felt it wasn't all that important. She didn't want to call Willette 'Mother' again, though. "Thank you for coming to be with me."

The next morning after breakfast they sat in the living room and Willette alternately read the paper and fanned herself with it. Suddenly she said, "You should sue this imposter of a newspaper! It says that although the paintings were taken, they left other valuable works of art, without naming them, thank goodness, and much in value next door in antiques and art and silver and other collectibles that were in the family for generations. Of all the irresponsible things to print! This is only inviting the thieves to return. You should have a security system installed immediately."

"I should have one installed next door," she said to placate her. It probably should be done, at that.

"Have one put in here, too. You've lived too . . . casually here all these years. This house is full of nice things. Family collections."

"I don't think I could live that way, all cloistered up –"

Willette laughed.

"Stepped into that, didn't I?" said Crystal, laughing too.

"It's time you thought of your own safety."

That was the most endearing thing she could remember Willette ever saying to her. She should have started a chart and made checkmarks for all the surprises Willette had given her lately. "Maybe I'll do it."

Willette turned to the stairwell. "You know, that wall does look lonesome without 'Baby.' I wonder if the thief knew he stole a mere copy?"

They shared a laugh at the bitter irony, and it was one of the few times – before this morning – that Crystal could think of when they'd found the same thing funny. If Willette didn't get out of here soon, they might end up appreciating one another.

FIFTY-SEVEN – Half-Sick of Shadows

As he had every day since the funeral, John dropped by. Today it was late evening. He was easy to be with. In spite of her new vision of him at Sarah's funeral she didn't stammer or trip over herself when he came around. When he talked she didn't watch his lips with desire. So now, and it was a huge step for her, he was a comfortable friend, only without Sarah and Miniver's irreverence. He was a preacher, for Chrissakes, she could imagine Miniver saying. She hoped she wasn't leaning on him too much because she didn't have either of her friends here when she needed them. And even Willette gone back to Memphis.

He'd kissed her cheek upon arriving and leaving after their porch interlude the night of Sarah's funeral. She wondered if she was leading him on by accepting those gestures of comfort and affection, even as she found herself expecting them. She let herself off by reflecting that as a minister he comforted people. And too, she hadn't found herself dwelling on his image, or she might as well admit it, his sex appeal. Which she thought now he wasn't even aware of. Maybe that outward appearance was the charm at first. Like the sleek lines of a sports car. But without a performance motor and satisfying interior it was only a lemon. She was beginning to understand. God was his cause and to him Jesus Christ was the draw. He was only the messenger.

Some days he wore a suit, the coat and tie left in his car; some days he wore casual pants and Polo shirt, slightly moistened with his sweat, as if he'd recently finished the golf course at a good country club, and perhaps he had. A couple of his members belonged to clubs in Memphis. Perhaps he had his own membership. She knew nothing of his background. Sarah hadn't found it necessary to tell her; or she hadn't let Sarah tell her. Today he wore brown dress slacks and a white button-down shirt, long-sleeved but rolled up, a yellow tie, and brown penny loafers. It was Wednesday. He'd made hospital rounds, she remembered, before going to church.

As he left this night, he drew her to him, as usual not too intimately, but hesitated for a second, and watched her. It dawned on her what he wanted. Instead of offering her cheek, she lifted her face to him. She felt she didn't want to disappoint him. His lips were soft and warm, and his face was full and smooth-shaven. She missed the thin firmness and heat and hair of Matt's face. He didn't kiss her long, or longingly, almost as if he didn't want to ask more or give more than she was ready for.

That night as she fell asleep, she felt lonelier than before. Maybe it was the kiss, inciting yearnings that had kept themselves in check the last week and a half, unwilling to overcome the fullness that was the absence of Sarah. Maybe it was some new fear of what she didn't want to accept – that she'd never be with anyone again as she had Matt. And now, a chance was rearing itself to her over the most improbable of odds, notwithstanding what Sarah had told her months ago.

But tonight she was filled with physical, bone chilling, empty longing for what she had done without for so long and then so unexpectedly received. She wanted to feel body heat next to her, fingertips against her skin. Her breasts felt as if they would burst like overblown balloons. She finally slept and later woke, almost certain someone was in bed with her, but it was her own hands on her tender breasts. In a dream her body began to fly apart but strong arms surrounded and held it together.

The next morning, she had to concentrate on what to do with her financial responsibilities. She'd had no idea of the scope of Sarah's wealth until she conferred with Ash Cooper. It seemed money, whether she didn't have it or did, was always going to be a problem. On the pleasant side were a few items. Bequests of two thousand dollars to each of her cousins. And trust funds for Miniver and for Tommy's and Tabitha's education. She had a big laugh when she saw stock in the casino they visited when Mr. Cooper showed her a monthly summary. He said Sarah had agreed because he'd convinced her that many unemployed and uneducated would find jobs there, even if low-paying.

A little unsettling was learning that she and Willette had lived primarily on dividends from a mutual fund that Sarah had set up as though it were from T. Oliver. Like Crystal, Sarah had not wanted Dad to appear financially incompetent to Willette. And she hadn't wanted anyone Dad loved to be in need. She must not have realized what a big spender Willette was. And that Dad's resources could never have provided for all her requests. But if it had been more, would Crystal have gotten herself out to work and done what she had? She remembered Sarah saying more than once that it was good Crystal was out working, mingling with people, rather than staying home, turning into a 'cave hermit' like her father had been.

A few days later she came up with an idea she wanted to discuss with Mr. Cooper. She called him and made an appointment.

She went back in the garden eventually, gathering the last of the ripe tomatoes and peppers. She remembered Ida frying the tomatoes that wouldn't ripen late in the season, and began to crave them. So she made fried green tomatoes every day for a week, slipping thick slices in an egg beaten with milk, and dredging them in salt and pepper-seasoned flour. She laid them in hot oil in a well-seasoned black iron skillet, carefully turning them only once to brown both sides without losing the crispy coating. She knew the craving was not only because of her pregnancy, but also a delicate treat she was trying to substitute for things lacking in her life.

She'd neglected the garden for so long that it stopped producing, so she hired Mr. Thrasher to clean it up. She wished she had been up to that task for the mental therapy it would have provided.

Matt didn't show up at work, but things were going smoothly so he wasn't needed. She had dreaded the possibility of seeing him and at the same time hoped to, so she was exhausted by the end of each day. She dropped to sleep on the couch and went up to bed hungry after eating only leftovers from the freezer or canned soup. She turned down John's invitations for dinner.

She planned to resign soon. Sooner than later. The month's end would be good, and only a few days short of two weeks' notice. She notified the home office. She could probably please Lydia by quitting tomorrow; and it would also be easier on Matt, wouldn't it, so he wouldn't be reminded that they had gotten together in spite of his misgivings. The town gossips would say, regardless, that it proved she had had no money before, and now that she was rolling in money, she was too good to work. She hoped that was all they would notice to say.

By Saturday morning after sleeping poorly and for two instead of one, therefore feeling the sleep she had was cut in half, she wished she had already resigned. While she was in the kitchen deciding whether to make bread in spite of her tiredness because Miniver and the kids were coming, or throw out the starter, which had somehow survived, leaving her to wonder if Willette had possibly scooped some out and made the additions to it, or if she should buy bread like everybody else did, John arrived. After taking the coffee cup she handed him, he placed it on the counter and pulled out a chair for her. He pulled one out for himself and sat facing her, then reached for her hands and said, "Will you marry me?"

FIFTY-EIGHT - Bells Rung Merrily

Miniver lay across the foot of the bed doing half-sit-ups under the guise of getting herself in shape. "Bob's gonna get me in bed one of these days," she grunted, "and my stomach's gonna be flat."

"Do you mean to tell me . . . I guess I'm such a moral slacker I expect everybody else to be!"

"I'm going slow. I have two kids. Half and half. You know what Bob thinks about that."

"You know Bob better than that by now."

"Yeah. But I'm still married. You're not."

"Not yet."

"Crystal! So Matt popped the question?"

"It's not Matt." She plumped her pillow and said, "I'm marrying John Half."

"Girl, you know people used to set their watches by you? You gettin' real unpredictable lately."

"He wants to make me happy."

"That's real admirable of him."

"I told him about the baby."

"Now *that's* admirable."

"I guess he's accustomed to all kinds of confessionals."

"Still, news like that from the woman he wants to marry. And him meeting Matt. Didn't he think you and Matt should marry?"

"No."

"Is he that sotten with you? Or is he just that good?"

"It's not Matt's."

"You mean . . . not Matt? As in the father?"

She'd had to tell John it wasn't Matt. She'd owed it to him, and to what he might think of Matt. "So now," she had said after telling him. "Still want to marry me? Don't you think I'm a slut? Carrying on with one man while pregnant with another's baby? And entertaining a third."

She had to admit *that* had startled him a little. Just surprise. In fact, that's what he'd said – "It's surprising. That's all. And it's sudden. I think I'm even relieved to know it isn't Matt's." "Because you think good of him," she'd said. "That, too," he'd answered. He didn't ask who, like

Miniver would now. And she didn't blame her. She had a right to know, after what she'd been through on her behalf.

"No. Not Matt," she answered Miniver.

"Then I know what happened. God, Crystal. You were raped. Weren't you?"

Miniver had faith in her. "There's some dissension on it."

"That's bullshit! You were or you weren't. And you were. But who in the – Horace! God! It's making sense now!"

"I'm so sorry you had to go through what you did because of me, Miniver."

"I only wish I'd known then! Bob would have that boy under the jail."

"It was my fault. He said I'd been showing I wanted him since he got here. I led him on that morning. When I realized I was making a mistake, it was just too late."

"Uh uh. That's his version. It ain't never too late. Unless he was drunk out of his mind. And you're married to him."

Crystal couldn't help reaching to hug her.

"But I know Horace don't drink."

"No, he wasn't drinking. But I was . . . drunk. On something. Want. Wanting to be wanted. I don't know."

"Still, a real man knows better," Miniver said, shaking her head. "You didn't tell John about this. Nor who it was."

"I couldn't."

"Didn't that tell you something about marrying him? If you couldn't confide it all to him? Especially him a minister?"

"I didn't want to put him in a position of thinking he would have to do something about Horace. I think. And it was so sudden, springing that on him. I believe he thought I uncharacteristically had a fling, a one-night stand. He said I'd know when the time came to tell him."

"You haven't had time to give this marriage much thought. I'm presuming it'll be soon?"

"My last day at work will be Friday. The wedding will be Saturday. A week from today."

"The sooner the better. More time to repent in leisure."

"I'm going to Memphis tomorrow afternoon to buy a dress."

"Uh huh. I see you now. Having the church ladies in for cake and coffee. Warmin' the front pew every Sunday."

"Sounds admirable to me."

"Girl . . ."

"But it won't be that way. He's requesting a year's sabbatical. He wants to research and write. He said he'd felt for a while that's what he was being led to do."

Miniver pretended she was going to throw a pillow at her.

"So, are you going shopping with me or not? Are you going to be my best woman or what?"

"Yeah, Girl, I've got to stand with you. I'll let Bob watch the kids tomorrow. Let the man see what *he's* up against."

FIFTY-NINE - Exegesis

She was standing on a small platform in front of the three-way full-length mirror in the dressing room of M. Rose's, *the* place to shop if you had the money, looking at herself in a calf-length, fitted, cream lace dress with long sleeves and high neckline with a diamond cutout over the bodice. Miniver had talked her into trying it on. "Get that preacher man all rattled," she said. She admitted she did look very curvy, and Miniver and the sales assistant, Ms. Winters, nodded satisfactorily to each other.

But then Evelyn Mae made it her business to look after Crystal.

"Do you mean to tell me *she's* M. Rose?" Miniver had whispered shortly after they'd arrived, when Evelyn Mae had gone to the back. "That short, fat, black lady looks like my grandma? She's the one has all the society women of Memphis dressin' down to their ankles or up to their ass?"

"That's her. She, that is," Crystal whispered back. "Some might not know. They just buy the clothes. I'm sure Willette does. She'd make it her business to know the owner."

"I believe that."

"I guess she can tell I need her help. Years ago, until she started ordering most of her clothes, and most of them from here, I used to come in here with Sarah."

Evelyn Mae – M. Rose – returned then with accessories, and said, "Did I hear you mention Sarah? Do you by chance mean Sarah Chancellor?"

"No chance about it," Miniver said.

"I expect you remember her from years ago. I'm her daughter," she added, even though there was a chance M. Rose might know Sarah had never been married.

"Why, I thought I should know you. You're Crystal. You still have your daddy's smile," she added, slipping her arm around Crystal's waist and squeezing.

Crystal and Miniver exchanged looks. "Who else knows who you were but you?" Miniver said.

"You knew?" Crystal said to M. Rose.

"Lord, Child. I knew it all along. I was fifteen, pregnant like her, and didn't have no man comin' to look me up like she did! I was her Aunt Bessemer's maid when she was taking refuge with her. The house was razed years ago when the state thought they'd run that highway right down her street. She helped put a stop to that, you know. Sarah didn't believe in lost causes. Vouched for me when I got my first salesgirl job at the old Lowenstein's downtown."

"Don't surprise me none," Miniver said. "I mean, it doesn't surprise me at all."

"Evelyn Mae, this is Miniver Tandy. My best friend since Sarah became my mother instead of my best friend."

"Who do you think funded me for this shop? Sarah. My best friend. Do you think some bank would lend money to a thirty-year-old black girl? They wouldn't even call me 'woman' back then."

Miniver was trying to picture it.

"Young women like you can't feature how it was," she said to Miniver.

"I can't even make it on my own today, without all that to bring me down."

"Miniver's going to college," Crystal said. "She'll be fine. She would anyway."

"Crystal, I'm so sorry about Sarah. I miss her, too. I was at the shows when it happened. I only found out about it a few days ago. Willette came in and told me."

"That surprises me."

"Well, she bought while she was here. I don't know which was the cover-up."

Two weeks ago Crystal would have known but now she wasn't sure at all.

Evelyn Mae shook her head. "I intended to call you soon. But I didn't know how much I could talk to you about, so I was putting it off. Sarah had told me she was going to leave a letter to be opened by you upon Willette's death, if it didn't come out sooner."

"I had wished it a thousand times. But we did have a few weeks to share it."

Evelyn Mae contemplated again. "Willette . . . poor thing. She's one of those people who never know to appreciate what they have until they've lost it. Not that we discussed any of this. She discusses her maid Barbara with *me*. But I saw a difference in her the other day."

"I wasn't sure she knew I found out . . ." She sat down on a pretty little chair with a nineteenth century scene embroidered on it.

"Girl, don't you go feeling guilty over Willette," said Miniver, turning Crystal to face the mirror and holding a dress for her to see.

Crystal stood and studied herself in the mirror again. Willette would say the dress was too much. Not too much money, but too much. Too elaborate.

Evelyn Mae said after a minute of turning Crystal around and looking her over, "You won't feel comfortable in this. Less is more, for some women."

Miniver looked skeptical. "She's been wearing Willette's hand-me-downs."

"She could have done worse," said Evelyn Mae, and then called for Ms. Winters. "Get her the Devore ivory silk suit. Size ten." She turned Crystal to the dressing room. "go put it on and we'll have a look."

"Oh, that's the one," Miniver said, touching the rolled satin collar, which plunged diagonally to cover the bodice and fasten at the side waist with a large pearl and crushed-diamond button. The skirt flared slightly at the hem, after curving around the thighs. "Both her mothers would feel good about this one."

Crystal hadn't told Willette she was getting married. That nagged at her, although it was going to be a private ceremony. Yes, she decided as she turned round in front of the mirror, she would get this. She looked at the tag. Good grief. She could get the house painted for this!

Miniver read her mind. "Knowing you, you'll only do this one time. Sarah would want you to do it right."

"Yes. I'll take it," she said, moving the side mirror to look at the back.

Evelyn Mae Rose said. "This is my gift for Sarah." She held up her hand to shush Crystal's protest.

SIXTY - Young Lovers, Lately Wed

Monday morning she was writing job specs for the position of manager to forward to the home office for their interviews. With Miss Annie on an errand to the bank, Mr. Elwood looked over Crystal's shoulder. "Man!" he said, laughing, "I didn't know I was responsible for all that!" He patted her shoulder. "You were underpaid."

She laughed, too, and said, "Oh, the two of us made a good one. Sorry you won't get to retire as soon as you planned. Thanks for agreeing to stay until they can get someone. I hope Sue understands."

"What Sue doesn't understand is why she's not getting invited to your wedding," he said as the door opened and Matt entered.

"Why, good morning, Matt," Mr. Elwood said. "We weren't expecting you. Didn't hear your truck. Air conditioner running so hard, I guess. Did you hear about Crystal getting married?"

"No. I didn't hear." He turned to Mr. Elwood's desk, took off his coat and placed it over the back of the chair. Then he began to remove it.

"It's all right hanging there," Mr. Elwood said.

"You're married?" he asked Crystal, turning back, precisely arranging the coat on the chair.

"Next Saturday," Mr.Elwood said, not waiting for Crystal. "Funny, I somehow thought – well never mind. Person sees what he wants to. Anyway, that preacher must have had Someone up above put in a good word to Crystal. Course, he's a good fellow they say. I'm Baptist. Haven't heard him preach. But he draws 'em in."

Crystal and Matt were quiet as Mr. Elwood searched for something else to say. Suddenly he said, "I bet you two would like some coffee."

"Thanks," said Matt.

"Be a few minutes. I'm going to make a fresh pot," he said, and went into the lunchroom.

"So. That's how it is," Matt said as the door closed behind Mr. Elwood.

"No. Well, not really. What I mean is, only very recently. Since Sarah. . ."

"Hell. I'm sorry. I made it sound like you did me wrong."

She rubbed her forehead then spread her fingers on her desk and stared at them, bare of an engagement ring. She had told John she wanted only a gold band.

He moved a chair close to sit, and covered her hand with his like the first time they'd touched. "You woke me up from something. It was like cold water thrown in my face. But you looked like you had just wakened, too." He said it like it was one of those favorite stories that never gets old to the person remembering it.

"More like I needed a cold shower?"

"I hoped that was it. It seems so long ago."

"I was ready for you. Only you." She saw it like yesterday.

"If that's true, I hate to think of you not wanting to be with whoever you're with."

"He's . . . like you. In ways." She put her other hand on his.

"Crystal . . . I'm sorry."

"You told me you were married. Showed me how conscientious you are."

"Obviously I'm not. I'm glad we were together. And selfish enough to say if you change your mind . . ."

She interrupted him before he could finish. "You were right about all those things you believed at first. How fragile I was." She shook her head from side to side. "Did I say that? Sounds so Tennessee Williams."

He kissed her cheek. "You're not like anybody else. But neither is anybody else."

"You turned me down that first time I wanted you. When you brought the painting back. I used my vulnerability to make you go against your better judgment."

"Hell. That's nonsense. I made the first move."

"You're a good man, like Sarah said."

"Are you saying I'm *too* good?"

She smiled.

"How does Preacher rank on the goodness scale?"

"Close. Think he should be warned about me?"

"I think not," he said. "He has God on his side."

"I'm not so sure, if he wants me."

She couldn't fathom how far she had come since that night in the kitchen. "I continued hell-bent, knowing we had no future," she said, "but don't be sorry. I'm not. What we had, it was too overwhelming. I don't know, too much of what we both needed, for us not to accept it while we could. I'm just now beginning to understand some of it"

He put his other hand on hers and they were stacked like loose bricks that didn't match.

The door squeaked, Mr. Elwood pushing it open with his backside, coffee mugs uplifted. The stack of hands collapsed as they jerked them to chair arms.

SIXTY-ONE - His Armor Rung

Friday, while Miss Annie and Mr. Elwood were at lunch, Lydia Hawkins called to say that she had selected a replacement for Crystal, someone Crystal was familiar with and who was already familiar with the brickyard, as he was a former foreman. Crystal held the phone away from her face and stared into it as if she could see Lydia in the receiver. Curtis Crull, Miss Annie's brother, had been the foreman for twenty-five years until he retired and Horace was hired, and he'd had a stroke since and was bedridden. That left only one. "You don't mean Horace? He was fired."

"Yes. Because of you."

"You haven't checked with Matt."

"He's with his wife and daughter in London."

Crystal heard something in Lydia's voice. It was either resentment or satisfaction. Maybe both. Resentment that she wasn't going to end up with him and satisfaction that Crystal wasn't either. "Yes, I know." Matt had called her the day after their conversation. He had agreed to go along with Helen on one of her tours, providing Hallie could be excused from school to go with them. That obviously had been arranged.

"Oh. So you're going to remain friends."

She didn't answer Lydia's sarcastic remark. She didn't want to not know what he was doing in his life, and had told him so. He'd said couldn't they be friends. And she'd said yes, but they both knew the answer was no. Life with other partners was going to keep them apart. But it wouldn't change how they had once brought each other back to life.

"One thing I won't miss when you're gone is your silence on the phone, Miss Bell," said Lydia Hawkins. "But here's something for you to think about. Sexual harassment is very serious."

"What do you mean?" Had Horace actually told her what happened? Even his version? "I didn't say there was any. There wasn't anything, really."

"He said you'd say that. But I've convinced him to take the manager's job rather than file a lawsuit against you for sexual harassment. I don't want the company's name involved in anything like that."

"What!" Crystal said, feeling as if she'd have to pick herself up off the floor.

"And I paid him a nice bonus to make sure. Just what is it with you? Going after men who don't want you."

Crystal stood up so fast the phone base fell off the desk and hung suspended to her receiver cord. She paced within the limits but couldn't think of anything to say.

"Let me be the first to tell you. Matt's decided to open an office in Nashville to enlarge our holdings there. He'll be with the one who really has his heart. His daughter."

SIXTY-TWO - A Knight Forever Kneel'd To a Lady on His Shield

That night John left at ten, just as a heavy rain began. They stood inside the door. She knew he wanted her to ask him to stay. He said he didn't like leaving her alone any more. He'd only lie next to her. Or in another room if she preferred. He thought God would understand if he spent the night, they'd be married this time tomorrow.

"I can think of a few others who would have a field day with it. Especially if they found out my condition!"

"I would have been happy if that were the case."

Shouldn't she turn now and go back inside? Was it leave him now, or leave him never?

"When Sarah first told me about you, I knew you're the only one I'll ever love. Or make love to."

She looked down to avoid his eyes, his words the most moving pledge maybe a man could make to a woman. Oh, God. Answer his prayers. Make this man happy. Could she possibly be the answer?

Her chest ached, her legs wanted to take her away, knowing she would have to tell him one day, of her casual tinkering with a man's desires that morning.

She continued staring at his shoes, unable to raise her eyes to his. Tassel loafers. Black. They were a little scuffed. Their imperfection made her consider them. She would have thought they'd be polished to a fare-the-well. The scuffs gave her hope. "Did you forget to polish your shoes, Reverend?" she said, bringing her eyes up his body. She didn't have to deny anything she saw in this man. Even his physicality. Muscular thighs, pressing against gray slacks. Flat stomach under a black belt. Large chest under a short-sleeved button-front silky shirt with pockets on each side. Smooth face and strong chin and eyes now the color of blue in Dad's stained glass with the sun on it. Well, now. How did she miss all that even one time? She had been determined to.

"One of my failings," he said, understanding that she was noticing him, giving her a second and enjoying the wait.

"What?"

He laughed, knowing she'd lost her train of thought and loving that he'd done that to her. "My shoes, they always need tending."

"I think that's a good character trait – for a minister, especially," she said, putting her arms around his neck. "Shows humility."

"Where did all the shoeshine boys go?"

"I used to shine Dad's. I'll do yours."

His eyes glittered like buckets of stars flung out of the darkest night sky. He hugged her so gently she could barely feel his arms, but his body pressed close and she could sense the tension in his restraint. She'd been aware of it all evening. Once he'd pulled her to him and she had felt the heat and solidity of him. But even then she'd not accepted him as human, she thought now. He'd been a man of God. A priest. A confessor. She'd already been more honest with him than she'd been with Matt.

She knew now he had been passionately controlling the want for her that flowed through him. She felt even more respect for him. But she'd needed something more to make him just a man who loved her. Was that the answer to her prayer, the shoes? He needed her. Well, that sounded silly. He didn't need her to shine his shoes. But he needed her to complete him. He was less than perfect. Of course less than perfect. But now he was human to her. And she knew at that moment that yes, she was going to marry him. Notwithstanding that she had already said she would. And had set the date and bought a dress. But it had always seemed like a time that would never arrive. It was too soon. She couldn't do that to him. She would postpone it long enough for him to know that she was marrying him because she wanted to. Not for refuge. He deserved that.

He stared down at her, aware, she believed, that something had been considered and decisions made. But he only said, "Don't come out on the porch. The wind sounds wild enough to blow rain on you. And you're tired."

"You're right," she said, more gravely than she had intended. Tomorrow would be time enough to let him know what she had resolved.

"God help me," he said, looking upward, "if that's your demeanor when I'm right."

She couldn't believe how chilly it was for late September when she woke on the couch, another new habit. Some blue norther or whatever the weatherman called it must be colliding with some warm front from the Gulf, by the sound of the wind, worse than when John left. She had fallen asleep soon after, with a mind at ease after so long.

She hurried, shivering, upstairs and changed into a fleece warm-up. She crawled into bed and uncurled a little at a time as she felt the sheets gradually grow warm. The wind and rain sounded like they were trying to get in the house and into bed with her. She was almost asleep when the phone rang. She answered it immediately. No not answering it these days. Hello. Flat and sleepy.

"Sweetheart," John said. "Sorry to wake you."

"'S'all right."

"Storm's fierce, isn't it?"

"Makes me think of when I'd run next door and we'd get in Sarah's cellar. For tornadoes."

"It's not supposed to get to that according to the latest. I have the television on – don't worry, I don't watch it all night." She heard warmth in his voice and hated that she was going to disappoint him. "I'm getting dressed."

Had he decided to come back? She almost hoped he would.

She heard a more somber tone when he said, "I got a call from one of my members – I'm sure you know her – Faye Ann Lipman? Her mother, Lorece Little – she's also a member – has been taken to the hospital in Memphis, a heart attack. Faye Ann asked me to be with the family."

Faye Ann. Faye Ann Little Truncy Lipman. Oh yeah, I know her. "I went to school with her."

"Would you like me to give her your regards?"

Faye Ann had made Crystal's life in second grade vie with her home life. Crystal could run faster than even Travis Wheeler, the biggest boy. So after recess she was always first to the water fountain. Dad praised her. But Willette said a young lady would never be first in line. "She is not too young to learn the facts of society life, Oliver. She should be in boarding school in Memphis." "It won't happen, Willette," he'd said. Then he'd put Crystal on his knee. "Bet you'll have a friend for life if you throw some of the races his way." Next day she let Travis dart ahead, and as he slid to a stop he turned and planted a kiss on her cheek as she came in behind him. The day after that, they were instructed by Mrs. Bennett to walk, not run, to the water fountain, and to not touch each other. Faye Ann had Crystal's new names ready for passing around like gold stars. Dumb Bell. Crystal Ball. Kissy Cryssy. But Travis had proven her father's knowledge of human nature again, and the others had eventually followed Travis's lead.

She hadn't understood that Faye Ann's eye was already on Travis. When Travis and Faye Ann started dating, Crystal offered to let their friendship slide, but Travis was more loyal than that. When Faye Ann broke up with Travis and eloped with A. W. Truncy, Travis's rival in all things, just after graduation, Travis joined the Army. She and Sarah were on a trip to Charleston and Savannah. Her best friend was killed in a helicopter crash before he was nineteen.

"Were you friends?" John asked when she didn't respond.

"Faye Ann and I weren't close," she said.

"I'll probably be all night," he said. "It appears serious. We may have to start our married life with a funeral."

"We won't," she said, wishing she had told him she was going to put it off, and thinking Faye Ann would probably gladly kill her mother if she knew John was planning to marry Crystal next day, to ruin the wedding.

"I like your faith."

"Call me in the morning?"

"Uh oh," he said. "I won't ask what you're not saying."

"I want to see you."

"OK. But isn't that against the rules? Bad luck?"

"Hey, if I didn't have bad luck . . ."

He laughed but said, "Weather's getting worse. They just flashed 'tornado watch' across the bottom of the screen."

"It's a tornado *warning* that's dangerous, I think."

"You should go downstairs anyway, don't you think? Sleep in the old maid's room?"

She laughed.

Then it struck him and he laughed.

"And on that note, I'll get back to sleep," she said.

But she couldn't go back to sleep. She thought of Travis, of her baby of so long ago, of Dad and Sarah and Willette, and let herself speculate about Matt and Hallie and Helen. Then she considered John and the life he expected them to have embarked upon by this time tomorrow night.

Finally she became aware that the storm's intensity had increased. She hoped John was already at the hospital and not out in it. Well. She was worrying about him. That had to mean something. She went downstairs and turned on the TV. To listen to the weather announcer, you'd think it was an incoming missile instead of a tornado warning. But you didn't live in northwest Mississippi all your life and take a tornado warning lightly. Especially when it appeared to be headed for the middle of your county where your town was. Just then she heard lightning strike somewhere close and everything went dark. She probably should get out of the cavernous living room of this house surrounded by trees and at least go in the maid's room as John had suggested, as it was almost an inside room, only one window, now facing north. Or maybe the basement. That would be better if a tornado actually did touch down. But she still hadn't repaired the steps and thought that's all she needed, to possibly get trapped down there until Miniver or John got here in the morning.

Why not go next door like she had the last several years? No doubt a good battery was still in the radio. She hurried to the kitchen for a flashlight and called Vernon to follow as she grabbed her umbrella and Sarah's keys from the hall table.

The wind blew the umbrella inside out before she got to the hedges and pushed Sarah's front door from her hand and banged it against the wall. While she shoved the door to, Vernon shook water off for all he was worth, which wasn't much if she was thinking about anything other than keeping her company. But that was a whole lot tonight. "Come on, Vernon. Let's get down there," she said, heading for the kitchen and the cellar steps. He stood, looking around as if waiting for Sarah. "She's not here. Now come on or the tornado will be over us."

She turned on the lantern and sensed the house vibrating and listened to the rain turn to hail. When the storm was over, the house hadn't been lifted off her and she had gone all comfy in the recliner and decided to stay where she was. But she woke after a while, stiff, needing to turn. Except for the rain, it was quiet. Even the radio had played out. The batteries must have been low, after all. She flipped the light switch. The electricity was still off. She didn't want to go out in the rain and dark. Vernon wouldn't, either. He was a sound sleeper. In fact, he was snoring. She might as well stay. She left the basement door open for when he did wake up, and went up to Sarah's bedroom.

Later, another storm rolled in and thunder woke her. She heard Vernon awake and roaming, looking for her. She had the first syllable of his name on her lips to call out when she heard a voice. Bob must have sent a deputy to check on her, looking here since she wasn't at home. But how did he get in? She got up and went to the open bedroom door and was about to call, "Here I am," when she heard yet another voice, her heart freezing in mid-beat as she recognized it.

SIXTY-THREE - One Bad Knight – and Another Good

One

"**D**og from next door," Horace said. "Wonder what he's doing here in the cellar?"

"Snorin' like an old man," the other voice said. "Close that door. We don't want him puttin' up a racket like he did before."

"Something could've happened to her." Thunder rumbled in the distance. "Another storm rolling in."

"Go over there and look if it's worryin' you," the man said. "Go. Maybe the old broad wanted the dog out the house."

"Gone back to Memphis. Probably had to get her hair done."

"Them Blacks still there?"

"They've moved."

"Man from work might be there. Don't like a guard dog."

"She's through with him."

"The preacher then."

"He wouldn't spend the night 'til he gets the knot tied."

"Shut up and go check it out. If she's there, bring her. She knows where the family jewels are."

"Let's keep her out of this."

"We ain't got all night. Get over there! Search for stuff we missed."

It was quiet now, so Horace had gone. This new man was the boss. His ruthlessness had crept up the stairs with his voice as he gave the orders. She wished to God she had followed Willette's advice and had an alarm installed. But when had she ever listened to anybody? Except now. She was listening to herself now. She must get out of this house.

She picked up the heavy flashlight – maybe she could use it as a weapon if she had to – and started down the stairs, clinging to the inside wall to avoid being seen, not to avoid the squeaks, as there weren't any in these stairs. She felt the thick carpet runner with her toes and carefully braced her heels against the brass rod at the base of each step. Halfway down, lightning struck just outside and she felt the thud as a tree fell. She stifled her outcry immediately. But she knew the man heard it. He'd honed his hearing for such as this.

She made her feet reverse their steps and closed the bedroom door. She slid the latch on the bottom of the old square lock the doorknob was centered on. She backed away just in time to keep from being hit by the door as it was shoved open.

"Didn't figure the dog to be here by his lonesome."

"The sheriff will be here any minute. I called him."

"I cut the line. Tornado blew half the poles down, anyway."

"I used my cellular phone," she said, the lie coming from she knew not where. Oh, God, why hadn't she listened to Miniver about getting one? If she lived through this night, she'd start taking some advice!

"If you don't show it to me you'll wish you did, even if that black dick's pullin' in the driveway!"

He made her wish she had one to show him! Heaven help her, she even wished Horace would get back.

"You ain't got one."

"You take what you want. All the keys are there on the table."

"Where's the safe?"

He'd find it anyway. "Behind the large painting in the dining room."

"What all's in it?"

"Some jewelry and a little money." Willette had insisted they open it and she'd said, "Nothing of real value," when only money and jewelry were there.

"What about the painting? It valuable?"

"I don't – "

He slapped her and though she knew it was coming, she'd never experienced one and never knew it could hurt like hell. "Yes," she cried out before her head had stopped rebounding from the blow, hating it although she knew Sarah would advise her to sell her moldering bones if it would protect Crystal. "It's a Milaro Landscape."

"Any of your pappy's around?"

"You already got them all! Listen. As you said, I can't call the police. I give you my word I won't leave the house 'til morning. Horace knows I won't turn him in. It's dark. I can't even describe you," she added, hoping he believed her.

"That's strange. I see you," he said, moving his lantern around. "You ain't bad. Makes no difference to me." He motioned toward the bed.

"You'd better not touch me!"

"You're not my type. I'm gonna watch you and the kid replay your happy day."

"The sheriff's like my brother-"

"That don't bother me. You convinced the kid, though. He ain't told nobody but me 'bout your rendezvous."

She was beyond fright now, getting angry. "You're responsible for Sarah's death!" she said, spitting blood, swinging at him.

"And I'll be for yours if you don't do what I say!" He grabbed her hand in mid-swing and squeezed so hard she buckled and whimpered. He tucked the gun in his belt and pulled her up and hurt every muscle and joint in her body as he yanked off her sweatshirt, slinging her hand around so hard another dagger cut through.

"Good tits," he said. "If you like such."

He rubbed himself between the legs. "Kid won't give this a try," he said. "Let's see what else you got that I don't." He pushed her onto the bed and jerked her pants off. "You don't look like no old maid!"

"I'm pregnant!"

"Hell you say," he said, about to slap her again.

"Horace!" she said, looking over the man's shoulder.

"Find anybody?" the man said, without turning around.

"No. Listen, man, don't hurt her!"

"You did."

"I didn't. She wanted me! You can't treat her like this!"

"I'll do what I goddam fuckin' want to. Get over here." He didn't even look at Horace.

"I told you the first time it was only a burglary. The old lady ended up dead. We ain't hurtin' nobody else!"

"You gonna do it to her one more time."

"You crazy homo!"

Horace was going to help her! She looked at him with gratitude, and recognized her father's old rabbit gun in his hands. Please God let him have loaded it!

"I don't take no from no pretty-faced kid!" the man said, pulling the gun from his waist as he turned. He fired into Horace's chest and Horace fell back in the doorway on the floor, even without time for a cry, the rifle still clasped in his dead hands.

"Horace!" she cried, sliding off the bed and darting past the man and kneeling by him.

But a toughened body like Horace's didn't die easily. He swung the gun up toward the man and squeezed the trigger, and she slapped at her ears from the noise.

"Fuck!" the man said, looking at his left forearm where blood trickled out. Then he fired into Horace's face. "Ain't so pretty, now," he said, putting the gun on the table. He grabbed a pillow and yanked the case off and wrapped it around his arm, holding it tight with his other hand, watching blood soak through. "Get up here and tie this!"

Horace had died trying to protect her! The animal standing behind her would do the same to her! Her baby would die! She wouldn't let it happen without God in heaven knowing she'd put up the fight of her life. She looked at the rifle. Could she lift it with her hurt hand? No! Quicker than she could even think of it, she twisted up and grabbed the man's gun off the table with both hands as he was saying something again like get up and fix this, and she fired just as she faced him. The shot into his lower stomach pushed him back and he fell. She pulled the trigger again, knowing it would take more than one shot to kill him and knowing she had to kill him. The third shot she aimed at his heart. She was attempting to fire again when the gun fell out of her hand and fired wildly, shattering a window as she came to her senses.

She screamed long and hard, as if she'd been holding it in for years. Maybe she had. But now she couldn't stifle it. A painful, mournful, "Oh."

She drew another breath and added another word, "No," to her scream. Then she darted out, jumping over Horace, and ran down the stairs. She heard her scream, horrible, piercing, echoing as she reached the front door, then realized it was Vernon, still locked in the cellar. She opened the door and he sat there on the top step, yapping for a hunt. As she hugged him his stiff coat down his spine made her realize she was naked. He smelled blood and turned toward the stairs, wanting to investigate. She dragged him across the porch.

Inside her house, she pulled a raincoat from the closet and wrapped herself in it, tried the phone – still dead – and started upstairs to get dressed. Just then she saw a car pull in her drive, overhead light spinning.

"Bob!" she yelled, running into the yard. "Bob!"

He hugged her to him, rain bouncing off his hat and slicker . "You get hurt in the tornado?" he said, noticing her holding her hand with the other one between them and giving her more room.

She started sobbing like she was a child when Dad picked a big splinter from her foot and she knew she was going to live, after all. "It'll be all right," Bob said, patting her on the back as he led her onto the porch. "Tell me what happened? The tree fall on you?"

For an eternity she shook against Bob but finally started drawing strength. The third storm front hit then like a wall, doubling the rain and wind. Lightning blasted and she noticed the tree, uprooted, branches sprawled in the yard, the tank and its gun having stopped its fall onto the kitchen.

"Let's get inside," he said. "Did the tornado set down here?"

"I don't think so."

"Do I have to investigate to find out what's happened?"

"You'll investigate," she sniffled.

"Girl, if you don't tell me! But I've got my hands full with the storm unless this is at least murder," he said in mock severity, less worried now that she was calming down.

"It's at least murder."

SIXTY-FOUR - All in the Blue Unclouded Weather

"Crystal, you're a hero," Miniver said a few hours later as she sat on the foot of Crystal's bed. "Can't you get that through your head?"

Crystal shook her head. "I don't know if I'll ever get it out of my mind."

"It was justice."

"Or the fact that I'm not sorry."

"I ought to kick your butt. Sarah would be proud of her daughter."

Crystal nodded. "But Willette will be angry. I should have followed her advice, for once."

"Sometimes things happen," said Willette, entering the room, "that no amount of planning can prevent. Horrible and tragic. The main thing is that you came through it."

"Willette! When did you get here? How did you find out?" She'd thought it was Vernon on the stairs. He was so unsettled, not knowing where to lay his head.

"Once more, Crystal. A mother should be the first one told something like this!" She looked at Miniver. "Although I'm glad you're here."

Crystal and Miniver glanced at each other, both wondering if she heard what they said. She went to a mirror and patted her hair and said, "I came the very minute I heard." But it was like her heart wasn't in appraising herself this morning. It was more a show of habit. Then she sat on the bed next to Crystal and touched her shoulder. "I am proud of you. Your father and Sarah would be, too. As usual, you did what you had to do. And from what I hear, you did it just right!"

"How did you hear?" Miniver said. "Aren't the lines down?"

"Sue Elwood has a new cellular phone."

Miniver nodded see, I told you to get one, to Crystal, then said, "You're O.K., Willette."

They all were silent for a moment, then Miniver said, "Are y'all hungry? You know I'm one who has to eat. Let's go make breakfast. Be good for you to get out of bed, Crystal. You know life going on, all that."

"The kids will wake up hungry," said Crystal.

"They're sleeping late," said Miniver.

"Tabitha and Tommy are watching TV," said Willette.

"I didn't even hear them," said Miniver.

"They have the sound off. They said they played "burglar" coming down so you wouldn't hear them. They wanted to watch Mighty somethings or other."

"How much did they hear?" Crystal said. "If this affects them . . ."

"Kids these days have to learn the facts of life. And I mean the facts of living life. So don't you worry. But they're going to learn they can't be sneaking past me anymore."

Willette nodded and said, "That's very wise, Miniver." Then she added, "They were hungry, so I made them cereal and milk."

Behind Willette, going down the stairs, Miniver did a fake stagger into Crystal and Crystal tapped her ear as if she hadn't heard right.

As Miniver and Crystal made breakfast, Willette said, "Crystal, there's something I want to discuss with you, and it can't wait. But you obviously have no secrets from Miniver."

"I'm sorry if I hurt your feelings," Crystal said. Obviously she had heard their conversation and wanted to discuss Sarah and herself after all.

"Then why wasn't I invited to your wedding?"

"Uh oh," Miniver said, busying herself getting cups and saucers and pouring coffee.

"Well, that won't be a point now. I'm not getting married."

"It is certainly relevant, at any rate. You must inform me of all impending marriages."

"Not getting married?" Miniver shrieked. "I was getting used to the idea!"

"How did you know?"

"Again, I found out on by-roads. Sue Elwood called last night to tell me she was disappointed about not being invited to your wedding, although she understood it was to be very private. She knew, I believe, that she must be the one to tell me. I tried to sound as if I knew."

Willette put such value on keeping up appearances. And Sarah had suffered to keep her own reputation from suffering. "I should have told you. I apologize."

Willette looked pleased, but had other issues to discuss. "Then Sue called me back to tell me about Lorece Little's heart attack, although I had not spoken to Lorece for years."

"I thought you were friends."

"Then why didn't you call?"

Willette had her there.

"But we weren't. Not since she refused to ask her daughter to rectify certain – oh, never mind dredging up unpleasant things from so long ago. Especially as she's gone to her reward."

So John's prayer hadn't been answered. More than one. "Are you talking about her daughter giving me nicknames? And you stopped speaking to Lorece because of it?"

"Any mother would have done it."

"What will we learn about you next, Willette? Are you one of those guardian angels?"

Willette shrugged off the comment, her spoon creating a silent maelstrom in her coffee cup.

"Do you want your prunes now?" Miniver said, picking up a small stewer from the stove. "I think they're tender. You can buy them already soft now, you know."

"Yes, thank you," Willette answered, holding up a small crystal dish. "And yes, I know. But it gives Barbara something to do in the morning other than make my bed." She cut a prune into halves with her knife and fork as if it were tenderloin. "If Sarah had known about what Lorece did, she'd have refused to bail out their dry cleaning business when Faye Ann's second husband embezzled it into ruin."

Listening to Willette make revealing small talk was engrossing in this place full of memories, and without thinking about it, Crystal trimmed the crust from her toast.

Willette looked at her toast, already trimmed. "Give these crusts to Vernon with yours," she said to Crystal.

Again, without thinking, Crystal cut her toast in half diagonally to make triangles, then in half again.

"Just like Sarah," said Miniver. "How could Sarah not know about it?"

"Know what? Oh. Because she and Crystal had gone on a trip, Timbuktu or some other practical destination. The talk had died down by the time they returned. I certainly wasn't going to tattle to Sarah."

"I wish . . ." said Crystal.

"What?" said Miniver, when Willette didn't ask.

Miniver knew, and Willette did, too. What might have gone differently if Willette had told her then, so long ago, that she had taken up for her? But Crystal only said, "Nothing." and Willette left it at that, too. Probably best at this late date. Things had already turned a corner between them, anyway.

"Girl, you've got the best of two women in you," Miniver said. "Night and day, East and West, up and down –"

"Some might simply say yin and yang," Willette said.

"No wonder you're like you are. And I mean that in the best possible way," Miniver added, "just to make things clear for one and all."

Willette actually dabbed at her eyes with the little white cloth napkin, saying the kitchen was hot. Miniver kindly said she'd turn on the air conditioner and Willette said never mind. In a minute, she continued with her rundown of slights. "Sue called to tell me about the tornado. I had planned to come down here this afternoon for the wedding." She gave a pointed look at Crystal. "I left when the storm was over in Memphis. I came the long way or I'd be sitting in some traffic jam now. I supposed correctly that the Broad Stream River would be flooding."

"You were worried?"

She looked exasperated. "Of course. Then Sue called on my cellular phone to tell me about all this next door. Doesn't it disquiet you to know that everyone in town assumes you wouldn't have called me? About any of this."

"Yes. I should have called you." Then she looked at Miniver before looking at Willette and continuing. "And while I'm confessing, I have something else to tell you. I don't believe Sue knows this."

"God in Heaven! Whose baby is it? Surely it isn't the Reverend John Half's. Although you two were to be married . . . Is it Matt Hawkins'?"

"Neither."

"Tell me this minute, Crystal!"

Willette was gripping the table edge as if she were holding onto a lifeboat.

"It was Horace. You met him at the funeral home."

"God in Heaven! I warned you . . . but it would have been too late by then . . . But you knew he wasn't to be trusted, I could tell by your attitude . . . Dear God. Did he rape you?" Willette rubbed her temples with her fingertips.

"He thought I'd been after him all along. I let him kiss me and touch me, I touched him . . . I wondered what it would be like to have a man making love to me. Then I changed my mind." She put her hand on her stomach. "I realized it was Matt that I wanted. So I don't know. I do know that he died trying to save my life last night."

Willette at last reached to touch Crystal's hand. "He redeemed himself, by saving you." Then with genuine need for clarity, she said, "But why would you not marry John? I'm certain you told him about being pregnant. He wants you. And he's handsome and accomplished . . . Being a minister's wife gave you pause, I expect, as you're not a church-goer. But you are a believer."

"I didn't love him when I said I would marry him."

"So, is it still Matt Hawkins? Will you marry him?"

"Not dignified to grasp at straws," said Miniver.

"Believe it or not, I sent him back to his wife and daughter."

"That was the best thing," Willette said without deliberation. "Even knowing what happened with Oliver and me. They should make that decision without anyone else muddying it up. Are you broken hearted? You mustn't take this 'one man' thing too far. Sarah and I . . . we both lost out on a lot."

"No. I'm not. I've come to think he was the only one for me at the time, the only one who could make me see my life for what it was."

She got up and did the bread dough ritual. The phone rang and Miniver went to answer it. Crystal thought it would be John. But Miniver came back shortly, almost breathless. "Crystal! Bob says the paintings are in a self-storage unit in Memphis. There was a receipt and key on . . . the man . . . and they went and checked it out."

"Thank God," said Willette.

"You can tell Sue some news for a change," Miniver said to her.

Well. That would cement the plans she talked to Ash Cooper about. Willette would be glad to hear it. "There's more you can tell Sue."

"What in the world?" Willette said. "I don't know if I'm up to any more news."

"I'm making a museum out of Sarah's house." And one of the Babies would soon be at home there. "Now that Dad's paintings are found, the rest of my plan can be carried out."

"Sarah would like knowing her house was being shown off," Miniver said.

"If she couldn't get Crystal to live in it," said Willette.

"Not a chance, now." Crystal said, shuddering.

"Yes. She wouldn't want you there to face that day in and day out. But what was the rest of your plan? Oliver's paintings . . ."

"I'll have an art gallery. Maybe in this house. I don't know that for sure yet. Maybe show all the other things . . ."

"Both will bring visitors to town. I don't think Oliver would object. But . . ."

"We'll still sell when an offer meets our price. Dad deserves that."

"I agree." Willette got up and went to the kitchen window and looked out at the tank. "I hoped that tornado had blown it away. But here it is."

"That tree didn't even dent it, I bet," said Miniver.

"I don't know that an army of tanks could have split us up, if I hadn't been so determined to do it myself."

SIXTY-FIVE - Bold Paces

It was still early, only a little after eight. She wanted to see the world just outside her door. The roses had been in their last good blooming. "I'm going to see what's left of the roses after the storm."

Miniver had said last week, and she had agreed, that they should be arranged in crystal vases with ivy for the wedding this afternoon in the church. Miniver and Willette exchanged looks and uncharacteristically waited for the other to ask what she was going to do with them. "Maybe I'll make potpourri as usual," she said.

She put on some of Dad's soft khaki pants because it was cool after the storm, and to keep her legs from getting scratched by the thorns. She looped a belt through them although they weren't as loose now that she was pregnant, and pulled on a white tee and a new white hat of fine, soft straw with a large floppy brim that Sarah had given her this summer, but which she had never worn, to replace her old straw hat that something had chewed on.

She looked the roses over in appreciation. The garden was on the east side and protected from most of the wind. The rain had taken a toll, but she saw several with life still in them. She went to the back storage building for her basket with garden gloves and snips and bottle of aspirin and Sarah's nail polish. She'd use clear today. Then she went to the spigot and half-filled a bucket and dropped in a couple of the tablets to dissolve to help keep flowers fresh as Sarah had told her so long ago.

She went way down the stem to find a five-leaf cluster, and cut at a slant just above it, awkwardly using her left hand, the right still hurting.

She was at ease, actually not thinking about last night, when she heard a car on the drive out front and then the door slam quickly. She stood up as he hurried around the corner of the house and saw her.

She went to meet him. "Crystal," he said, pulling her to him. "Are you all right?" He leaned back to look at her face and she nodded, catching the hat as it slid back when she looked up at him, then he pulled her close again. "I'm sorry I wasn't here with you! I felt I shouldn't leave you last night. But I thought it was my heart and body talking."

She could have let herself sink against him and into his desire to protect her today and from now on. But instead she blurted out, "I've killed a man!"

"You saved two lives."

"I don't regret what I did. I can't regret it. But I took revenge. I shot him, killed him again, after he was dead."

"You couldn't have come through this, done what you did, without God's intervention."

"There's more. Horace. Horace was the father of my baby."

He nodded, not with surprise or contempt or anger.

"You knew already."

"I thought maybe he was. That you'd given in during some moment of need . . . but after last night, I don't think that was the case."

"That's close, close to how it happened. How it began that day."

He squeezed her shoulders and shook his head and looked down, perhaps praying again.

She looked down, too, and in a moment realized she saw his shoes as usual. As usual, they were sorely in need of care, especially after the night's weather.

"I don't know how to make it better . . . for what he did . . ," John said. "I'm sorry that any man will do that . . ."

"He was killed trying to help me last night . . ." And she faced for the first time what she knew. Like a child who only wanted a cookie but whose precipitous climb had resulted in the broken cookie jar, her actions with Horace that day in the office had ended up killing him.

John touched her face, perhaps understanding what she was unable to voice, and said, "We aren't meant to understand why. But Horace's death is on one man." Then he looked up at the sky and said, "Thank you, God, for letting the man who's the father of Crystal's baby show redemption. When the questions come, as they will, from the child who grows from his deed, Crystal can answer that he was a good man. We ask you God to have mercy on his soul." Then he looked into her eyes and she felt, not absolved, but forgiven, as he said, "As always, it's in God's hands. Let Him handle it."

She couldn't believe what she did then. She put her head on his shoulder and boo-hooed her eyes out, with his arms around her. After a while she stopped and said, "Good Lord! I haven't slobbered like this in . . .well, since last night."

He handed her a handkerchief.

A handkerchief. Was he perfect?

"We were in IC waiting room through the storm. I tried calling you, but couldn't get through."

She nodded. "I was sure you were still in Memphis."

"A tornado struck there after the one here. But it was six before the news mentioned there had been one here, too. I left right away to come here."

"You did?" That was over two hours ago.

"Seems like days," he said, digging into her eyes with his. "But trees were blocking streets everywhere up there, so many detours. And a section of bridge was out over Broad Stream River. I was trapped in traffic before I knew it."

"So you didn't stay to find out about Mrs. Little?"

"I'll never choose anyone over you, Crystal."

"She didn't make it. Sue Elwood told Willette. You already knew what happened here. Next door. How did you hear about it?"

"I hate to tell you," he said, with a bare hint of sarcasm, locking his hands behind her back, but more than that still locking her with his eyes, "probably what you always dreaded finally happened. You made the news."

"You make me think I can laugh again."

"I hope always to."

"Even at something so bad? Murder? Death?"

"No. We're not laughing at that. We're happy about other things."

"I wanted to talk to you, you know."

"Do you still want to?"

"No, I'll see you this afternoon."

"Will you wear that hat? You looked like a bride in it."

She turned it in her hand. "Sarah gave it to me. Miniver and Willette can put some roses on it."

"Is there anything I can do to help you?"

She shook her head no, then thought of something. "Yes. I want to carry Sarah's bible. It's on her nightstand."

"I'll get it." He walked to the hedges but turned to look back at her just before he went through.

END

Excerpt from
BOUND FOR EBENEZER

ONE

S hep snapped awake. A woman in a black shroud turned her legs to slide out of a long black car. She looked at him and pitied him at first, but then smiled. She walked to him and sat next to him on the bench. She put her arm through his and leaned her head on his shoulder.

What? Instantly he became aware that he had been asleep in a vacant place in his mind that hadn't even let any memories in, and he didn't know where he was, but that he had been wakened, and not by explosions. No. Not tanks and machine guns. It had only been the smooth sound of an engine that did not have to strain to carry its load, unlike the army vehicles that he had grown accustomed to. But it was more like a recruit driving it who didn't know yet how to handle the vehicle.

He did a double-take, if only with the one seeing eye it could be called that. Damn. In his hallucination of waking, he had imagined what he wanted to see happen, he supposed. Because in fact, a woman was sliding out of the car. But she didn't come to him.

She wasn't in a shroud either, but dressed in black high heel shoes, a strap around the ankle peeking out of loose-fitting dark gray slacks as she stretched her legs to the ground. A white short-sleeve blouse was tucked in. She was like a magazine advertisement of a female who was taking advantage of freedoms the war was bringing, no matter who she was. She lifted a chauffeur's cap, revealing thick black hair in long, smooth curls. And no matter what else she was, she was young and he couldn't deny, beautiful.

He almost wondered if he could still be dreaming. The huge black Cadillac LaSalle was preposterous in this backwoods, like an emperor's carriage would be in a hinterland. It was a '40 or '41 he'd guess, by far the nicest vehicle he'd seen since he'd been on the road. Probably would have been even if the automobile factories hadn't converted to build war machines. The little group inside was exhibited like a framed photograph behind the expansive windshield. And if that wasn't revealing enough, you only had to look through one of the six side windows or large rear window.

Why in Heaven's name did it come to this wide spot in a dirt road in a Kentucky valley hidden between two hills? This unincorporated community hadn't even felt the need to identify itself with a welcome sign. They didn't expect, probably didn't even want, any strangers. Especially such as the little group lighting on the place in front of their eyes.

The license plate on the front bumper said the car had started in Washington, D. C., the very place he had begun his odyssey. Was that some kind of God's irony? Certainly this was not its destination any more than it was his, or any more than a steer would deliberately run into the slaughterhouse gate. Could it be they were having car trouble?

And how did the young woman get a job driving the damn car, if she couldn't do any better than she'd done pulling in here? It had crunched to a not exactly smooth stop on the gravel in front, even with its hydraulic brakes, even a bit of grinding of gears as she shifted too early.

He should have been used to strange sights by now after serving the past two years in Uncle Sam's army, but this beat all. The car might as well have been pasted with a banner identifying it as Trouble. The dust wasn't settled and already the talk between the two men inside the cluttered little gas station had stopped, their conversation hanging like balloons over cartoon characters.

They were already in aggravated mode, having been kicking the bald tires of an old pick-up parked in the shade not far from where he sat, when Shep had limped up about half an hour ago. After a few minutes the two men had gone inside discussing a dirty Ford sedan that was suspended over the work pit, and owned by the hefty man in tan pants. Shep's glance at the impotent car had put him in mind of a behemoth pig blackened and ash-blown, being removed from its burial cooking by the black workers on his place down in the delta.

The two men's voices had floated out the open window of the small building with the careless assurance that their viewpoint was the only relevant one, as they calculated the cost of rebuilding the car's transmission, versus simply adding oil and taking it up to Ohio to sell. "Damn Yankees deserve it," the big man had avowed, ignoring the reality of Kentucky's loyalty to the Union in the 1860's. "And don't forget ole' Jeff Davis was ours," said the petite man, who had introduced himself to Shep as Mr. White, owner of the station. Shep wondered if that was to counter the fact, apparently troublesome to them, that Lincoln was theirs, too.

"Fed'ral gov'ment got no right telling states how to run their business," the big man had added.

Sure, this war was different, they had concluded. Had to join the Yankees in this one, like in the Great War. Shep wondered if maybe they'd added that for his benefit as a soldier; he wasn't certain.

"Reckon it's true about the Jew-killing?" Mr. White had asked, raising his voice enough that Shep had realized he was to answer. "Papers say so," he had replied, without opinion in his voice. Not going to get anything started. Just rest in the shade, enjoy a cold drink, be on his way in a few minutes.

"Now that would be one to ponder out back over your catalogue in the mornin'," the big man had stated, accepting no opinion of someone he didn't know, directing his theorizing back to Mr. White. But loud enough to show he didn't really care if Shep heard.

And the voices had never tired of the subject, reaching him even now as he snapped awake: "And what if Hitler was to say after the Jews and Polaks comes the Ni – !"

Shep could practically see their hackles rising as the two men had given up their diatribe to witness the black apparition descending upon them.

All things considered, it might not be such a strange sight in certain sections of Washington, Shep thought. But around here, just like where he was headed, you just didn't see this.

A fine car, led as if in flight by the winged goddess of a hood ornament.

And three Negroes as its occupants.

And, "Parking in front pretty as you please!" according to Mr. White, accompanied by the other man's exasperated, "What the hell is that?!"

GLINDA MCKINNEY

While teaching some of world's great books to high school students in Mississippi and Tennessee, Ms. McKinney decided to try her hand at writing about some of the characters she had nurtured in her imagination. She enrolled in creative writing and began her first novel.

 These days, she continues writing; substitute teaches; teaches four-year-old Sunday School; helps coach the local high school tennis team; "reads 'til her eyes bleed;" revels in her circle of friends; recently bid farewell to Babycakes, her cat of almost 24 years; and most of all spends as much time as possible with her family.